THE OGRE
AND
THE DRAGON

Also by Keith C. Blackmore

Mountain Man
Mountain Man
Safari
Hellifax
Well Fed
Make Me King
Mindless
Skull Road
Mountain Man Prequel
Mountain Man 2nd Prequel: Them Early Days
The Hospital: A Mountain Man Story
Mountain Man Omnibus: Books 1–3

131 Days
131 Days
House of Pain
Spikes and Edges
About the Blood
To Thunderous Applause
The Ogre and the Dragon
131 Days Omnibus: Books 1–3

Breeds
Breeds
Breeds 2
Breeds 3
Breeds: The Complete Trilogy

Isosceles Moon
Isosceles Moon
Isosceles Moon 2

The He-Dog Chronicles
White Sands, Red Steel
Savage

The Bear That Fell from the Stars
Bones and Needles
Cauldron Gristle
Flight of the Cookie Dough Mansion
The Majestic 311
The Missing Boatman
Private Property
The Troll Hunter

131 DAYS

BOOK 6

THE OGRE
AND
THE DRAGON

KEITH C. BLACKMORE

For my dad

Cover design by Alexandre Rito

ISBN: 978-1-0394-9203-5

Published in 2025 by Podium Publishing
www.podiumentertainment.com

Podium

THE OGRE
AND
THE DRAGON

LANDS
OF
GREAT ICE
ARROWHEADS
SHIGA
NORJOS
ICE
KINGDOMS
ZHIBERIA
PERICIA
OSGAR
NORDUN
ORVASIA
ANVAR
MARRN
BALGOTHA
GHEDA
SUNJA
VALENCIA
PAW
(TRIBAL LANDS)
THE
SPIKES
VATHIA
HARUDIN
GREY
TEETH
KREE
DESERT
OF THE
BLIND
BORJA
MADEMIA

1

The sound of sloshing water filled the dungeon.

Torchlight grew stronger outside Arrus's cell, revealing the dirty, ankle-deep water flooding the cellblock. Beyond iron bars, a shadow lurched across damp brickwork, where it bobbed and weaved and, at times, split into two or three. Voices then, a low, well-placed string of words, no doubt curses. The Sunjans cursed a lot, or so Arrus thought.

A scratching at his throat seized him then, and he coughed into the wall. Harsh, hacking notes that stung his sore throat. Each expulsion left him rumbling without any relief, and his gullet filled with what felt like raspy needles. Arrus swallowed painfully, thumped his head against the wall he'd been cleaning, and wished for another taste of beer. Just a drop, like they had flung at him days ago while he was leaving Sunja's Pit.

Beer. A distant, pleasant memory.

Blessed Curlord, he could use a drop of that now.

Since that time, the waters plaguing the dungeons underneath the arena had receded to his ankles. There it lingered, refusing to drain any further for some mysterious reason. Masked jailors carried torches or swinging lamps as they waded through the flooded corridors. They supplied the Nordish prisoners with buckets and cleaning materials, and with Rullik the Norseman interpreting, ordered them to scrub down every surface above the waterline.

The prisoners, pallid and sickly, did as told.

Water bobbing with split lemons and other mysterious seasonings filled those buckets, and when one was emptied, it was replaced. The jailors, dressed in their leathers, resembled orange-hued ghouls that haunted those flooded corridors. They cursed and splashed away at the filth drifting too close to them. At times they peered into the cells, lifting their torches to inspect the prisoners' efforts.

And one of them was approaching Arrus.

Torchlight shone upon water and gleaming stone and revealed the Nordish man leaning against a dungeon wall. The fierce glare forced him to avert his eyes, while droplets fell from the rag he held.

The jailor spoke, a harsh stream of syllables that ended in a chuckle.

Another cough scratched at Arrus's throat, and he let it out with a bark. That one explosive note grew into a violent hacking and forced him to double over, his hands going to his knees. After a time, he finished, growling and wincing with every swallow. He wheezed a sigh, holding his hitching chest, and felt that annoying rasp still tormenting him.

That outburst prompted the jailor to move on, perhaps a touch fearfully. He swished through the depths to the next cell, taking his torch with him.

In that lessening glow, Arrus stared, hollow-eyed and miserable, before something scraped his throat again. Another coughing fit followed, where the explosive force scrubbed his gullet raw. It stretched his ribs and buckled him, rattling his entire frame. In time the spell passed, leaving him dazed and unsteady and leaning against the wall. He spat in dribbles, a string of knobs that stretched to the water. With a gasp he wiped his mouth and tempted another storm with a few pained and wheezy breaths.

Curlord above, he thought, knowing he was well and truly miserable. The worsening cough was only part of his deteriorating health. Something had seized him over the last few days.

Every swallow clicked and ached. Every raspy breath threatened a paralyzing fit of coughing. At times, his head burned to the point of boiling, while his innards crystallized with chills. Worse still, the relief between those instances of burning and freezing seemed to be growing shorter, while the periods of suffering were growing longer. He knew one thing, however. He wasn't the only one sick. The Norjos man Rullik constantly barked and yowled as if he were attempting to summon fire from his throat. Heelslik coughed just as much but, even more worrying, when he started he couldn't seem to stop.

Men suffered in the same fashion throughout the dungeon, and just when it seemed all settled down, when the sounds quieted to nothing more than wheezy rattles in the dark, one began again. Great whooping expulsions that blasted the throat raw and left one near senseless.

Outside his cell, the torchlight strengthened again. The jailor sloshed his way back, perhaps to see if Arrus had died. The Sunjan stopped a step away from the cell bars, thinking matters over. After a beat, he held up his torch for a better look. Arrus cleared his sparkling throat, expelling soft curds and grimacing. He hoarked again, wanting to wash his mouth, his whole person, really, but lacking the clean water to do so.

"Get back to work," the jailor said, or so it *sounded* to Arrus, though he didn't rightly understand the meaning.

Message delivered and perhaps unwilling to risk his own health any further, the jailor sloshed away.

"Aye that," Arrus rasped back in the Nordish tongue, just before another outburst bent him over. The coughing forced him against the wall. His throat bristled and stabbed as if he'd choked down a cupful of dusty clay shards.

"Blessed Curlord," he muttered weakly and wiped his bearded face.

Then he remembered his water bucket. The one used for drinking.

With a splash he lurched to his bed and grabbed the empty container at the end. From there he sloshed back to the cell door, every step a struggle, the water fighting his every stride. The bars felt cold to the cheek as he mashed his face to them, searching for the departing jailor.

Off in the distance, the glow winked out of sight.

Panic flared in his chest. Arrus shouted and raked the bucket across the bars . . . but the Sunjan was gone. Quick as that.

"Blessed . . ." he trailed off. Again he doubled over, miserable to the core, and released the bucket. Holding his knees, he swallowed back his sickness and remembered the bed. The bare pallet once had straw covering it, but now only a single blanket lay there. A day ago, he had cleared the filthy strands away and stuffed them into a sack a jailor had provided, which some nearly naked Sunjan then carried away. The straw hadn't been replaced, not that Arrus cared. It only prickled him through the blanket anyway. He waded over to the bed and sat down with an exhausted grunt. There he wrestled with the damp blanket trapped underneath one ass cheek. Once freed, he lay down on bare planks and was thankful he rested above the water.

"Still alive over there?" Heelslik asked from the nearby darkness, sounding close to death himself.

"Aye that," Arrus replied, dragging the blanket up to his chest.

More coughing erupted nearby.

"That one sounded . . ." Heelslik paused, his words lost in a spell of hitching and wheezing. "Sounded bad . . ."

"Was bad," Arrus said and squirmed until his back touched the wall he'd cleaned that day. There he rested for a breath before rumbling. "My chest . . . feels like . . . it's filled with hot, watery shite. That eventually turns cold. And bubbles into my gullet."

"Mine as well."

"I've sucked down whatever was fouling the air."

"We all have," Heelslik said. "I can taste it."

"The taste . . . isn't as bad as before."

"No. Not as bad. Because of . . . that slop . . . we're scrubbing the walls with." Heelslik started coughing again. "Almighty Curlord," he finally gasped. "This is unfit."

"You have your water?" Arrus asked.

"I do. Hurts to drink it, though. My gullet is *raw*."

6

"Drink it anyway. I knocked over my water bucket."

"Did you now?" Heelslik said in an exhausted voice. "Unfortunate. Why not try . . . the slop in the other bucket?"

"Don't make me laugh. I'll have another coughing fit. If I do, I'll piss myself."

"Apologies."

"I wonder what they mixed in there . . ."

"As do I," Heelslik said as another prisoner broke into coughing, a violent discharge that lasted a long time.

Arrus waited until the noise stopped. "Probably tasted blood on that one," he finally said.

"Probably did. Maybe they'll take a few of us aboveground. To fight."

"I said . . . don't make me laugh."

"Apologies."

"I'm barely able to squat."

"It would be worth it," Heelslik said. "To be aboveground, I mean. Just for a breath of fresh air."

"And then we'd perish," Arrus groaned, the planks pressing into his face and side. *Misery upon misery*, he thought. Something crawled over his thigh and he feebly swatted at it. The flooding hadn't killed off all the crawlers in the dungeon, and that dampened his spirits all the more. Worse, that heaviness in his chest returned. Perhaps even heavier, as if thickened.

Someone slogged toward him through the corridor.

Arrus rose on an elbow. A jailor with a torch returned with five others at his back, the leather *X*'s across their chests flickering orange against the light as they filed in. Masks hid their features, and everyone was looking at him. In one hand, each quietly brandished a short sword or club, the faint wavering suggesting a readiness to use them if given the chance, and in the other, each carried a bucket. One jailor opened Arrus's cell while the others crowded in behind.

Arrus struggled to sit upright and held out his bucket. "I need fresh water."

That stopped the lead jailor. He emptied Arrus's cleaning bucket into the floodwater and backed away.

"Water," Arrus begged, rattling his container on the edge of the pallet.

The group scrutinized him and, for an instant, the Nordish prisoner thought the lead jailor might take a swing at him.

Rullik called out from the dark then, sounding distant, even though he occupied the cell next to Arrus's. The Norseman translated the request, his once strong voice stricken and hoarse.

The lead jailor muttered a few words to his companions, drawing soft chuckles from the lot of them.

Arrus's chest flared again, but with anger.

One of them snatched the bucket away from the Nordish man. The lead jailor spoke then, a string of gibberish lost on Arrus. Once the Sunjan finished, he closed the cell door, locked it with a clatter, and moved on to the next.

"Rullik," Arrus said.

"Yes?"

"Are they going to bring me water?"

"They will . . . ah . . . when they feel like it." Rullik answered.

Anger festered into hatred. "My thanks. For asking."

The Norseman didn't reply.

"How are you feeling?" Arrus asked, grimacing at a sharp pinch.

"Terrible," the unseen man said. "But my cell is clean."

"Well, there's that."

"I'm still jealous . . . of you . . . getting a taste of beer."

"Seems like weeks ago . . . but . . . it was only Sunjan beer."

"Any beer would be grand," Rullik said. "A whole mug would be as grand as a barrel. I would drink it all. Dare I even think of a drop of mead. Or firewater. That would be very fine."

Arrus agreed. "Better than any slop a healer might give you."

"Aye that. Very much so."

They quieted then, listening to the sick in the dungeon.

"The whole place is diseased," Arrus muttered.

"So it seems."

Snores came from Heelslik's cell, oddly comforting.

"Heelslik?" Arrus asked.

"He's sleeping," Rullik answered.

"I was just speaking with him."

"So I heard."

"He's fortunate he can sleep."

"He is that."

Arrus listened to the sleeping Jackal. "Rullik," he asked. "A word with you?"

"Certainly."

"I feel unfit."

"We all feel unfit."

"I suppose, but . . . I mean . . . in a way I've never felt before. There's the sickness part of it, to be sure, but then . . . there's a darkness as well. Clinging to my chest. Smothering it. Weighing down both my heart and mind."

"That's dire, indeed," Rullik noted quietly.

"What do you make of it?" Arrus asked.

"Have you felt like this before?"

The death of his brother, Kra, came to mind. "Yes."

"Did you get better?"

Had he? "Yes," Arrus said and believed it to be true. "In time."

"Then face it. Confront it. And fight it off. You're a Nordish Jackal, after all. And truly, what's death? You know it. You've faced it. Fed it. Countless times over. Don't let some inner torment take you. That's a path to ruin."

Arrus supposed it was, knew it was, but the feeling tormented him still. "I don't know what to do."

"Just do . . . what I *said* to do," Rullik insisted, his voice closer. "You're a Jackal, blessed Curlord above. Even more . . . you're *Arrus*. You went into the Pit expecting to die. You came *back*. With a story that left us envious and . . . and longing for *beer*, of all things." The Norseman chuckled, a light and pleasant sound, and did not break into a cough. "Don't think about a week from now. Think only of *this* day. Make it through this day. Then make it through *tomorrow*. Then the next. You're made of hard stuff. Much harder than whatever's tormenting you. Starve it. Defeat it. Then . . . throw it aside like the useless skin it is. That and the sickness."

A coughing fit finally broke him, and Arrus waited until the man finished.

"Apologies," Rullik wheezed. "Talking brings it on. As I said. You're made of harder stuff. Sleep. Rise. And push. Then do it all again. Each day. Until you shove that darkness away. And become stronger for it. You hear me?"

"I hear you."

"Will you do it?"

Arrus sighed, not quite convinced. "I'll try."

"Will you *do* it?"

He sighed and nodded. "I will."

"All right. That's fine enough for me. And here."

A rustling of movement turned Arrus's head, and a filthy spider of a hand, barely seen in the dark, extended outside the bars to his cell. There it waited.

"Take it," Rullik whispered.

Unsure of what to expect, Arrus reached out and gripped that hand, the flesh hard and calloused. On the other side of the shared wall, Rullik held on, transferring warmth that was far better than mere words alone, and very much needed.

He squeezed back, and the two men held on to each other for a time.

"Words can stay with one," Rullik said, his grip unrelenting. "But then there's the strength. And spirit. And dare I say . . . *comfort* in the touch of a friendly hand. You mind this day, young Arrus. Survive it. Know that you survived it, and then . . . tomorrow . . . do it all again. And if you need me, I'll be here with a good word or two. Just to let you know all is well."

Arrus squeezed harder, which wasn't very much considering how weak he was. "My thanks, Rullik."

He held on for a few heartbeats more before releasing the Norseman's hand.

Not long after, someone strode through the water again, marring the waves and coming closer. Arrus lowered himself to his bunk. The sloshing stopped directly outside his door.

A jailor appeared with a water bucket. Two buckets, in fact. A handful of Skarrs slogged into sight, their armor gleaming in the torchlight.

The jailors spoke.

"He says, here's your water," Rullik reported, "and that he decided to bring you two buckets instead of one."

". . . Good of him," a wary Arrus replied.

The jailor continued speaking while one of his henchmen shuffled to the door and produced a key.

The darkness flared within Arrus again.

"He says," Rullik translated, "now that he's done something for you, you must do something for him . . ."

The cell door squealed open.

Daylight shone through the portcullis above, casting a pattern of sun and shadow upon stone steps.

Half of the gatekeeper's unruly beard was flattened, as if the man had slept on that side of his face the whole night. The old bastard sensed Arrus's scrutiny and glared a question. Not needing the trouble, Arrus looked to the stairs. The disappointed shouts of hundreds, perhaps thousands, reached his ears from above, informing him of all the Nordish man needed to know.

The crowd was not looking forward to another fight between prisoners.

Arrus agreed with them.

The familiar darkness enveloped his heart and gave it a worrisome squeeze. A round of coughing took him as well, but not so severe since he was clear of the dungeon. When the coughing passed, a nearby Skarr offered a short sword, the blade resembling the one he'd used before. Perhaps it was even the same one—old and practically without an edge, resembling more of a club.

Frowning, Arrus clasped the leather-bound hilt.

The gatekeeper pulled a lever and unseen gears groaned into motion. The portcullis cranked upward with a rhythmic rattle.

The Skarr jerked his head, signaling for Arrus to get moving.

The Jackal climbed the stairs, fearing the effort would kill him. A dewy sheen of perspiration coated him despite breathing better since leaving the dungeon. Halfway to that yawning opening, he stopped, hoarked, filled his mouth with a vile wad, and sent it flying.

"Get out and walk," he muttered.

On impulse, he chanced a look behind him.

Below, six soldiers watched him, along with the gatekeeper. Visors hid the guards' expressions. The gatekeeper did not have a visor, and he appeared doubtful, probably expecting Arrus to collapse at any time.

The Nordish man turned and continued climbing, grunting the higher he got. Blinding sunlight greeted him, and its heat damn near stole his breath, steaming his all-but-naked body. Gasping, almost finished by the stairs alone, Arrus staggered onto the arena's sands. He avoided inspecting himself, knowing he was filthy. He was long used to his own stink, but the sun-loosened sweat released a bodily stench that repulsed even him. If he lived to return to his cell, he promised himself he would use that lemony slop water to scrub himself down. Worse still, that troubling darkness within his chest had sunk its claws deeper, bleeding him of both strength and spirit. His forehead went tight for reasons he wasn't sure of, and a mysterious pressure bore into his temples. A breeze whistled in his ears, like a woman's hot breath, but he wasn't sure if it was real or not.

A figure emerged across the way, beyond the shimmers of the scalding sands. Bare-chested, loin-clothed, and carrying a short sword. Probably one with a much better edge to the steel.

The crowds savagely voiced their displeasure at the offered combatants. They shook fists and swore. Tossed gurry into the arena and spat wine. One hairy lout, half pickled from drink and sitting in the lower section of the arena, pressed his thighs against the rim of the wall. The Sunjan unsheathed his manhood and pissed into the sand, cursing all the while.

Arrus looked away. His nagging cough returned, rocking his frame and filling his mouth once more. Sunbaked and sweating, he spat the gob away and trudged toward his opponent.

Who stayed where he was.

That soured Arrus's mood all the more. *Unfit*, he thought—or at least the Nordish equivalent—and blinked away a dribble of perspiration that attacked one eye. All he needed was a damn *poltu* unwilling to meet him halfway. With the fury of both sun and crowd, Arrus didn't think it wise to linger. The spectators wanted blood and they wanted it *now*.

The sand burned his feet as he crossed the midway point, while the people swore oaths upon the whole affair. Arrus didn't care anymore. The darkness in his chest had relaxed somewhat, but the rest of him still wasn't fit for this.

And still his opponent didn't move.

That puzzled the Nordish man . . . until his opponent started coughing.

Truly coughing.

Powerful enough to set the lad's frame shivering. The very sight of it slowed Arrus to a stop.

His opponent was sinewy, his upper body resembling a stretched-out knot of muscular cords without a trace of fat. He was pale, far too pale, really, and festered with flowering sores. The prisoner bent over while his sword sank to the sand. There he stayed, seized by another fit of hacking, until he checked on his foe. That one look revealed eyes red and sunken, set above puffing cheeks. Spittle freckled his bearded face.

The sick man cringed just before another bout doubled him over, ignoring Arrus completely. The force of each blast robbed him of his strength and he dropped to both knees before putting hands and elbows to the sands.

Amid the angry urgings of the spectators, the Nordish man did not know what to do. His opponent clearly wasn't fit to lift a sword, let alone fight, and Arrus hesitated to go any farther. Continue on he must, however, else the Skarrs would march out and finish them both.

"Can you fight?" he asked, making himself heard over the noise.

The man didn't seem to hear, but that was understandable since he had lowered his forehead to the ground, his shoulders shivering with every cough.

His concern growing, Arrus glanced around. "I said, can you fight?"

The prisoner stopped coughing and turned his head.

Good, Arrus thought, eyeing the angry onlookers spilling over the lip of the arena wall, not twenty strides away. The Sunjans there leaned over the brickwork and shook fists, goading them to get on with the butchery.

Arrus took a tighter grip of his blade and regarded his opponent.

The sight of a blood-covered hand sparked a chill despite the heat.

The sickly prisoner studied the grim surprise coating his palm, which he held stretched out before him. He clenched a fist and looked about, as if searching for something. Then he lifted his face to Arrus. Blood speckled the man's lips and beard as he managed a red smile.

Arrus retreated a step, unsure if his foe's sickness was different from his own.

The Sunjan spoke, the words and meaning lost in the roar of the crowd. He swallowed and coughed once more. Blood sprayed from his mouth. The episode didn't last long, but it clearly drained his strength. With a feeble effort he rocked himself back onto his knees, his head hung between sagging shoulders.

Something flew out of the crowd. Arrus ducked as a bottle flew past his face, a wet line lashing one cheek.

The sick man looked up, chest and shoulders hitching. He spoke, too weak to be heard, and frowned in weary frustration.

Arrus knew the other was also a prisoner but didn't know his crimes. He suspected the lad might be Sunjan, not that it rightly mattered anymore. He met the gaze of those weary, unwell eyes, and realized one sad truth . . . whatever the man *might* have been before was gone, and all that remained was someone ready to get on to the next existence, wherever that might be.

The very air trembled with shouts and screams, needing no translation.

The prisoner swayed, perhaps one coughing fit away from falling over. He said something, but Arrus shook his head, unable to hear a word.

So the sick man pointed.

Arrus looked over his shoulder.

Skarr. Emerging from an opened portcullis. Armored, bearing a sword and shield, and walking with purpose toward the two prisoners.

"Skarr," the sick man mouthed.

Arrus agreed with a nod. He took a firmer grip of his blade.

The sick man closed his eyes.

And with whatever strength the Nordish man could muster, he brought that club of a blade down upon the prisoner's skull. Bone split in a shocking clatter, scattering secrets across the ground. The other prisoner toppled and Arrus nearly joined him.

In the bloody aftermath, the audience quieted for a beat before bursting into cheers. They approved. Somewhat. No doubt glad the contest was finished.

That one killing blow took everything from Arrus, however, and he staggered a step before righting himself. Looking around, he realized he had another problem.

The Skarr still marched toward him, visor lowered, face unreadable, sword and shield at the ready.

Arrus had no idea if he was about to be herded back to the gate or killed right there and then. He wavered on defending himself or dropping the blade and surrendering.

The Skarr, his armor bright under the sun, came within two dozen strides. Sensing violence, the crowds warmed to the approaching soldier, eager to see a second killing.

Arrus realized he really didn't have to do anything. The Skarr had already decided what would happen, and all the Nordish man had to do was accept it. His chest rumbled with sickness and, considering the execution he'd just performed, Arrus didn't care what happened in the next few moments. If the Skarr decided to kill him, he hoped it would be quick.

Coughing, Arrus plunged his blade tip-first into the sand, meaning to sink it. The resulting deflection nearly twisted his wrist off when he failed to penetrate the ground at all.

The soldier drew closer, sword and shield raised.

Weaponless, Arrus got to his knees and nearly fell over.

The Skarr stopped within three paces of him.

The crowds roared, *pleading* for his death. A smattering of something pelted the back of Arrus's head, stressing that very thought.

Crushed nutshells.

The flurry distracted the Skarr. The soldier sized up the unarmed Nordish man then inspected the corpse splayed across the white sand. The angry cries grew so loud, Arrus would not have heard a word from the soldier anyway.

Decision made, the Skarr regarded the waiting Jackal.

And motioned for him to rise.

"What happened out there today?" a dismayed Soranthus demanded. The representative of the Gladiatorial Chamber clearly wasn't pleased with the dismal showing in the Pit. He wasn't yelling. Not yet. But anger was not far off. "What *happened*?" he repeated. "I mean, that was rubbish. No, that's not right—that was *shite*. Pure shite. Did you see that match? The one between the Jackal and that other one? Prisoners selected by *you*? That wasn't a fight. That was a damn *execution*. And what did I say about executions in the Pit? What did I say?"

Hiding the nerves clanging inside him, Balazz gnawed upon his upper lip while nodding. Runson stood alongside him, head lowered, weathering the barrage like a child hoping the storm would soon pass. They all gathered within the jailors' common room, where Soranthus had confronted them.

And trapped them.

"Apologies, Master Sore—" *Ass*, Balazz *almost* said, and the fatal slip frightened him badly. "Soranthus. I did not see the fight. I did hear what happened, however. As for your other question, you clearly said you would permit an execution."

"To bring the others in line," Runson added.

Soranthus glared and the temperature within the room became that much cooler.

"Let me clarify one point," the Chamber member said, taking a moment to compose himself. Balazz appreciated the effort, but he was already making plans for someone to replace Runson, whom he would gladly toss to the Skarrs if it meant saving his own hide.

"They have to be *able* to fight," Soranthus stressed. "Not like what happened out there today. That wasn't a fight. That was a sorry meeting between two dying pissers, where one just happened to perish. And it's not the first time this has happened. I *had* hoped that the contests might improve. They have not. And the audience? They know gurry when they see it. They were demanding the deaths of both those dogs when the Skarr appeared."

"It's not our fault," Runson muttered, inspecting his feet before squinting at parts of the room—anywhere but where Soranthus stood. Along with a dozen or so soldiers accompanying the Chamber member.

Runson abruptly stopped looking about, as if realizing who he was addressing. "There was a flooding, Master Soranthus," he quickly explained. "A monstrous flooding. The dungeons here were built years ago. Hundreds of years ago. Everything was floating—"

And on he gushed, damn near drowning the Chamber member with the retelling of how the recent rainstorm had all but submerged the dungeons. All the while, Balazz nodded in support, still ready to offer up Runson if he had to—in one fluttering heartbeat, guaranteed.

When Runson finished, Soranthus sighed and studied the ceiling, unsure what to make of it all. The Skarrs at his back, however, seemed a step closer to the jailors, on the verge of encircling them. Balazz didn't notice them moving, however, and their subtle repositioning very much disturbed him.

"All right," Soranthus granted. "All right. None of that can be helped. No one could anticipate a storm of that size. Or its effects upon the dungeons. Or the prisoners. Understandable. I'll return to the surface. The Free Trained will entertain the masses for the next few days until the prisoners get back to some state of health."

That was news to Balazz. "Ah . . . begging your pardon, Master Soranthus, but . . . how exactly will they get back to health?"

"I'll send down a healer."

"A healer, Master Soranthus?"

"Yes."

"You're . . . going to *nurse* them back to health?" The very notion stunned the jailor.

"I'm not, but the healer will."

That left Balazz at a loss. He was far more used to smashing and outright killing the rosy pig bastards in his dungeons. Not . . . *caring* for them.

"One healer isn't enough, Master Soranthus," Runson said, supporting the idea. "Far from it. Best to send more. Many more. As many as you can spare. Not that I care, mind you. The prisoners are all flecks of maggot shite to me. But if you want them taking the heads off each other, out there on the sands, best send down a group of healers. To speed matters along."

"They are a sickly group," Balazz muttered, shaking off his initial shock. "Terribly sick. And it might take time for them to get better."

"A terribly long time," Runson said.

Soranthus looked from one to the other.

"Very well," the Chamber member grumbled.

2

Inside a Salish temple, robed priests walked about with ceremonial grace. A small gathering of onlookers waited, enduring the holy men as they recited their prayers for the dead. The Salish, twelve of them, had arranged themselves on either side of a wooden plank, where the recently deceased rested.

A black blanket covered the first corpse, a man called Borchus. The priests blessed the body and mumbled through a prayer meant to protect the dead in the next life. They anointed the corpse with holy herbs and lifted it off a low table. From there they guided the body into a waiting oven. The fire within flared briefly as the priests fed it with the corpse and closed the iron doors. There were no tears. No words of grief. No family or friends with long, miserable faces. The attendants who had brought the body to the Salish simply left and that was that. It wasn't an uncommon occurrence.

The second corpse of the day, brought in with the man—well, that one was different.

Sindra had been wrapped in white from head to toe and adorned with flowers. A thin cloth covered her face. A second stone oven waited to receive her body, her feet no more than an arm's length away. The open oven resembled an unhappy mouth, where orange teeth fluttered and crackled. A solemn murmuring rose just above the rumble of the fire, as did Telda's uncontrollable grieving. Novus, her husband, a builder of chairs, held his sobbing wife close, feeling her terrible sadness moisten his shoulder. Young Barrud, the barkeep, stood nearby, transfixed by the oven's fire, still in disbelief that Sindra was no more. Mori and his small group of enforcers were in attendance as well, their heads lowered.

Then there was Gurga.

Standing a head over the other mourners, the bearded enforcer stared at the crackling flames, his hairy features set like grim stone, eyes as piercing as polished marble. He wore his best clothing—which meant his cleanest—that being gray pants and a white shirt opened halfway down the chest. Curls of chest hair poked through, mostly black but some silver.

The fire mesmerized him.

The prayers stopped and Telda's sobbing intensified with a pitiful wail. Novus drew her closer.

"She wasn't supposed to die," Telda cried, clutching at her man. "She wasn't supposed to die. She wasn't *supposed* to—"

Novus pressed her face to his neck.

Unaffected by the emotional display, the head priest signaled for the ceremony to continue. Twelve priests carried Sindra's body to the mouth of the oven. Her feet went first, and they slid her inside without issue. One of the Salish closed the oven's ornate doors as the flames rose over the deceased. A puff of smoke lingered upon the air, the last of the very essence of the alehouse owner.

The head priest concluded the service with a few final words and a respectful bow. None of the priests left the burial chamber, however, as the custom was to wait until after the family and friends departed.

Mori the enforcer sighed and glanced around. With a despondent look at Novus and Barrud, he gestured that they should leave.

"*No!*" Telda wailed. "Not yet, *not yet!*"

She didn't resist, however, when Novus guided her to the door and the stairs beyond.

The enforcers followed them out, and Barrud stepped in behind them. One of the last to leave, Mori hesitated. He studied

Gurga's intimidating bulk, taking in those massive arms and build, eyeing the stern, stonelike expression fixed on the iron doors of the oven.

"Ah . . . Gurga?" Mori asked gently, very much unsure as to how the other would react. "Gurga, is it?"

No response. Not even the Salish moved.

Mori doubted he could count on those temple slaves if the big man turned violent. Seddon above, they'd *all* be praying if that happened.

"Gurga," he tried again. "It's time to leave."

Gurga stared on.

"She's . . . gone, Gurga. To, ah, a better place. I would imagine. Unfortunate, this one. So very unfortunate. She was . . . she was too good to die. Far too good. Aye that. Come on, now . . . let's leave."

Gurga didn't appear to hear. He certainly didn't move when Mori gestured for the door. The mighty enforcer stood fast like a stone pillar.

Seddon above, Mori thought. He reminded himself that he was in a temple of the holy one. A different approach would be needed.

"Gurga," he began. "I know you miss her . . . but remember her in other ways. Not like this. Not . . . stone and iron and smoke. Sindra smelled nothing like smoke. So that won't do, and truth be known, I don't think Sindra would *want* you to remember her that way. She'd want you to remember her as she always was. Smiling and—"

Gurga turned and walked from the chamber, leaving Mori to stare with his mouth open. He watched the enforcer's broad back as he climbed the stairs. The big man did not look back.

Shrugging at the Salish, and after one last parting headshake at the closed oven, Mori followed.

Outside the temple they gathered behind a stone wall that shielded the Salish from the tide of busy Sunjans traveling beyond. Telda bawled into her husband's neck, wet and loud enough to distract anyone hearing her. Barrud placed a hand upon her shoulder. Red, streaming eyes appeared as she lifted her head at the contact.

Seeing who it was, Telda left her husband and latched onto the barkeep, startling him with a powerful hug.

"She's gone, Barrud, she's *gone!*" she wailed, burying her face in his neck.

"Aye that, she's gone," Barrud winced, regretting his words the instant they left his mouth.

Telda bawled in his ear and squeezed even harder.

"You're going to deafen the poor lad," Novus said, touching his wife's shoulder.

Trembling, hitching, Telda slowly released the barkeep. She wiped her face with a wet cloth and once again latched onto her husband.

"Can't really blame her," Barrud said, suddenly red-eyed. "Sindra was . . . well . . . she was . . ."

"She was the best," Mori finished, squinting at the tall spires of the Salish temple.

"Aye that," Barrud agreed.

Mori looked at where Gurga stood, off from the rest of them. Lost in his own thoughts, the big man stared at the crowds walking past the open gate. The brutish enforcer still hadn't said a word.

Mori spoke to Barrud. "I know it's an unfit time, but . . . what will happen to the alehouse?"

With the exception of Gurga, they all regarded Telda. Even Mori knew she was Sindra's second-in-command when it came to the business.

Barrud studied the stricken woman before clearing his throat. "Sindra made it known, time and time again, that if anything ever happened to her, or if she decided to give up the business, Telda would have the alehouse. If she wanted it."

Telda released another miserable roar, one quickly muted by burying her face into her husband's wet shirt. They waited for her to control herself, which took a while.

"I'll have it," she finally whispered, red-faced and pitiful. "I'll have it."

And that was that.

"Barrud, what about you?" Telda asked in a hitching voice. "Will you . . . will you stay?"

"I'll stay," the young man said. "Can't do anything else. Filling mugs and wiping tables are all I know. I'll stay if you'll have me."

"I'll have you," she said with a sniffle. "Mori? You and your lot? Feel like doing a . . . a bit of enforcing?"

Mori hesitated before nodding at Gurga. "You have an enforcer."

"Oh," Telda said and vigorously wiped at her nose. "You're right. Yes. Oh, I'm sorry, Gurga. So terribly sorry. I should have asked you first. But I just thought . . . just *figured* you would . . ."

Her pleading turned Gurga's head. The dense scruff of facial moss hanging off his chin shifted just a bit as he scowled that familiar scowl of his.

"Will you?" she implored.

Gurga merely stared on.

Later that day, in the room that had been his home for a very long time, Gurga leaned against the closed door. The huge bed before him creaked and groaned with every turn he made upon it. The same bed had clean blankets that Sindra insisted on cleaning for him on a regular basis. His hard features softened just a touch at the memory. Softened even more when he remembered Sindra bringing him his meals. Or a drink of something good. He remembered her hard reprimands of how he dealt with troubling patrons—which he still believed the punces deserved. She was the owner and mistress of the alehouse, however, so her words were law, and Gurga's duty was to obey them.

That brought back the familiar scowl.

Here and there, dust speckled in the corners of the room, but it met his standard of cleanliness. Sindra constantly reminded him to clean his room and, while he did, he often left a few corners untouched. Until the dust became webs, whereupon he would tidy up immediately. More memories then, of her standing in the doorway, talking to him while he dusted. Talk of the day before, the day that was, or the approaching night and what might come of it. When he guarded the alehouse entrance, she always made it a point to check on him, perhaps offer a face towel or a drink, especially during the hot summers. If there was an argument between him and customers, she always took his side at first, but questioned him thoroughly to get to the truth of the matter. She could fearlessly scold him at times, but always left him with a good word, magically motivating him to do better in the future.

Not too many could do that.

The trainers and taskmasters at old Tilo's had striven to do that very thing and failed, back when Gurga had tried his hand at being a gladiator. Back then, he was too slow of foot. Easily fooled by a feint and a touch too uncoordinated. Without question, they said, he was powerful beyond measure, and certainly possessed the brutal nature necessary for the business. Still, after watching him train, they knew well enough that the first skilled gladiator to face Gurga upon the sands would cut him to pieces. So they said.

That resulted in Old Tilo passing him off to Sindra to hire as an enforcer. Thinking back, it was the best thing to have ever happened to Gurga. The very best thing. He'd gotten fortunate. So very, very fortunate.

That thought tightened his cheesepipe, painfully so, the ache stretching deep into his chest and moistening his eyes.

Sindra. Lovely, fair-minded Sindra.

The corridor still had her scent upon it, and that very smell both saddened and relaxed him. Made him believe, just for the cruelest moment, she was somewhere below, moving about the tables or talking with Telda over the mysteries of the kitchen. Gurga remembered Sindra's soft, pleasant laugh, as well as her scowl. He'd earned enough of those.

He'd earned many more smiles, however.

So he waited, quietly, for her to come walking up the steps, where the creaks would announce her every footfall. He kept waiting, hoping it was just a bad dream, a nightmare, truth be known. In the end, however, he knew she would not be visiting him today. Not now. Or ever.

His throat constricted just a touch more. He cleared it, sniffed, and cleared his throat again. At some point, he dabbed the wetness from his eyes and wiped his hands on his pants. Once certain he'd gotten some measure of control, he went to his chest and threw it open. Inside was a sack, which he took and stuffed with the last of his clean clothing. He jammed a spare belt into the sack, as well as a much wider belt, one that he wore around his midsection to protect against knife thrusts. Once he had gathered his few possessions, he reached down into one corner of the chest and felt a sizable purse there. One of a dozen.

He took the purse and hefted it.

Sindra never officially paid him for enforcing the peace within the alehouse. He'd heard her say it many times over. Truth be known, however, on the good nights, the *very* good nights, when the coffers were overflowing, she would give him what she called "his share" to spend as he wished. Gurga never really thought much about the coin. Never really needed it. He was constantly provided for—food, drink, and even clothing of all things (chosen by both Sindra and Telda, and uneasily approved of by Barrud). And all he ever had to do was look frightening and put fear into a punce's head every now and again.

Or toss the unfit pig bastard into the street. Little bit of that never hurt anyone. Not in Gurga's mind, at least.

Sindra, however, insisted that he take the coin and spend it on something he liked or save it for when times were difficult. *Times will be difficult*, she had told him, but never too difficult if one prepared for them.

His scowl deepened as he tucked the purse away inside his shirt.

Difficult times had arrived.

The most difficult time he'd ever come across. The *worst*.

The sadness returned, welling up inside him, squeezing his throat and wetting his eyes. He closed the chest, locked it with a key, and took one last look about the room that had been his home for many years. Floating in the dust were the thoughts of a woman who had welcomed him and treated him fairly and decently and had given him a purpose. A purpose at a time when he thought he had none.

Gurga sighed heavily, sniffed again, and scrubbed a finger across his nose. His dark eyes dimmed further.

He had a different purpose now.

His attention settled upon his spiked club for a long, considering moment. After a while, he reached for it and grasped the end. Having made that decision, he left the room.

And, as Sindra had warned him so many times before, he closed the door as softly as possible behind him.

Telda, Barrud, and Novus sat around a table on the ground floor, staring at nothing, lost in memories. No patrons were present this afternoon, as Telda had placed a sign outside the entrance and barred the door. Three pitchers and four mugs were before them, but they barely touched the drinks. Sunlight streamed inside through half-opened windows, casting lonely beams across a clean-swept floor.

Gurga descended from upstairs, his slow footfalls breaking the silence.

Their heads lifted upon hearing him, and they watched him step into a single swath of sunlight.

"Gurga?" Telda asked, her voice raspy from grief.

The enforcer shifted the sack, a great bulbous thing slung over one shoulder, and looked to the window. His other fist held the great spiked club.

"Won't you sit with us?" she asked. "Just for a bit? It would make me feel better."

Gurga didn't appear to hear.

"Gurga?"

The enforcer left the sunlight and walked over to the table. There he stopped and eventually held out a key.

"Oh . . ." Telda said in a little voice. "Not you."

Gurga said nothing to that.

"Please, no, don't go," she pleaded.

"Keep that," he rumbled. "For when I return."

Telda stared at him. "That room is yours. Always yours."

Gurga supposed it was. Telda was a good person. She could talk anybody to sleep if allowed to, and she certainly made him feel as if hornets were trapped inside his skull at times. But . . . she was a good person. A good cook as well.

He continued holding out the key and she reluctantly took it.

"Where are you going?" Barrud asked.

"Out there," Gurga said. "For a bit."

That confused and alarmed Barrud, for he knew the big man rarely ventured far. And he couldn't imagine, for the life of him, the alehouse without the grim enforcer.

"For how long?" Telda asked.

But Gurga didn't answer. He studied Telda's sad face and remembered happier times. He then studied Barrud's sad face and remembered happier times. Gurga stopped at Novus. The singular weight of the enforcer's glare froze Telda's husband in place. Gurga couldn't remember much about him. Not that it mattered. He was Telda's husband. That was enough.

Having said his awkward goodbye, Gurga left them all. He went to the door, unbarred it, and walked out without a glance back.

Enduring the heat, Gurga lumbered through the busy streets using his spiked club as a walking stick. He had no trouble navigating the crowds and clutters of wagons, being the sizable brute that he was. Knots and tangles of faceless city folk split apart upon seeing him approach. Occasionally he had to wait behind the busier ones, those too oblivious to notice his shadow looming over them. The children were the worst. They stopped and stared at him without fear, unwittingly becoming low obstacles that reached his thighs. Gurga didn't mind the stares—he'd long since gotten used to them, in fact—but he did have to exercise caution around them, not wanting to knock any down as he passed. Then there were the mothers, also staring, usually with distrust, or the fathers, uneasily hoping beyond hope that they wouldn't have to be called upon to defend their family. Soldiers, mercenaries, and other assorted punces who thought themselves dangerous glowered at Gurga, scrutinized him warily as if remembering him. Some of them were tall by Sunjan standards, reaching as high as his jawline, but the majority of heads surrounding him leveled out at his upper chest. Some even attempted to talk to him for some unfit reason.

He walked by them all.

A wagon driver wearing a broad hat spotted him and gave him a dirty eye, warning him to keep clear. The driver sat in the wagon's perch, and a small hill of caged chickens clucked merrily at his back. When the big enforcer reached the wagon, the driver—an older man with a swarthy face—realized just how big the brute was. Unconcerned with the alarmed look, Gurga walked by. It was always that way for him, especially among crowds, and he'd grown numb to it. He'd grown the beard and kept it untrimmed to look even more savage, and that quelled most of the conversations others tried to start with him. Gurga wasn't one for conversations. He knew that. Knew he had a very limited capacity for social engagement. Knew he had patience, but no time for talk.

His strengths lay elsewhere.

Later that day, with a healthy sheen of perspiration soaking through his clothing, Gurga neared his destination. He lumbered down a wide lane, where retreating shards of sunlight revealed floating dust. He turned at a corner, and the lane narrowed while the shade deepened, granting just a little reprieve from the heat. Gurga followed a high wall of sandy stone until he reached a closed gate, where battlements loomed overhead. It was a good wall. Well-cut and fitted. A fortress within a fortress, truth be known, surrounding a sizable plot of land and bespeaking the owner's wealth. The gate was a tall and dark thing, with planks of heavy Hrand timber reinforced by iron bars. A vile coating of pitch stained the wood, warding it against the elements. The builders had inserted a wicket gate inside the larger door, and within that smaller portal was a slotted peephole, currently closed.

Gurga rapped upon the hard surface exactly three times.

The iron covering the slot snapped open and a set of eyes stared out. They blinked in confusion for a moment, before angling upward, making an effort to do so. The gaze narrowed into a squint as the owner stooped, to better take in the towering visitor.

"Eh, who are you?" asked the guard, mouth unseen, but his eyes taking it all in.

"Gurga," the enforcer answered.

"Gurga?"

Gurga nodded.

"You're a right big bastard."

He didn't respond to that, having heard it all before.

"Well, what do you want?" the guard asked, perhaps secure in the knowledge that the giant couldn't get through the gate.

"Want to see Tilo."

The eyes narrowed even further. "That's *Master* Tilo to you."

". . . Master Tilo, then."

"What do you want to see him about?"

"Need to talk to him."

"About what?"

Gurga didn't answer.

"Look," the guard said, taking a breath to explain matters. "I'm not being saucy here, all right? If I go to Master Tilo and say, 'Oh, excuse me, sar. There's a bearded giant at the gate and he wants to see you,' he's going to say to *me*, 'Well, what does he want?' Right? 'Course he is. Except I won't be able to *tell* him . . . because I don't *know* what you want. See the problem? Especially someone like you. You're a right intimidating pisser and it's still daylight. Wouldn't want you to come visiting at night. Right? *Right*? So what's all this about then?"

"Tell him . . . it's Gurga."

"All right. It's Gurga. And what does Gurga want?"

Truth be known, Gurga wanted to strangle this punce of a guard, but what he said was, "Sindra's perished."

"Sindra's perished. All right. And your name's Gurga. Anything else?"

"He'll know."

"He will, will he?"

Gurga didn't answer.

"All right, I'll go tell him. Just to prove to you I'm not being saucy. Because I'm not. Even though the heat's hard enough to cook one's head. I can use the walk, anyway. Wait here, then."

Metal snapped across the slot.

Gurga sighed and examined the thick timbers of the gate. Then the battlements above. The walls stood about two and a half levels up, if he remembered right. Far too high to climb, and he didn't intend to do any foolishness like that. He just wanted to talk to old Tilo. *Master* Tilo, as the guard so rightfully reminded him.

So he waited, eyeing those dark timbers stained with pitch, smelling it in the heat of the day. A few street-farers trod by, slowing as they beheld the size of him. Gurga didn't pay any attention to that gurry. A fly buzzed by his ear and he didn't flinch. His wait ended with the heavy grind of timber being removed from an unseen latch. The smaller portal swung open and a guard stuck his head out, grimacing at the size of the visitor.

"You truly are a big pisser," he grumbled, sounding like the one who'd spoken to him earlier. "Think you can fit through here?"

Gurga did, lowering himself and slipping through sideways, backing up the guard and three others carrying spears. It was tight, and the opening clawed him at points, but he got through. When he straightened, the men arched their heads.

"Leave the masher there," the guard ordered, pointing toward the portal wall. "Can't have you walking about with that thing. You're too damn frightening as it is."

Gurga put his club down as ordered.

"This way then," said the guard. The man walked on, relaxed enough, though sweat beaded the back of his neck. Into a grand courtyard they went, following a wide flagstone walkway built along a line of Vathian marble columns. Beyond the columns and not so far away, trainers whipped a dozen or so gladiators through their exercises. Bare-chested men squatted and lifted heavy timbers in a small clearing. In another corner, men wielded blunted blades and hacked out complex combinations upon wooden figures. A few others held wooden cups as they stood around a water barrel, eyeing the large visitor as he was led to the main residence. Servants moved about nicely landscaped lawns dotted with a few trees until they took notice of the big enforcer. When they did, they lurched to a stop, the wonder plain upon their faces.

Gurga spared them a glance and nothing more. He'd tried being a gladiator, had failed miserably, and didn't miss the sport in the least. He had something much more important. Or, at least, he used to.

They continued on, the gate guard and Gurga, treading past a large stone building before turning at a corner. The columns ended, but another structure loomed, one they approached from the side. A pair of armored men guarded a wide, red-ocher door. Gurga's guide acknowledged both before opening the portal, revealing a sunlit floor of stone tiles beyond. A whiff of some earthy fragrance enveloped him, not sweet or too heavy, something ladies would certainly like. An older woman, wearing robes and a shawl of flowered white, walked into sight and balked at the thing lurking upon the threshold.

"He's good enough," said the guard accompanying Gurga. "Just big is all."

The woman nodded but remained wary all the same. "This way then. Both of you."

The guard shrugged as if not expecting to go any further but did as told. He left his spear at the entrance and gripped the pommel of a short sword hanging from his waist scabbard.

Gurga took no offense.

The woman led them through a finely cleaned interior, much cleaner than Gurga's room at the alehouse. They stepped through a white archway that forced him to duck. The woman then indicated the pair wait before a wide set of stairs, one that ended at an open platform that rose to about waist height. There, the entire wall had been cut away to allow a view of the training grounds. A pair of marble fountains resembling sitting lions dribbled water on either end of the platform. A wide canopy stretched out, providing plenty of shade for whoever sat beneath it. And sitting alone at a fine table, between a pair of burly protectors already watching Gurga, was Master Tilo himself.

Old Tilo turned in his chair, attempting to get a better look at his visitor, and almost knocked over a lovely clay pitcher no doubt filled with wine. A robe of resplendent red covered his ancient frame. His gray beard looked even more slovenly than usual, and his black eyes squinted in puzzlement. Wood clattered off wood in the background, while trainers sporadically shouted instructions and moved among gladiators.

The woman hurried up the steps to the table and quickly righted the pitcher. Tilo waved to not make a matter of things. Then he considered his visitor once again.

"Gurga," he said, inspecting the enforcer with sage interest. "Been so long I barely recognize you. What business brings you here to my house?"

"Sindra's dead, Master Tilo," Gurga answered.

That summoned a frown to the old man's face. "Sindra?"

"She owned the alehouse," Gurga said. "The one where I worked."

Understanding dawned across Tilo's face. "Oh my. She's dead? How?"

"Killed by three knifemen. They're dead now."

The older man's mouth hung open and his black nubs of teeth glistened. "Sweet Seddon above," he muttered, his face turning sour. "Three knifemen, you say? Three?"

Gurga nodded.

"Where in Seddon's name was the street watch when this was happening? Unfit business. Unfit. Poor, poor Sindra. She was a lovely one. Simply lovely. Well. Thank you, Gurga. For telling me this bit of very bad news. I remember Sindra. I remember. A shame. A right and proper shame. You've darkened my morning. Darkened it quite a bit."

Gurga stared, his expression unreadable.

"So . . ." Tilo drew out, as if wondering how to best ask his question. "What are you going to do?"

Gurga thought about it. He'd been thinking about it for a long time.

"Are you looking for work?" Tilo asked. "Hm? My memory says you weren't quite fast enough to be a gladiator. And that was years ago. You're much too old for the Pit now. Much too old. I can give you a bit of work if you need it. Guard work. Something suited for you. Around here, that is. We'll find something for you."

"No."

The reply plainly surprised Tilo. He studied the man in a new light. "No?"

"No."

The owner shifted in his seat and exchanged looks with the lady standing nearby. "You wish to be a gladiator, then?"

"Not a gladiator," the big man answered. "Never was."

"Well, I might have other work for you then . . ."

"No."

"No?"

"I have work," Gurga replied with the subdued calmness of an executioner.

Gladiators continued to train in the background, their noisy efforts filling the uncomfortable silence.

"I see," Tilo finally said. "Well. Then. Thank you for bringing me that terrible, terrible news. I'll be thinking of Sindra for the rest of the day. She'll be missed. She'll be sorely missed."

She will, Gurga thought, and that damn near cut out his heart.

Tilo watched him. "No doubt you have . . . your work . . . to attend to, good Gurga, so I'll leave you to it. Guard. Escort this fine man back to the gate. See that he's not lacking for anything. He's one of the good ones. Thank you again, Gurga, although your news has . . . ruined me . . . for watching the lads go through their paces. Goodbye."

The dismissal didn't seem to reach Gurga, however, and he continued to stare at Tilo for long heartbeats. Then he considered the two guards upon the platform. He even regarded the woman wearing the flowered shawl.

"This way," said the guard from the gate, indicating that he should follow.

That unlocked the big man.

With a solemn nod to the owner, Gurga did so.

Tilo watched the towering brute as he shuffled out the door. When he was gone, the woman, Tilo's favorite servant, covered her mouth and shook her head.

"Bring me another pitcher of wine," Tilo said.

She left at once, leaving him with his thoughts.

Sindra was dead. He remembered the woman. Shame, really. She was as lovely as she was intelligent. Killed by three knifemen, no less. Knowing full well the service she provided for him, and the role of Gurga at her alehouse, he wondered if her death had anything to do with the recent disappearance of Senturo, his agent. Though Senturo was good at his work, Tilo didn't miss that two-legged street snake in the least. Tilo's instincts told him it was indeed all related.

He'd only really know the truth if the asslicker returned to him, and he believed the man was already quite dead. Perhaps packed away in some forgotten hole in the city's sewer system, never to be found again.

Or fed to pigs.

Another favored method of disposing of gurry.

Tilo sighed, idly checked the mug he held, and turned back to the activity upon the training grounds. He supposed he would need a new agent.

3

Daylight filled the cell, warming the wrecked form of Pig Knot. He stirred under the light, grimacing, before releasing a heavy sigh. The last thrashing left him on his side—where he woke up—facing the bars of his cage. Pig Knot cracked open swollen eyes. Snorted. Lifted a hand and saw the rags he'd bound around his broken fingers. Three broken fingers, all red and bloodied and swollen to the size of sausages. In fact, his entire hand looked like it had been mashed through a bloody press before being yanked free, leaving only his pointer and thumb intact.

For now.

Another long, miserable sigh leaked from the man who had wished he'd perished long ago.

Pig Knot lowered his hand and positioned it so it didn't hurt so much. He had to be careful of where he placed his hand. Sleep, true sleep, was elusive, as he discovered he moved his crippled paw while he slept. Twice he even flopped onto it. Those unconscious, traitorous acts resulted in him waking up with a song on his lips.

Well, a hissing, truth be known.

Once he had rolled over onto his bruised chest, every bit as tender as the rest of him. That resulted in a series of hot warning stabs that damn near robbed him of his breath. Both his broken fingers and his ribs reminded him to be more careful in the future. From then on, he slept on his other side or his back, keeping his abused hand stretched out and away from the rest of him.

Simply because the rest of him was a mess.

His tongue probed the holes of missing teeth, forcefully removed by some very hard fists. He suspected a boot or two had contributed to the ruination there. At one point in time, he'd believed himself to be a handsome man. Dashing, even, in a coarse sort of way. Not so now, and it bothered him enough that he tried not to dwell on it. The damage Kelmo had done to his face would be permanent. A work of legend, really. And since Pig Knot woke up breathing once again—much to his disappointment—he lay there in a perpetual state of agony and exhausted dread . . . of when the next bashing might occur.

And it would. Guaranteed. Kelmo had hammered him into his very personal slab of meat. Had repeatedly conveyed the sentiment that the legless length of fur-crusted gurry would perish in his cell. Pig Knot might have been able to fight back, but Kelmo had tenderized him to an incapacitated state. The Koor struck hard, struck often, and only stopped when Pig Knot's consciousness had departed . . . or the officer became too tired to continue.

No doubt, Machlann would have approved.

Head propped up against the wall, Pig Knot groaned at the sight of his battered torso, festering with angry blooms of purple, red, and unfit yellow. When he had enough of that, he looked through the bars of his cell. A stone wall waited beyond those bars and a passageway that forked left and right. Sharo, one of Kelmo's jailors, entered and exited from the left when he came to feed the prisoners. That scratched a little smile across Pig Knot's smashed features, one that quickly faded. *What did he eat before,* he wondered, *before he bedded the Koor's missus?* He remembered bread and apples. *Luxury* compared to what they were throwing at him now. Apples half rotten. The gristle and fat off a day's old roast. Bread soaked in piss, which Pig Knot lobbed at the squatting hole at the back of the cell. Even his water had yellow gobs of spit floating in the bucket. Water was water, however, so he closed his eyes and drank, telling himself the gobs were rotten berries.

Lords above, he'd fallen. Fallen hard, and still he drew breath.

His nose itched, so he lifted his right hand, the one still intact, and brought it in close to his face. A sigh left him as he frowned, yet the itch demanded to be serviced. He scratched, gently, and even that got him mewling. Even caused water to run from his eyes. *Tender.* As tender as overripe boils.

With a miserable groan, Pig Knot lowered his hand and stared beyond the bars of his cell.

"Are you all right?" a voice whispered. His neighbor, Zepedos, the thief.

"Aye that," Pig Knot said.

"I thought you were dead."

Pig Knot wheezed, wishing for that very thing.

"Can you talk?" Zepedos asked. "For a little?"

Pig Knot arched his back and let his breath go. "A little."

"Was she worth it?" the thief asked in a cautious voice.

"What?"

"Was she worth it?"

"Who?"

"The woman. The Koor's missus."

Oh. Her, Pig Knot thought. Lords above, he only just remembered her. Jana was her name. Sweet, lovely Jana, who snored the likes of which he'd never encountered in all his travels. Or would again, if he was fortunate.

Still . . . "Aye that," he said wearily. "She was worth it."

"I thought they'd killed you."

Pig Knot had hoped for that.

"Are you hungry?"

"Hurt . . . too much to eat."

"Thirsty?"

The thought of drinking anything caused him to shudder. "No."

Zepedos paused, perhaps thinking of whether or not to continue the one-sided conversation.

Pig Knot made the choice for him. "How long . . . have I . . ."

"Been unconscious?"

He grunted as an answer.

"Two nights."

That arched Pig Knot's brow. Kelmo and his lads had left him alone for that long?

"They come in to check on you," Zepedos explained. "They spare a glance for me but they're more interested with you. They watch you. Oh, they watch you for long moments. Talk to you, even."

"Talk?"

"Well, talk *at* you. You never answer them. They thought you were dead. Kelmo even went into your cell and kicked you. Kicked you hard. I heard it over here and thought . . . well . . . *I thought* you were dead. But Kelmo did something and said you weren't. Then . . ."

Pig Knot waited.

"Then he said 'good' and kicked you again. Left the cell and locked it. I saw his shadow leave and didn't say a word. Dared not to."

"Wise."

"I thought so. Truth be known, he's solely focused on you. I mean, with Sharo? I believed I would be here for a few months and then released. Perhaps even earlier. With you? What I've heard? Every time Kelmo enters, every time I hear someone unlocking the main door, I lower my head and wait. Wait until . . . I don't know. Wait until they decide you're done and drag you out by your heels. It reminds me of . . . sleeping next to a castle, one under siege by an army. And that army is lobbing catapult shots at the castle, without concern as to where they fall. Or what they hit."

Seeing as he was underneath that unfit storm, Pig Knot understood the sentiment. His nose itched again, but he didn't scratch it. Didn't have the strength.

"Well," the thief said. "I'm happy to know you are still alive."

"I'm not."

"We should not be talking for long."

That wasn't a bad idea.

"They could come back at any time," Zepedos said.

Pig Knot suspected they would. Kelmo had a taste for inflicting pain upon others. Perhaps he enjoyed it. When given the proper motivation. Like when he had a prisoner who had once rolled about in bed with his missus.

"I said they could—"

"I heard . . ." Pig Knot assured him.

"Apologies. I thought you'd gone on again."

Pig Knot shook his head, forgetting the thief next door could not see him. "You . . . asked . . . if I was hungry."

"Aye that, I did. Are you?"

"I . . . am."

"Hold on then . . ." Pig Knot heard the barest rustling of material on bare stone. Then the softest grunt. "Can you reach this?"

Pig Knot raised his head until a sharp stabbing seized his neck.

A grubby set of fingers stretched around the edge of the cell bars. Those fingers jiggled a half-eaten apple up and down.

"I held on to this," Zepedos explained. "Just in case. I would've eaten it this evening if you had not awakened. The rot would take it otherwise."

The sight of the apple summoned water to Pig Knot's mouth, much to his surprise, as if the wretched meat that was his nearly dead carcass wasn't quite ready to perish.

But the food was so far away.

"Can you throw it?" he asked.

"Throw it?" Zepedos asked. "My shoulder's tight to the stone as it is. No, I can't throw it."

Seddon above. Pig Knot shifted onto his good side, sparking a ripple of needles that sank deep into everything else. The sensation ripped a gasp from him and left him motionless for a beat, until things settled. He fumed and whimpered like a hurt dog while those dirty fingers waved that bit of fruit.

And he wanted that bit of fruit.

Huffing, bracing himself for the next part, he lowered himself onto his chest so that his hands—especially the one with the broken fingers—were ahead of him. It was slow work, achingly slow, where every exertion rubbed a little more hurt into his bruises, threatening to transform those prickling needles into dagger thrusts.

"What are you doing?" Zepedos asked.

"Moving."

"Sounds like you're dying."

Despite his predicament, Pig Knot's devastated face broke into a smile. With a winded huff, he collapsed just short of the cell door, taking a moment for the next part.

"Pig Knot?" the thief whispered.

"Yes?"

"Hurry."

"This is as fast as I go."

"Then be quieter . . ."

Kelmo, he realized. And his jailors. Closer than he thought.

"Then . . . stop *talking* to me . . ." He looked up and spied the apple. Still there. Sooner or later, however, Zepedos might lose his nerve. Or change his mind. The man was a self-professed thief, after all. So Pig Knot dug in his elbows and arched himself off the stone, killing himself a little more with every movement. Baring his teeth and grunting, he pulled himself along using only his elbows. Pain lanced through him, warning him to stop, as his lower back stretched out, dragging everything else along.

That pain intensified after a few pulls and he eventually dropped to the floor, one ear mashed to the stone and his crooked hand splayed before his head. Pig Knot rolled his eyes. The whole venture was becoming too much work. Another intake of air and he pulled himself forward again. Then again . . . before collapsing. Once more he pressed his face against an indifferent flagstone, barely missing his nose.

"I said be *quiet*," Zepedos warned.

Seddon above. Hurry. Be quiet. The thief was starting to annoy him. Pig Knot glanced up. The apple was still there. Elbow over elbow he hauled himself forward, mindful of his hand and oozing sweat. The floor rubbed his underside raw. There were no edges about, no harsh bits in the stones, and yet the image of him dragging himself over all manner of sharp things entered his mind.

"*Hurry*," Zepedos insisted. "I think I hear someone."

"What?"

"*Hurry.*"

Pig Knot dragged himself another bit, then another, his entire frame stretched out on the floor, and while it hurt terribly, it didn't kill him. He dug in both elbows and lurched forward the final bit of distance. He landed hard, his chin rubbing stone and pulling his lower lip down with it. Gasping, Pig Knot reached up and snatched the apple from a trembling hand.

"You have it," Zepedos said, yanking his fingers out of sight.

Pig Knot stuffed the fruit into his mouth, not bothering to answer. The first chew was a stinging reminder of his many missing teeth. The apple wasn't the softest. Or the sweetest. The second chew went easier, as did the rest after that. Pig Knot lay back, savoring the sharp flavor and taking it all down.

When he was done, he turned himself onto his good side. "My thanks, Zepedos."

"You're most welcome."

The clatter of an opening door startled him. He could not retreat back into his cell, so he closed his eyes and lay absolutely still.

Boots halted near his head, just beyond the bars. Breathing, then, deep and considering, as if the guard had just finished a grand meal and wondered if there was anything sweet about.

"He moved himself," a voice said, perhaps well-suited to singing.

"He did," a rougher voice replied.

"All the way from back there to here."

"Quite the effort," said the rough voice. "And now he's sleeping."

"*Pretending* to sleep."

Seddon above, Pig Knot thought and strained to keep still.

"Aye that," agreed the rough voice. "Guaranteed. Probably heard us. Listening right this moment."

"You sleeping down there, Pig?" asked the singer.

Aye that, Pig Knot thought, forcing every fiber of his being to look dead.

"No doubt in my mind," said the rough voice, and in another place and time, Pig Knot's memory remembered a Skarr. One of Kelmo's trusted lads called Slok. Hard-looking man, with dark hair cut close to the scalp, revealing a jagged piece missing from one ear as if it were bitten away.

Which meant the *other* voice belonged to . . .

Keys clattered in a lock.

Odusk.

Hinges shrieked and boots scuffed across the flagstones. A grunt perforated the air an instant before a hard foot slammed into Pig Knot's chest, putting him onto his back. The unexpected blow stunned him, emptying him of air, and hurting far more than expected. Pig Knot sputtered and balled into himself, leaving his broken hand in the open.

Which Odusk stepped on with a bootheel. Not that the punce was an overly large man or anything. He wasn't. But Pig Knot had decided a while ago that Odusk liked to hit people. Liked to inflict pain. Perhaps even more than Kelmo, and for very little reason, if any at all.

That boot crushing his hand widened Pig Knot's eyes and pulled a strangled cry from him.

Which was right about when Odusk kicked his forehead, stretching his neck for a rattling instant.

"He's awake now," Odusk huffed.

"Looks like it," Slok said.

"You're awake now, aren't you Pig?" Odusk asked, making himself heard.

Pig Knot lowered his hand from his brow—where a new cut bled—to cradle his fiercely throbbing fist to his chest.

Odusk loomed over him, as if deciding on where to strike next without getting any of that slop on him. "You best answer me," he warned.

Pig Knot rightly believed the man's eyes were the most insane set he'd ever had the misfortune of looking into. Pale blue, perhaps gray, and intensely clear. The eyes of a man who enjoyed his work, especially when work meant kicking heads and stepping on fingers.

"Aye that," Pig Knot managed over the agony of his hand. "I'm awake."

"Thought you were," Odusk said and pulled a dagger from his waist. Curved steel flashed in the fading daylight.

"Hold on," Slok hissed. He sounded annoyed.

And much to Pig Knot's relief, Odusk actually held on, his fair but weathered features clearly puzzled.

"What are you going to do with that?" Slok demanded.

"What?" Odusk asked. "This?"

Slok nodded, with an exasperated *Of course I mean that* look upon his face.

"Well . . ."

"That's Kelmo slice of meat there," Slok reminded him.

"I wasn't going to *kill* him," Odusk protested.

"What then? Hammer his melon with the pommel?"

Odusk eyed Pig Knot's bleeding and swollen melon. "Well—"

"Look," Slok interrupted. "If it was anyone else, I'd let you have at him. But Kelmo's claimed this one. You know that. This shagger packed his missus. Maybe even more than once. And you put the boots to him two days ago, which left him *senseless* for two days. Kelmo was checking on him ever since, and you know why?"

A defeated Odusk sighed. He knew.

"That's right," Slok continued. "He's been waiting for him to wake, so *he* could put the boots to him. That's what I'm saying. This pig here? You smash his nogs any more than necessary, which is to say hard enough to leave him senseless for another day or two or, Lords forbid, *longer* . . . well, you'll anger Kelmo. And Kelmo's got more reason to hate that crust of maggot shite than you do."

The words sank in as Odusk's dagger dropped, and the torturer with the fair but weathered complexion put the weapon away.

Thank Seddon above, Pig Knot mentally prayed.

Which was right about when Odusk grabbed Pig Knot's chin and held it tight . . . before jamming his little finger up the prisoner's nostril. That hook of flesh and bone and fingernail right and proper hurt. Odusk forced Pig Knot's face *back*, and he released a squeal not unlike his namesake.

"You're fortunate, Pig," Odusk whispered, pushing deeper, the gouging nail painfully making its presence known, "that Slok is here to save you. Hear me? If he wasn't—"

Pig Knot's eyes watered fiercely as the finger pushed *deeper* into his head, but he couldn't worm his fish-hooked face *off* that excruciating digit.

Until Odusk yanked it away in a thick string of red, leaving Pig Knot cringing and covering his beak with both hands.

"Odusk . . ." Slok warned.

Still wanting to do more, Odusk's upraised fist trembled as the soldier gazed upon the prisoner. He glared, his features red and steaming, baring teeth before tucking them away, making it known he wanted to continue hurting Pig Knot. Pig Knot didn't doubt that he did, but the whole posturing and gesturing thing struck him as being, well, overcooked.

"I heard you," Odusk whispered with forced bluster. He leaned over Pig Knot. "When Kelmo's tired of you . . . you'll be mine. Until the end." With a nod and a look that was best suited to some poorly acted Perician stage, Odusk smiled his best cold smile, perhaps believing it was terrifying. It probably was, to most.

Thing was, Pig Knot had been smiled at in such similar ways *plenty* of times, and by scarier people.

Odusk, however, did have the advantage, so Pig Knot returned to nursing his current hurts without so much as a sly wink in return.

"He's smart," Odusk said.

"He's bleeding all over the place," Slok muttered in annoyance. "Get out of there before you step in it."

"Let him soak in it," the other said as he exited the cell.

"Let him soak," Slok scoffed. "He's wallowing in his own filth every *day*. Really, Odusk. Take your fingers out of your own nose for once. Smell all that?"

"S'all fresh air."

"Fresh air," Odusk slammed the cell door. "You're unfit. Tell you what. You can clean out that pisspot of a cell once he's dead, since the stink doesn't bother you."

"Doesn't bother me."

"You listening to yourself?" the other one asked as the pair wandered away. "'Doesn't bother me'. You probably *like* the stink . . ."

"Never said I *liked* it. I said—" a door closed, and the voices diminished to nothing.

Pig Knot lay there, gasping, as his nose buzzed and ached. He dabbed at that tortured piece of property, checking for blood and finding plenty. A hesitant sniff sucked a gob down his throat, and that unexpected surprise got him coughing.

"Not dead?" Zepedos asked from the other cell.

". . . Not yet," a weary Pig Knot replied after a time.

"They don't like you," the thief said, sounding like he was smiling. "I mean, I know Kelmo hates you, but . . . I don't understand why Odusk and Slok don't like you."

". . . Odusk . . . hates me. Nearly ripped my nose apart. With his finger."

That stunned the other man into silence.

Pig Knot nodded, until he remembered the thief couldn't see him. "Oh, aye that," he whispered.

"They know you're awake now," Zepedos said.

". . . They know."

"*Kelmo* will know you're awake."

Pig Knot's tongue probed the holes in his mouth where his teeth used to be. "Aye that," he finally agreed, and lost all interest in the conversation. In the silence that followed, his blood pattered against the floor.

4

Neither Kelmo nor any of his lads returned that day, and the sunlight withdrew from the cell, allowing the darkness to creep in.

The regular jailor Sharo entered with the prisoners' evening meal. He attended to Zepedos first, filling a bucket of water and then feeding him from another bucket. The thief thanked him, to which Sharo grunted before moving to Pig Knot.

There the jailor stopped and stared in quiet awe. ". . . You alive in there?"

The devastated mask that was Pig Knot's face cracked into a smile. "Still alive, good Sharo."

That uneased the jailor, as if he had spoken with a corpse.

"Something good this evening?" Pig Knot asked weakly.

"What?"

"To eat . . . I mean."

Sharo didn't answer. Instead he remembered something and stepped out of sight. He reappeared after a bit, fussed with the lock, and opened the cell door. Hinges creaked as a wary Sharo entered. With guarded precision, he filled the water bucket.

Pig Knot watched him.

When the last few drops dribbled in, Sharo straightened and blatantly studied the mess at his feet. He started with Pig Knot's face and moved down over a frightful collection of bruises. Then, as if remembering his duty, he sighed and stooped.

"Hold out your hand," Sharo said.

"Don't pass anything to him," Slok warned from the shadows, startling Pig Knot. He hadn't noticed the Skarr at all. "He doesn't deserve that bit of courtesy."

Sharo didn't argue, though his expression said otherwise. The jailor tossed a chunk of bread onto the prisoner's chest.

Pig Knot placed a hand over the food and was about to thank him when the jailor lobbed a piece of fruit onto his stomach. The lack of aim disappointed Sharo, and it showed upon his face.

"Don't worry," Pig Knot smiled again, the sight no doubt sickening. "I'll get it directly. Many thanks, good Sharo."

Nodding, Sharo withdrew from the cell. He locked it, glancing at the one occupant, and with a parting look, moved from sight. Another door opened and closed and all became quiet.

"Good man," Pig Knot mumbled. "Good man."

He inspected his supper. The bread was a little smaller than his fist, with spots of green about the edges. Dirt speckled the ends where gouging fingers had torn the loaf apart. The fruit was another apple, already half eaten and bruised, edging toward rotten. Pig Knot regarded one then the other. He placed the apple on his chest and went to work on the bread, pinching away the worst of the mold. He ate slowly, carefully, ignoring the stiff dryness which softened over time. When he finished, he studied the apple to determine the safest place to bite. He nibbled away the rotten parts, as much as he dared, before eating the remainder. Despite the discoloration and soft, wormy texture, it went down all the same.

After a time, he wondered if Slok was still out there, lurking. He could not hear the man. Unable to bear the mystery, Pig Knot cleared his throat. "You there, Slok?"

No answer.

"Slok? You there? Keeping to yourself?"

Again, no answer.

"He's gone," Zepedos answered.

"Are you sure?"

"I'm sure."

"Slok," Pig Knot said, the spite welling up inside him. "You enjoy shoving your arm up a sick cow's blossom?"

The words flew out of him, probably because he needed to say something, to release the building fury at how they were treating him. Then the fear returned and Pig Knot braced himself, eyes and ears on high alert, waiting for the Skarr to appear. Perhaps with Odusk.

Nothing of the kind happened, however.

His fluttering heart measured off the passing moments before he realized Zepedos spoke the truth. "He's not there."

"Said he's not," the thief said. "But don't say such things again, just in case he's leaning against the door outside. If he is, if *anyone* is, well . . . you'll know."

Pig Knot swallowed and checked on his nose. The bleeding had stopped, but it remained as tender as a boil lodged in one's ass crack. On impulse, he reached over and pulled the bucket in close. A moment later, he propped himself up on one elbow and peered inside. Gobs of putrid matter floated in the water. Pig Knot frowned at the sight. At least the toppers hadn't pissed in it.

He dipped his good hand into the bucket's contents, fishing out one bit of filth after the other. Just a bit of spittle. When the water looked presentable, he took another handful, sniffed at it, and deemed it clean. Cleaner than before, anyway. The first sip was as tentative as it was noisy, but the water tasted as it should. The lads took mercy on him after all.

Pig Knot took in a mouthful. He swished it about before expelling it, toward the latrine—that dark and dreary hole meant for squatting at the back of the cell. He missed the squatter with the first shot but hit the edge with the second. Twice more he did this, until he finally drank. *Warm.* Warm as piss, truth be known, but at least it wasn't piss.

He splashed a little bit over his bloodier wounds, and wished he had something to wipe himself down. The mat he'd once lay upon had become far too crusty for such scrubbings. So he did the best he could with what he had. It took time, but he removed some of the mess around his face, being extra cautious around the tender bits. When all that was done, he left himself to dry and stared at the wall.

The silence deepened, broken by the Sunjans in the streets going about their business far beyond his cell window. Even that diminished as the night deepened, and very little could be heard at all outside the jail.

"Did they feed you?" Zepedos asked at one point.

". . . Like a king."

"I saved a bit of apple."

"Where are they . . . getting all these apples?"

"No idea."

"They have a tree nearby?"

"Maybe. You want this?"

"No, good Zepedos. I'm full enough."

"They say if you don't eat, your stomach becomes smaller. In time."

"They say a lot of things," Pig Knot said.

"That they do," Zepedos agreed, perhaps with a smile about his words.

"Until the morning then."

"Until then . . ."

The banging of the cell door jerked Pig Knot awake. He lurched to one elbow, minding his broken fingers. Torchlight cast a fiery hue over the stonework and the shadows became men. Several men, some wearing armor, even.

One of them leered, and Pig Knot recognized him as Kelmo, the jealous husband of Jana, from so long ago. Vengeful husband, truth be known. His two torturers, Odusk and Slok, flanked him, their eager faces half hidden by shadow.

Kelmo gestured at the cell door and a fourth man moved in to unlock it.

Pig Knot's breath quickened, his eyes locked on all of them. He edged back until his head thumped against the wall.

Kelmo watched him all the while.

The jailor pulled the door open and the officer gestured at the prisoner. "Hold him still."

Men flooded over the threshold so fast that Pig Knot barely had time to move. They swarmed him, pinning his arms and the nubs of his legs and holding him fast. One Skarr trapped an arm under his own and his side, placing his back to Pig Knot's head. Someone clutched his ruined hand, and that vicious squeeze of his broken fingers sent a blast of fire up his arm and seared his face.

Pig Knot did his best not to resist. Knew they'd hurt him more if he did.

"Little, little Pig," Kelmo muttered, entering the cell. "You're awake, I see. Good. It's not good to sleep so long, anyway. Bad for the health."

Slok and Odusk moved into the cell. Odusk looked unfit evil in the torchlight.

"Did you eat well this evening?" Kelmo asked.

Pig Knot huffed, licked swollen lips, and nodded.

"Speak when you're spoken to," Slok warned, raising his voice.

Kelmo's brow arched, indicating it was good advice to follow.

"Aye that," Pig Knot rumbled, wondering what it would be this night. Would it be just a beating about the face or hard boots to the body? Or both? Perhaps a swift kick to the bells, ringing them for all their worth. If it was a pounding to the face, would it be knuckles wrapped in leather, or the mind-rattling thunderclaps of open palms? They had done it all to him before, but they all knew they could do much, much worse.

Pig Knot feared tonight would provide fresh nightmares until his dying day.

"The lads informed me of your fingers," Kelmo said, nodding at his prisoner. "You've bound them together? With a bit of cloth?"

"Aye that," Pig Knot released, barely suppressing the urge to scream.

"Which hand is it? I forget."

Pig Knot set his jaw and nodded at his left.

"That one? Slok."

Slok came forward, holding a torch aloft, while the Skarr holding Pig Knot's afflicted arm angled the limb into the light. Kelmo leaned in and scowled.

"Doesn't look good," the officer declared. "Doesn't look good at all. All crooked. Didn't you try to straighten them first?"

Pig Knot fumed, his breath firing from his nose. He shook his head.

Odusk stepped in. "You were warned . . ." he said and stomped on the stricken hand. The resulting snap, quiver, and bell-shriveling scream that escaped Pig Knot threatened to deafen all who could hear.

Until Odusk slapped him across one cheek, silencing him.

A hand gripped the filthy hair atop Pig Knot's head and yanked up his face.

"Do I need to repeat myself?" Kelmo asked, his brow lowered to better send his warning.

"No," Pig Knot gasped.

Odusk reared back an arm, looking to slap him again.

"Couldn't straighten them," a huffing Pig Knot winced. "Hurt too much. Hurt too much. Couldn't do it."

Slok looked at his commanding officer.

"Bring the light in closer," Kelmo instructed and leaned in. His frown deepened into a scowl. "Looks bad."

"Very bad," Odusk agreed.

"Never seen anything so bad," added Slok.

"Can you move them?" Kelmo asked.

Pig Knot cringed. "No," he puffed in agony, and pressed his head against the Skarr's back.

"You're in a terrible pinch, Pig," Kelmo informed him as he straightened. "A terrible, terrible pinch."

Pig caught the unmistakable delight on Odusk's torchlit face.

"I've seen broken fingers like yours before," Kelmo went on. "They never really heal right. Not really. Especially when left alone without a proper healer to set the bones straight. They get all crooked. Like yours. Men can't hold a *spoon* right, let alone anything else. My suggestion, if you wish to hear it?"

Pig Knot didn't dare hesitate. "Let's hear it."

"Those fingers will never heal. Never. Be more of a problem for you when they do mend. You should . . . just remove them. I think."

Pig Knot turned his full horrified attention upon the officer.

"What do you think, lads?" Kelmo asked his men.

"I agree," Slok said with a mocking expression of sadness.

"I'll do it right now," Odusk offered brightly. "I've got just the blade."

"No," Kelmo said. "I wouldn't let you do anything I wasn't willing to do myself."

"I don't mind. Truly."

Kelmo glared back, silencing the man. "Let's see this blade."

Nodding, Odusk pulled a small knife from a sleeve. He promptly turned the weapon over and offered it handle-first.

Kelmo took it. "Hold him still."

Pig Knot tried to squirm free, but the men holding him down were stronger, fresher, and had not been so soundly trounced. They tightened their grips and bore down upon him, and his mangled hand felt all the more exposed. He still attempted to pull it back, until Odusk grabbed his chin and held a second blade . . . just below his right eye, of all places. Torchlight turned the steel orange and beyond that, Odusk's evil smile.

"Hold him, I said," Kelmo repeated as he dropped to a knee.

Pig Knot sputtered, wondering if a good bout of pleading might work. The hard, calloused grip about his wrists informed him otherwise. Someone pressed his palm to stone and dragged it to straighten the fingers. All that brought water to his eyes, and he started whining.

"Stop *moving* it," Kelmo warned. "If you don't, Saimon below as my witness, Odusk will scoop out one of your eyes."

Upon hearing his name, Odusk edged the blade a little closer. That sharp pressure stiffened the prisoner.

"Stay still," Kelmo said. "This isn't the first time I've had to cut something off a man, for his betterment. I only mean to take your fingers, so listen . . . if you pull your hand away, Odusk there will blind you. Half-blind you, anyway. There's not much left to you, Pig. Not much at all. Which would leave me with an even greater problem of sorts. One that every farmer of livestock has . . . that is, when to butcher a favorite animal. One that's clearly suffering."

Kelmo lowered his head, focusing on the next part.

The grip and pressure about Pig Knot's wrist increased, keeping his hand in place. His breath quickened as the knife's edge touched a finger . . .

Then came down in a dreadful crunch.

5

An angry sun hung over the arena, baking white sands sullied by a handful of uninspiring fights. Spectators filled every row of Sunja's Pit, appearing as faces and shoulders, stacked upward in wide sweeping rings until great awnings shaded them. Up there, they lost all features, growing into a long, undulating mass. Shouts and angry insults salted the air as they dismissed the disappointing carnage thus far.

Borl Grisholt, of the Stable of Grisholt, stroked his wispy beard, watching the offended masses in those seats, listening to their annoyance. He leaned forward, taking care not to press his chest—and his new and very fashionable red robes—against the lower brick sill of the arched window. Even then, peering out from the private chamber assigned to his stable, the heat was stunning. Breath-stealing. The kind of heat that would melt the soles off bare feet if one walked across the arena sands. Though he was shaded from the full brunt of the sun, he still perspired, and heavily, very much aware of the dewy cracks and crevices underneath his clothing. That annoying moisture threatened to undo the magical scent of rose water he'd rubbed on himself before venturing to the day's games.

On impulse, he straightened and sniffed at one wrist then the other, unimpressed with the mild fragrance. The merchant who had sold him the shite declared it was a powerful scent. A very popular one, if not enticing, with the ladies of the day. Even allowed Grisholt a sample sniff from a vial, and yes *that* was strong, but the vial he had bought wasn't nearly as potent, and the strongest smell wafted from the lip of the container itself. That little discovery annoyed him and ruined his mood. He had been promised he'd smell of fresh roses. If he detected a scant whiff of perspiration off his person, he would find that merchant and insist his coin be returned. Forcefully, if needed. Not that it would come to that. His personal guardian, the one-eyed once-gladiator named Brakuss, would ensure Grisholt would get his coin back. Maybe an additional vial of some other scented water for his trouble and continued business, for free. Perhaps even two. That was fair. In his mind.

Grisholt tugged on his beard, squinting at the harsh glare of the sands.

Maybe he would do that after his matches this day. Maybe on his way to the brothels. Or, just perhaps, he would send for a wagonful of honeypots. Bring them out to his villa, where they could entertain him and his lads for a time. In between fights.

A slamming door startled him. Brakuss had returned. Grisholt didn't bother turning around and instead waited. Someone stopped behind him, someone stinking like the festering blossom of a dead cow left rotting in the heat.

"Placed the wagers, have you?" Grisholt asked, reaching for one of his pockets.

"All done, Master Grisholt," Brakuss reported.

Grisholt fished out a hand cloth and dabbed at his neck. "Many wagers being placed?"

"There are. The Domis was very busy. Very long line for wagers."

"Apologies," the owner said but didn't really mean it. "Caro couldn't place them. He was indisposed. Doing things best kept secret. He'll return when he can. See anyone you know?"

"No one."

Grisholt ceased dabbing at his throat and covered his nose. He could smell *something* resembling rose, but certainly not as powerful as he had been led to believe. He inspected the damp cloth before eyeing his dangerous henchman. Imposing and grim with a thick chest, stubbly chin, and one narrowed eye. Brakuss stood half a head taller than most and every bit of him was sweltering from the short trip to the Domis. The bodyguard wore light clothing, in anticipation of a hot day, but sweat had soaked through the layers in great, wet splotches.

Grisholt did not approve.

Feeling the weight of his master's inspection, Brakuss waited while rivulets slid down his well-cooked profile.

"Next time I'll send Caro," the owner promised.

"My thanks, Master Grisholt."

"Think nothing of it," he replied, and briefly considered handing over his hand towel. Thought that would be right nice of him. He did nothing of the sort, however.

Taskmaster Turst stepped into view. A blocky stone of a man dusted off but still of service. Sun-wrinkled and scowling, Turst flexed his thick jaw and eyed his employer. "Nearly that time," he growled.

"So it is," Grisholt said and nodded at Brakuss.

His bodyguard went to a bench, where a small chest waited. He opened it and took a moment to examine the contents. Then, with the greatest of care, he lifted a metal flask with a brass stopper resembling a crown. Holding it up, he glanced at his employer.

Grisholt twirled a finger, indicating he get on with it.

Brakuss carried the container to a gladiator standing with his back to the wall. A young pit fighter, shallow-chested with narrow shoulders, but possessing strong, bulky arms and legs. He wore a hardened cuirass over his torso and iron-studded greaves and bracers about his wrists and shins. An open helmet with a broad nose guard granted opponents a view of his battle-hardened face. One sip of the potion and his face would warp into something truly terrifying.

His name was Kossa, and, like Brakuss, Kossa was an imposing sight. With a taste of the Sons' wondrous potion called Victory, however, Kossa would become a monster. Days ago he had butchered Stonum, a pit fighter belonging to the House of

Vandu. Today, Vandu wanted revenge for the killing. The blood match was the fourth since Grisholt's lads had begun their run of slaughter among the gladiatorial ranks. Barros had destroyed three of Razi's dogs—Shoor and Jonca and the most recent asslicker, whose name Grisholt couldn't recall. That last killing, however, had greatly stung old Razi, and the owner was forced to delay any further attempts at revenge. That might change soon, Grisholt suspected, since Barros had lost to the Perician Wonder. That surprising defeat scalded Grisholt to no end, especially since he had wagered heavily on his man being victorious. Not that it mattered. Grisholt knew he was well on his way to becoming wealthy. *Unfit* wealthy.

Of all his fighters, however, Kossa had been considered the Stable's strongest entry in this year's games, with the potential to advance deep into the competition. Perhaps not win it all, but Turst initially believed Kossa could place well enough to at least line the bottom of the Stable's empty coffers. Even deposit enough to offset the cost of preparing for next season.

That was before.

The potion had changed all that.

With the potion, Kossa could be champion.

Grisholt stroked his beard while his thoughts whirled. With the potion, *any* of his brutes could be champion. What a problem to have.

Kossa lowered his long-necked war hammer and small, rounded shield, and steeled himself for the drink. Brakuss adjusted his grip on the container before removing the stopper.

"Wait for the knock," Turst said, meaning the door.

The words jarred Grisholt from his thoughts. "Yes, wait for the door," he agreed, widening his eyes at his taskmaster. "My thanks for that, Master Turst. Wouldn't want Kossa reaching his, ah, *peak* before time."

Turst arched his own eyebrows.

As effective as the potion was, the recent match with the Perician Wonder lingered in all their minds. That one had not only defeated Barros, but Junger had allowed the man to *exhaust* himself upon the sands, revealing a limitation of the potion. The timing of when to use it needed to be observed, to maximize its effectiveness. To make use of every heartbeat of power the potion bestowed, before it left.

Scratching at one ear, Turst joined the owner at the window. "Eager," the taskmaster said under his breath.

"As he should be," Grisholt said and grimaced. "Unfit hot out there. How do they ever manage to sit through a full day of fights?"

Turst grunted, inspecting the spectators crowded into the stands.

Grisholt understood that sound immediately. "Something bothers you, taskmaster?"

Turst clenched his thick jaw. "Only the use of the potion."

"Victory."

"It wasn't victory against the Perician."

"That was fortune favoring him."

"That was *intelligence*," Turst stressed from one corner of his mouth. "Make no mistake. But I wish to have a moment of your time after the day. To talk further on this."

"About the potion?"

Turst nodded.

"Done. Later this day. When we're clear of the events."

Turst nodded again.

"Don't you have any words of encouragement for Kossa?" Grisholt asked.

"With respect, Master Grisholt, I feel that . . . any thoughts I might impart upon him . . . would be lost once the potion takes hold."

"Yes," Grisholt smiled. "Most wicked, isn't it?"

Turst cocked an eyebrow as someone knocked upon the chamber's door.

"It's time." Grisholt looked at Brakuss.

Orders received, the one-eyed man removed the stopper and held the potion out to Kossa, who took the drink.

"Just a sip," the owner warned. "Remember, just a sip."

"Only want a sip of this gurry," Kossa grimaced as he raised the bottle to his lips. He hesitated, bracing himself, then tipped the thing back and embraced the foulness. Just a sip, but his features twisted and turned in disgust as he forced it down. He cringed, gasped, rolled his head, and stomped a foot. "*Gahhhh*," Kossa released savagely and wiped his mouth. "That's unfit. That's *so* unfit."

No sooner did the words leave him when he bent over and grabbed his knees, his whole frame shivering.

Expecting the worst, Grisholt backed up and waited for the retching, He could not imagine how horrible the potion tasted. Didn't care. He didn't have to drink the shite. What was it the Sons had called it? *Liquid fire*, he believed. The Sons should have been merchants. Barros had said it tasted like bloody piss filled with pulpy chunks.

Brakuss snatched the flask away from the convulsing gladiator, shielding the container from what was to come.

Grabbing his stomach, Kossa released a strained moan. He slammed a hand against the wall for support. There he trembled, violently, while straining to clear his throat.

Those standing nearby backed away, pressing themselves against the brick.

Grisholt exchanged concerned looks with Turst and Brakuss.

Then the trembling stopped and Kossa lifted his head. He ceased his uneventful retching and slammed a fist against the wall. He bared yellow teeth and snapped mightily at the air. With an evil groan the pit fighter straightened, armor and bones creaking as he did. His eyes blazed madness and the tendons along his neck popped forth as if engorged by a flood of blood. He jerked his head left to right before he steadied himself and snatched up his weapon and shield.

Turst had the presence of mind to signal the gladiator next to the door . . . who immediately flung it open.

Seeing the way clear, Kossa released a bowel-quivering "*YES!*" and hurried into the hallway. In no time he was gone from sight, roaring all the way.

In the shocking wake of the departing pit fighter, Grisholt relaxed against the windowsill and released a long and thankful sigh.

Then he turned around to watch . . .

At the far end of the arena, on a tall podium of sand-dusted brick and wood, Qualtus, the white-haired Orator of the games, consulted a scroll of parchment. A thick, gray blanket, spread out between four posts, hung over his head and blunted the power of the sun. Though the canopy shielded him, it did little else, as he perspired heavily beneath his robes. His sallow but clean-shaven features twisted this way and that, perusing the information before him, absorbing the details of the next match. As he read, the odd fly buzzed around him. He swished his robes, mostly to get a little air under there, and idly scratched at his left ass cheek, forgetting there was a crowd behind him.

When he found what he was looking for, he cleared his throat and raised both arms, the sleeves falling to his elbows.

Within moments, the mutterings of the audience died away.

"Men and women of the Pit," Qualtus called out, his voice crisp and carrying. "If it pleases you, allow me to introduce a match of retribution. A fight for revenge. Where one of our honored houses has taken the life of a gladiator and now must face the wrath of offended sword brothers. Days ago, the pit slayer known as Kossa, of the Stable of Grisholt, took the life of Stonum, who fought under the banner of the House of Vandu. A house one takes care *not* to offend. This day, this time, the House of Vandu demands vengeance and has sent a hellion to take it. You know him as Jundal of Sunja. The Stable of Grisholt will know him as . . . the one they wish they will never encounter again. He is a *shredder* of flesh. A *destroyer* of wills. He is *Jundal*, and he *will* have vengeance for his house."

The audience shouted approval, and Qualtus let them chew on that bit of gristle he'd just spat to the ground. It wasn't his best bit of theater, but given how his robes were clinging to his elderly ass, he didn't rightly care. With that thought, he pinched and pulled damp material away from the more sensitive places, allowing fruit to dangle, before further consulting his parchment.

The portcullis to the west rose in great, cranky lurches until it was wide enough for Jundal to step onto the hot sands. A black iron helmet covered his features, the eye slots dark and dreary. A vest of chainmail gleamed, revealing muscular arms with bronze bracers. Broad of shoulder, Jundal walked forth swinging a battleaxe. He halted a dozen strides away from his entrance and faced the opposing portcullis.

Which was already opened, no doubt because of the opponent.

"Men and women of the Pit," Qualtus began again, his voice low but gathering strength. "This year, the Stable of Grisholt has decided to take the games by the throat and *squeeze* it for whatever juice—"

A deep bellow ripped from somewhere inside the opposing entrance, one that not only distracted Qualtus but silenced the audience to a person. The roar ended, deprived of wind, before a second infuriated blast exploded from the brick and iron opening. That one surged in strength as Kossa drew closer, and an answering rumble of anticipation rippled throughout the onlookers.

Qualtus drew breath. "He—"

Kossa rushed out onto the arena floor. He halted, kicking up sand, and threw his arms wide, shrieking pure rage at the sky. The audience exploded with their own excited greetings.

Qualtus shut up, his ego bruised at being interrupted, but recognizing good theater when he saw it.

And Kossa was good theater, even without the introduction.

The pit fighter from the Stable of Grisholt continued screaming at the day, as if it pained him with its light. He shook his war hammer and shield, turned, and shook everything and screamed again. Once he got that out of his chest, he sighted his adversary—the one meant to exact revenge—and charged.

Jundal stood ready. His battleaxe flashed as he cocked it to one shoulder, looking to end his foe with one fell chop. Only a handful of the regular spectators knew of Jundal's history in the games. It was his fourth year in the competition, and while he had never won the champion's title, he'd once finished within a fight of entering the rounds of the final eight. An accomplished showing he no doubt sought to improve upon this year, once he took the life of the screamer rushing at him.

Which was to say, Jundal wasn't one to piss himself at the sight of his foe, despite the surprising string of deaths the Stable of Grisholt had recently collected.

And if Jundal *was* nervous, his helmet hid it well.

Kossa stormed straight across the steaming, gleaming breadth of the arena, raging every step of the way.

A waiting Jundal held his ground, bracing for impact, his fingers flexing upon the shaft of the axe.

Kossa's arms pumped with every stride.

And as the distance shortened, as the mayhem was about to commence in earnest, the cheering swelled to impressive levels.

Jundal waited, waited, and just when it looked like he would sidestep Kossa's headlong rush, in those last few strides before bloody contact, he did the last thing *anyone* expected.

He lashed out, seeking to sink the scratched edge of his axe deep into Kossa's face.

Except Kossa stopped the blow—*one-handed*—with his war hammer. The hard connection of steel upon steel rang out, sharp and stinging and causing many to cover their ears. Kossa smashed Jundal's heavy battleaxe away an instant before crashing into his opponent's larger bulk. They embraced, before Kossa discarded his hammer and lifted Jundal off his feet. Kossa carried him three paces before slamming him into the sand in a spray of grit. He landed on top of Jundal, to better bludgeon the fighter . . . with the edge of his shield.

The first strike drove Jundal's flailing weapon arm back.

The second crashed into his armored face.

As did the third.

Gonging notes rang out, heavy and devastating, and even before the dust settled, it was clear Jundal wasn't able to defend himself. Truth be known, he had gone limp the moment his back had hit the ground.

That didn't stop Kossa from hitting him—*pounding* him— like a hammer smashing out a tune on an anvil. The iron band of Jundal's shield fell off in a bent strop. The wood splintered. Then shattered. As the shield broke apart, Kossa bent over to compensate the distance and kept on smashing. Fragments of his destroyed shield flew into the air, until nothing remained. Kossa used a fist then, then both, raining down strikes. A dozen blows fell and the gladiator screamed impatience.

He got to his feet.

And stomped.

Qualtus straightened and blinked at the massacre transpiring within his beloved Pit. He'd witnessed savagery aplenty, even blatant butchery, but what was happening before his eyes *this* day was . . .

Well, *unwatchable.*

Stomach-turning, even.

Evidently, the whole of the arena agreed as their cheering choked off in horrified fascination. Shocked gasps and words of protest flared from the onlookers. The raging gladiator didn't hear any of it, however. He continued to stomp, driving his bootheel into everything above the dead man's shoulders. Every strike spattered gore in a lumpy pool.

That Jundal was dead wasn't even a thought anymore.

Eventually, Kossa slowed, stricken by exhaustion. He ceased his heavy dance and swayed, as if near senseless from a downed bottle of firewater. He listed before righting himself and staggered away from the mess at his feet. The clingy remains stuck to him, however, and every step dappled the sand.

Kossa might have run headlong into the arena, but he walked out of it much slower, leaving a bloody trail behind him.

And not a person in the arena cheered his name.

Just before the moment of impact, when Kossa tackled Jundal and lifted him off his feet, Grisholt stopped breathing. He clutched at the brick sill when Kossa slammed Jundal into the ground and began smashing him. Grisholt watched the rest in unchecked wonder, not bothered in the least by a little bloodshed. Not at this point, and not when he'd wagered a sizable fortune on Kossa's blackhearted hide. The unmistakable chalky note of a breaking skull sucked all the excitement out of the audience, but not Grisholt. His breath hitched in his chest and threatened to choke him dead as he nearly pulled the beard off his chin.

"Lords above," he exclaimed as a warm, sparkling realization overcame him, like diving headfirst into bathhouse waters. *I'm rich*, he thought, clamping down on the words before they escaped his mouth. A glance at Brakuss revealed the one-eyed shagger watching the aftermath of the appalling fight in horrified wonder. Taskmaster Turst appeared darkly perturbed, staring on with his mouth slightly open.

Grisholt didn't understand the uneasy faces. "Another victory, lads. *Another* victory. Blessed Lords above, we . . . are . . . a *force* in the arena now. A damn unstoppable *force*."

The once-gladiator and taskmaster regarded the owner at the same time.

"Why the dour looks, good Turst? Brakuss? We've won another match. A *blood* match, in fact. Oh my, Vandu must be pulling bricks out of the walls right now." Grisholt turned to the few gladiators standing near the doorway. "Go get Kossa! Help him back here. The lad looked ready to collapse. Carry him if you have to. Go on now, go!"

They left to do just that.

"Brakuss," Grisholt continued. "Take Seel and Hease there. Get a marker from the Domis. Inform them we'll be by later in the day. Then go to the market and look into purchasing a few fine chests. You know the kind I like. Quality. All right? Understood? Excellent. Off with you then. Olibo, you stay here, to ensure you're still here when it's time for you to fight later this day."

Brakuss and the two other gladiators left.

Grisholt looked into the arena. A number of attendants dragged the corpse away, leaving a trailing mess. "I'm enjoying myself more and more this season, good Turst," the owner said with a broad smile.

Turst didn't speak.

"What?" Grisholt asked. "Nothing about Vandu being angered by this? No lecture about how we should be careful from here on?"

A pensive, squinting Turst shook his head.

"Not that you would, you understand," Grisholt added. "I just thought you might."

"When I become worried," the taskmaster said, "I'll tell you. If you'll listen."

"Listen? What's this about? Why wouldn't I listen?"

Turst said nothing to that.

"We'll all feast like *kings* this night, good Turst," Grisholt promised. "You have my word."

Turst sampled the inside of his cheek before filling his chest with hot air. "Though I'm not as pleased as you, Master Grisholt, I am pleased with the run of victories for the Stable. One gets . . . tired of bad fortune."

"Our bad fortune is behind us, good Turst. Behind us."

"Ah, Master Grisholt? Master Turst?"

The voice turned both men around.

There stood a concerned Olibo, glancing from one to the other. Rough-faced, with a number of unflattering scars, and a sepia-colored bruise fading away about the right cheek. A nick of flesh was missing from a cut lip, a parting gift from a flashing sword. When he spoke, he flashed gaps of missing teeth. In preparation for his fight later that afternoon, Olibo wore a dependable vest of leather armor, with matching bracers and greaves. Thus far this season, he had been defeated five times, while winning only twice. In private conversations with Turst, it had been revealed to Grisholt that the man trained as hard as any other but remained a touch clumsy. Grisholt kept him, however, as there weren't a great number of warriors asking to fight under his stable's name. In truth, if the stable's finances ever dropped to a truly horrible level, he planned to wager against Olibo on the sands, in hopes of keeping at least a few coins in the coffers.

"Yes, good Olibo?" Grisholt said, his spirits soaring.

"Was wondering, Master Grisholt, sar," Olibo said in a respectful tone, his brow lowered. "If it is possible, as I fight later this day . . . might I get a taste of that flask, sar?"

"You what now?"

Olibo hesitated, certain he'd been pleasant enough. "The potion, Master Grisholt. The, ah, *Victory*? Just wondering if I might get a sip of that? To help me win? Like the others."

Grisholt's soaring spirits leveled out as they all regarded the small chest on the nearby bench. The same chest to which Brakuss had returned the iron flask.

The owner reconsidered Olibo and shook his head. "Not this day, good Olibo."

The pleasantry exuding from the gladiator dwindled just a touch, before he glanced at Turst and then the owner again.

"Something else?" Grisholt asked.

Olibo cleared his throat. "It's just that . . . I've seen what the potion does, Master Grisholt. We all have. And if we haven't . . ."

"Master Grisholt has heard your request," Turst said sternly, eyeing the pit fighter. "And he's given his answer. You fight your best fight this day, Olibo. Win it. Win it on pure skill of arms, and perhaps the good master will consider your request another day. When it suits his plans."

The mention of skill of arms got Grisholt's attention.

Olibo absorbed all that and seemed he might argue, but then he nodded his acceptance. "My thanks, then, to you both," he said and returned to where his weapons waited.

Grisholt watched him before glancing at Turst. "Was this the matter you wished to talk about?"

"Later, Master Grisholt."

"We'll talk now," the owner said, lowering his voice while keeping an eye on Olibo.

"Very well. Aye that. This was the matter."

"Then, as you've said. I'll decide who gets what, when it suits me. Can't give them all a taste. I'll be needing a *refill* before the games are even *done*."

Turst nodded. "Just be aware, Master Grisholt, victory on the sands . . . is an infectious thing. To see a fellow gladiator win? It's not only good for him and you, but all the others competing in the games. It . . . *inspires* others, dare I say, to work even harder, so that they might win."

Grisholt's eyes narrowed. "All right. Understood. I still decide on who partakes of the potion. You even cautioned me on using it too often, if you remember."

"Oh, I remember, but that was before. This is now. The lads all know about it now. They all understand what it does. And for someone like Olibo . . . having that sip greatly increases his chances of victory. He wants to win, Master Grisholt. They *all* want to win. Not all of them will win, however, because of individual weaknesses. The potion, though, offers a chance of victory *despite* their weaknesses. A *very* good chance." Turst furtively glanced around and leaned in. "They're talking among themselves," he whispered.

"Who?"

Turst frowned and, with a subtle flicker of his eyes, indicated Olibo. "They are wondering . . . why haven't you given them all a taste? I cautioned you about using the potion too often. Now, it seems if you don't use it *enough* . . . it might cause dissension in our ranks."

Grisholt's brow crinkled.

"Consider it," Turst said. "For later. I'm not suggesting have them *all* drink the gurry. Ration it out. At least once. Even in the following blood matches if they happen."

Grisholt nodded, slowly understanding.

"Make no mistake," Turst continued. "When this season is over? If the other houses don't suspect any wrongdoing? If the Gladitorial *Chamber* doesn't suspect any . . . ? We should *all* retire from the games, with our fortunes made. And consider moving far and away from this place."

"And our silence forever held?" Grisholt asked.

To that, Turst locked gazes. The chamber door opened then, and the handful of men brought in a ragged and exhausted Kossa.

Grisholt glanced at his taskmaster before heaping praise upon his victorious gladiator.

6

Above the arena, sitting in the viewing box reserved for the top-three ranked houses, Dark Curge tipped back a silver goblet and gulped his wine. When the last drop went down, he stretched out his arm and gestured for more. A manservant with a clay bottle appeared at his side and poured. He filled the goblet and then backed away, leaving Curge to his drink.

The imposing house master squirmed in his chair, his tunic sticking to his considerable frame. He slapped the sole of one huge foot against the low wall before him, kept it there, and leaned back. With a frown, he took in a mouthful of wine, swished it about, and set the goblet down with a grimace. All the while, he gazed over those once-rabid onlookers, those feature-less faces of the audience, from one end of the Pit to the other. *Once*-rabid, he thought, as the last fight had quieted them like a hard slap across the bells. That brought a smile to Dark Curge's swarthy features. He rubbed his nose with the stump of his left arm. The tastes of the crowds could both please and sicken him. They were like nagging children. *Give us carnage*, they cried. *Give us blood.* But when they got a right and proper *faceful* of it, as they all just had . . .

Well . . .

Just like a heavy slap, it stunned them. Left them red, quivering, and marked. Shocked to the core, even. *Didn't need to see* that, they would later say. *No need for* that *much blood.*

Maggots all, Curge judged with contempt, his mood souring. They even resembled maggots, when you thought about it. Especially from where he sat. Freshly disturbed maggots, writhing, ever hungry, and clinging to the moist underside of an overturned cow kiss. And yet, they would soon forget those appalling scenes. Quick to *want* to forget, and to demand the next serving. As they were right now—the collective murmurs growing, swelling in volume, building toward the next match. Curge sighed, sweltering, knowing he would need to bathe when he returned home. Witnessing firsthand how unfit *full* the Pit could become with spectators; it was a wonder how anyone could endure such heat. Especially on scalding days like today. It wasn't merely the heat but also the *contact* among strangers, some well and truly pickled from too much drink, soaked into a mindset that they were pit fighters. Even believed themselves to be *good* pit fighters, though they might barely understand how to swing a blade. The Skarrs patrolled the walkways of the Pit to quell any such pissers looking for a fight, and even that thought annoyed Curge. Such pissers would be looking for a fight, which annoyed Curge to no end, even though the Skarrs that patrolled the walkways of the Pit would quell any over-eager punce.

Another drink of wine. He bared teeth at the bite while his thoughts turned to *Grisholt*. He remembered his talk with old Tilo, when they all met to discuss Nexus and how to deal with his . . . acquirement of the gladiator called Prajus. The same dog who had killed his house master, the golden masked Gastillo.

"Did you see that lavender-dipped weasel at the end of the table?" the older man asked.

"Grisholt?"

"Aye, Grisholt. See his finery?"

"I don't really notice how another man dresses, good Tilo."

"Well, you should. Your father would. You can tell an animal by his clothes, and that's one maggot who's enjoying life far too much. For a maggot."

Fuming, Curge decided Tilo was right. His father *would* have noticed Grisholt's clothing and questioned how he managed to pay for it all when the punce had been financially skewered through the guts at the beginning of the season. Grisholt's fortunes had changed dramatically in a very short time, which, Curge allowed, *could* happen during the games. Fortunes had been won and lost over the course of the season.

But the puzzling thing was his gladiators.

They had become right . . . *vicious*. Displaying a feral eagerness to not only dispatch their opponent, but, well, to tear them apart. Or just stomp them into the ground, as evidenced by the last fight. Curge had noticed this before, when Grisholt's animals were trouncing Razi's dogs. And Vandu's. Both owners did what they could with what they had, but Curge believed Vandu's pit fighters were better trained and skilled than any of Razi's lot.

For the blood match between Kossa and Jundal, however, Curge made it a point to watch with greater scrutiny. Kossa was a screamer, but that was no matter. What was surprising, however, was the man's hatred for his opponent. Anger could power a man, power him quite well, in fact, but only for a short time. Curge remembered the fight between Grisholt's man called Barros and Junger, the Perician with the House of Ten mongrels. Barros had also displayed terrible energy and swiped and swung for the Perician's head, looking to rip it from the man's neck. He had failed, however, and Junger simply evaded everything until Barros collapsed from exhaustion.

Thinking matters over, Curge took another drink, staring at the arena but not seeing it.

Barros had fought the same way as Kossa had—power forward and quickly, brutally, to overwhelm the foe. Thing was, during that contest, everyone, including Curge, was watching the Perician. To see how he would fight. There was no strategy involved with Barros. No skill of arms. Simply charge in and start smashing. Granted that would win some fights, but Junger had proven that, against skilled opponents, it would not do at all.

Grisholt employed a capable enough taskmaster called Turst, a Sunjan and veteran of the games. Curge wondered if Turst had decided upon a different manner of fighting during the season, since the previous one clearly wasn't working. The owner sighed and sucked on a tooth. One more matter to keep an eye on. He would assign the task to his agent Bezange, to see if any of his spies might discover something.

Curge went for another drink and discovered his goblet empty. Frowning, he stretched out his arm, signaling for another refill.

The manservant did so at once.

While he poured, the fearsome owner glanced over his shoulder, at the entrance to the viewing box area reserved for the owners of the top-ranked houses. Of which only Curge presently occupied.

On each side of the door stood four guards, recently hired by the house master. All eight wore the armor representing the House of Curge. Leather bands crossed their torsos while bronze greaves and bracers protected their limbs. Full helmets hid their grizzled faces. Rounded shields hung off their arms while short swords remained sheathed at their waists. The head of Curge's household guard, burly Demasta, paced before them all. Thick of arm, leg, and body, with dark hair and a short black beard, Demasta glared this way and that. His hairy hands hung off a thick belt around his waist, where a broadsword jutted from the left side. Unlike the paltry coverings for the masses gathered for the day's fights, the viewing box had much better awnings, draping all with an oppressive shade.

Realizing his master's eyes were on him, Demasta halted and shook his head. *No sight of Nexus.*

Good, Curge thought.

Reflecting on the day's schedule, and with his goblet refilled, Curge regarded the arena again. A new bottle had been cracked and the wine tasted tart but not wholly unpleasant. He drank and enjoyed it, mostly because he knew Nexus did not. The unpleasant topper. An unwashed scrub brush for one's ass crack was more pleasant. The merchant no doubt watched the games from his chambers at ground level. Best place for that silver shite weasel, as far as Curge was concerned. The viewing box was *his* now. And Demasta and the eight guards behind him, as well as the other sixteen posted *outside* the entrance, would convince even a soft-skulled knob like Nexus to keep well away.

Unless he wanted a bit of bloodshed.

Curge stroked his chin while the wine warmed his guts. *Nexus.* The other house owners had talked and decided the wine merchant was unworthy of their circle. The decimation of his ranks had been planned, and anyone fighting for him would have marks on their heads. Punishment for granting shelter and providing purpose for the maggot called Prajus.

None of the wine merchant's asslickers would fight this day, however. And that was fine.

Curge's hatred for Nexus blotted out thoughts for his other nemesis in the games—the House of Ten. It was one thing that the brazen Free Trained meat was able to buy their way into the games, but it was another to convince old Clavellus to return to the very place he'd been cast out of . . .

Curge tightened his grip on his goblet.

What was worse, however, was that the Ten actually had a pair of toppers who showed promise. And one of those men— dare Curge even believe it—could *win* the games. The thought of that hurt his head. Poisoned his guts. He checked on his goblet. *Seddon above.* He'd downed the last refill without realizing it. Fuming, he stuck out his arm again and the manservant appeared with the bottle.

The Orator lifted his arms and called for silence. The audience responded, waiting for the introduction of the next fighters.

His drink filled yet again, Curge shifted and watched, red eyes darting from one end of the Pit to the other.

This day, one of his own fought. And his name was . . .

Gair swaggered out onto the sands to warm applause, soaking in the adulation. His heavily muscled frame cast a bulky *V*-shaped shadow upon the sands. A band of leather protected his torso, to keep his guts inside in case of a fatal slash. A red faceplate, adorned with a brutish silver jaw with short, troll-like tusks covered his features. Instead of the usual bundle of cloth around his head, Gair wore a helmet that trailed black beads over his shoulders. Spiked gauntlets armored his hands. He carried a pair of thick knives, just a hand's length short of being swords, and the steel shone brightly in the sun.

Many considered Gair impressive.

The pit fighter he fought this day, however, was a monster.

From the School of Vorish, Grigo, the one they called the Punisher, stepped into view. A rousing cheer went up at the Orator's introduction, though Grigo appeared not to hear it. Tall and grim, a shirt of polished mail hung off wide shoulders, while a rounded helmet hid the man's features. Beneath the wide metal mesh that protected his eyes was a grill of razors fixed in a broad smile. What really caught the audience's attention, as it always did, was the dreaded spiked mace the Punisher carried in his right hand. A shield that could serve as a door protected his left side.

Amid crashing cheers, an unhurried Grigo approached the middle of the arena. His indifferent stare and metal smile fixed upon his unfortunate adversary.

Gair studied the task before him, knowing the man had amassed an undefeated record. Five victories, killing three in the process. Grigo was part of a handful of gladiators that were performing quite well for the School of Vorish. Gair didn't take his eyes off him. As Grigo closed the distance, it became apparent he stood a full head taller.

The insectile eyes of Grigo's helmet stared, while the razor smile conveyed anything but goodwill. He readied his shield before him and held his mace downward, the spiked end close to his shin.

Steel flashed as Gair brought up his knives, flexing his arms as he did so.

As an answer, Grigo whipped his dreaded mace straight for his opponent's crotch.

Gair nimbly sidestepped the blow, which the crowds praised with a booming "*Oooo!*"

The knife fighter went to work, seeking the bigger man's weapon arm.

Knives clicked and screeched off shield and mace as Gair pressed his attack, backing Grigo up. Blocking all of Gair's attacks, Grigo lowered his head and edged forward, mace cocked and ready at the shoulder.

Sensing danger, Gair relented and darted away.

Grigo nodded. "You're a nimble little bastard, make no mistake," he rumbled in his metallic voice. "Like a black-bellied gnat. Or shite fly. Come here, little shite fly. Come here. So I can—"

Grigo lunged.

And even though Gair thought he was out of harm's way, Grigo's imposing height and *reach* allowed him to close the distance in an instant. Gair ducked under the sweeping mace, the prickly bauble missing his skull by a scant finger.

They passed each other, but Grigo whirled as he went, to block the expected counterattack. His foe did no such thing, however, choosing to turn at a healthy distance, his blades held before him.

Grigo peeked over his shield while readying his mace once more. He lumbered into a run, scuffing up sand as he went. He swung for a shoulder and missed, then bashed his shield at a head and got only air. But Grigo was closer to his foe, and he swung for everything offered, powering each bone-breaking strike with a heaving grunt.

Gair twisted and dodged, ducked and backpedaled, eluding every swipe of that spiked ball of iron, every slap of that door-sized shield.

Until he dropped to one knee and lashed out with a spiked fist.

Grigo stopped that on his shield, slamming the barrier down like a falling portcullis. The fist landed flat, the smack ringing across the sands.

"*Gah!*" the big man blurted as he looked to crush Gair's head.

Gair, however, was already moving. He yanked his fist free, misting the air with splinters, and sprang from his crouch. Like some bent over sapling released, Gair came up into Grigo's face and punched that smiling grill. The blow twisted Grigo's head aside, staggering him in a wave of sand. Grigo flailed, purely out of reflex, and connected with Gair's armored thigh.

The blow blunted Gair's momentum but only for a moment, as he recovered quickly and stabbed for the big man's head.

Grigo slapped the blade away with his shield. He did not stop the *other* blade, however, looping around to hammer an armored profile.

The audience cheered again as Grigo staggered away.

Gair pressed forward, swarming his larger foe. He struck at everything, the strokes ringing, the steel twinkling. He slashed a leg, an arm, and repeated but on the opposite side. Up and down, high and low. He got in close, rammed his shoulder into Grigo's shield, and heaved him up.

That revealed a pillar of a leg.

Gair drove his boot into the exposed ankle.

With a forward lurch, Grigo dropped to a knee, awkwardly kept upright by his shield.

His head was right there, offered as if bowing to a king.

Gair punched that smiling helmet, repeatedly, swinging from the hips while flinging aside his daggers. Grigo's head snapped from left to right, weakening with every blow, dazing him a little more. Then the punches fell straight from the shoulder—heavy, one-shot hammerblows that sought to crumple armor. A sheet of blood spurted from underneath Grigo's helmet, staining everything below. Unable to defend and too stunned to counter, Grigo held on to his shield and sagged a little more, absorbing more and more damage.

And with every punch that landed, the crowd cheered.

Sensing the end, Gair grabbed the neckline of Grigo's armor and held on. He redoubled his efforts, rocking his foe as if he had a hold of someone well and truly pickled. After a time, he stopped punching but kept one fist cocked while looming over his sagging opponent. He shook Grigo once and, after a deciding moment, released him.

Grigo toppled backward, his legs twisting awkwardly beneath him.

The onlookers leaped to their feet and roared in approval.

Gair seized Grigo's throat and aimed a shivering fist at his face.

Ready to continue if needed.

Somehow, Grigo had the sense to lift a trembling arm.

And the audience erupted again.

The victory delighted Dark Curge and he slapped his stump off the nearby brick. A quick fight and a good win over a dog who had been undefeated. A rare smile spread across Curge's face. He could almost hear Vorish's indignant squealing. To that, he drained the last of his wine and considered another.

The manservant waited with a ready bottle.

Giving the nod to get on with it, Curge held out his goblet, and the servant poured without a word.

Demasta stopped at the owner's other side. "A lady wishes to speak with you, Master Curge,"

"A lady?" the owner blurted, spit-spraying a few drops.

The head of his household guard nodded.

"Who?" Curge demanded.

"A lady *Zelia*. Says she's the wife of the dead gladiator called Sorban, just recently deceased."

Curge remembered the man. As an afterthought, he checked on his goblet and dismissed the manservant.

Sorban. Belonged to the Stable of Salwark. No, not Salwark, Curge corrected himself. Stable of *Slavol*, once belonging to *Vavar* Slavol. Vavar and old Tilo were the last living owners from a time Curge considered the golden age of gladiatorial combat. An age where his own father, Old Curge, had cut out a chunk of bloody history for himself and established his house as the very best. Tilo still breathed and showed no sign of perishing, still managing the affairs of his own successful house. Vavar, however, was bedridden and close to death, while his son Salwark oversaw his father's stable. Salwark was an overeager—if not a touch skittish—punce, plying a trade he knew nothing about.

Sorban fought and died under Salwark's ownership. Killed by Goll, in fact, who formed the upstart House of Ten.

"Bring her here," Curge rumbled with curiosity as the wine took a greater hold.

Demasta returned after a moment, escorting the lady. She was short, dressed in tasteful robes of red from neck to ankles. A fine leather belt hung about her waist, accentuating her hips. Blue eyes, short lashes, and a round face freckled by the sun. Her hair, light and long, was pulled back into a tail behind her, displaying a high forehead.

Slightly pickled, Curge's eyes widened, not expecting one so lovely.

"Lady Zelia," Demasta introduced stoically. "Master Curge, of the House of Curge."

They exchanged nods of greetings and Curge waved a hand. "Bring her a chair."

The manservant complied, and Zelia sat next to the house master, her knees pointed at his.

Curge minded his manners despite his steady indulgence in an afternoon bottle.

"Thank you for granting a meeting, Master Curge," Zelia said, her voice pleasant to the ears, but her expression one of wary courtesy.

"I'm not . . . used to meeting a lady here," Curge admitted. "Some wine?"

She shook her head. "Thank you but no. That is not the nature of my visit."

"I assumed as much. Well then, what is it?"

"You are the owner of the House of Curge," she said. "And these are the games. My husband, Sorban, fought and died during these games, not so long ago."

Curge held up his stump. "Apologies for your loss," he said, and genuinely meant it.

The sympathy took Zelia off guard. "Thank you, Master Curge," she whispered before taking a fresh breath. "The one called Goll killed him. Once a Free Trained pit fighter but now calling himself and those with him a house. Sorban fought for the Stable of Slavol. Once an honorable establishment of these games, but no more. Slavol . . ." she took a steadying breath, "could not avenge my husband's death. He did not even inform me that Sorban had died. I found out through other means, whereupon I went to Slavol and demanded revenge for Sorban. I had to demand revenge, Master Curge. *Demand* it. From the very one who *forgot* to inform the wife of his best gladiator about his death. Perhaps his very best. In the end, Slavol abandoned his revenge against Goll, as he did not have anyone capable of killing him. Nor did he have anyone *willing* to fight the Kree. Well, except one, and he lost."

"That one was called . . . Harook, I believe," Curge supplied.

"Aye that. That's his name. Which brings me to you."

The owner waited, already guessing the reason for the visit.

"Goll killed my husband," Zelia stated, flashing teeth. "The Stable of Slavol cannot avenge my husband's death. Worse, they are gutless. They . . . sling about talk of being sword brothers, but only when it serves their purpose. They have forgotten my husband, but I have not. I want Goll dead, so I come to you with an offer of coin. If any of your men face Goll in the arena in the coming days, have them kill Goll for me, and I'll pay you generously. Use your best gladiator. Use whoever you wish. Butcher him as he butchered my husband. Avenge him, for me. Humiliate the ones who could not avenge one of their own, and the coin is yours."

That lifted Curge's brow. He blinked and, with a glance at his wine, carefully placed the goblet on the ground. He then faced her and gathered his muddled thoughts.

"You're offering me coin to kill Goll?" he asked.

"I'm offering coin to *all* the houses to kill Goll," Zelia said. "The first house to kill him can collect. I'm telling you of this bounty *first*, however. Since my husband considered your house to be the best in these games, this year and years past. He had a great respect for you."

Despite the amount of wine in him, Curge concentrated very hard on what the woman was saying. "Lady Zelia . . . I am . . . truly sorry for the death of your husband. As owner of this house, I knew firsthand how skilled Sorban was. And I knew of

Slavol's failure to avenge the death of his best fighter. And, aye that, Sorban *was* his best. We all knew it." He paused. "What if Salwark learns of this bounty?"

"He will not care. He'll be delighted he doesn't have to risk any more of his maggots. He has no faith in any of them."

"No, clearly," Curge agreed. "Goll killed his best when he . . ." the grizzled owner faltered, realizing his misstep.

"When he killed Sorban, yes," Zelia finished.

The Orator shouted something, signaling the start of the next match, but Curge concentrated on the lady before him.

"You don't see it yet," he said, "but war has come to the Pit this year."

"Does it include Goll?"

Curge thought about it. "No. Not yet."

"Then I'm not interested in your war."

"And, sadly, my war is more concerning to me than your revenge." Curge allowed that to simmer for a moment. "You may not be aware of it, but the games have grown longer this season. Much longer than before. And they will *not* end until King Juhn decides it so. My lads will eventually meet Goll on the sands. When they do . . . I will tell them to take his head. In memory of your husband. You keep your bounty."

Zelia stared at him, "Thank you, Master Curge."

"It may take some time, however," Curge admitted. "A very long time. Truth be known, the Kree is well-experienced with a blade. He would have gutted Slavol's entire roster if Slavol had sent them after him. One by one. Slavol could not afford to lose any more fighters to Goll. It would ruin him in both morale and, more importantly, coin. Look. I will save you offering the other houses a price for the Kree's head. Goll has already been wounded. He's hurt. A healer can only do so much in the time between fights. Some of those licks will never heal in time for his next match. Some will never heal at all. These games have always been a contest not only of skill but of endurance and *will*, to push on despite the cuts and scratches. The further you advance, the more relentless the adversary. Only the very best make it to the later rounds unscathed. The houses all know Goll has a history of killing his opponents, so they will show him no mercy. And every bloody lick he takes will slow him down just a little more. What I'm saying is . . . just be patient, good Zelia. Someone will take the Kree bastard's head. In time. For *nothing*."

"The only thing that matters to me is Goll dying," Zelia countered. "During these games. Or after, if needed."

That admission surprised Curge. "You're a fierce one."

She said nothing to that, and in the silence they studied each other. Somewhere far away, the Orator continued with his introductions.

"Thank you for this meeting," Zelia said abruptly and stood. "I must leave now. I have to visit the other houses."

"You'll still make an offer to them?"

"I will."

"All of them?" Curge asked.

"All," she replied without pause. "Goll will perish during these games, Master Curge. By someone's hand, because I demand it. And I will pay well for it to happen. I will not risk someone allowing him to live if they have him at their mercy. I came here first because your house, your fighters, are the best. My husband said so, many times."

"Well . . . if my lads meet Goll in the Pit, they'll kill him. I'll order them to take his head. And they'll do so for Sorban's memory. I hope that is enough."

She waited for more, but Curge had nothing more to say on the matter. "Then we are done," she finished, surprising him again.

"Lady Zelia?" he asked.

She paused.

"You said you were going to all the houses. Does that include the School of Nexus?"

"It does."

Curge held her gaze. "Think again on that. The name of Nexus is . . . not a popular one this season."

"Kill Goll and I won't have to visit him," Zelia said evenly. "Good fortune to you, Master Curge."

With that she walked away.

Curge sought to rise but sank back in his chair instead. He nodded at Demasta, who followed the lady to the door. *Nexus*, Curge thought, wishing death upon the wine merchant. Then he remembered Lady Zelia's personal bounty on Goll's life.

He sighed and frowned at his wine, knowing he'd drunk too much to commit to such a thing. Oh, he would give the order, but in the end taking a life was a gladiator's decision. Fear would stay the hand of whoever might have Goll at their mercy, for anyone killing Goll would openly invite the Ten to seek a blood match with the killer.

They would send their best for that contest.

That meant the Perician.

There were only two surviving pit fighters remaining in the House of Ten; thus, whoever killed Goll would have to face *him*. And, though Junger had shown he was unwilling to kill a man, even in a blood match, there was always the first time. Junger might even choose to hurt the offending gladiator so badly that the defeated man would be unable to continue in the games. For some, having their chances ended before the final eight was worse than death.

Curge sighed. As much as he hated to admit it, he suspected no one would dare risk being hunted by *that* one. He doubted Zelia had enough coin to rival the riches that came with the title of champion.

And, truth be known, Curge would need all his killers to fight Nexus and *his* killers, until the merchant was forced into defeat and withdrawal from the games. Spending time hunting for the likes of Goll would only put his lads at risk when they would be needed elsewhere. Curge would have been far more interested in Zelia's offer if it were for the Zhiberian pig bastard *Halm*. That pisser had left the games, however, to live in some shite-crusted squat hole called Karashipa. That one had no desire to return this season, since returning meant facing an immediate blood match.

Even then, killing the Zhiberian meant having to face Junger, but Curge found himself willing to risk a pit fighter for that one.

The cheering brought him back to the fight currently taking place in the arena.

There, two men battled, but one was clearly on the offensive. One was called Olibo, from Grisholt's pack of rats. Olibo fended off a series of cuts and slashes from a much larger man, wearing a black shirt of mail that seemed all the dustier in the daylight. Curge concentrated on him. *Wocello.* That was his name, a lad belonging to Burco Ustda, the overly cheerful owner of the House of Ustda.

Wocello whipped a huge greatsword about, backing Olibo up on his heels. Despite the vocal crowd, Curge knew that frightening blade hummed as it split the air.

Something caught his eye, however.

The owner frowned and rubbed his nose with his stump. Grisholt's lad wasn't screaming his head off like the others from that nest. In fact, Olibo was clearly overmatched, doing everything to regain the initiative while still retreating. Olibo ducked and parried, using his shield often, occasionally stabbing or feinting with a short sword. Nothing deterred Wocello, however. The fearsome gladiator pressed forward, swinging in wide sweeping arcs, forcing Olibo to duck and sidestep, but he was unable to close the distance to his foe.

Perhaps sensing the same, Olibo gambled and darted to his left, seeking to strike an exposed leg.

Springing his trap, Wocello whipped his blade up and over his head in a bowel-loosening arc before he slammed it down.

Olibo attempted to block the weapon with his shield.

The greatsword split the upraised platter in a crow's squawk of metal, powering through it and the arm underneath, to shear Olibo's shoulder from the rest of him. That length of steel sliced a spurting, dribbling, lopsided *V* into the smaller man's chest. The pit fighter slumped to his knees, leaning into the sword killing him, as if pleading for mercy.

Wocello held the pose for a reckoning moment. Just a moment, before he placed a boot to his adversary's chest and shoved him off the sword.

Scowling, Curge's attention flickered between the crowd and the victorious gladiator. The carcass staining the sands red clearly hadn't had the same enthusiasm, the same eager *glee* for violence as others fighting for Grisholt.

Deciding that nothing was amiss, Curge held out his goblet once again to be filled . . .

7

The evening faded into a tired orange sky, flattered with streaks of purple.

The window remained open, but not a breath of a breeze came through. Shadows lengthened upon the bare floorboards. Gurga lay on a bed, sticky all over from the sweltering, lingering heat, and studied the ceiling timbers of the room he paid for earlier that day. His hand strayed through the unruly garden that was his chest, at times scratching at troublesome roots.

After visiting Tilo and declining an offer of assistance from the gate guard—who wasn't a bad fellow in the least—Gurga had searched for lodgings. There was no desire to return to his old room at Sindra's. Not yet. The memories were still too fresh, the ache too deep. Also, Telda would doubtless try to stop him from leaving again. He didn't need that. New accommodations would be essential for what he intended to do next.

Sons of Cholla, Sindra reminded him from another, better time. *Men with ink upon their skin. Up and down their arms. Even their necks.*

All color left the sky, leaving his room in darkness. Soft clicks, clacks, and the murmurs of passersby drifted up from the streets. Gurga waited, listening, taking in the peace of it all. When he had had enough, he pushed himself up with a grunt.

A nearby pitcher of water waited for him, and his thirst was a mighty one. After a series of great gulps, he wiped his mouth and dumped the remainder into a wide wash pan. A hand cloth lay nearby, neatly folded, so he took that and scrubbed himself with warm water. Once clean, Gurga looked out the window.

It was still early . . . but dark enough.

Sniffing, he opened his sack of belongings. The first thing he pulled out was a thin but exceptionally long towel of coarse fabric. With great care, he wrapped the material around his midsection twice and tucked the ends away so that they would stay in place. Next, he extracted the broad leather band and draped that around his waist as well, covering the towel. That slab of gut armor had three small buckles, and he took his time fastening and adjusting them. Once done, he rubbed a hand over the snug piece. Every scratch and gouge stirred up a memory. If there was anything he had confidence in, it was the armor's ability to stop a knife.

With another glance at the dark sky above, Gurga cleared his throat and undid his trousers, letting them drop. From the sack, he pulled out an iron cup stitched into a leather sheath and padded with cloth. The armor had been fashioned for him when he was with Master Tilo, and they had let him keep it when he left the business. Gurga fitted the piece to his fruits until all was in place. Straps and a single buckle kept everything in order, and he fumbled to secure everything—as he always did—with his oversized fingers. When he was finished, he hauled up his trousers and fastened his belt. Leather on leather. The same trusted protection he'd worn while on duty at Sindra's alehouse. A different duty but the same purpose. Seemed right to use it now. Felt right. To *not* use it felt like . . . ignoring the help of old friends. Gurga pulled on a shirt and left it untucked so that it hung past his waist. He buttoned the clothing only to the sternum, where only a hint of the armor showed. Once finished, he lay a huge hand against the tough leather and tapped it with a finger.

A loud chatter of voices coming from the street below drew his attention. A few peals of laughter, then everything died away.

Gurga wiped his nose and went back to the sack. He strapped on leather bracers, each one reinforced with a strip of iron stitched into the back of the fabric. These he laced up, drew the strings tight, and judged with a hard slap. A pair of fingerless gloves were next, black paws with small squares of iron stitched into the knuckles. These, he'd hired a leather worker to make. Gurga was an immensely strong man, and he hadn't met anyone able to defeat him, but when he was working the main entrance of the alehouse, every little bit helped keep the peace. Or enforce it, when needed.

Leather creaked as he hauled on his gloves. Straps were pulled tight and buckled. He laced his fingers together to ensure the fit and finished with a soft punch to one hand then the other. Another pause before he extracted a dagger from the sack. Short and lethal, the steel scratched and worn from years of sharpening. His spine crackled as he bent over and eased the thing into a hidden scabbard inside his right boot. Once tucked away, he moved about a few steps and deemed it secure.

A leather collar went on next. He fumbled through the sack and located the armor as well as the cushioning cloth underneath the piece. A touch annoyed for forgetting such an important item, he fought with his shirt until he had everything in place. With that done, he straightened out his shirt again. His beard hid most of the collar in the front, but the piece was easily noticed from the sides. He knew he'd get looks because of it, but he got those anyway, and he preferred stares to a blade across the cheesepipe.

Finally, he pulled out the cap, leather like most everything else, with a thick cloth inlay that always smelled of rancid sweat, no matter how often Gurga soaked and cleaned it. Sindra had suggested scented water to mask the smell, but he'd scoffed at the thought. In his opinion, real men didn't wear scented water, which always earned a scowl from her.

That little memory stopped him, and he stayed that way for a while, a statue in a dark room, leather cap hanging from a hand. Voices drifted in from the streets. After the moment's reflection, Gurga pulled the leather cap tight over his head. That, along with his huge beard, created a sight not many would forget. He didn't care about that. In fact, he wanted to be remembered . . . by those wearing the ink. The Sons of Cholla.

That got him fuming.

It was dark enough now, although the longer he waited, the deeper his prey would be into their cups.

He decided to wait a little longer.

Then he would go.

A hunched giant of a shadow slunk through a maze of unlit alleyways, underneath a night filled with stars. Gurga shambled through fragrant puddles and kicked unseen slabs of wood. In one instance, he hooked the leg of one senseless punce laid out on the alley floor, jerking the figure sideways. The weight and startled grunt surprised Gurga, but the enforcer didn't linger and continued on his way. Being quiet was proving to be more difficult than he first anticipated, but he resolved to do better, despite his mounting frustration. When the alley ended in a wide street, he looked both ways before proceeding. If the street was too wide with too many people, he would backtrack and find a less traveled path. He avoided the pockets of torches and lamplight when he could and kept to the dark.

It took time. More than he expected.

At one point, Gurga emerged from between two stone buildings, his meaty arms swinging, and startled a pair of city workers. Both men, who were replenishing an oil lamp, froze upon seeing the huge enforcer. Gurga ignored them and crossed the street, turning a few heads as he went, and disappeared down another dark alley. The place he was heading for, however, would be darker. He didn't rightly know where these Sons would be, but he had an idea. Over the years, he'd overheard enough patrons talking about the rough places to avoid. The shite troughs. The crusty holes. Alehouses that charged a little too much for their drinks and filled their mugs a few fingers less than full, and whose customers were brazenly robbed by toppers hunting for the pickled and the senseless.

The very thought of a robbery happening inside *his* house angered Gurga. Boiled his juices.

Well before midnight, he reached what he believed to be an area rampant with street clan activity. Somewhere to the southeast was the Pit, but Gurga didn't need to go anywhere near there. Not yet. He stopped at the corner of an unlit building and studied an alehouse across the way. Streetlamps warmly illuminated the scene, coloring the cobblestones brightest beneath their posts. The alehouse was a tall stone structure, some three levels high, with long ribbons hanging from the overhangs. Warm lamplight glowed in every open window. A crowded interior could be seen through the lower windows, and figures moved amid the rumble of happy conversation.

A pair of enforcers guarded the entrance, muscular and stern, stopping each person trying to enter the premises.

Gurga studied the two men. He had no real plan of how to find anyone wearing the ink, except walking about and looking for them. Annoyed by the enforcers, he sighed and reluctantly pulled his leather cap from his head. He'd have to go inside, get among all that unfit drinking and shouting and pickled merriment. Worse still, he'd have to wade through the foul muck of someone *else's* alehouse, *without* authority. *Without* permission to toss saucy nogs out into the street. All that soured his mood. Unable to think of any other course of action, he tucked his cap within his shirt. With a scowl and pat of the hidden armor protecting his guts, he stepped into the open.

A few cautious glances came from those walking by but he ignored all that.

The enforcers noticed him straightaway. The two men exchanged wary looks and unfolded their arms before focusing on the approaching ogre.

Gurga stopped a few strides away. Even though the alert guardians stood on a raised deck two steps high, they were only slightly taller than Gurga. They were big men, blocky and intimidating. One had a scar that ended in a chunk of missing lip, where a bit of tooth gleamed in a fixed snarl. The other flaunted a well-trimmed beard and a questioning scowl. Both wore black shirts without sleeves, to show off their powerful arms. Arms without ink.

The bearded one spoke first. "Going inside, are you?"

The question distracted Gurga from their arms. He eventually nodded.

"No weapons on you?" the bearded one asked.

Gurga shook his head.

"Not going to cause any trouble?"

Again, Gurga shook his head.

"I ask because you look angry."

"Unfit angry," added the one with the piece missing from his lip.

"And we don't want unfit angry folks inside," resumed the other. "That might start trouble. We don't like trouble. We stomp on trouble. If you go in there and start trouble, we'll stomp on *you*. Understand?"

Gurga's eyes flickered from the bearded one to the other. "Aye that."

"All right, then."

They parted and waved him through.

Gurga studied his feet. "I have a question."

The two enforcers traded looks again.

"What was that?" asked the one with the beard.

"I have a question."

"All right. What is it?"

Gurga hesitated. "You, ah, see any lads wearing ink?"

"Lads wearing ink?" the bearded one repeated.

"Aye that. On their arms. Hands." He looked the man straight in the eye. "Necks."

"You mean . . . street clan ink?" asked the one with the piece missing from his lip.

"Aye that." Gurga nodded at the alehouse. "In there."

The enforcers regarded each other again. Gurga thought they did that a lot.

"What if there are?" asked the bearded one. "You're going to talk with them?"

One of Gurga's many faults, which Sindra often reminded him of, was his endearing . . . *unwillingness* to tell a lie. Ever. So he thought over his answer very carefully, while his mouth tightened into a button. "No," he said after a time.

"No?" repeated the one with the piece missing from his lip.

"No."

"Are you going to cause trouble?" probed the bearded one.

A sighing Gurga had to think it over. "Not in there." And he meant it. *If* he could help it. Knowing the business firsthand, he didn't want to start any trouble for these two lads, who were only there to keep the peace. Only doing the same job he'd done for Sindra.

Another exchange of looks between the enforcers.

"All right, then," the bearded one said. "In you go."

Somewhat surprised, Gurga ascended, the steps protesting his weight. The enforcers arched their heads as he walked by, but neither man backed away. Gurga appreciated that. Understood it without question. One couldn't show fear in their business. Fear invited trouble.

The smells hit him upon entering, of beer and mead and other good drink. Of clean sweat and pipe smoke and seasoned roasts, fresh off the spit and sliced into tasty slivers. A lovely haze enveloped Gurga as he strode forth, hunched over just a bit to avoid the low-hanging cross-timbers.

The reaction was immediate.

As always, people noticed him. Smiling faces slackened with shock or turned serious. Conversations stalled or were entirely forgotten. Women hanging off men and men hanging off women moved closer to each other. The drinking continued, but eyes watched him as he went about his business. He looked over faces and necks, shoulders and arms, whatever bared skin there was for ink . . . and saw none. The masses parted as he wandered through, earning a nervous smile here, a pickled grin there, all to the low murmurs of "Seddon above" and similar such remarks. The hard ones tracked him too, as territorial as any wild animal, wondering if they would have to fight for what they considered theirs.

Gurga had no trouble reaching the bar. The nervous souls standing before it moved before he got there. The revelry had subsided considerably by the time he stopped at the counter and gazed down upon the two barkeeps. The two men looked up and waited for whatever was about to happen. Gurga regarded one then the other, and let out a heavy, contemplative sigh that lifted his chest and shoulders in a worrying manner.

"Water," the big man grumbled. ". . . Please."

The barkeeps regarded each other. One of them placed a mug before Gurga and promptly filled it. Gurga offered to pay, but the barkeep nervously waved him off. The huge enforcer drained half the drink before he paused and glanced around. Four more burly enforcers prowled the floor, passing through smoky lamplight or leaning against thick posts. Each man eyed him, letting him know he had their attention. Knowing the business firsthand, Gurga expected no less. He actually approved of such vigilance. Clasping his mug in his oversized hand, he again examined the crowd.

The crowd stared back. Someone coughed. A clay mug clattered upon a table. A chair squealed briefly as it was pulled across the floor. What had been a rousing good time had bled away to wary silence. The attention uneased Gurga, and the heat off all those bodies warmed him enough to perspire a little more heavily. So he finished his drink and returned the mug to the counter, where the nervous barkeeps had taken a step back. Gurga nodded thanks at them both.

Sensing his plan had failed, he straightened and flinched, barely missing one of those low-hanging cross-timbers. Scowling this way and that, he wandered back through the crowd. Not a bit of ink to be seen. Just cautious revelers.

The smells stayed with him as he left the alehouse. The enforcers at the entrance watched his every step.

As did the four others shadowing him.

"Find anyone in there?" asked the one with the beard as Gurga's boots hit the cobblestone street.

The big man turned about. "No."

"No," said the bearded one, as if knowing that very answer. "Not in there."

His companion with the piece missing from his lip shook his head in agreement.

"The owners like keeping the shite away from this part," said the bearded one.

That surprised Gurga. "They do?"

"They do."

"Since when?"

"Since forever," the bearded one stated, to which his companion's headshaking switched to solemn nodding.

"When was the last time you were about these parts?" the bearded one asked.

Gurga thought about it. "A long time, I wager?"

"Suppose so," admitted the big man.

"The gangs and clans *were* here, years ago," the bearded one said. "But that was *years*. The street watch cleaned everything up, in the most violent way you can imagine. What needed to be done was done. Boundaries set. The gangs and the clans know not to come around these parts. Oh, they still linger about the Pit and parts of Arbin's Row and the Lords know where else, looking like animals hungry for scraps, but not here. Know better not to."

"The Pit and Arbin's Row?" Gurga asked.

"Lots of coin to be had on the games," said the one with the damaged lip.

"He knows that," scolded the bearded one.

"He looks like he doesn't."

They regarded Gurga for his thoughts on that matter.

"My thanks," the big enforcer replied and got moving.

"Hey . . ." called out the bearded one.

Gurga turned again.

"Did you once work an alehouse?"

Gurga thought about it.

". . . No," he answered and walked away.

8

About the same time Gurga was returning to his room at the alehouse, Grisholt sat slumped over in his study, where musty tomes of history and forgotten poetry lined the shelves of the surrounding walls. Those books—filled with an odd mixture of knowledge and gurry—soured the very air if the windows were shuttered, but Grisholt dared not throw the things away, as they belonged to his father. Still did, in his mind, even though the man was long gone.

He stared at those old books, thinking about nothing, well on his way to being truly pickled. He kept his goblet close, the broad base resting on his belly. Five bottles, two emptied and three untouched, rose from the middle of his desk. Candles and lamplight brightened their shiny curves. At times, his fingers wandered to the arm of his chair, hunting for frayed threads. When he found them, he stretched their lengths out before plucking them free. After a quick inspection, he fluttered his fingers and let the gurry fall to the floor, then went on the hunt again.

After a bit of that, he stopped and thought about matters.

It had been a long trip back.

Well . . . not that long. Not with all the drinking along the way. Celebratory drinking . . . the likes of which he hadn't wanted his lads to see. It was one of two reasons he decided to ride in his private koch, the other being so he could open one of the half-dozen chests he'd purchased unseen, to gaze undisturbed upon its luminous contents. Its *considerable* contents.

Gold, with a handful of gemstones sprinkled throughout. Gemstones of luminous green and icy blue, each one worth a hundred gold pieces. Or so the Domis had explained. Perhaps even more, depending on who might later buy them, but a prized commodity to have in one's treasury. The Domis had also explained that, instead of laboring with chests brimming with coin or notes that could easily be lost, gemstones were an acceptable form of payment. If the person who won the sum was agreeable.

If the person was agreeable. Grisholt smirked and had another drink of wine. Though he had purchased fewer chests than he wanted, he had certainly bought enough wine before returning from the games. Wine enough for all his fighters, in fact. Beer and firewater as well, the spoils of a very successful day. Oh, aye that, they'd lost Olibo, which had lengthened the faces of the lads and soured their spirits, make no mistake. Once Grisholt started buying wine and firewater for all, however—well, that lifted their moods. Somewhat.

Sitting near the door to the study with his own bottle, Brakuss crossed one leg over the other, a smile on his rugged features.

"Something amuses you?" Grisholt asked without slurring.

The one-eyed guard shook his head.

"Something is making you happy over there. You haven't had enough of that, yet." He pointed at the guard's bottle.

Brakuss half shrugged.

"Out with it, good Brakuss," Grisholt pressed. "We've been through too much together to keep secrets now."

Still, the guard didn't reveal what was on his mind.

Fine then, Grisholt shrugged. He studied the bottles before him, considering cracking open one with firewater.

"We're rich," Brakuss finally said.

"Well, *I'm* rich, truth be known," Grisholt corrected. "But I'm also generous. So, aye that, *we're* rich, if it pleases you."

"It pleases me."

"And so it should."

"At the start of the games," Brakuss continued, "this house, this home . . . this very *room*."

Grisholt gestured to hurry along with it.

"This room was leaking, Master Grisholt. *Leaking*. The roof, I mean. And now?"

"Now, it does *not*."

Brakuss smiled again, a rare sight indeed. "No, it does not," he repeated and tipped his bottle back. He took a long drink. *Had to be wine*, Grisholt thought. He *hoped* it was wine. That much firewater could kill a person. Or unleash a deluge of scutters to fill an entire shite trough.

"It's unfit what a few wins in the arena can do," the head of the household guard said.

"What a few *victories* can do," Grisholt corrected with a knowing smile, one which Brakuss answered with a wetter one of his own. That sight dimmed the house master's own merriment, but only for a moment.

"I can't . . ." Brakuss said, shaking his head. "I can't . . ."

"Believe it?" Grisholt supplied.

Brakuss chopped a thankful hand at him.

"Ohhh I knew we would recover," Grisholt explained with drunken confidence. "The stable is too good to *not* recover. Was only a matter of time. A question of when. A puzzle of *how*. All I had to do was . . . keep us in the games. For just a little while longer. Keep pushing. Pressing. Day after day. Push. Press. Until . . . this. All this. No leaks in the roof. In any of the roofs. The outer walls are being restored. All the aging timbers replaced by new. New doors, new shelves, new quarters . . ." He thought more on it. "New weapons. New *armor*."

"New wine," Brakuss added.

Grisholt pointed at him. "New *wine*. New everything. Same old games, but new coin makes it all grand again. All *glorious* again. Lords above how good it feels."

"Marrok nearly perished with shock when he saw the wagons," Brakuss said.

"He did, didn't he? Oh, that was a sight. Holding a chicken in one hand, cleaver in the other, and nothing to shut his mouth. It's probably still open."

"He's enjoying the night."

"As he should," Grisholt said with a nod. "As we *all* should. Enjoy this one and all the others that follow. Right to the end. These games are *ours*, dear Brakuss. *Ours.* If I didn't know before, I know *now.* Oh, if only my father were still alive to see all this."

Brakuss met that with a suddenly doubtful, if not disbelieving, eye.

"Perhaps not," Grisholt said and smiled with pickled knowingness.

A heavy knocking upon the door distracted them both.

Brakuss looked at the owner, who released a heavy sigh and nodded. The guard rose and, with one hand on his sword, opened the door. There Turst the taskmaster waited, his features only partially revealed by lamplight. He looked Brakuss up and down before shaking his head in disapproval.

"Mind yourself, boy," he warned and started forward, expecting Brakuss to move aside. When he did not, the taskmaster slammed right into Brakuss's unmoving bulk.

Scowling bewilderment, Turst stepped back and glared a question of *Well?*

Brakuss stepped aside.

"Well met, good Turst," Grisholt chuckled. "I see you've met my other door."

"The *bells* of your door almost met my boot," Turst rumbled. He stopped at the table and studied the bottles. "You favor any of these, in particular?"

"Have a bottle of whatever is there, taskmaster."

The older man's face screwed up in thought as he examined the selection. He placed a finger on one bottle before going to another. That one he turned about. He took it, uncorked it, and sniffed at the contents.

Grisholt was about to offer a goblet when Turst tipped the bottle back. He gulped noisily for moments.

"Good," the taskmaster croaked upon finishing. "I'll have this one, then."

Grisholt gestured it was his.

Turst spotted a chair. "Caro hasn't returned?"

"Not this night," Grisholt answered. "He remains in the city. Doing agent things."

Turst settled down and took another swig of the bottle, the gulping causing Brakuss and Grisholt to trade looks.

"That's fine gurry," the taskmaster whispered upon finishing. A soft belch followed.

"Much better than the previous swill," Grisholt said.

"Or the swill Marrok was brewing."

Grisholt *tsked.* "Marrok did what he could with what he had. Now . . . he'll have much better. And we'll *all* have much better, dear Turst."

The taskmaster grunted neutrally.

"Are we having that talk this night?" Grisholt asked.

"Best we do."

"Well then . . ." the owner waved again. "By all means."

"Olibo perished this day."

"And I've grieved his loss . . . only as long as it took to collect the wagers placed on his losing."

That darkened Turst's features. "Never liked that part of the games."

"What part? There was no part. I simply made the right wager. Wocello was the better fighter and Olibo was plainly outmatched."

"Wocello would have spared him, but he didn't . . . because he believed he was fighting for his own life."

"Perhaps."

"And Olibo *would* have won, if you had given him the sip."

Leaning back in his father's chair, Grisholt spread his hands and glowered, not appreciating the souring of an otherwise good time. "We've already had this conversation, good Turst. Unless you have something new to say . . . we should be drinking. In Olibo's memory, of course. And his parting gift to the stable."

Turst waved that off like the stink from an unwashed ass crack. "There's something else afoot. I realized it when Wocello put Olibo into the dirt. Something you need to know about."

"All right . . ."

Before continuing, Turst glanced at the standing Brakuss. "The other houses *know* we've changed our strategy in the arena. They don't know *how*, but they *know*. At the very least, they suspect. As I've said, Wocello wasn't a killer."

"He killed a man this year," Grisholt countered.

"One man," Turst scoffed. "That's *nothing*. You know this as well as anyone. Even him," he nodded at Brakuss. "To the common peasant, our lads are entering the Pit screaming long and loud, enough for their nogs to drop off. To our opponents, however, they know something's afoot. Wocello was sent out there with orders to defend himself, because our fighters were *destroying* others before him. Smashing them dead and flat. Not a drop of mercy given. Wocello knew this. So he fought like it was to the death and rightly so. Any other time, it *might* have been to the death. *His* death."

Pickled as he was, Grisholt's eyes narrowed as he concentrated on what his taskmaster was telling him.

"If the House of *Ustda* is telling their dogs to kill *ours*," Turst went on, "then we can expect *every* match, from this time forth, to be to the death. Because of what our lads have done. And if you decide to . . . continue exercising caution? Choosing who gets a sip? Well, our lads who don't have the potion in them? They will be at greater risk than those who do. Unlike you, unlike *us*, the other houses don't know who has drunk from the flask. They'll come out looking to take our heads regardless, because they'll expect it done to them. In the most brutal fashion."

Grisholt shrugged. "So if it happens, we'll have a blood match and end it. Or two or even three blood matches and end it."

"With our lads strengthened by the potion . . ." a nodding Turst said.

"Of course."

"Well. We can prevent all of that, and save a few of our hellions in the bargain, by giving them all a taste before they fight."

Grisholt blinked in confusion. "All?"

"*All*," Turst repeated. "Don't you see? Our own rosy bastards will realize what the other houses are doing. Sooner or later, they'll know they all have marks on their heads, sips or no sips. When they realize that . . . they'll look at *me*. But mostly they'll look at *you*, and then the grumbling will begin. Why didn't you give them a taste before sending them out there? Hm? Why didn't you give *all* your lads every chance at winning instead of picking and choosing who perishes?"

Unbeknownst to him, Grisholt began tugging on his beard.

"That . . ." Turst punched home, "will *rot* this stable to its very heart and bring it down from within."

Brakuss's one eye flickered from the taskmaster to the owner.

Grisholt blinked at the implications. He stopped playing with his paltry chin whiskers and drank more wine. Without warning he drained the whole goblet before reaching for the bottle. "Hadn't thought of that," he admitted.

"That's why you have me," Turst rumbled. "But I've only described one problem we have. There is one much worse. I've had my misgivings about that flask of sorcery from the beginning, but coin is a strong persuader. I'm still in this plot of yours, since it means riches for us all. And clearly it does. You know the lads wager on themselves?"

"Of course I know."

"They'll start wagering *more* on themselves, but only if they know they're getting a taste of the flask. A damn near *guarantee* of victory. And because of the advantage they get, because of their wagers upon themselves, their *larger* wagers, they'll start to *demand* a sip before every fight. Olibo did. You didn't give him one and he perished because of it. His death was bad enough, but Lords save us all if our hellpups suspect *you* are wagering on their opponents when they *don't* get a taste."

"What do you mean?"

"Are you listening to what I'm saying?" Turst snapped. "What I'm talking about is ensuring the lads' continued loyalty to you. Keeping their *silence* about what you've done this season. What we've *all* done. Because if the Gladiatorial Chamber discovers what we are doing, they will have our *heads*. Starting with *you*. And *me*. And the best way to keep the lads' loyalty? Now and after the games? Especially after? Well, you best start giving them *all* sips from that damn flask. That's my thinking. They all get a taste from this time onward. And not just a taste. Regardless of win or lose . . . life or death . . . At the end of these games, you best consider giving those remaining a generous gift of coin. To hold their tongues about this season and the potion."

"Pah . . ." Grisholt scoffed. "They'll hold it regardless. Anyone hearing their story will know they had taken part. Especially if they remember any of our matches."

Turst set his jaw. "I saw what you pulled aboard those wagons this day, good Grisholt. If I saw, *they* saw. Remember, it's *their* blood they're risking while you're profiting. It would be very wise on your part to share the wealth. At the end, of course. A pot of coin. Perhaps even a strongbox. Enough to bring about smiles. Enough for them to leave the games and never return, if they so wish."

Grisholt squirmed.

"Else," Turst shook his head, "only the worst will happen. To us all. It would only take a whisper from one sour tongue to get us all killed, by the Chamber itself. And if you need any proof of that, consider what's being mustered against Nexus and his maggots."

In the uneasy silence that followed, a muffled cheer went up from a not-so-faraway section of the villa.

A drunk and petulant Grisholt let off an annoyed sigh. "You certainly know how to kill a fine time, good Turst."

9

The humidity of the previous night had faded just a bearable touch. Light from the open balcony door stretched across the swept floor, setting the polished marble aglow. Nala lay beside her sleeping husband and watched his profile. Clavellus lay on his back, mouth open, the shadows darkening his leathery features while his dense beard remained starkly white. A few mutinous whiskers stuck off that bush, and she restrained herself from plucking them. Blissfully oblivious to her quiet examination, Clavellus slept on. His chest rose and fell in a peaceful rhythm, and his left arm had pushed the silk sheet down to his waist.

Nala squirmed onto her side and pushed her silver hair out of her eyes. Her gaze fell upon his hand, the same hand which trembled constantly while he was awake but remained oddly still while he slept. She'd mentioned that to him once, which led to more than a few curious discussions. In the end, Clavellus was just glad it didn't bother her when she slept, and that was that.

Nala reached over, pinched the end of the sheet they shared, and slid it up and over her sleeping husband. Clavellus didn't move, not even when his wife's hand caressed him, running fin-gers along his chest, to his whiskers, before tracing the outline of his ear. Some mornings, when she felt mischievous—and he looked far too comfortable—she would torment him. Just little things. Yanking a contrary hair from his beard. Sticking a finger into an ear or nose. Or simply kissing his cheek.

Not this morning, however. She was too pleased to have him back home.

He had returned to her last night with the others, wagon-rattled and weary but happy to be back. Clavellus had greeted and hugged her and asked of the affairs at the villa. She kept nothing back, informing him of everything that had transpired with the sickly Brozz, from her own attempts at helping the Sarlander to the unexpected healing skills of the dour little armorer called Ajik. Despite how late it was, Clavellus had led her back to their private chambers. Once behind closed doors, he bade her to turn around while he fiddled with gifts wrapped in fine cloth upon their bed, all for her. A short time later Nala opened them, one at a time, and pressed a hand to her chest. Her husband had brought her a new robe of silk along with several elegant bottles of scented waters.

"Did well, did you?" Nala had asked, very much impressed.

As an answer, he wrapped his arms around her waist and pressed himself against her.

"Aye that," he whispered against her neck, his breath hot and pleasant.

Smiling at the memory, Nala pushed herself up from bed and swung her feet onto the cool floor. There she sat, inspecting her bare knees, thinking it took increasing effort to rise every morning. She rubbed her thighs, checked on her man, and reached for the same robes she had worn yesterday. She took her time getting dressed, intent on further examining her gifts from the night before. Clavellus always brought her back something from the city. It was his way of apologizing for being gone, especially if it was during the games. Any games. She never asked for such things, because his safe return was always gift enough, though she kept that to herself.

The edge of her robes whispered along the floor. She stopped and inspected the hem, noticing a few loose threads. Perhaps Clavellus had noticed them as well, prompting him to replace the clothing. He continued to sleep as she tied a rope belt around her waist.

A clatter turned her toward the balcony. There, framed in dark timbers, was a bright morning.

Curious, she stepped outside onto that perch, stopping at the stumpy pillars supporting a white railing.

Below, marching around the sands, was Master Goll.

And Master Goll was exercising with a furious energy. He rounded the corner of the training grounds, arms swinging, his bare, muscular back turned to her. His face gradually came into view as he moved along the edge of the sand, revealing a glistening layer of ointment smeared over a brazen black eye. Nala stared at it for moments before looking anywhere else, frowning at her lapse of control. She remembered how the Kree's face had been partially hidden by darkness last night. There were no issues seeing his features this morning, nor the beating he'd sustained in his last fight.

A rack of wooden swords stood near Goll's path, and he snatched one free without pausing. He marched toward a practice man, snarling at perhaps some other concealed injury. There he stopped and lined up the figure. Without pause, Goll hammered out a combination of strikes upon the target, both high and low, right side and left. Wood rattled off wood for a good dozen connections. He ended the flurry by smashing the sword against the neck of the thing. There he held the pose, shoulders heaving from the brief but meaningful contact. Then he broke away and resumed pacing.

"Who's working the sticks this morning?" Clavellus rumbled from their bed, turning Nala around.

"Master Goll, dearest."

A sleepy smile spread across her husband's features as he lay on his back, eyes flickering from the ceiling to her. "'Dearest' . . . I like how you say that in the morning."

"I know you do."

"I know you know."

Nala walked to the bed. She traced a finger along a freckled shoulder sprouting scraggly hair, no longer as muscular as it once was, but still firm. Still her man.

A contented Clavellus gazed up at her as her fingers slid over him.

Another lengthy clatter shattered the moment.

"What's that punce doing?" Clavellus fumed in sleepy annoyance.

"I'd say he's training."

"There was supposed to be *no* training. We discussed it last night."

"Perhaps he changed his mind?"

Clavellus sighed, flashing an expression of *Obviously so.*

"Well," Nala stressed. "He's out there now."

"Supposed to be a day of rest," he said with mild irritation.

"Maybe he forgot."

"He's the one that needs it most."

"You usually have a day of rest after a night of drinking."

"We were going to drink *today*."

"I see," Nala smiled, enjoying his sleepy grumbling.

"I didn't even drink much last night."

That creased her features, as she regarded the nearby bed table and the empty bottle upon it.

"That was nothing," Clavellus muttered, his eyes closing again.

"Shall I ask him to stop?"

He cracked open an eye, just as Goll again ripped away at a target. "Well . . . only if you're going that way . . ."

"I'm going that way. Once I get below."

"Oh. Well, then. Please . . ." he settled back.

Nala bent over, kissed her husband's hairless head, and left the bedroom while rubbing at an ear. Her robes swished across stone tiles as she descended to the ground floor. The sun blinded her upon opening the front door of her home. Shielding her eyes with a hand, she went outside and stopped a few strides from the training sands.

Goll had already stopped, a puzzled frown upon his face. "Good morning, Lady Nala," he greeted.

"Master Goll," she returned. "Up a bit early, aren't you?"

An awkward silence answered that, so she continued. "My husband is still in bed, but since I was up . . ."

"Apologies if I woke you," Goll said, his shoulders sagging.

"You didn't wake me. I was already awake. My husband isn't, however. Not quite yet, and he asked me to remind you that this day was supposed to be one of rest? Or something like that."

That straightened the Kree's back as he nodded. "A day of rest for some, perhaps. Not for me."

Nala squinted under the powerful sun. "Couldn't you do with at least one?"

"Yes, couldn't you do with at least one?" repeated Shan the healer, stretching his back while emerging from the barracks. Dressed in a plain tunic and breeches, the healer switched to leaning one way and then the other. "And wasn't that the reason you all agreed to a rest day last night? Something about that crack to your skull? And those stitches of yours? The ones I sewed up for a second time. After you split them apart in your last match."

"I didn't split them apart, good Shan," Goll replied calmly. "The dog blossom I was fighting split them apart."

Shan's sleepy demeanor hardened into a glare. "Who do you think you're talking to, Goll of Kree? Hm? I know well enough who did what and when, because *I* was the one piecing you back together. I was the one slapping the saywort to your hide. Which reminds me, if you wish to continue with this season of madness, you best *have* that day of rest. And that means keeping still long enough to allow *some* healing to happen, before you return to that unfit bloodletting."

Goll shook his head. "I'm fine enough."

"You look like sun-blackened shite."

"Harsh words."

"It's clear it'll *take* harsh words to get you to put arse to ground and stay there."

"I'm fine, I tell you."

"You're *not* fine," Shan blurted with heat, pointing a finger. "Listen, will you? A day's rest is nothing. Nothing! You might not think it, but you *need* a day to recover. At *least*. I'd prefer a week but I know that won't happen. So just a day, then. You won't wither away into nothing, and no one will think poorly of you for doing so."

That volley appeared to sink through, to a point. "The stiffness will work into me," Goll countered.

"Then walk about the grounds here," Shan said with exasperated wonder, setting his hands to his hips. "But light exercise only. Swing your arms even, as you've been doing. But easily. All right? That will be enough to keep the stiffness away. And I have medicines to counter such aches, regardless. Just let me know what's troubling you."

"You're troubling me now, with your gurry. I'm not some youngster coming into your house with a bloody knee."

"No, you're not, but if I'd known . . . the . . . *savagery* of the games like I do now? The bloody brutality of it? I would be there for those youngsters. And their bloody knees. And hands. And whatever else they might have. And they would listen to what I tell them to do, and they would do it. Without question."

That silenced the gladiator, who glanced at Nala.

"One day, Goll," Shan said sternly. "One day and no more. The games won't forget you. Look. Even your opponents have to rest, and they're stronger for it. Would you let them have that advantage? However meager you might think it is?"

"You do look like a fright," Nala added quietly, very much meaning it. While the house master and healer exchanged words, she saw the extent of damage Goll had taken. A black eye fading to a diseased shade of sepia. Bruises and a touch of swelling all along his right profile. Careful stitches resembling a hairy crawler stretched over his right eye, just above the brow. And that was just his face.

Shan gestured *You see?* before nodding thanks to the lady of the house.

Huffing defeat, Goll inspected his sword before sinking its tip into the sand. Even that bit of effort seemed to pain him. He grimaced, recovered, and deliberated on what to say next. "Does it look that bad?" he finally asked.

"It does to me," Nala replied. "And I'm not a healer."

"I've heard otherwise," Goll said with a smile.

"Brozz was merely . . . good fortune," Nala said, suddenly flushed. "And that wasn't me. Good Ajik saved him."

"She's a modest one," Clavellus said from above, his voice carrying across the stillness of the morning. "One of the reasons why I married her. And you truly do look smashed, Goll. Listen to my missus. And your healer, before he stomps off back to Sunja. I know our armorer can do a bit of healing, but I prefer the ones I can talk to."

A grateful Shan nodded his thanks.

Goll considered them all before settling his gaze on Clavellus. "Apologies for waking you."

The taskmaster dismissed that with a wave.

"He'll only start drinking sooner," Nala said.

"Not until noon," Clavellus announced, studying the horizon before switching back to Goll. "Rest yourself today. For Shan's sake. Our healer is getting a touch contrary, I think. And like he said . . . the games won't forget you. They certainly won't forget us. So let's have a little peace before we go back to war. Hm? Before the games remember us . . . and send us word of your next opponent. What say you to that?"

In the warm calmness that followed, in that swelling expectation of an answer, Goll reluctantly nodded.

"Done," Clavellus said and sipped from his silver mug. The flash of metal in the sun caught Nala's attention.

"Just water, my love," her husband said and went back into the house.

Nala frowned. "I have a feeling noon has begun."

"Perhaps you should go back to him then?" Goll suggested.

"Oh, he won't stop for me. The best I can do is slow him down. Not that I would. If he wants to relax then here is the best place for him. Under my eye. My thanks, Master Goll. You've made an old man happy. Given him purpose again."

The healer stopped before the gladiator. "Stand still," Shan ordered as he examined his patient. He touched and prodded the bone around Goll's eye, causing him to flinch.

"What was that?" Shan demanded.

"What?"

"What? Don't say 'What'! You know what!"

Goll scowled. "Nothing."

"Saimon's hole that was nothing," Shan seethed. "You wait right here. Right *here*, Goll. If you're gone when I get back, I'll save my efforts for someone who appreciates them. Oh, you heard me. I'm a healer, Goll. A *healer*. I made no joke when I mentioned the savagery of the games. I was never interested in them. Never understood why others had an interest. Unfit season. Unfit *sport*. Not truly a sport, either. Not when you get to the bones of it."

"Get your medicines," Goll interrupted. "Do what you have to do and leave me alone."

That quieted the healer in a most dangerous manner. "Don't you dismiss me in such a way, Goll. Don't you ever. Do so again and I *will* leave. All the way back to Sunja. Just remember, my house is still there. My wife is still there. As are patients who will *listen* and *follow* my instructions."

Goll lowered his eyes and wisely kept quiet. The healer resumed working on the battered man.

Shan abruptly stopped. "Stay there," he warned and hurried away, arms chugging with purpose.

"Is he usually this way?" Nala asked as the healer left for the barracks.

"No."

"You must be the reason for it, then."

". . . Suppose so."

"Suppose he's not the first."

That earned her a soft glare. "Suppose not."

"I understand him, though," she said.

"Really?"

"Certainly. You would as well if you gave it thought."

"My thoughts now are only on what to do with the day."

"And there you are. His thoughts? 'Why are my boys placing themselves back in harm's reach after I've sewn them together? Why do I nurse them back to health, only to have them return to me in an even worse state than before?'"

Goll frowned. "Not the worst state I've been in."

"It's not?"

"Far from it, but . . . it is the most recent."

"Clavellus says you're good," she informed him in a low voice.

108

That hooked Goll's attention.

"And . . . he says you could go far in the games. That you have the potential to even win it."

"He said that?"

"He did. He said similar things about that one there." Nala indicated the barracks.

There, stepping into the sun, was the Perician himself. Dressed plainly, Junger squinted at the sky before noticing the others. He smiled, raised a hand in greeting, and started walking around the edge of the sands.

"I imagine he did," Goll grumbled, eyeing the Perician as he rounded the far corner of the training area.

"He doesn't look . . . as bruised as you do."

Goll's jaw clenched at that.

"Apologies," Nala said. "I spoke without thinking. I didn't mean anything by that, Master Goll."

"It's all right. You spoke the truth. He's not as bruised as I am. Not yet."

"No, not yet."

Junger rounded another corner and marched toward them. As he did, the blocky shape of Ajik appeared, moving under the arched roof of the open smithy. The man's dark head stilled as he took stock of the little gathering. He spared them only a heartbeat of time before returning to whatever work he'd been at from the day before. Metal clattered on wood, breaking the morning quiet once again.

"They rise one by one," Nala observed fondly and turned to the approaching Junger. "Good morning to you, good Junger."

"Good morning, Lady Nala," the Perician said pleasantly. "Master Goll."

Goll scowled back.

"The stitches look better this morning," Junger noted. "Let Shan work his sorcery on you this day. Stay off the sands if you can manage."

"He best manage," Shan remarked, returning with a satchel in hand. He stopped before Goll and opened the bag. A moment later, he produced a jar, removed its lid, and dug two fingers within. "Keep this on you," the healer warned. "And don't touch it. Not even if it itches. If it does, find me and I'll see what I can do. Now then," he warned, with a gob of pinkish salve on his fingers. "Be still . . ."

As Shan carefully applied the ointment, Nala regarded Junger. "May I walk with you a bit, good Junger?"

"Upon the very ground that belongs to you? Apologies for not asking first."

"You flatter me."

"Because you deserve it, my lady."

She smiled, and with that they strode off.

"I have no real interest in the games," Nala admitted as they strolled. "I don't follow them at all. So forgive me when I ask . . . how is the season going for you?"

"I'm unsure as to what I'm to forgive, Lady Nala. The games aren't for everyone. I'm not even sure why I participate, truth be known."

"So why do you?"

"Ah . . ." he smiled broadly, peering at the sky. "That's a question I've asked myself many, many times. I think it's the sport of it."

"The sport? People perish during the games."

"They do. All the time. But not by my hand. Truth be known, no one has to perish at all, but the games have evolved into that. Or fallen, I should say. Not for me, however. I'll rattle a few heads in their helmets but nothing more."

"For the sport of it."

"For the sport. Nothing more."

"I suppose that's reason enough. But it's all so confusing to me."

"How do you mean?"

Nala gathered her thoughts. "How is it you . . . train yourselves into near perfect physical condition, or as close to it as you can, only to . . . risk harm to yourselves? Even death? In moments."

"Another riddle I ask myself every day, but I do have an answer. I enjoy the training. Very much so."

They turned, placing the sun at their backs, and strolled along the barracks.

"It's hot," Nala said, watching the ground.

"It'll be hotter soon enough. Your Sunjan summers can be searing."

"Where are you from? Within Pericia, that is."

Junger thought about it. "I don't rightly know. Not really. I suspect I was born in Sunja. My first language is Sunjan. I know that as I remember speaking to my parents in that tongue, but I later learned Perician. No great matter there. The two languages aren't all that different. In any case, I tell people Pericia when they ask. In a small village far from the main city."

"Do you have a wife there?"

His eyes widened. "Lords, no. Not yet anyway. Perhaps when all this is done and I return home."

The barracks and nearby bathhouse passed by as they talked, then the northwest corner of the grounds. The thick outer wall and battlements, nearly the height of two men, loomed overhead as they made their way south. By this time, Nala's breathing came a little faster and sweat beaded upon her forehead.

Junger slowed his pace and stepped to the outside, in an effort to shield her from the sun.

"Well," she said, the word coming out a little more breathless than she'd wanted. "I hope you survive the games. And return to your Pericia. And that you find a wife. You're pleasant enough. Not hard on the eye. Certainly mindful of manners. You'll do well . . . if you look."

"My thanks, Lady Nala," he said. "I've noticed there aren't so many ladies about here."

"No, there aren't. Most women have the sense to stay away from such. And it's to be expected, since it is a gladiatorial school. Can't distract the boys from their ongoing efforts here."

"That sounds like something Master Clavellus might say."

"Master Clavellus said exactly that. But . . . we talk at times. The nearest town is a place called Pynn's Brook." She stopped, halting Junger beside her. "That way," she pointed southeast and resumed walking. "Half a day away. A bit of a travel in the winter. My husband and I, we talk about starting a village here. A little one. Bring in the tradespeople. Perhaps a little marketplace. Just talk, but it would greatly please me."

"Especially the marketplace."

The sun wrinkled her expression as they turned east. "Was that a jab?"

"Maybe. Probably. Aye that. It was."

She smiled and didn't comment.

"Thank you for that," a relieved Junger said. "Far be it from me to upset the taskmaster's wife."

"No, that wouldn't be wise. In the meantime, you'll have to do without a lady's company while you're here."

"I don't mind. In any case, I have Brozz for company."

They approached Goll and Shan. The healer still held his jar while dabbing at spots on Goll's forehead, further annoying his patient.

"You're not nearly as battered as Master Goll," Nala observed.

"He's fought much more dangerous opponents."

"I see. Well . . . I leave you here, good Junger. Thank you for the morning's exercise. I think I prefer the shade."

"Thank you for the company, Lady Nala."

They parted then. She headed for her doorway while Junger continued onward.

"Be gentle with the grease, good Shan," the Perician warned with a little smile as he walked by the healer and his patient. "That lad's angry enough."

That creased the foreheads of both men, but Goll looked even more annoyed.

Later that morning, other members of the house showed their faces as the sun rose and applied heat across the sands. Stepping out of his home, Clavellus paused and held his hips. His beard twitched as he screwed up one corner of his mouth and then the other.

"Unfit," he muttered, snarling at the harsh temperature. Wasn't even midday and it was already scorching. He briefly considered the figures moving about the training grounds and waved at two. "Marden. Listus. Bring me a table. And some shade. Set it up here. Right here. Off with you, Ananda."

A few strides away, the young woman and the house trainer, Koba, talked. Hearing her name, Ananda ceased her conversation with the towering trainer, who straightened and nodded at the taskmaster.

"We brought in a few kegs of Sunjan Black last night," Clavellus said. "Clurik knows where they are. Get him to bring out a keg. And bring me a platter with meat cuts, fruit, and cheese. A large platter."

Ananda nodded and disappeared into the house. Koba watched her go.

"That wagon unloaded yet?" Clavellus asked.

The big man shook his head.

"Go on with her, then," the taskmaster said. "Nothing is planned this day, good Koba, so . . ." he nodded in the direction Ananda had taken. "Enjoy your time together."

Clearly pleased with the suggestion, Koba went after her.

A day of rest, Clavellus thought and scratched at his nose. A right fine idea that was. A moment's peace within a season of carnage. Might as well make the most of it, for they might never have the time again. And there were plenty of hands about to do the unloading. All he had to do was choose the unfortunate gits.

The household guards Marden and Listus returned with a round table, rolling it out of the living quarters. Another guard brought chairs, which was good thinking indeed. Clavellus stood back while the three of them arranged matters. They set up poles and a thick cloth canopy, which would provide ample shade for six or seven people beneath it.

"Good, good," Clavellus nodded. Every now and again, he would glance about the courtyard and hold up a hand at whoever caught his eye.

The thickset armorer called Ajik, rummaging about the smithy, actually nodded back at the taskmaster.

The guards on the wall lifted their spears in greeting.

The once Sujins—Clades, Pratos, and Valka—all in regular clothing for once, gathered at the wagons and proceeded to unload both the supplies and strongboxes filled with coin. Which was excellent, as it saved Clavellus from ordering someone else to do it.

The one-legged Garl hobbled forth from the barracks, followed by Torello, still favoring a twisted ankle. Clavellus narrowed his eyes, wondering how it was that healers had ointments and salves for cuts, bruises, and even broken bones, but nothing for injured joints. *Punces*, he brooded, but he still smiled at Shan when the healer waved.

Ananda and Koba returned, with the trainer carrying a beer keg. Ananda placed a platter of food upon the table while Koba planted the keg upon the ground.

"Careful with that, lad," Clavellus growled. "That's gold you have there. *Gold.* You know what I mean."

Koba nodded that he did, and set the keg upon a chair, next to Clavellus.

"It is the Black, correct?" the taskmaster asked.

"That's what he told me," Koba replied. "Said it's your favorite."

"It's all his favorite," Nala said from the balcony above, the canopy hiding her from her husband's sight.

"Not true," Clavellus said and sat. "My thanks, dear Ananda, dear Koba."

That drew the barest frown from the trainer.

"Have a seat," the taskmaster invited. "Both of you."

The couple exchanged looks.

"If we may, Master Clavellus . . ." Koba began.

"Aye that, of course," he said. "Go on, then. Enjoy the day."

Happy to be excused, the couple walked away while Clavellus idly checked his fingernails. He then picked up a knife near the platter and flipped through some of the more appealing cuts. "You coming down for any of this?"

"Any of what?" Nala asked from above.

"Meat cuts," Clavellus said, inspecting the goods. "White cheese. Some yellow. Fruit. Grapes. Apple slices."

"Perhaps later."

"May not be any left."

"Then I'll just go to the kitchen," her voice trailed off, suggesting she'd gone back inside their bedroom.

Clavellus grunted and picked up a cut of beef. He slapped an uneven wedge of cheese to its tender hide and popped the entire thing into his mouth. *Lords above that was fine.* As he chewed, he fiddled with the keg's spout and poured himself a drink. *Sunjan Black.* Not a finer choice could start a day of drinking.

A chair rattled across stone as it was pulled out. A weight plopped down beside him. *Machlann.* Aged, grizzled, and already scowling from the heat. His impressive mustache hung off his face like a thick winter pelt.

"Lad," Clavellus greeted, enjoying his chew.

The old trainer grunted in return.

"Want some of this?"

If he heard, Machlann didn't show it. He stared ahead, locked in a morning daze. Then, as if finally understanding what was being asked, he leaned forward to better examine the morning feast. Mustache twitching, he picked at the grapes and popped a few into his mouth. A few chews and he rubbed at his nose before selecting a few more.

"Some of the Black?" Clavellus asked.

Blue eyes flashed at the taskmaster and then the keg. After a deciding moment, Machlann nodded. Clavellus poured him a drink, filling a cup to the brim. He carefully placed it before the old trainer. Then he lifted his own mug and sampled it. "Lords that's good," he declared. "So very good."

Machlann gathered up a few choice cuts of meat before helping himself to the cheese. A handful went into his face, and he struggled to chew through it all before remembering his drink. Smacking loudly, he took his cup and sipped, earning a curious glare from the taskmaster.

"That's all good," Machlann remarked when he got everything down.

Clavellus nodded. "It is."

"Clurik make that?"

"I'm not sure. He might have. Or they might have bought it from Pynn's."

"He's getting better if he did make it."

"He is," Clavellus agreed.

So they sat and ate, enjoying their beer and food. Clades went into the living quarters and returned shortly with a few other household guards behind him. Those men waved at their employer and Clavellus raised his mug in greeting.

"Lads are late rising," Machlann rumbled.

"Goll was up and battering the wood there."

"I heard that."

"Everyone heard that."

"Probably the blossom's intention."

"Nala got him to stop."

Machlann grunted. "Where is he now?"

"Eating perhaps, with the rest."

"Best place for him."

"Oh, he won't stay there for long. Daresay he's behind Clades and the others unloading the wagons."

They quieted, watching the men work across bright sands. Clavellus wiped at his brow, feeling the heat despite the shade. Something rattled from the smithy, and Ajik's head bobbed in and out of sight.

"What do you make of it all?" Clavellus asked quietly.

"Of what?" Machlann asked.

"The season."

Machlann grimaced. "Started with ten. Down to a pair, with no end in sight."

". . . But what a pair."

The trainer grunted agreement and scratched at his mustache. "Where's Koba?"

"Sent him off with his missus. For the day."

"For the day? Decent of you. Nala?"

"Upstairs somewhere, probably listening."

They exchanged looks and waited for the lady of the house to say something. When she did not, they went back to nibbling, certain that she *was* listening.

"They'll be coming for us," Machlann rumbled after a while. "Especially the Perician."

Clavellus nodded sagely and sipped his drink. "I say they'll go for the Kree first."

"They'll think he's the weaker?"

A squinting Clavellus inspected his mug. "They'll think he's the weaker. They'll think they can kill him easy. Or force him out because of his wounds. They'd prefer to kill, make no mistake. They know he started all this. They'll go after him first, claim victory either way, and then . . . concentrate on Junger."

"They'll want the Perician," Machlann said. "He's becoming very popular these games. Very popular. The lad that beats him? If there is such a person? He'll be champion."

Before Clavellus could respond, a scraggly Muluk stepped out from the living quarters. The Kree man rubbed at his hairy forearms before combing his fingers through his unruly black beard. He scowled at the sun and limped over to the men unloading the wagons. Clades met him and they talked for a bit, before Muluk spotted the two older men. Leaving Clades to work, the disheveled house master hobbled over to the table, baring yellow teeth in a broad smile.

"Good morning boys," he said cheerfully. "Not too early for a bit, I see?"

"You see correctly," Clavellus said, lifting his mug in greeting. "Why don't you go inside the house there and bring out another chair?"

Muluk's dark face brightened and he went off to do just that. He returned a short time later and sat with a heavy thud. Clavellus had a drink waiting for him. Raising his cup to the two older men, the muscular Kree drank it all down without pause and asked for more with a look.

"Drink away, Muluk," the taskmaster gestured at the keg. "And if you finish that, there's plenty more about."

Muluk drained half a second cup before putting his elbows on the table and rubbing at his face, stretching his features this way and that. Once settled in, he addressed them both. "A day of rest, 'eh? Fine idea. Very fine idea. Goll wouldn't have called for it. He's inside there now. Eating. Giving orders. When he's done, he'll be out. You'll have a chore to keep him sitting."

"He's a determined one," Clavellus agreed.

"Aye that, he is, but . . . if it wasn't for him," Muluk glanced around before leaning in, "I wouldn't own part of the riches going into your cellars right now."

"If you have need of another room below," Clavellus said, "just ask. We have others. If needed."

"I will. Ah . . ." Muluk rubbed his chin. "Master Clavellus, we may need another room. To separate our accounts from yours. Just to keep matters . . . you know."

Clavellus knew. "I'll have Pirrus show you the storerooms. Is one enough?"

"Should be."

"How much did you win, anyway?"

Muluk smiled widely. "A lot. Ah . . . Master Clavellus?"

"Yes?"

"Just wondering . . . how many guards do you have here?"

"Ten all told, but thirteen if you count Clades and his two once Sujins. Then, of course there's the obvious . . ."

"The obvious?"

Clavellus smiled.

"We're a house of gladiators, you punce," Machlann rumbled.

Muluk quieted, if not a touch scalded, not caring for the jab so early in the day.

"Stop that," Clavellus said to the trainer. "Please. It's a day of rest so keep your tone civil."

"That was civil."

The taskmaster ignored him and regarded the Kree. "Have no fears about the safety of your coin here, good Muluk. Only the vaults of Sunja would protect it better."

"Oh," he said. "Well, that's good."

"And we all know what you're about if someone does try to take your coin," Clavellus reminded him fondly before he lifted his drink at the young master.

A pleased Muluk returned the gesture, his hand, minus three fingers, resting upon the table.

A guard headed for the main gate and Clavellus waved him over. It was Pirrus, the same who had gone looking for a healer in

Pynn's Brook not so long ago. "Pirrus, lad, you know what's on for the day, right?"

"A day of rest?"

"You have it. A day of rest. So, arrange the shifts fairly between you and the boys. And make certain that whoever is on the wall watches the road. For messengers. Namely Naulis, or perhaps even Borchus. Or both. Understood?"

"Aye that, Master Clavellus."

"And before you do all that, free up a storeroom down below, for this one's riches." He nodded at Muluk.

"I will."

"Off with you then."

The three men watched the guard leave for the lower chambers. Machlann downed a mouthful of beer and sighed.

"Don't say it," Clavellus warned him. "Don't even think it."

"Think what?" Muluk asked.

"Nothing," the taskmaster said with a glare. "Leave it be. A day of rest, though daresay tomorrow will be a struggle enough. The best thing that could happen? The best? They schedule our fights the day *after* tomorrow and leave us be for a bit."

"Will they do that?" Muluk asked.

"They might."

Machlann slowly nodded and flicked his thumb across his nose. "They might," he repeated.

So they drank, ate, and talked, at times pausing to watch the few hands unload the wagons.

10

Morning exercise at the School of Nexus.

Prajus stood all but naked except for his loincloth, clenching a wooden sword and shield. Though made of wood, the training tools were weighed down, which Prajus didn't rightly like. Especially the sword. Though the trainer Rezzo had assured him that it was properly balanced, he could feel it was off enough to bother him. But try telling Rezzo that. Or the other trainer Bernd. Or the taskmaster, who ruled over all when Nexus wasn't present.

And this morning, Nexus was present, sitting in the shade on a raised platform, in the very chair Taskmaster Tino usually sat in. Tino sat nearby while Nexus seemed to be cursing directly into the older man's ear.

Twenty-four fighters lined the training sands before that platform. Two rows squared off against each other for a bit of mayhem. Purely practice, to keep one's skills sharp, but Nexus had gathered a rather competitive bunch of killers under his banner, and more than once tempers had flared, dispensing with the rule of half strength only.

Rezzo swiped his fist through the air, signaling for the drill to begin. All at once, the two lines erupted in cuts and slashes, every footfall stirring up dust.

"You looking about this morning or are you fighting?" scowled an ogre of a man called Greygar. He was tall, perhaps a couple of fingers taller than Prajus, but then all of the school's gladiators were big. He was also muscular, definitely much more so than Prajus. A black beard shorn down to the quick covered his chin and throat, while equally black hair drizzled his meaty chest. Ointment gleamed upon a scattering of bruises upon the pit fighter, as well as a lengthy cut straight across his lowered brow. A cut stitched together and shining wetly.

Prajus studied his training partner. "It's obvious, isn't it?"

"Then start swinging at me."

"Apologies, I was waiting for you."

"Then raise your weapons."

"What's that?"

"I said raise your weapons."

Prajus smiled. "These things? Good Greygar. These aren't weapons. Not real ones."

Grimacing as if he'd just stepped in the sloppiest cow kiss, Greygar swung for Prajus's head—who darted back. "Not sporting at all, good Greygar. I wasn't ready. Now then . . . I'm ready."

Greygar bared a surprisingly full set of teeth and rushed him.

The larger gladiator thrust and slashed, punctuating each strike with a burst of breath, looking to punch that stick through a chest or shatter it over a skull. Prajus parried each blow, the wood clacking and splinters flying, until one mighty stab forced him to retreat.

"*Prajus!*" shrieked an indignant Bernd, his voice high-pitched enough to split rocks. "*Get back in line.*"

Prajus spotted the trainer, the man's tanned arms and legs splayed as if expecting to be tackled. Bernd liked to shout, where Rezzo—Nexus's other trainer—would stop alongside a man and address him in a voice lethal enough to tighten one's blossom. Bernd clearly thought shouting was a more effective means of communication. Red-faced, as if mortally offended, the man practically shouted all the time, especially when calling upon or scolding a pit fighter. In prolonged fits of screaming, a worm of a vein protruded down the middle of the trainer's forehead, while more veins as fat as roots made themselves known about his neck. In the short time Prajus had known him—or, rather, heard him—he suspected the trainer would one day shriek loud enough to pop something important inside his head, whereupon he would perish on the spot.

Prajus believed Bernd, like all of them here, didn't care for him very much. That puzzled the gladiator. He was usually much better at hiding his true self from others. Killing off Gastillo, however, the owner of a once-powerful house of pit fighters, did leave something of a mark upon his head. Or so he supposed.

And Bernd watched Prajus like a wide-eyed Harudin bloodfish smelling bloody meat in the water. Bernd, wearing a vest of leather armor for some reason, placed his left hand on the short sword hanging from his waist on the same side.

"Apologies, good Bernd," Prajus said loudly. "This one's raw power forced me out of line."

"*Get back in line this instant*," Bernd shouted, froth flying as he strode forward. "*Before you feel my bootheel on your throat.*"

Prajus bowed more apologies, not too low as his pride forbade it, and returned to face Greygar.

Greygar looked ready to crack his skull open.

When you're ready, Prajus gestured, and immediately parried a cut for his head.

Apparently, Greygar was *more* than ready.

So they fought, as did the rest of the gladiators, hacking at each other at full strength when only half was required. Only when a shield shattered or a sword snapped did anyone step out of line, and that happened often enough. When it did, the others didn't slack off in the least. They continued to test each other, pushing their partners until their arms ached and their sweat flew in the sun.

"*Stop and step away*," Bernd shrieked above the clatter, which immediately ceased. The men training with each other reached out and clacked swords in a complimentary gesture of well done, when they were too breathless for words. They did this after every exercise. It was an act of respect, similar to mashing fists together, recognizing the shared effort. They did the same thing upon the training grounds of Gastillo . . . when the gold-faced tit was still alive.

Within the School of Nexus, however, there was one exception.

Not one of the gladiators offered to tap swords with Prajus. Or even offered a fist. They would either look away or glare at him while huffing pure, exhausted disdain. Some would turn their backs or hitch up one corner of their mouths in dislike. Prajus learned quickly, after the first man he squared off against ignored him completely. Every shagger after that did the same thing, sending the same message.

Prajus didn't belong.

Not that Prajus cared. He did not. Didn't before and cared even less now, but it did tickle him—in a purely poisonous way—to think that *they* thought it might rankle him. Or just outright break him.

Fools.

Greygar was no exception to the others. When Bernd gave the command to stop sparring, he turned from Prajus and ignored him completely.

Prajus backed away from his partner's hairy figure drenched in perspiration. He huffed and winced, his own skin shimmering, before sticking his sword into the sand and looking about.

Beyond the heads and shoulders of tired pit fighters, Nexus lounged in the shade, speaking at his taskmaster while sipping on something most certainly not water.

"Oh you brazen fig, you," Prajus whispered with a wet smile. He reminded himself that Nexus was a successful merchant. Very successful, in fact, which warned Prajus to be careful about the man. He wasn't a complete punce, like some of the fragrant he-bitches grazing around him.

As if sensing that very thought, Nexus observed him over the rim of his cup.

Prajus glanced away before the trainers could say anything to him. And they would, as they'd made it clear they sought to break him from the first day.

Fools all.

All of them. They walked around his ankles, in Prajus's mind. They just didn't—

"Get some water into you," Rezzo called out, rubbing his chin as if harboring deep thoughts.

Water, Prajus thought, and decided that wasn't a bad idea. He went to a great open tent where a pack of near-naked animals had gathered. They stood in a herd around three wet barrels, sharing one of several wooden ladles. The men passed the dipper around among them, some taking a drink, others pouring it over their heads in sweet relief from the heat.

Prajus halted a few steps away, smelling his skin cook under the sun. There was a game afoot here as well.

When one of the men hung the ladle off the barrel, he entered the tent, made a path around the three bears who had grown quiet, and reached for the ladle. The gladiator closest smoothly took it before Prajus could touch it.

The brazen lad then dipped the ladle, drew it up, and poured it out at Prajus's feet. His two companions watched for a reaction.

Prajus backed away without a word or gesture, however, even though he'd caught their knowing smirks. He skipped the next barrel over, also crowded by thirsty, overheated pit fighters, and went straight to the last barrel. Two unused ladles hung off the rim where three men stood, finishing their drinks. When they saw Prajus they smoothly blocked him from passing as they left. One's shoulder came within a finger's width of brushing against his chest. Eventually the men departed. When the way was clear, Prajus went to the barrel, scooped up the ladle, and fished himself a drink. Then another. The other gladiators dispersed, strolling into the sun. One lingered, however. Tall, with huge shoulders and arms, appearing powerful enough to split boulders in a single embrace. Dark of eyes and of complexion, he leaned in Prajus's direction and spat into the sands. He straightened, flashed a dangerous look, and walked away.

Oh I'll remember you, Prajus mentally promised and emptied a cupful over his head. *Glorious. Simply glorious.* So he did it again.

"Wash yourself in the baths, you slick knob of shite!" Bernd shouted at him. "Then you can clean your cracks as much as you like."

A few chuckles at that, and more than a few nasty smirks.

I'll remember you all, Prajus thought, waving at the trainer before going for another drink.

"Perhaps he's best suited for the baths, Master Rezzo," Rigger sneered, contorting his ugly collection of facial scratches and stitches.

"Scrubbing the ass cracks of others," added another.

"Probably did that with Gastillo's lot."

Chuckles erupted all around.

Taking it all in, Prajus hooked his dipper on a barrel and left the tent.

"What do you say to that, then, boy?" Bernd asked loudly, enjoying the moment.

"To what now, Master Bernd?" Prajus asked.

"What I just said."

"Apologies, I was thinking about other matters."

"I wager he was thinking about other matters," Rigger smirked, dangling a wooden sword from his crotch.

Prajus ignored that gurry, breathing in sharply as if smelling fine flowers. He glanced over at Nexus. Still there, enjoying his wine, watching him intently. His fine silver hair appeared dull under the shade of the tent, but he sat stock still, waiting for a reaction.

"What other matters might be troubling that ugly head of yours then?" Bernd asked for all to hear.

Prajus addressed the trainer. "Wondering what you might have us do next, Master Bernd."

"No more training for you, maggot. You fight this day."

That was a surprise. "This day?"

Bernd looked to Rezzo and then to Nexus. "This one must be partially deaf." He glared at Prajus. "You deaf, lad? Or merely unfit? Up here." He tapped his head.

"Without question, unfit, Master Bernd."

"Maybe a mace to the jaw will help him," Rigger chirped, and got a few mutters of agreement.

I'll most certainly remember you, Prajus grinned as if believing the threat a great idea. He distracted himself with thoughts of splitting the dog blossom's head down the middle.

"A word with you, Master Bernd," said Rezzo, walking over to his fellow trainer. The two older men talked in low voices, with Bernd's expression brightening.

"*Prajus!*" Bernd shouted, turning heads. "We've decided you'll practice again this morning. Get your blood right and proper hot for your fight this afternoon. Since you seemed a little sluggish in the earlier drills. Did I say a little? You moved like thick shite. Frozen and hanging from the inner lip of an Ice Kingdom pisspot. Can't have you fight like that. Not for the School of Nexus. You'll go again. And again, until you're right ready. What do you say to that, maggot?"

Prajus smiled. "Well, we best begin."

More snide looks, but he ignored the faces and went for his sword and shield, feeling Nexus watch him the entire way.

The rest of the morning sped along with the usual slights and insults, all hurled directly at Prajus . . . who absorbed them all with a smile or shake of his head. His training partner was called Mison, the same black-bearded shagger who had spat in his direction at the water barrels. From the onset of the drill, Prajus challenged him, exchanging quick cuts and faster thrusts, pushing him to the limits of his ability, but not enough to best him. He didn't want to beat Mison but rather judge his skill. At the end of several exchanges, in which Prajus held back from striking, he deemed Mison far beneath him. Not surprising. He suspected they were all beneath him. And when Mison broke off contact for a quick breath, Prajus graciously allowed it and took the opportunity to study the fighters nearby.

Skilled, to a point, but heavy-handed. Ponderous, but believing themselves to be swift of hand and foot. The grunts of effort sounded louder than they should have, in an attempt by the men to convince their handlers that they were working. Prajus saw through the lies of it all.

The morning drills finished a short time later, when the gladiators went to the baths. In the cool waters of the pool, Prajus kept to himself, placing his back to one corner and quickly scrubbing himself down.

Surprisingly, the other gladiators left him alone.

When he was done, he left the bathhouse and immediately faced the trainer Rezzo.

"Follow me," the older man commanded. "And don't dawdle."

"Barely out of the bath, Master Rezzo," Prajus said.

"Shut your guts."

So Prajus shut up and followed the trainer to the school's armory—a single-story building next to the smithy. Rezzo ignored the two Marrnite guards on either side of the portal and motioned for Prajus to follow him inside. Stale air lingered, not yet banished by the fresher stuff, carrying the smell of rusty metal and old leather. The trapped heat was another matter, powerful enough to summon sweat to Prajus's face and back.

"Armor's there," Rezzo said, nodding at the racks. "Weapons there. And there . . . are your shields. Pick whatever suits you and be quick about it."

Prajus frowned. "Nothing fitted?"

"For you? Now? No. Maybe when you've proven yourself, but not before. No time, anyway."

No time, indeed. Prajus frowned, inspecting the armory. No time at all when he was being put through the paces that morning. The same day of his first fight for Nexus.

"I said be quick," Rezzo warned.

"So many choices, Master Rezzo. One hardly knows where to start."

"If one doesn't start soon, one will be fighting this day without a stitch."

"Understood," Prajus said and picked his way deeper inside, examining the wares. Vests of toughened leather and heavy shirts of chainmail hung off racks. Those he left for later and went straight for the swords. Along the way, he stopped at a window and threw open the shutters. A warm breeze blew through while daylight scattered the shadows, allowing a better look at a sizable rack.

Blades. Long and short. Serrated and curved. All well-kept. All ready for the cutting. The amount of edged steel collected underneath that roof sent a shiver through Prajus despite the heat.

This was his kind of marketplace.

He felt a moment of regret then, as he remembered his old broadsword from the House of Gastillo. His armor as well, finely crafted scale mail that shimmered under the sun. He set his jaw, missing every piece. When the moment passed, he regarded the rack of blades and hefted a broadsword. Heavy, but balanced well enough. A curved blade caught his attention then, so he returned the broadsword for that. He lifted it and swished it about the confines, ignoring the stern look from Rezzo at the door.

"Hurry up," the trainer ordered.

"One can't rush these choices," Prajus informed him. "Must be careful about it. A blade too heavy and—"

"Shaddup my son," Rezzo said in a tired voice. "The day you lecture me on choosing a sword is the day I shove one through my own guts."

That didn't bother Prajus, and he kept silent. The curved blade was his choice, so he gathered up its scabbard. The shield was a sad affair. A rounded barrier with no distinguishing features upon it. Painfully plain and without a shred of character.

Lords above, he winced inwardly. He missed his dragon's head.

"Hurry *up*, I said," Rezzo warned.

Prajus glanced back at the trainer. Just a flash, a harsh flicker of annoyance, before he caught himself and returned to the task at hand.

That single look, however brief, silenced Rezzo. Startled him, truth be known, enough for him to wonder what he just saw.

He said not another word until Prajus was done.

Later, beneath Sunja's Pit, Nexus led them all into the private chambers assigned to his school, leaving a dozen Marrnite mercenaries outside to guard the door.

"Ahhhh," Nexus said, strolling toward the arched window looking out onto the sands of the arena floor. He smoothed down his hair and stretched out his arms as if addressing rapturous applause. The merchant stopped at the brick sill and peered outside, cringing at the heat. The men behind him filed into the room, unloading their equipment on benches or the floor.

"What a fine, fine day for a little bloodletting, hm?" Nexus said.

"So it is, Master Nexus," Rezzo agreed from the owner's flank.

"A fine day," added a restrained Bernd.

"Old Tino doesn't know what he's missing," Nexus snapped. "Eh? *Eh?* Doesn't know. Or maybe he does. I wager he'd be here if he could. Not feeling well today, he said. The trip might kill him. Wouldn't want that. Then I'd have to appoint one of you unsavory kogs as taskmaster. For a lesser amount of coin, I might add."

Smirking, Nexus regarded one trainer and then the other before facing the window.

"Kogs," he repeated to himself, studying the brickwork. The entire room had a rough edge about it. A certain coarseness. Most certainly rougher than what he was used to, but that was to be expected when walking among the peasants. On impulse he tried leaning out the window, palms flat against the hot sands, to see if he could spot the viewing box he had vacated to Dark Curge. A cunning merchant he might be, but he saw no benefit or favorable outcome in openly battling Curge and his minions for that lofty perch. He knew his lads, especially his Marrnite mercenaries, would slaughter Curge's minions, cracking open their skulls like cheap pisspots, but that might rouse the wrath of the Gladiatorial Chamber. Or some such gurry. Nexus would have his agent Bojen look into the matter, just in case it ever did come to that, upon Chamber property or beyond. It was best to move only when one was well aware of the consequences, and he knew the Pit had its rules.

He'd already squatted on a few of them by acquiring Prajus, who'd killed his previous owner. Since taking him in, Nexus had watched the houseless he-bitch. Assessed him. Tino was somewhat reserved with what he'd seen on the training grounds, stating that he believed the undefeated Sunjan was holding back for some reason. That the man was ignoring obvious openings, even feigning disappointment after letting opportunities slip by. It was the taskmaster's opinion that the man was, in fact, doing so to determine the skill level of his opponents.

And yet, when Tino was muttering through his observations, Nexus realized that exact truth for himself. Prajus, the greasy little slick of shite that he was, was playing a role of sorts. One fit for Perician theater, hoping to convince all onlookers of his mediocrity. Prajus was good enough to fool both his trainers, Rezzo and Bernd. That was concerning enough. That little bit of knowledge reminded Nexus why he had hired Tino in the first place. It also instilled, dare he admit it, a grudging appreciation for Prajus. The pit fighter knew that by entering an established school, there would be an amount of physical and mental abuse put to him, and that he could either lash out or endure it all. As far as Nexus could tell, Prajus had taken every verbal jab with ease. Every sour insult. Every nasty, despicable look of loathing, and not once had he lost control. Even better, the man appeared faintly amused by it all. Nexus decided that Prajus was biding his time, waiting for the perfect moment to strike back, and strike decisively. Until then, he suspected Prajus would remember every slight. Every insult. Every rancid look.

Or so he thought.

Nexus could appreciate that kind of patience. The man had killed his house owner easily, after all, without fear of scorn or retribution. Such an individual would have to be watched constantly. He would no doubt excel at being a merchant.

This day, however, Prajus would fight for the School of Nexus. The very thought sent an evil shiver of anticipation through the owner.

Truth be known, he could not wait.

Head lowered, Prajus sat on a bench at the far end, enduring the ill-fitting greaves and bracers of his hastily chosen armor. Lords above he wished he still had his old metal hide and trusted weapons. That summoned a bout of regret, as those items would be difficult—if not impossible—to retrieve. Immediately after killing Gastillo, the owner's house staff and most of his gladiators had sought a bit of righteous retribution. All three score of them. Before more blood hit the dirt, however, a patrol of street watch entered the house grounds, drawn to the racket of Prajus's fight with Gastillo. Those dozen city guards prevented an even greater round of bloodshed. After listening to various stories and asking questions, the street watch judged Prajus innocent of any wrongdoing and allowed him to leave.

All while those loyal to Gastillo watched.

We'll see you again, maggot, Giannus had said, one of Gastillo's gladiators, with a scowling Jaco nearby. Those were two faces that stood out from a wall of angry pit fighters and household guards. As furious as they had been, not one challenged the judgment of the street watch. Nor did they stop Prajus and his group from leaving. If Prajus had asked for his equipment then, however, he suspected the resulting fight would have been memorable.

Still . . . he wished he had his equipment back.

His current helmet had no visor and felt overly tight, but it was the best of the lot. The leather cuirass he'd chosen felt loose on him, even with the cloth padding underneath—cloth that stank of old sweat. His shield was a small and rounded thing of wood, reinforced with and banded by iron. He chose that over the other larger and much heavier shields, which were better suited for large-scale defensive formations than fighting in the arena. In fact, the dismal selection of quality equipment made Prajus wonder just where Nexus might have gotten it all—and where he kept the good stuff. The man might have taken all that ill-fitting gurry from the armory below the Pit. The same armory that supplied the Free Trained rabble. The same armory that obtained all their pieces from those who perished in the arena.

Prajus frowned at wearing some dead topper's armor. There might have been better picks in the armory, but he simply hadn't had time to find it. He blamed Rezzo for that. The trainer should not have rushed him. Prajus would remember that as well.

In the days to come, he would be doing a lot of remembering.

He leaned over and regarded the sword lying across the leather strips protecting his thighs. Somewhat disgusted, he took the weapon, examined it once more, and placed it tip-down into the flagstones. He knew it might blunt the point, but at the moment he did not care.

Nexus and his school had two fighters competing that day. The first one would be Ansut. Like most of the school's gladiators, Ansut was a tall lad with broad shoulders. Brown-haired and bearded, he forever wore the expression of a guard enduring boring sentry duty. He wasn't as overly muscular as some, but what he lacked in mass he gained in speed, being exceptionally fast with his strikes. In the fleeting moments Prajus stole to study the other gladiators training around him, he noticed Ansut's rapid attacks right away. Harsh combinations that flew at his foe, usually forcing his partner to retreat rather than parry.

Ansut was one gladiator Prajus watched when he could.

Ansut was also one of the rosy pissers who watched him in return, and not kindly.

The same hellpup paced back and forth in the middle of the room. Unlike Prajus, he wore armor fitted for his frame, and that alone made Prajus despise him. Black vest of toughened leather with a fancy lace design along the ribs. A caged helmet decorated with some creature's curved fangs. Brass greaves and bracers, etched with arcane characters, protected the whole of his limbs. A thick-headed war hammer swung from one hand, while a square shield hung off his opposing arm.

Ansut stopped at a wall and released a deep grunt of satisfaction, as if he were thinking dire thoughts for his upcoming match. That, or he was about to let slip a massive cow kiss. Right there in the chamber.

The image of the pit fighter having a squat summoned half a smile to Prajus's face.

Two gladiators from the school fought this day, but Nexus allowed ten more to attend the games. All ten stewed in the room, waiting for the mayhem to commence. Rigger, Greygar, and Mison gathered about the door, conversing among themselves in low voices . . . until Rigger noticed Prajus.

"Something amuses you, blossom?" Rigger sneered, moving closer.

Prajus was of a mind to ignore the question until he realized the punce was trying to frighten *him*. That notion was more offensive than the effort.

"Nothing," he answered, not meeting those eyes. He hoped the trainers would soon intervene with stern reminders of who was fighting that day.

"What was that?" Rigger asked, the sneer even more exaggerated, as if he were fish-hooked through one cheek.

Lords above. Prajus scratched at his lower lip with his teeth. "I said . . . nothing."

"Look at me when you talk to me."

"That . . . isn't necessary."

"What did you say?"

Saimon's hell, Prajus inwardly groaned. The unfit punce had learned *his* preferred way of annoying someone. He looked to the door.

Rigger stepped before him, gazing down a crooked nose.

Not needing to see any more, Prajus checked on the trainers. Neither Rezzo, Bernd, nor even Nexus himself was aware of the fiery sparks flickering at their backs. All three gazed out the damn window, captivated by something or other.

Rigger poked a hard finger into Prajus's chest. "*You* look at me when I'm talking to you. Understood, maggot? Right here," he said and touched the upper bit of his cheek.

Prajus leaned back until he hit the wall, very much aware of the punce before him, one who believed himself to be more dangerous than he truly was. That riled Prajus. To think this flake of maggot shite believed himself a threat . . . to *him*. Even more insulting was Rigger's attempts to threaten him with a few hard looks.

A warm feeling spread across the back of Prajus's neck then. A familiar, welcome, sensation of lethal amusement where he asked himself with cold honesty if his existence would improve if he removed whatever it was annoying him. He'd asked himself that very question often, the last time being when Gastillo challenged him to a fight.

Gazing up at that half-hitched face looming over him, smelling every rotten expulsion of breath, Prajus wondered if he should make his presence known right there . . . starting with Rigger.

That resolve strengthened by the heartbeat, despite Nexus's warning days ago.

Prajus realized he no longer wished to play the game, and without warning, he whipped his sword up and halted the cut a mere finger's width from the man's fruits.

Rigger froze. Greygar and Mison tensed, their hands reaching for blades.

Prajus stopped them both with a show of teeth. "Pull that steel, boys," he warned, "and your lad here *will* scream."

"*Master Rezzo*," Rigger yelled, turning heads and disappointing Prajus to his core.

"What are you *doing*?" Rezzo blurted in flowering rage. "Put that blade *down*."

Now *the blossom looks*, Prajus fumed and reluctantly did as told.

"You unfit knob," Rezzo growled, spittle flying, as the rest of the gladiators crowded in around him. "I asked you what you were doing?"

"He pulled steel on me," Rigger informed the trainer. "The maggot pulled steel for no reason."

"None," Greygar said while Mison shook his head.

Lying maggots, Prajus smiled, impressed.

"You don't pull steel on your fellow *dogs*, he-bitch," Bernd said, his voice rising as was the color to his cheeks. "You don't—"

"Bernd . . . shut up," Nexus commanded from the window, leaving them all muted and staring. Staring mostly at Prajus, that is, who glanced from one to the other, wondering how many he could kill before they killed him back.

"Back *away*, all of you," Nexus ordered, and the lot of them complied, unblocking a path straight through the dozen or so bodies in the room. There, with his back to the arched window and elbows hitched on the sill, was the owner himself.

And he did not look pleased.

"I'll say this once more," Nexus rumbled, mouth puckered as if about to spit poison. "And once more only, so you all best listen, since the message clearly wasn't understood the *first* time. *That* one . . ."

He chopped a hand at Prajus.

"Is fighting for me now. *Me*. And I expect him to *win* . . . a good pot of coin. For *me*. A damn fine sum, truth be known. So—and this is the important part I want you *all* to understand—if any of you *hurt* him, thereby *hinder* him, so that he does *not* win that fine pot of coin for me . . . well . . . I'll have the offender's head. I'll have his head and have the skin boiled from his very skull. I'll have the top cut off and use the thing for a pisspot. Or I just might stick my pisser through the eye socket instead. Every time I need to piss. And I tell you all, with harsh modesty . . . these days I piss a great, *great* deal."

Silence at that. A respectable if not fearful silence, when you got down to the bones of it. A stillness where not one of the killers gathered dare to so much as clear one's throat. Not only did that little speech quell whatever violence was on the cusp of breaking out, it left the group visibly uncomfortable. Heads eventually looked to the floor or glanced at companions, but no one said a *word* in the wake of the warning.

"Understood?" Nexus put to them all. "Rezzo?"

That jerked the trainer's head up, purely shocked at being included with the pack, and he quickly nodded.

"Bernd?"

That infused an even greater amount of flush into the other trainer's cheeks.

"*Answer* me."

"Aye that," they rumbled together, even though Rezzo had already given his answer.

"You," Nexus prodded, pointing a finger. "You are . . . ?"

"Rigger, Master Nexus," the gladiator said and cleared his throat, his sneer nowhere in sight.

"No, you're *not*. You're an overripe berry of shite is what you are. An overripe berry of shite. Near bursting with rancid juice. I know. I've beheld my unfair share of rancid berries, just clinging to whatever unfit vine they sprouted from. So you remember this well . . . If you're not training with that one *there*," he indicated Prajus with a nod, "then keep clear of him. Keep your rancid blossom clear of him. Or I'll have your bells as gambling dice and your bell *sack* as a purse for small coin. Understood?"

Looking as if he were forced to swallow a mouthful of gurry, Rigger nodded. "Aye that, Master Nexus. Understood. Clearly."

"*Prajus . . .*" Nexus said.

That caused Prajus to stand, if only for the show of it.

The owner locked eyes with him. "Be civil," he seethed. "Sweet Seddon above . . . be *civil.* Understood?"

If it were Gastillo addressing him in such a way, Prajus would have given a much saucier answer. But then Gastillo was insufferably weak with his warnings and Nexus was so refreshingly . . . *not.* So Prajus did nothing of the sort to defy the impressive air of total authority. "Understood, Master Nexus. And . . . my thanks."

Nexus focused on Ansut. "You there, you armored tit."

Ansut didn't flinch.

"I usually let Rezzo fill your head with whatever fiery gurry you need to swing steel. But this day? You'll hear it from me. You know who you're fighting? Hm? You're fighting a man-child called Sergur. Spawn of the House of Vandu. My agent tells me the other house owners have been not-so-secretly meeting *without* me. No doubt because of my decision to appropriate *him.*"

Nexus pointed at Prajus, turning heads once again.

"So . . . make no mistake . . . we're on the cusp of war here today. *War.* Sergur will be looking to take your head, because of him."

Prajus suppressed a smile, as he was very much enjoying being the center of such murderous gurry.

"You take his head instead," Nexus ordered his pit fighter. "Understood? You. Take. His. Head. *Instead.* Either whole, halves, or in bloody pieces. But you take it. Understood?"

"Understood, Master Nexus."

Finished with Ansut and tonguing the inside of a cheek, Nexus nodded and eyed the rest of his pack. "You all take their heads. Of whoever you're fighting. This day and the next. Prajus?"

Prajus lifted his chin.

"I most certainly mean *you*. Do you understand me?"

"Aye that," Prajus replied, allowing his smile to surface again. "Perfectly."

11

Within the chamber belonging to the House of Vandu, the owner turned away from the window and inspected Sergur, his gladiator fighting this day. A sleepy-eyed Vandu hooked his thumbs inside his thick, straining belt, and remembered the meeting of house owners not so long ago within Dark Curge's home.

Dark Curge.

The thought of that one-armed asslicker brought a scowl to Vandu's scarred face. In his mind, Dark Curge was a younger version of Old Curge, but with a single difference—Dark Curge was still alive. Only one thing would brighten Vandu's mood *more* than having one of his gladiators become champion of the games . . .

And that would be learning of Dark Curge's death.

Preferably something fitting for one he so disliked. Like . . . oh, he didn't know what, but something exceptionally unusual. Perhaps drowning in his own pissy bathwater. And being found days later, well after his body had voided itself, floating in a ripe sludge of its own filth. Vandu sighed and rattled off a short tune upon his belt. *Drowning in one's own pissy bathwater*, he reflected. Not very imaginative, but then he wasn't a very imaginative person. Never had been. Not in his chosen profession. Not when he'd battled gladiators in the Pit himself, not when he started training them, and not when he finally managed a house of them.

Vandu shook his head with a touch of regret.

He didn't like Curge. Not in the slightest. Didn't like Curge back in the day, when he was killing gladiators under the banner of his then-living father. No one could defeat the brute when he did kill a gladiator . . . and that included Vandu himself. Oh, many had tried, and many had either perished, been crippled, or simply pounded into the dirt. When Curge had killed a gladiator and friend of Vandu, belonging to the long-gone House of Ballum, Ballum sent his next best after Curge.

That pit fighter had been Vandu.

By Curge's own account, Curge defeated Vandu handily. But in the days that followed that fight, spectators informed him that they believed he had killed Curge. In fact, depending on who he talked to . . . Vandu learned he was perhaps a hair away from taking Curge's life.

Instead of half his arm.

Time loses all meaning in a fight, and the only thing a pit fighter is truly aware of is the hellpup they're facing. And the growing tiredness in their own limbs.

Recalling the match, Vandu supposed he didn't do so badly after all . . . but he wanted to kill Curge to avenge his friend. Wanted to send a message to Old Curge, that no one—not even he—could do such to the House of Ballum. But Vandu's life-taking stroke missed Dark Curge's head entirely and lopped off his arm instead. Curge had whipped that bleeding stump about in a panic, flinging blood into Vandu's eyes and blinding him for a critical instant . . . before smashing him upside the head with a mace.

Vandu survived only because of two things. The stout helmet he wore, and Curge himself, who ran for the portcullis instead of finishing his opponent.

To this day, the scars marking the point of impact upon Vandu's cheek still ached for some unfit reason.

A hair away from killing Curge, he thought, hot regret flaring every time he remembered.

Perhaps even worse . . . the Chamber declared Curge the victor in the blood match, as he was still standing, even though he fled the sands while clutching his fountaining stump. The blow to the head left Vandu unconscious for two days. Gone from the world for two days and unbalanced on his feet for two weeks, with no assurances that he would ever be the same. When he finally did regain his senses and righted himself, the games had finished, and no blood match could be carried over to the next season.

Curge had won that, as well.

The memory didn't consume Vandu, but it did burn him every now and again, especially when he had to tolerate Dark Curge's presence. Every time he looked upon that one's face, he remembered just how close he'd come to ending him. No doubt Curge thought the same of him. Both men regarded the other as unfinished business, and Vandu, at least, wondered if he would ever get a chance to hack at that fleshy neck. *Probably not*, he supposed with a deflated sigh, as those days were long gone. So he strove for the next best thing—challenging Curge's legacy during every fighting season since then, by any means possible.

How he hated to be lectured by that oversized pig bastard. How he hated it even *more* when what Curge was saying was the *truth*.

Vandu opened his mouth, feeling things pop in his ears, and stretched his jaw to the fullest.

Nexus, he thought darkly. *You wine-drinking punce. What were you thinking?*

Didn't matter. Vandu knew Nexus didn't really care about the games. Didn't care about the manner of men fighting under his name. Clearly didn't care about the history. As much as Vandu despised Curge, the bald-headed topper was right on that point. He remembered their talks and final decision regarding Nexus . . . and the killer of gold-faced Gastillo. Nexus had to be punished for taking in Prajus. He had to be punished most severely for pissing on the history and spirit of the games.

Sighing, fuming, Vandu rapped fingers off his belt. He strolled through the dozen or so men filling the chamber, their ranks parting for the owner and taskmaster. Each man nodded as Vandu passed by them. His expression grew even more dour as he stopped before Sergur. With a distasteful eye, the owner inspected the bindings of his gladiator's leather vest, the studs of iron speckling his shoulders, and the dull shine of his belt buckle. Finally, he studied the tarnished pommels of twin short swords hanging from the pit fighter's waist.

All the while, the men at his back watched and waited.

His inspection finished, Vandu's sleepy eyes flicked upward to gaze upon Sergur's faceplate, molded in the visage of a hellion howling into the fury of a storm. Metal braids hung off around the back rim of Sergur's helmet.

Vandu gripped his belt and rolled his shoulders. "You know what's happening at the games . . ." he rumbled, studying that frightening mask. "Today you fight a bastard. A corruptor of what was. Is. And what will remain to be. You fight one . . . belonging to one . . . who squats upon these games. The entire history of the games. One who will allow *murderers* to fight under his banner. This shall not be. This will not be. Today . . . you will deliver a message. And that message is *pain*. Not death. *Pain*. Do *not* kill the gladiator you fight this day. I forbid it. But see to it he does not fight again this season. At all. Nexus believes his house—his school—will emerge victorious at the end of these games. Show him he is wrong."

The hellion mask nodded once.

"He believes you are *nothing*," Vandu whispered, stressing the word. "He believes these games are *his* to own. To purchase like a goblet of cheap wine. You show him he is wrong. So very wrong. You hurt his warrior. Give him the first taste of the war . . . *he* asked for."

A knock upon the door then, measured and ominous. No one moved within the room.

"Go on, then," Vandu finally said, breaking the spell. "Bring us victory."

Gray clouds moved across the face of the sun, granting rare shade to the next event. The Orator finished his rousing introductions, his dramatic words rivaling any performer of the local stages or those of distant Pericia. Once given the signal to begin, the two combatants, Ansut of the School of Nexus and Sergur of the House of Vandu, swaggered toward the center of the arena.

Ansut kicked sand with every step, war hammer and shield swinging, eyes set upon his opponent.

Sergur's screaming hellion faceplate stared back, his armor dark and his twin short swords swishing.

The distance between the two shrank.

Sergur, Nexus thought, his hands spread across the warm bricks of the window, watching the two men. *You unfortunate shagger*.

Nothing was guaranteed, but Nexus demanded the best from his killers. Made it well-known that he demanded the best, and that alone would motivate Ansut to finish the fight decisively. Nexus wanted a death. He had no flimsy belief that the games would remain the same after taking in Prajus. Didn't care as long as the man won. If all went well, Prajus might very well inspire his other hellpups to win a few matches.

"We'll know soon enough," he said under his breath.

"What was that, Master Nexus?" a nearby Rezzo asked.

"What?"

"You said something just then?"

Nexus fixed his trainer with a withering look. "Not to you."

Rezzo diverted his gaze to the arena. Nexus eyed him for a few heartbeats more before doing the same.

Excited murmurs from the audience—a full crowd this day—spread across the expanse of the arena as they waited for the impending clash.

Ansut and Sergur steadily marched toward each other, raising their weapons once they were some five or six strides apart. Then they slowed to a more guarded pace.

Ansut circled first, watching his foe over the rim of his shield, his war hammer cocked at his shoulder and ready.

Sergur clacked his short swords together, signaling his own readiness.

Ansut launched himself at his opponent. He swung for a head, the hammer whistling before shouts from the crowd drowned out the sound entirely.

Sergur darted out of harm's way. He feinted right, then left, before Ansut swiped at a head, an arm, and ended with a swing intended to shatter the ribs beneath the armor.

Sergur scattered sand as he dodged everything.

Ansut backed away, looking to reset. Sergur pursued, however, and the two fighters exchanged pleasantries in close quarters. Short swords flashed and clattered off shield and war hammer. When Sergur faltered, Ansut hooked one blade and forced it down—and punched the edge of his shield at the hellion's screaming face.

Sergur jerked himself back, backpedaling to halt a few paces away. He weaved his blades in a complex pattern, and that swishing, darkly scintillating wall stopped Ansut, who held back and waited for the opportunity to strike.

The instant Sergur ceased waving his swords about, Ansut charged.

Another flurry of blows then, faster than before, either deflected or dodged entirely, until Ansut put his shoulder into his shield to stop a sword. He whirled, showing Sergur his back, before whipping his war hammer at the hellion helmet.

Cracking Sergur behind the ear.

The blow staggered the gladiator, wobbling him, until one leg buckled and he fell to a knee.

Ansut rushed in and Sergur—not quite as done as first suspected—slashed at the legs of his oncoming foe. Sword clacked across metal greaves as Ansut twisted and tumbled to the ground. He rolled, stirring up dust as he went, and regained his feet while Sergur did the same.

Both men shook heads and limbs and resumed their contest. They circled each other, hunched over with weapons ready, looking to exploit any weaknesses. At times, Sergur jabbed a sword at Ansut's face.

Until Ansut grew tired of those annoying probes. He bashed one sword tip away and lashed out. Sergur ducked under the incoming hammer and rang a sword off an armored leg. He spun and struck with his other blade, bouncing it off hard leather protecting a spine.

Ansut twisted to face his adversary and the pair traded blows again, blocking and parrying, the connections ringing across the arena.

Until Ansut parried high with his shield while swinging his hammer low. The scratched weapon smashed into Sergur's greave and knocked the legs out from under him. The fighter fell to fists and knees and rolled clear.

Ansut moved in, his hammer high and aimed for a head.

But Sergur, sputtering and all but kissing sand, slashed at an ankle. That looping cut sank halfway through leather, meat, and bone. Ansut straightened with a scream, only to topple from a foot half hewed off from his leg.

Ansut fell hard and clutched for his nearly severed foot, while the audience erupted with a blend of cheers and groans.

Sergur stood, shook out his arms, and studied his opponent. Flailing, dealing with the agony of his lower leg, Ansut hunched over as if shackled to a very short chain. His greaves scuffed sand. Every movement pulled his nearly severed foot from his ankle, stretching, testing red bone and tendons while the sand soaked up a torrent of scarlet.

Ansut glanced about to check on his foe, when Sergur cracked a heavy sword across the fallen man's helmet. Ornamental fangs flew as the blow flattened Ansut in a puff of dust. With his opponent at his mercy, Sergur methodically stabbed at exposed spots, twisting Ansut one way and then the other. Swords punched through armor in places but failed to pierce others. Blood spritzed from opened wounds, and Sergur eventually backed off.

In that brief respite, Ansut slowly rolled onto one side, his stained hands clutching at the worst of his wounds. It took effort, but he flopped out one arm and managed to lift it—signaling he was done.

Sergur made it official. He flipped one sword to an underhand grip and nailed Ansut's exposed calf to the ground.

Far above the carnage, Curge froze in mid-sip of his wine. He leaned forward while a satisfied smile crept across his face.

In his private chambers, Nexus saw the sword flash downward, into the lower leg of his fallen investment. Ansut's head snapped back, perhaps releasing a scream that was never heard, swallowed up by the roar of the approving crowd.

"You . . . unfit . . . *bastard*," Nexus raged in a barely controlled whisper, shaking fists at the unfolding scene.

The ass-splitter called Sergur pulled his sword free in a black spray, leaving Ansut writhing upon the sands. The Vandu gladiator retreated, ready to do a little more cutting if needed. In the end he did no such thing, however. Pleased with his win, he took a moment to bask in the loud and lengthy adoration from the audience.

When he'd had his fill, he strode for the rising portcullis.

"Seddon's rosy *ass*," Nexus spat, livid with the result, and put a hand to his chin. A dewy wetness distracted him. Two of his fingernails were bleeding. Confusion diluted his anger, just long enough for him to realize the reason for his dripping fingertips. There, along the rough edges of brick, lay a generous dappling of blood, as well as a shred of fingernail. At some point, Nexus had clawed at the grain hard enough to rip one nail free and leave the other dangling and oozing.

"*Master Nexus*," Bernd blared as if he'd just fish-hooked his own pisser. The trainer reached for the owner's bleeding hand, but Nexus pulled away. Gnashing his teeth, he bit away the hanging sliver and spat upon the floor.

Rezzo stood nearby, with a hand cloth at the ready.

Nexus snatched it from him. "Seddon's almighty crack. What was that? What was *that*? *Bernd*. Gather him up. Find out if he's dead."

Bernd hastily turned for the door.

"Not *you*, you nog," Nexus winced in hateful dismay. "Send someone *else*. You! You go. *Now*."

A gladiator hurried out the door, leaving the trainers to face the wrath of Nexus.

"Ansut isn't dead, Master Nexus," Rezzo said. "Not from what I can see."

A livid Nexus turned on him. "How did he lose that? How did he *lose?*"

The trainer swallowed. "Mistakes were made."

"*Mistakes?* I don't *pay* you for mistakes. I *pay* you to train these toppers to be *unbeatable*. Daresay *invincible*. To transform them from mortals into mortal *monsters*. Saimon-spawned fiends that will weaken knees and turn shite to water upon the very mention of their names! *That's* what I'm paying you for. And, thus far, I'm not seeing any damn return on my investment."

Rezzo absorbed that, while Bernd looked at the floor.

Nexus continued to rage, spewing frothy lines of hateful vitriol, at times waving the bloody hand cloth at his trainers' faces.

Prajus watched it all from the corner of one eye. He remained expressionless, not needing the storm cloud called Nexus to thunder over his head. A man could only endure so much of that gurry before someone got killed. Instead, he listened to the hot deluge of insults and threats directed at the trainers as well as any nearby pit fighter. It faded in time and a steaming Nexus faced the window, downing wine from a bottle that was no doubt intended for a victory that had not happened.

Lowering his head, Prajus waited for his time.

The next two fights flew by. Gair, a knife fighter from the House of Curge, defeated Rune from the House of Razi. Zilos, the spear-wielding spectacle from the House of Tilo, met and bested Urson from the Stable of Slavol. Prajus didn't see either one of those contests, but he heard the hard ringing of weapons as well as the cheering crowds.

But mostly, he heard Nexus continue to rant and roar.

Near the end of the fight between Zilos and Urson, however, one of Nexus's gladiators returned with word about Ansut. The arena attendants had delivered the pit fighter to the infirmary. Ansut lived, but his season was over, if not his entire career within the arena. The Vandu fighter had cut up Ansut quite badly, leaving him a bloody mess—the worst of the injuries being the nearly severed foot. A wound that, according to the infirmary healers, would probably leave him limping for the rest of his days.

The news brought out the worst in Nexus.

"They *meant* to do this," he raved, waving his hand about as if fending off a swarm. "They meant it as a *message*! A message, the brazen pissers. That's why they had their little gathering, to talk all this through. To plan all this out. They like messages? We'll send them a message. We'll send them a message of our *own*."

He whirled upon those at his back. "Out of my way," Nexus growled, and the trainers and gladiators fell back, like fearful dogs knowing who held all the bones as well as the whips.

Nexus cut through them all and stopped before Prajus, who lifted his head.

"*You* . . ." the merchant said in a low and lethal voice. "You'll fight next. When you do, you kill the man. You hear me? Kill him. They want a message? You send them one *back*."

Prajus studied the owner for a few lingering heartbeats. "As you wish," he said quietly.

Gears and chains clicked and rattled as the rising portcullis withdrew its dreary shadow upon the steps. Prajus casually ascended those stairs to the arena, at times glancing at the opening. Beyond that stony framework, gray clouds thickened, blotting the sky and granting a little respite from the blistering Sunjan sun. The air remained dense and soupy, however, and unpleasant to breathe. The Orator's voice boomed in the distance, introducing Prajus at length, to an indifferent reception. A few jeers soured the already weak applause. Some remembered him or knew of his recent history. Not that he cared. The crowd meant nothing to Prajus.

Onto the sands he strode, sword and shield swinging at his sides.

The jeers erupted into hostile curses.

"I hope he splits you down the middle!"

"May Saimon's hell suck you down by the bells!"

"Shite has better worth than you!"

A half-eaten apple landed a stride away from him and signaled the start of it. More heavy patters all around, partially devoured fruit and chicken bones, even a few empty skewers. Something bounced off the back of his helmet and stopped him. Prajus rolled his shoulders and turned with stern intent, searching for the offender in the stands. Hundreds of angry faces greeted him from that quarter, waving arms and shaking fists, as if cursing him was a sport in itself. More food scraps rained down, enough to draw the attention of the few Skarrs standing upon the stairs.

Well, Prajus thought.

They recognized him for something.

So he smiled and showed them his back. He resumed his march toward his opponent—his very first while fighting for the School of Nexus.

Brontus from the House of Ustda.

Picking through his scattered thoughts, Prajus remembered the name. A veteran of the arena, Brontus had no issue with cutting a throat or two if needed, having already taken at least a couple of lives this season. No reservations at all about putting a gladiator into the dirt. That was all Prajus knew about the man. He did not follow who was doing well this season, having had enough distractions to occupy him. And Nexus had not provided any information that might help him defeat the pit fighter other than the name.

No matter, Prajus thought, scuffing sand as he went.

It was clear that Brontus was a tall man, and he grew bigger with every step. Large and meaty, with broad shoulders, he wore a vest of leather like Prajus, except his was no doubt fitted to his frame. Doubled up strips of leather protected his thighs. Spikes, long and prickly, protruded from bronze greaves. A closed helmet hid his features, and a beard of dusty chainmail hung from the helm's iron jaw, all the way around the neck.

The curses and jeers transformed into cheering, which intensified as the two fighters closed in on each other, leaving no doubt as to who was their favorite.

Brontus halted half a dozen strides away, leaning into a round shield while holding a spiked mace at the ready. Dark eyes glinted in the metal sockets of his helmet.

"Prajus," he called out over the voices.

"Brontus," Prajus greeted, readying his own weapon and shield.

"The people dislike you."

"Clearly."

"I usually ask if this is to the death. Not this time."

"No? The crowds sway you that much?"

Brontus shook his head. "Not at all. I know it's merely a waste of breath talking to you. Everyone knows about you, maggot. And how you killed Gastillo. Everyone. Us. Them. Daresay, all of *Sunja* knows by now."

Daresay, Prajus thought.

"I knew Gastillo," Brontus continued. "Not well, but enough to talk with him when I saw him in the streets. In the off-season. He was a good man. Pleasant enough to talk to a kernel of shite like me. And he always remembered my name. Always. Daresay, if I hadn't joined the Ustdas, I would have gone with Gastillo."

Prajus smirked. "You'll be with him in a few moments."

"Oh-ho," Brontus nodded, the chainmail beard shivering. "I was foolish to expect anything less from shite like you. Such is my nature. Come on then, you treacherous kog. You'll sleep in Saimon's fiery shite trough soon enough."

"Come on indeed," Prajus muttered and raised his guard.

Amid the roaring crowd, the pit fighters closed the gap between them.

Brontus flexed his shoulders in a feint before swinging for his foe's head.

Prajus ducked, the mace whistling over his helmet. He slashed for a leg, but Brontus stopped that on his shield. Prajus twisted, righted himself, and lunged back into the fray, stabbing for guts.

With a grunt, Brontus slapped that away with his shield as well.

Prajus skipped out of reach. No sooner did his heels strike the ground than he sprang forward, sword poised like a dreadful stinger. Prajus stabbed, stabbed, and stabbed again, all at the body. Three quick thrusts meant to double the larger man over.

Brontus knocked the first one away, then the second and third, but a *fourth* thrust clipped his helmet with a startling clap, straightening his spine.

Whereupon Prajus went low and chopped at the tall man's legs. Edged steel hacked downward, dimpling the hard leather protecting a thigh and biting meat as well. Brontus staggered and swung at his opponent's head once more.

Prajus ducked under it, shoved Brontus's arm away by the elbow, and punched the edge of his shield over the arc of the mace.

To smash his adversary's profile in an explosion of iron bands and shattering wood.

The impact silenced the crowd's cheering and stunned Brontus, his knees buckling for an instant. He backpedaled, arms flailing as he strove for stability. Prajus shook off the remains of his destroyed shield. He rushed Brontus and leaped, his feet slamming into the gladiator's shield. Both men fell in a swirl of sand.

Prajus regained his feet first. He chopped downward, into the chainmail mesh protecting the neck of a rising Brontus. Though the armor saved him, the force sent the bigger man sprawling.

Brontus landed on his chest, his blood dappling the ground, and quickly sought to stand.

Prajus brought his blade up and over his shoulder for the greatest cutting power, and again hacked at the man's neck. That time, edged steel bit flesh, dropping the larger pit fighter flat on his face and shocking the audience. People groaned at the sight. A few horrified screams went up. None of the noise arrested the prowling Prajus. He struck again, sword flashing, slashing, targeting Brontus's exposed weapon arm.

The blade drew a frightening, gushing line from inner wrist to elbow.

The big man collapsed.

Prajus stomped on the hand holding the mace. Brontus released it with a grimace. The fallen gladiator turned onto his side, slapping a hand to his bleeding forearm, sand sticking to the wound.

Prajus put a foot to his opponent's chest and forced him onto his back. Screams of protest erupted from the audience then as he dropped a knee onto Brontus's stomach. He loomed over the gladiator, clutched his helmet, and held it fast.

A dazed and weakened Brontus made no effort to defend himself, and Prajus shoved a length of sword through the eye slot of the helmet. Steel shrieked as the dreadful blade sank deep into the opening, nailing Brontus's head to the ground.

Brontus's legs kicked once before becoming still.

Prajus bore down on his weapon. He held the pose for several heartbeats, soaking in the horrified mutters from those who had cursed him only moments ago. He glanced about, seeing a few shocked faces. Then he stood, yanking his blade free as he did. The extraction jerked the dead man's head from the ground before it landed with a thump.

Chest heaving from the effort, dripping sword held at his side, Prajus examined his work. As an afterthought, he took care to avoid the pool of blood around the corpse. The audience regained their voices and shouted their disapproval.

Prajus half turned at the noise, gauging it, enjoying it.

When he had had enough, he tossed away his sword and strode toward the rising portcullis.

"He did it," Rezzo said, barely heard over the wailing of the audience.

His features partially darkened by shade, Nexus nodded, chewing on the inside of his mouth. "He did indeed," he said, watching the people hurl curses at the departing gladiator. Nexus lost interest in that, thinking of the coin he'd just won from Prajus's victory. It wasn't a large wager, but that was fine. In his mind, it was best to keep the wagers modest until he saw what he had there—what Prajus was capable of.

The offended yelling grew even more distant then, as a dawning realization filled him, curling a corner of his mouth into an unchecked smirk.

He suspected the hellpup was capable of so much more.

Standing at his own arched window, Burco, owner of the House of Ustda, covered his mouth with a trembling hand and gazed upon the crumpled husk of Brontus. Death was ever present at the games, and it wasn't the first time it took one of his lads, but Brontus had been a personal favorite. The man could talk for days but somehow never bore you. Now, no more, and it shocked Burco badly, even more than he could have expected.

A chill pierced his usually cheerful demeanor to the core. "Torgul," he eventually said, breaking the rigid posture of the taskmaster standing next to him.

"Master Burco?"

"We'll have to respond . . ."

"Aye that. I'll send a lad right away. Issue the blood challenge."

"See if Wocello will do it."

"Imagine he will. Brontus was his friend."

"I know. And Torgul?"

"Master Burco?"

The owner turned and faced his taskmaster. "Tell Wocello to gut that maggot . . ."

The death of Brontus disappointed Curge.

He had watched with interest and some margin of hope upon the start of the fight, but his heart quickly sank. Brontus was clearly outmatched. Thrust, cut, parry, over the top with a shield's edge to the skull, and the disparity in skill became painfully obvious. Prajus had merely been playing with the man until he finally dispatched him. Without hesitation, Curge noted. The man was a killer, make no mistake.

And now Curge knew it.

He lifted his cup, replaying the fight in his mind. Prajus might be a worrying handful. He would have to watch that topper closely when he fought again, which would be soon. From what he understood, Brontus had been well-liked by the House of Ustda. It would be a long time before young Burco would smile again.

Still, Curge reckoned, *two matches against Nexus. War has begun with one victory and one loss. One crippled. One dead.*

The houses would have to do better.

Curge tipped his cup for a drink and discovered he'd already finished it.

12

With the information provided by the alehouse enforcers, Gurga decided to hunt around Sunja's Pit. Thus, the next morning he went to the arena, ignoring the usual stares and gawkers along the way, until the venerable grandness of the Pit revealed itself above the many lesser rooftops. The sight of the towering structure urged him to walk a little faster, until he turned a corner and strode along the street leading straight for the arena. Constructed of red brick, massive timbers, and black-veined Vathian marble columns, Sunja's Pit stood some four levels high. Brick archways ringed the very top with plunging waterfalls of sparkling blue stone decorating those heights, separating warrior figures of gleaming copper. Painted murals covered the lower walls, portraying bloody scenes from its violent past, depicting men and beasts alike in heroic or ferocious poses.

The closer he got, the more vibrant those scenes became, stirring some unease within him. He wasn't one for the arena. Never was, despite his earlier ambitions of being a gladiator. Tilo had done him a huge favor by releasing him from their agreement and later introducing him to Sindra. The Pit would have only cut him to pieces.

Life with Sindra, however, had been the best years of his life.

Shadows stemming from those inspiring heights darkened the cobblestones as Gurga crossed the grand fairway, moving for the southern end known as the Gate of the Sea. *Gate of the Sea.* He didn't know why it was named that. Perhaps no one did. Figured the "Southern Gate" would work just as well. Then again, he wasn't much for naming things. A public pool was a short walk away from it, but that was no sea. There *was* a sea somewhere to the south, but to get there, one had to travel several days, through several different countries.

As it was early, there were fewer people about the arena, which was something he appreciated. He lumbered through a short tunnel, sparing glances at the numerous wall paintings, and emerged into a wide walkway stretching east and west. A great inner wall faced him, its length broken into sections by tall archways of red brick and more thick timbers. Dull daylight poured through those openings, brightening the steps leading to the many seats that circled the arena. Columns of Vathian marble lined the walls at Gurga's back, spaced out much like the timbers, supporting the slanted ceiling and the thousands who would watch the fights later in the day.

Thousands.

Gurga rubbed his neck. Thousands was a *lot.*

Barely a soul wandered the halls at the moment, however, and that was fine with him. The thought of thousands struck him again and he examined the timbers and columns. Those supports stretched out the whole length of the passage, perhaps even all the way around. He wondered how they were strong enough to hold up the weight of, well, *thousands.*

An uneasy Gurga inspected a nearby column from base to top. Even reached out and patted the thing, feeling the cool, unyielding stone under his calloused hand. Vathian marble. Said to be the best. The prettiest. The strongest. Even the most expensive. Gurga hesitantly leaned against it, eyeing that ominous ceiling all the while. The main passageway stretched both ways until it turned north at either end, hiding the rest. Light from the many archways split the shadows and left a pattern upon the floor.

From here, few would get by without him seeing them, without him giving them a good look over. Gurga approved. He had his perch to watch people.

Now, he figured. *We'll see what we'll see.*

With that, he folded his arms . . . and waited. He looked up every now and then and tried not to think about all that weight overhead. Weight which would only get heavier as the seats began to fill.

Gurga sighed and went back to watching the passageway.

Waited.

Time dragged on, measured in the dreary shifting of light and shadows upon broad flagstones. People gradually appeared in the far ends of the passageway. In spotty trickles at first and walking straight on through to the seats, too far away and too fast for him to see anything. Gurga wondered if he should follow but decided to stay where he was . . . under all that weight.

Eventually, he needed to empty the bull, so he left his spot to find the nearest public piss trough. When he finished that bit of business he decided on a walk and did the complete passage encircling the arena. As expected, the columns went all the way around, holding up all that mass, which seemed even greater than before.

Those troubling thoughts stayed with him as he returned to his original post.

And there he waited again.

More people arrived. Women, men, and even children. The trickles thickened into streams as the day's events grew closer. The streams became a river. A noisy, fragrant river of smiling, chattering heads and torsos with no end in sight. They poured through the Gate of the Sea, drawn to the promise of extreme violence. The sheer number surprised Gurga. There were far too many for him to inspect for ink, and the afternoon had darkened the passageway, making it a touch more difficult. Still, he did what he could as they went by him. Some eyed him warily in return, giving him and the pillar he leaned against a wide berth.

More time passed, quickened by the grim concentration Gurga applied to his studies. *So many people*, as if the city was emptying the whole of its population into this one building. Certainly wasn't like the alehouse. There, he only had to deal with a hundred folk—a hundred and fifty at most—mucking about beneath Sindra's roof.

Roof.

Gurga lifted his worried gaze to the ceiling. *Thousands* flashed and thundered within his mind. Of every shape and size, especially size, as some looked very large indeed. And *every one of them* was gathering right over his head, where they would place ass cheeks to seats.

Adding to the weight.

Any moment he expected to see a sinister wisp of dust falling from above.

A voice roared from beyond the archways, startling the enforcer, breaking his distressed thoughts. That powerful voice continued blaring, perking Gurga's hairy ears, but damn if he could understand what was being said. Too far away and too much in between. The voice soon stopped, replaced by a rock-splitting cheer of thousands. *That* unexpected boom straightened Gurga's posture and widened his eyes, and its power prompted the big man to again check on the ceiling.

Nothing fell, but the roar continued. In fact, the roar didn't stop.

Roar. A constant, ear-rupturing blast that enveloped the whole of the arena, smothering all conversation. A shocking wave that drowned the conversations of those still entering the arena. Oh, it lessened in between fights, enough for Gurga to hear that one distant voice addressing the gathered masses again, and again he puzzled over what was being said. The noise never completely died away, however, refusing to return to the sleepy stillness of earlier, becoming at best a low, skin-tingling rumble, just before the voice returned. Always the same voice, rising above the excited murmuring, speaking at length before being buried in the next explosive barrage of cheers.

At times, someone shouted over the voice, an outburst of some sort quickly forgotten. Other times, after the voice had finished, Gurga could hear the tinkling of metal, not unlike crooked chimes being swung about and battered by a stormy wind.

But the cheering, the *noise*, did not end. Not ever.

At one point in the day, however, the cheers soured into a brow-arching boom of *jeers*, every bit as powerful and perhaps even more so. It was a bitter sound. A poisoned one. A blend of curses, hisses, and groans all rushed into one fell uprising of displeasure. After hearing so much cheering for so long, the abrupt change in tone, from spectacle-charged enjoyment to hateful protest, Gurga wondered the reason for it all.

He scratched his beard and stopped near the base of his neck, just above the collarbone. There he discovered a fleshy protrusion and proceeded to dig into it with a fingernail. As he scratched, the unhappy noise flooding the corridors faded into a vengeful grumble. People continued to walk the corridor. Some held drinks. Others ate. Some did both. Gurga always wondered how a person could do both while walking. Puzzling over that little mystery, he sniffed and rubbed at an eye while watching those walking past him. Standing as he was, somewhat tucked behind the column, some passing by missed him entirely. The girth of the pillar concealed him somewhat from the flow as they strolled west to east, which most seemed to prefer. Oh, there were a few dissenters going against the tide. Always a few pissers. Those who did easily spotted the giant of a man leaning against the column.

When Gurga noticed their stares, however, they quickly glanced away—even hurried along, as if in dire need of a squat. He made it a point to get a good look at them, but they were normal folk like the rest. Farmers. Cobblers. Bricklayers. Clothing makers and woodworkers. The people of the city, hardworking and mostly honest, out for a day of entertainment. They wore regular summer clothing, like short robes or loose, sleeveless tunics, all with open necks to help with the heat. Some wore nothing above their belts at all, walking about half naked, freely perspiring and glistening in what light there was. The summer styles left little to hide, at least from Gurga's vantage point, and no one wore any ink. Not a single line or design could be seen. Not a stroke or even a misplaced drop.

Nothing.

They still stick about the Pit and parts of Arbin's Row, the enforcer had told him. *And the Lords know where else.*

Gurga scratched again at that annoying little bulb sticking out of him and glanced about. A half-dozen Skarrs charged with keeping the peace marched against the current of spectators. The armored men approached Gurga, who continued scratching himself, at times checking his fingers. When the guards walked by, eyeing him as they went, the enforcer eyed them back. Even gave them a nod—which one returned—showing all was good. Gurga had no issue with the Skarrs. They were keepers of the peace, just like him, really, when you thought about it. Even friends when truly needed. He gave them no more thought and they let him be, eventually marching out of sight. Gurga thought he could have been a city guard once. Part of the street watch. It would have meant a lot of walking, though, on hot days like this one, while dressed in armor.

That darkened his sweaty face.

He resumed his watch.

The clouds continued to thicken until they blotted out the day entirely, ending the events of the Pit. Feeling a touch despondent over failing to find anyone wearing ink, Gurga left the arena and started the long walk back to his lodgings. Along the way, he spotted a cart and a pair of women behind it. A middle-aged man sat on a stool at the rear of the cart, fiddling with a knife and stick. They blocked the opening of an alley, where bare clothes-lines webbed the space a level over their heads. Their cart was, in reality, a small wagon, pulled along by whoever wanted the exercise the most. A stout cauldron sat in that wagon, near the rear, and two cooked chickens lay upon spits over the top. Near that black pot was, of all things, a small wooden bin half filled with huge heads of cabbage.

Gurga stopped alongside the wagon. The two women, older sorts, perhaps in their forties, slowly ceased their fussing over the food as they grew increasingly aware of the presence looming over them. They lifted their clean but uneasy faces, taking in the enforcer's menacing height. The middle-aged man behind them stopped fiddling with his knife and stick and blinked at the ogre before the food cart.

"Hello," one of the women greeted with a nervous smile.

"Hello," said the other.

"Ah, feeling hungry, are you?" asked the first.

Gurga regarded the roasting chickens. "Aye that."

"Feel like a bit of bird?" asked the first.

"Well-cooked bird," said the second.

"With a lovely sauce on it."

"Lovely sauce."

"You can smell it," said the first.

"Smell it all over," said the second.

Gurga *could* smell it, and it smelled right and proper fine, and because he'd had nothing since morning, he discovered he was damn near famished.

"How much for the pair?" he asked.

The first one named her price.

Which wasn't bad, not in his mind, remembering how much Sindra asked for one of Telda's meals.

Sindra.

"Something wrong?" the first one inquired cautiously as the other woman paused over the crate of cabbages.

Gurga unclenched his jaw as a lump filled his throat. He shook his head.

"Will you eat that here, sar?" the other woman asked.

Gurga shook his head again.

"Taking it home, then?" she asked again.

"For the family?" asked the first.

He nodded.

"Lovely feast for the family," said the first.

"Lovely," agreed the second, who took a cabbage and tore away several leaves. She then handed them over to her friend, who promptly used them to wrap a whole chicken. She secured everything with a bit of string and went to work on the other. Gurga, dealing with his unexpected sadness, simply watched her.

"Here you are," said the first woman, handing them over. "Enjoy the food."

"Enjoy, enjoy," said the second.

"Get it home before it goes cold."

"Best when it's hot. And mind the bones."

"Mind the bones," the first one repeated with a note of scorn, eyeing her companion.

"What?"

"Foolish thing to say. Of course he'll mind the bones."

"Well, I was only *saying* . . ."

With the chicken wrapped up and in his hands, Gurga nodded thanks and walked away. He returned to the alehouse where his little room waited. The enforcer guarding the door was a tall one, young and well-built, with barely a scar on him. He watched Gurga carefully as the much bigger man entered the establishment, the floorboards loudly announcing his arrival.

No warm greetings or waves of a hand. No questions about how he was or what might be on his mind. Only cautious looks. Gurga crossed the floor to the clean-shaven barkeep perhaps in his fifties. There, he fetched his key, nodded thanks, and proceeded to the stairs, very much aware of the silence inside the establishment, as if everyone was holding their breath at once. Gurga meant to get out of their sight quickly. Every step creaked as he climbed to the second floor. He located his door, unlocked it, and went inside.

A plain bed, barely big enough to hold him, but clean, with the blanket straightened out and the feather pillow fluffed up. Next to the bed was a small table with a wide wash pan and cloth towels upon it. A jug of warm water was next to that, either for drinking or washing. A handful of candles sat on an otherwise empty shelf. No memories. Just a place to sleep for the night and nothing more.

Gurga gazed upon the sparse furnishings, hearing muffled voices down below.

Realizing his supper was getting cold, he closed the door.

In the morning, he ate the last of his chicken and washed it down with water from the jug. He dressed, hiding his armor under his loose shirt. The leather collar went around his neck, but he held on to his cap. Considering what to do with it, he eventually jammed it inside his trousers until needed. Not sparing a look behind, he left the door open as he vacated the room, sack of belongings in hand. The barkeep accepted the key without a word of greeting, and Gurga walked out into a cloudy day, using his spiked club as a walking stick.

By early afternoon, he'd found another alehouse, paid for the night's lodgings in advance, and left his club and meager possessions in the room.

From there he proceeded back to the Pit.

It was afternoon by the time he got there, and the crowds inside were screaming their faces off once again. Gurga wasn't sure he could endure another day of all that noise. Nor was he confident he'd spy any street clan members strolling around the passageways. Last night he'd had a thought and it seemed a good one. Someone wearing the ink might very well have seen him *first* and decided to keep clear of him, as if he were a Skarr. Maybe.

In any case, Gurga thought—and thought hard—the best place to find the ones he wanted would be the place that interested them the most.

That place was the Domis, where most of the wagering upon the games took place.

The Domis was not a hard place to find. Located to the right of the Gate of the Sun, a name that puzzled Gurga just as much as the other. The importance of the Domis, however, did not puzzle him. The Domis consisted of four fortified booths built of stone and timber. Perhaps two dozen Skarrs guarded those booths while another dozen patrolled the fairway beyond. Those inside the Domis interacted with their customers through a barred window, taking all official wagers placed upon the contests.

Gurga stood back from the lines of people dozens long. Beside each window stood a Skarr with his visor down and weapons ready. Scratching at his neck yet again, Gurga studied those closest to him, waiting to place their wagers. Some felt the weight of that powerful scrutiny. A few were confused, a few annoyed, a few even smiled, but most were clearly nervous. In time, the smiles disappeared, the angry ones turned their attention elsewhere, as did the confused ones, but the nervous ones remained.

Ignoring their reactions, Gurga sized up what he could until he detected movement on his right.

The Skarrs. A handful of city guards watched him in return. A few exchanged glances.

Sensing it was time to move on, Gurga wandered away from the Domis, sparing a few parting looks at the lines of gamblers. Nothing. No ink on any exposed skin he could see, and he could see plenty. Bare arms and shoulders. Necks. Shirts opened wide to reveal sweaty mats of hair. Some were naked from the waist up.

Not a lick of ink on any of them.

The Skarrs continued to watch him from afar. Not wanting to further rouse the city guard, Gurga returned to the open grounds surrounding the Pit, inspecting whoever caught his eye, whenever they crossed his path.

Not long after, the fights commenced, marked by the overwhelming explosion of sound from thousands upon thousands of spectators. Several from the audience roamed the fairway, some eating and drinking around booths selling such wares. Children ran wild around the place, slapping each other before scampering off in all directions. Gurga frowned at the sight and hoped they would stay clear.

Shouts of excitement rose and fell, marking the slow passage of time. The clouds thickened again, threatening rain as powerful as just a few days ago. The heat lingered, however, trapped between cottony heavens and the stone-bandaged earth. Gurga repeatedly wiped his face and brow and dried his palms on his shirt. He eventually left the open area and walked toward a narrow lane, between what smelled like a barn and a boarded-up smithy. The smell he didn't mind so much, as it would keep people at a distance. So he chose the corner of the smithy where the exposed stone foundation jutted out and offered a perch. That bit of rock was just big enough for him to sit upon, so he did, putting his hands to his knees. From there, he watched Sunja's citizens teem around the building. Gurga knew the city was huge, but the number of people all in one place quietly shocked him.

The day grew older, and one thrilled outburst of cheers became the last. Shortly after that, thousands spewed forth from the gates. *So many*, Gurga thought in growing awe. So very many, while the smell of the nearby barn wrinkled his nose.

"What are you looking at, my son?" rasped a voice nearby, sending a fright through the big man.

"Ha! Easy boy," chortled a beggar. "Nothing to fear from me. Not you. You could break me over one knee if you like. Break me and toss me aside like rotten kindle."

He flashed a near-toothless smile as he spoke, and what teeth he did have were yellow-black stumps, wet and glistening. Black eyes crinkled about the corners. A full head of hair and a great gray beard masked most of his face, but he looked to be in his fifties. The stained rags of an open shirt exposed a chest frizzled with even more filthy gray hair. Breeches, as tattered as his shirt but holding in the important places, looked as rancid as a rat's pissy nest and were perhaps just as old as he was. As Gurga studied him, he realized the stink from the barn wasn't from the barn at all, but from the unwashed knob standing a couple of strides away from him.

When Gurga guarded Sindra's alehouse, he'd had dealings enough with beggars. Some were in a deplorable state, some were insane, and some were a combination of the two. One or two were even savage angry upon being denied entry to the alehouse, and those he shoved back into the street to get his point across. Wasn't something Gurga enjoyed doing, but if the need was there, he would do it, and do it right, to send a message.

The one before him was clearly in a grubby state, and the way he was smiling put Gurga on alert.

"What I'm saying, boy, is that you're *huge*," the beggar went on, lips puckering to stress the word. "*Huge*, I say. I watch people. Watch them all the time. Not much else entertains me these days so there you have it. In all my time of looking about, you, sar, would make any three look small. *Small.* I imagine if you remained still long enough, the youngsters would be crawling over you. *Climbing* over you I meant to say. Swinging from that rug fixed to your chin. Your beard is greater than *mine*, truth be known, and that's saying a lot."

He ended with a chuckle and a quick pick of his nose.

"So what are you looking at?" he asked again, rubbing his fingers in those awful breeches.

Gurga frowned. He couldn't see any weapons upon the man, nor any ink upon his skinny limbs. The enforcer sighed, torn over answering the street louse or driving him off, like he was supposed to do . . . if he still worked the front door of Sindra's alehouse.

"Looking for people—" he finally said.

"Plenty of them around."

"Who wear the ink."

That stilled the beggar, and he stared at Gurga for a few beats. "Ink, you say?"

Gurga nodded.

"What do you want from them?"

Gurga rubbed at his nose, enduring that potent blend of sweat and whatever other juices an unwashed body will produce over time. "Just talk," he finally said, squirming with the half truth. *Talk until he started smashing* is what he meant, however.

"Talk?" the beggar repeated. "To them? Lords above, you brute. You looking to purchase something from them?"

"Purchase?"

"Buy something?"

Gurga's frown deepened, and he shook his head. This one right and proper *stank.*

The old man eyed him dubiously. "No one simply *talks* to those who wear the ink."

That got the enforcer's attention. "You know them?"

"Know who?" the beggar winced while scratching vigorously at his ribs.

Despite the smell, and probable fleas, Gurga reached out and grabbed the distracted man's festering chin fur. The street louse's eyes widened as Gurga pulled him close. The louse did not resist for fear of having his very jaw ripped off.

"The ones who wear the ink," Gurga glared, his words low and lethal.

"You have a long arm," the louse whispered back, his breath even fouler than the rest of him.

Wincing, Gurga turned the beggar's face toward the barn. "You know them?"

"I might . . ."

Gurga rattled the head.

"*I do, I do*. Aye that I do. Lords *above* . . ."

"Where?"

"What do you want from them?"

Gurga rattled the head again.

"All right, I know where you might find them, but . . ."

Something crawled over the back of Gurga's hand, but despite the sensation, he held on.

"But it's the Sons I'm talking about."

Grim satisfaction flared through the enforcer.

"You don't know about them?" the louse asked.

That brought on a few painful memories. "I know about them," he answered.

The louse showed the whites of his eyes as he turned against the grip holding him, just enough to meet his captor's stare. "They're killers," he whispered.

Killers. They were indeed.

"Where are they?" Gurga rumbled.

So they walked through the tangled alleys and cluttered back-streets of Sunja, sometimes avoiding puddles of mysterious liquids, sometimes walking straight on through while the day faded. The street louse led the way. Gurga followed, his hand clamped upon the smaller man's shoulder.

At one point, the smell of something roasting over a fire hooked Gurga's nose, despite the stink coming off his guide. Gurga's stomach rumbled, reminding him he'd eaten nothing since the morning. Water was freely provided in the many public fountains around the arena. There had been food merchants as well, but Gurga had concentrated on his hunt so hard that the thought of eating never entered his head.

Which his stomach again reminded him of, grumbling a second time and sending a dull ache through his guts.

So he stopped, halting the other with a lurch, and peered down one alley before considering the way they'd traveled already.

"Something bothers you?" asked the louse.

"No," Gurga answered and sniffed mightily.

"Smell something?"

"Only you."

The enforcer pulled the louse in the direction of whatever was cooking. Beneath clotheslines with sagging loads they went, past knee-high stone foundations and tall brick walls garnished with flourishing greenery. Ahead, the alley opened into a street, where a row of buildings faced them, their peaks darkened by the evening.

Gurga and his prisoner stopped at the alley's end as men wandered by. Those homeward bound few saw the big man first, then the louse, before hurrying off. The smell of something cooking grew stronger and turned Gurga's head to the left. There stood a fat little man, standing beside a big cauldron fixed to wheels, with a grill splayed over the top. He held a long fork, used for stabbing and flipping, and blinked at the monster-sized man before him. The rest of him stayed motionless, paralyzed by the appearance of the pair, before realizing he possessed the very thing they no doubt wanted.

Gurga guided the louse to the street cook while studying what was on the grill. Chunks and thinly sliced strips of roast, seasoned with sweet-smelling herbs that set the mouth to flooding. As long as you were hungry . . .

Gurga waved a finger. "How much?"

The cook blinked again. "Well . . . how much do you want?"

"All of it."

". . . Oh. Well then . . ." and the cook named his price.

Gurga turned the louse around and glared at him. "Stay here. If you want to eat."

The louse said nothing, but his fluttering, darting eyes suggested he very much wanted to eat.

So Gurga bought whatever the cook had and stuffed his face without tasting any of it. When he finished, he paid the man, then asked for a second helping. The cook, smiling weakly, gave it to him on a wooden plate, and Gurga thanked him with a nod.

Holding the plate in one hand, the enforcer pulled his beggar guide into the alley, shoved the louse up against a wall, and offered the plate to him. Without a word, the louse snapped up two handfuls, taking half. He bit off great portions, chewing savagely, before swallowing with effort and taking in more.

Gurga watched him while eating his own share.

"Many thanks," the louse said in between gulps. "So many thanks. Oh Lords above, many thanks. My first real bite in days. Days, I say. Which I didn't have to steal. I don't want to steal, mind you. Who does? Stealing's no good. But when you're without coin and hungry and see an opportunity . . ."

Gurga supposed so, pausing to pick a piece of gristle in his teeth.

"Oh, you got a bit of that," the louse said, scratching feverishly at his beard. "I did as well. With the first bite. Still swallowed it down. I tell you, starving will make you appreciate every damn morsel. You think you would get better quality with the coin you paid. Still tastes good, however . . ."

They finished eating, the evening twilight turning them into shadows. Gurga glanced about until he decided on a spot. He left the wooden plate there, putting it so that it would not fall.

"What's your name?" the louse asked, scratching at an armpit.

Gurga ignored that and pushed his captive back the way they'd previously walked, keeping a hand on his shoulder.

"I'm Darsho," said the louse, believing that might grease the wheels.

It did not. By the time they crossed the street, walked down another alley, and turned right, the introductions had long been forgotten.

"Are we close?" Gurga asked.

". . . Not far now."

He pulled the smaller man around to face him, flea-ridden beard and all. "Just know . . ."

"I know, boy, I know," Darsho groaned. "You'll kill me. You'll smash me. You'll take my head and use it as a pisspot. Fish-hook my eyes and use them as soft marbles. Perhaps even rip my bells free and send them rolling along the street. I *know*, I tell you, I know. I've heard every threat on the Lords' holy ground. And chance a guess on who I've heard most of that from . . . ?"

Having no response to that but sensing he'd been understood, Gurga ignored the question. He righted Darsho, tightened his grip on his shoulder, and let him lead the way, through the darkening maze behind the main walkways. Lamps and firelight glowed through open windows and outlined the shuttered ones. Low conversations and laughter reached their ears, but they walked on, their eyes growing used to the dark.

Then another sound. One of meat striking meat. Repeatedly. A sound Gurga was quite familiar with.

They turned a corner and Darsho stopped, abruptly enough to surprise Gurga. The louse pointed to a section of the alley drenched in darkness, where two shapes appeared even darker than the surrounding night. One shadow held the other by the throat and was slapping his face with his free hand. Repeatedly, each crack ringing out in the dark.

"And *this* one as well," the slapper whispered in a vengeful tone before he hauled back, way back, enough to arch his spine and let his open hand fly.

That blunt smack of skin on skin shattered the otherwise peaceful night.

The slapper gripped his prisoner and slammed him against the wall. There he leaned in. "That's all for you. *All* for you. You dewy little maggot. After all the stupid he-bitches who have been caught before, after all of them disappearing, you think you would *realize* what would happen, 'eh? No one holds back a single coin from me. No one. But you either didn't care or were too stupid to think . . . and here we are. Here we are. The very thought makes me . . ."

Upon that, he growled and hauled back again, this time his hand knotted into a fist.

Which Gurga grabbed with one of his own.

That sudden, irresistible grip upon the slapper caused him to look up, and though it was too dark for details, Gurga glimpsed a flicker of surprise about the eyes. Just before he shoved the smaller man against the wall with all the force of one arm. One arm, but the slapper slammed into it and crumpled. The person being pummeled slunk a few steps away as if stricken with far too much firewater.

Gurga focused on the man at his feet. He grabbed a fistful of shirt—the seams ripping in places—and pulled the dazed topper off the ground. Whereupon he slammed him into the wall again and caught him by the neck before he fell.

Gurga leaned in, squeezing, ignoring the desperate wheeze of someone frantically trying to breathe.

Something stabbed a blade into his lower back, the point deflecting off the leather armor hidden beneath his shirt. That pointed thrust straightened the enforcer. He knew what it was the moment it pressed into his armor and whirled upon the attacker. He punched a face, backing up the whole head up upon its shoulders, and smashing the body beneath it against the opposing wall.

Where he crashed to the ground.

"I couldn't stop him!" Darsho pleaded in a near hysterical voice. "Apologies! *Apologies!*"

And ran for his life.

A scowling Gurga let him go, unable to catch the louse scampering off into the night. Instead he felt the point of contact and deemed the knife didn't get through. He glared at the pair of unconscious pig bastards at his feet. The one who had stabbed him was the same who'd been tenderized by the slapper, which greatly confused Gurga.

The slapper pushed himself up, gasping for breath.

Gurga grabbed him. Mashed him against the wall, teeth to brick, nose to crumbling mortar. There he held him, hard, pressing one meaty forearm into the base of the little blossom's skull. He ignored the peals of pain emanating from the man and inspected what little skin he could see.

Dark. Too dark to see anything.

"You *kog*," the slapper squealed in a half-livid, half-pained voice. "I'll skin your *topper* for this. No one—"

Gurga shoved his elbow into him, cutting off the threat, transforming the words into a squeal of agony. The enforcer leaned in. "You wear the ink?"

A nonsense mewling answered him.

Gurga lessened the pressure and the slapper gulped down a breath.

"What?" the man whispered in dazed discomfort.

"The ink. Do you wear it . . . ?"

"Ink?"

Gurga shook his head. "You with the Sons?"

". . . Aye that."

That one grunt unlocked a frightening wellspring of anger. It narrowed Gurga's vision and bubbled up into his gullet. It enlarged his very heart and strove to take control of his hands. He fought down the impulse, however, to drag this one the length of the alley with his face still pressed to the brick. Shaking himself, Gurga set his jaw before whispering the next question.

"Where?"

"What?" the slapper groaned.

"Where are the Sons of Cholla?"

"You want to meet them?"

Instead of saying yes, Gurga mashed the face up and down against the wall, *twice.* Juices best kept inside spattered the surface, while teeth fell to the ground.

"I'll take you," the slapper slurred when he got his chance. "I'll take you to them."

"Where?" Gurga insisted, applying pressure again.

"They're *close*, they're close. Not far. Not far at all."

Gurga whipped the slapper around. He adjusted his grip around the man's neck, his fingertips nearly touching at the rear. Thus held, the enforcer pawed at his captive, feeling this and that. A dagger fell to the ground. Another dagger. Then a thin spike of a blade tinkled off the stone. A fourth blade hidden in the small of the slapper's back, just above his beltline. The buckle of the same belt came apart, revealing an unpleasant shard of sharpened steel, nearly indistinguishable from the rest of the garment.

All the while, the slapper did not resist.

"That everything?" Gurga asked.

"I think so."

Gurga squeezed the slapper's neck, producing an eye-bulging hiss. He held it, listening to the strained groan whistling from the man. The slapper's eyes narrowed and widened again. Blood from several raw rashes dribbled down Gurga's hand, but the enforcer held on. An organic creak perked his ears an instant before the slapper's eyes slowly closed, as if a great and heavy weariness had finally caught him.

Gurga relaxed his grip.

The sudden gasp for air was noisy and unmistakable.

"Everything," the slapper croaked. "That's everything."

Gurga lifted him off the ground. "Bring me to them," he said, glaring into the smaller man's face. The enforcer dropped him and spun him around. Arms flailed and, for a moment, the slapper might have collapsed, but Gurga grabbed his neck from behind. He shook the slapper, an irresistible force that jangled arms and head alike, urging him to walk. The man did so, and together they moved along the alley.

Not before Gurga stopped beside the one who had attempted to stab him, halting the slapper as well.

He studied the unmoving man lying upon the ground for one deciding moment . . . and stomped on his neck.

The slapper's breathing improved as they walked along in the dark. He spoke only when they reached intersections of streets and always took the unlit alleys and narrow lanes through the city. Gurga held on to his guide by the neck, mindful of the pace and the surroundings. They splashed through something once and at one point trudged over broken planks that rattled underfoot. The squealing of an unseen rat perked their ears before it scurried off.

"This way," the slapper grumbled, stopping at an alley half the width of the one before.

Gurga eyed the dark over his prisoner's head.

"What?" the slapper asked. "You scared?"

"It's dark."

"So it is. That's the trouble with night. You should have done this during the day."

"What's there?"

"The Sons. Some of them, anyway. There's a door at the end."

"How many?"

"One or two."

Gurga thought about it before pushing the slapper forward. Into that narrow passage.

The slapper kicked a slab of wood out of the way, either intentional or not. Gurga stepped on it a moment later, the piece creaking underfoot. Another splash through an unseen puddle as the walls grazed his shoulders, plying him just a touch sideways.

"Here it is," the slapper said, stopping at a large door. "Your worship."

"Open it," Gurga ordered, sensing a brazen smile around his prisoner's words.

"Only opens from the inside."

"How do *you* open it, then?"

"I knock. Punce."

So Gurga slammed the slapper's face against the door. Repeatedly. He grabbed a fistful of oily hair for that little extra grip and pounded the barrier before them. Three hard blows upon the wood and the slapper ceased all movement. After three more, Gurga wasn't sure the salty little pisser was even breathing, so he let him drop.

A scrabbling at the wood beyond, followed by a thread of light, outlining a rectangle.

That rectangle slid across and a mouth, then a set of eyes, came into view.

Gurga jammed his hand into that slot, the edges stropping skin. He got a hold of a neck, hard enough to produce a short grunt of shock and pain. Then he yanked back, cracking the face against the upper lip of the slot. He yanked a second time, then a third and fourth, his victim's eyes squinting shut. A scalp burst apart, staining the wood. Feeling that spill over his fingers, Gurga squeezed, squeezed with whatever strength he possessed in his one hand, and heard a soft, pleading hiss of escaping breath. Then an even softer pop, followed by the muffled crackle of something organic.

The enforcer released the neck and the body dropped.

Then came the dangerous bit.

Gurga hunched down and peered inside, baring teeth as he did so. A small room waited beyond, lit by lamplight and empty. With a touch of urgency, he pushed his arm through the slot and groped about the lower part of the door. His fingers touched the plank barring it. Leaning into the wood, he twisted and reached, utilizing every bit of his arm, while the slot bit into the tender bits of his bicep. *There*, he felt the lower edge of the plank. Setting his jaw, he hooked his fingers underneath it and lifted . . .

Until it fell free.

The heavy clatter froze him for a heartbeat. Then he pulled on the door. It didn't open so he pushed. Inward it swung but only half a stride, blocked by the dead man on the floor. Gurga forced his way inside with two hard shoves. Light from an oil lamp placed upon a nearby shelf spilled over everything. An old table and a chair lay to the right, with a half-eaten apple and a shiny dagger beside it. Two stairways waited beyond that, one going up a level while the other went down.

Gurga looked up.

There, at the top of the stairs, stood a pair of men framed in weak light from the room behind them. Shadow hid their faces.

Gurga charged up the stairs.

One of the lads pulled steel—a short sword—while the other retreated.

"Oh you lovely—" the lad with the sword started to say, when Gurga grabbed his ankle with that extralong arm of his.

He yanked the nog off his feet. The lad bounced his head and spine off the steps in a noisy tumble, his eyes squeezing shut at first impact. Gurga pulled him close and punched the fallen man's throat, producing a deathly gurgle. Not content with one blow, he struck again, plowing iron-shod knuckles into the face, stamping those hard squares stitched into his gloves deep into skin.

Not many could stand after a pair of Gurga's heavy punches, so he stomped up the steps while pawing at the walls. A beat later he reached the landing and rushed into the room.

A mace blurred for his chest.

Gurga caught the shaft in mid-swing, just below the spiked head. He yanked the weapon out of its crushing arc, pulling the wielder off his feet. With a vengeful grunt, the enforcer whipped his attacker into the nearby wall. The lad bounced off the surface and crashed onto a table, conveniently placed there to catch him.

Gurga kicked the piece over and turned to face the room.

Three men stood behind a table filled with dice and bottles. Lamplight shone off a few coins scattered across the surface. Like most during the Sunjan summer, all three wore sleeveless tunics or shirts opened to the navel. Black ink covered their skin, starting from their shoulders and reaching all the way to their elbows. Intricate designs of serpentine coils, thick chains, and crossed knives. The markings on one lad stretched from the side of his neck and ended at the wrist of his right hand. Their shocked expressions twisted into rabid anger. Blades came out—short swords and daggers.

Gurga charged, booting the table before them and scattering all three. He knocked aside a short sword and smashed the owner across the room, his head flopping about as if suddenly boneless. The two others tackled the enforcer. Grunts then as their momentum staggered Gurga into a wall. Knives stabbed into his waistline, blunted by the thick band of leather hidden underneath his shirt.

But then Gurga righted himself.

The enforcer spiked an elbow into the back of a neck, driving the man to his knees.

He punched the other, slamming his oversized fist into the smaller man's profile, smashing an ear and ripping it off. Blood gushed as the lad fell, reaching for his ear which dangled by a shred. With both gang members senseless on the floor, Gurga took his time selecting his targets. He kicked the one-eared lad in the ribs, eliciting a grunt and rolling him into the nearest wall.

The other one slowly climbed to his feet while fumbling with a dagger.

Gurga cracked a fist off the lad's jaw. The lad collapsed, his dagger rattling free. Gurga stomped on the hand, producing a piggish squeal. Livid with agony, the lad clawed at the enforcer's leg to free his squashed appendage. Gurga drove his foot into the lad's head and ended the struggle. He loomed over the fallen, fist poised and ready, but saw that there would be no further danger from that quarter. Before he could catch his breath, the screeching grate of wood grinding against the floor whipped Gurga around.

The first lout, the one with the mace, had shoved aside the table he'd landed upon. Snarling, spitting blood, and furious at being tossed about so, he brandished his weapon at the big man, wanting another go.

Gurga stomped across the floor and clamped a massive hand about the lout's neck.

Over his years as an enforcer, he'd learned to time his choke-hold just long enough to knock his victims out. It didn't take long at all when he really held on, held on *tight*, like he was squeezing for juice.

Like Gurga was doing at that exact moment.

The lout's eyes widened at the overwhelming power pinching off his throat. His first instinct was to swing his mace—an awkward attempt which Gurga easily deflected. The lout tried again. Gurga caught the pig bastard's wrist and held it—watching him squirm in that crushing grip. The pig bastard's eyes narrowed. A spotty snarl then, red and foamy, as he tried and failed to breathe. He clawed at Gurga's wrists—the same ones protected by leather bracers—and his fingernails came free in burps of scarlet. He kicked feebly, clipping Gurga's shin but failing to move the bigger man.

The frantic clawing slackened off.

The kicking became sleepy nudges.

Blood seeped from the gang member's split lip as his face relaxed and his eyes closed.

The enforcer held on for a few beats longer knowing the trick was when to release his victims. Too long and they didn't wake up at all. He'd killed three in such a way over the years. Two by mistake . . .

Thoughts of Sindra, dead and gone in a pool of blood. The little man called Borchus lying next to her.

A scowling Gurga regarded the purpling face before him . . . and let him drop. The unconscious sack of blood and bones flopped to the floor. One leg twisted up behind his rump in a way suggesting a trip to a healer's house would be needed.

Sucking in great chestfuls of air, Gurga glanced about the room. Two of the men groaned, barely moving. They all wore the ink, but by Gurga's thinking he had only found a small nest of them. A small nest, which meant he would have to ask a few questions. Not that he minded asking a few questions.

Rolling his shoulders, he grabbed the nearest one by the foot.

It took a little bit of wrangling, but he disarmed the stunned topper, whose head rolled upon his shoulders as if seized by a feverish dream. Gurga freed a pair of knives from the man's waist and tossed them aside. Once done with that, he slammed his captive against the wall and held him there by his neck. Just enough to allow him a breath.

Minding the others, Gurga rattled the bloodied man. Rattled him until the man released the barest groan and opened red eyes. He glared at his attacker.

Gurga glared back. "You a Son of Cholla?"

The man smiled brazenly, baring stained teeth.

Gurga shook him.

"Aye that," he said weakly. "One of them."

"How many?"

The Son probed the inside of his cheek while studying his captor. "You're dead."

Gurga shook him again.

"Dozens," the Son croaked, meeting the enforcer's eyes. "Hundreds, even. You picked a war with the biggest street clan in Sunja."

"Where are they?"

"Where?" the Son sputtered. "We're *everywhere*, you *punce*."

Gurga checked on the ones still on the floor. "Where are they?" he repeated, adding the barest squeeze to the question. Just a touch more, but the pressure contorted the bloody face before him.

"*Everywhere*," the Son sneered. "*Ev . . . ree . . . waa.*"

The men on the floor stirred, slowly returning to life.

"Where do I find them?" Gurga demanded.

"You . . . don't . . . We . . . find . . . *you.*"

If Gurga could render a man unconscious with one hand, it wasn't surprising what he could do with *both* hands around a neck. He wormed his big fingers around a very pliable throat and secured a much firmer grip.

Knowing his time was done, the Son's eyes flared wide, attempting to issue one last threat.

Having no time or patience for such gurry, Gurga snapped the man's neck, the muffled pop surprisingly loud in the little room. He squeezed once more, vengefully, and tossed the corpse aside. The noise of the falling body roused another, one who cradled his squashed hand close to his chest.

Gurga stomped across the wooden floor as he went for him next.

When that bit of work was done, Gurga descended from the room, his footfalls heavy upon the stairs. Disappointment soured his mood. None of the Sons had revealed where the rest of them might be, despite his best efforts. So he finished them all, one by one, annoyed at their stubborn secrecy, but resolved to find the remainder on his own. The house was a puzzling affair. The main level held only a table, chairs, and a tavern bar with a few shelves behind it, stocked with bottles of what looked to be mead and beer. He located another room downstairs, filled with, of all things, bales of hay stacked one upon the other, and with no other door. A top floor held a half-dozen beds, paltry things stuffed full of straw and covered with thick blankets.

And nothing else.

Scratching at his neck, Gurga puzzled over what he'd found as he returned to the entrance at the bottom of the steps. A corpse lay there, and, as an afterthought, he nudged the dead man with a boot. Nothing. Not that he expected him to move. Thinking about what to do next, Gurga stepped outside and breathed deeply of the night air. He glanced about and spotted a shadow moving, bobbing, against the lightless confines of the alley, toward the far end.

That confused Gurga for a moment, but then his breath caught in his throat.

The slapper was missing.

He'd left him for dead on the ground, which was clearly *not* the case, as he was making a very good attempt to escape. Perhaps to return to another nest belonging to the Sons.

That thought urged the enforcer to give chase.

Not too fast, Gurga told himself, moving along the narrow alley. Shapes sped by in the dark, and the walls grazed his shoulders in a whisper of contact. He slowed, not wanting to alert the escaping man. Nor did he want to catch him. Allowing the battered topper to go where he wanted to very much appealed to Gurga. All he had to do was stay back, keep out of sight, keep his quarry *in* sight, and let the little—

Gurga splashed through the same unseen puddle he'd mucked through earlier, the sound startlingly loud in the alley.

The shadowy figure ahead lurched to a stop—perhaps even turned around—the outline just barely visible.

That halted Gurga in his tracks.

Distant sounds of the city filled the night beyond. No light bled around closed shutters, and no stars shone overhead. Gurga stared, stared hard, refusing to move, to even twitch, for fear of driving his rabbit to run.

The slapper did not move either. Not to Gurga's eyes, and his eyes were doing odd things, mashing shadows together before separating them, making new shapes in the dark. After a few heartbeats, Gurga thought the slapper might have slipped away. So he edged forward a step, his hands brushing the walls.

Another step and still he saw nothing.

So he took another.

Gurga stopped and stared, stared hard at what might have been a crouched figure, but he was no longer certain. So he took another tentative step, placing his foot squarely down on a familiar piece of loose wood, the crunch freezing him to the spot.

Ahead, a shadowy mass fled.

Gurga hurried after him.

Through the alleys they ran, kicking debris and skidding along the tighter spaces. Gurga suffered the worst as a jutting brick hooked his shoulder, slowing him down. The slapper moved faster and reached a faintly lit intersection. There he turned a corner and was gone from sight. Not long after Gurga reached the same corner and halted.

There.

Against the dim light of streetlamps, people strolled past an alley mouth, and the slapper's outline hurried toward them.

Gurga lurched into a run.

The slapper reached the street and bolted right.

Fuming, his hands gliding along rough walls, Gurga hurried into the open street as well, surprising perhaps a score of people out for a nighttime walk. He looked over their startled expressions and regarded the busy street. Scores of souls wandering the night.

Gurga pushed through them all, searching for the escaping slapper somewhere ahead.

And couldn't see him at all.

He stopped before a pair of buildings with shuttered windows long closed for the night. Barrels and other mysterious debris cluttered the lane between them. The gurry strolling by didn't seem disturbed in the least, so he turned and hurried along, hoping to spot the escaping man.

Nothing. Nothing ahead, except faces staring back at him. Scared expressions, all of them, and no hint as to which direction to take.

Looking around, Gurga slowed in a stream of individuals enjoying the night, while frustration welled up inside of him.

Damnation. He'd lost sight of the man.

The slapper had vanished.

13

The slapper, whose name was Gallwin, held his aching head as he weaved through the wandering nighttime crowd. The bleeding had slowed to an annoying dribble that found his eyes, and his nose throbbed mercilessly and trickled blackness. His mouth, however, worried him more. Several teeth had been mashed down to jagged nubs, and every breath felt like a whetstone stropping the edges.

What worried him the most, however, what truly terrified him, was being caught by the same giant who had hurt him in the first place.

Lords above, he thought in a panicked daze and glanced back to see if he was still being pursued. The giant had killed them all. *Had* to have killed them all. He was the only one left. The only one who *knew*. And he had to alert the others. Before he dropped on the spot.

His strength waning, Gallwin halted near a wooden post, before a closed storefront of some unknown wares. Blood found his eyes again, forcing him to take a moment to scrub them clear. He then turned this way and that, blinking mightily, wondering where exactly he was and if the giant was coming after him. At the very edge of his vision, where the streetlamps cast warm, orange hues upon the roaming crowds, he could see the giant, searching for him. A bolt of fear bent him over and he lurched away, avoiding the pockets of light. *Lords above*, his mouth pained him and his nose was becoming worse. He tried touching it, but the resulting agony was as sharp and stunning as a fist to the face. In the drunken rabble wandering about, however, his condition went largely unnoticed. He swayed through the shadows, passing clumps of people sitting on porches, drinking, smoking, and talking. He avoided a few unfortunate toppers retching loudly in the street.

All that moving, however, left him feeling faint, so he slunk around a corner of some darkened structure and slumped to the ground. The world tipped and wobbled, and at some point Gallwin lost consciousness. He woke with a lurch, staring at the surrounding darkness. All seemed quiet and the nearby street wasn't so busy anymore. Slowly, using the wall for support, Gallwin stood. He leaned out and cautiously checked on matters. No one. Not a person in sight. Even the lamps were dark, their nightly allowance long spent.

Rubbing his nose and immediately regretting it, he staggered out into a featureless street, where the nearby buildings were darker than the starless night above. He turned a corner and sighted the waning light of a solitary oil lamp. At the edge of the light stood one large structure, flickers of firelight visible inside some open windows. A pair of men stood about a doorway. As Gallwin got closer, he recognized them as enforcers, both bald-headed and bearded, wearing leather armor that bulged around the paunches. Broad-shouldered and menacing, the men eyed patrons stumbling through the doorway.

Alehouse, Gallwin realized and hobbled for it, knowing exactly where he was.

One of the enforcers spotted him. The guard straightened, alerted his companion, and moved to block Gallwin from entering the place.

"It's me, you punce," Gallwin growled, but what came out was *Ishmee y'puncssh*. The sound widened his bloody eyes, as he barely recognized his own voice. Worse, the bit of breath he used had fired up the jagged ends of his teeth and brought water to his eyes.

He stopped before the pair and waved his hands about as if that might help.

"Gallwin?" one enforcer, Corlak, muttered in disbelief.

"That's Gallwin?" asked the other, called Barrick.

"Yes, yes, it's me, let me in," which *sounded* like *Yesh yesh, ishme, lemmein.*

"Who did this to you?" demanded Corlak.

"And why didn't they finish you off?" asked Barrick with a smirk.

Both bastards chuckled then, flashing spotty teeth, perhaps a full set between the pair of them.

Gallwin glanced from one to the other, the effort nearly causing him to fall over.

"What do you want?" Corlak asked.

"Bit late, isn't it?" added Barrick.

"Early for this one," Corlak said. "Probably only got up a short time ago."

"Before or after the thrashing?" Barrick wanted to know.

They chuckled again.

"So what do you want?" Corlak asked again.

"Let . . . me . . . in," Gallwin said, enunciating hard enough that it hurt.

"In you go then," Corlak said while rubbing at an eye. "Mind you, it *is* late. Practically tomorrow. Morg won't be happy to see you."

Gallwin attempted to climb the first of two steps and fell to his knees.

"Here then," said Barrick, helping the man up. "Come on."

"Hold onto the punce in case he falls over again," said Corlak.

"He's all bloody," Barrick complained, hooking an arm underneath Gallwin. Together, the enforcers walked him inside. The smell of spilled beer hit Gallwin then, despite his nose being smashed, but the lamplight seemed out of focus to him, his vision smeared. The interior glowed eerily, as if seen through a fog. No one sat at any of the tables and chairs, some of which were overturned. Barrick swung Gallwin close to a thick post, a hoarse giggle as he pulled the injured man away at the last instant.

The bar came into view, with lanterns hung behind it, the light shimmering magically off rows of bottles.

Until Morg stepped into view.

Pallid Morg, tall and stiff as the planks he stood upon, blinked at the sight brought to him. And with every passing moment, his scowl deepened.

"Lords above," he sneered as the group came closer. "What happened to you?"

Barrick shrugged free of Gallwin, who plopped both elbows hard onto the counter. Even then, he seemed on the verge of falling, if not for Corlak steadying him and keeping him in place with a hand.

"Got smashed," Gallwin groaned, his words coming out all squished.

"Clearly," Morg agreed. "You're an unfit mess."

Barrick smiled in agreement.

"Look," Morg offered as he reached underneath the counter. He brought up a polished mirror and angled it before Gallwin's features.

"Muh," the battered man got out, stunned by the sight. A right and proper state. His poor face, red and purpled, was grossly swollen on one side, one eye narrowed to a slit. His lips resembled fat worms flattened upon cobblestones after a rainfall. His nose was most certainly broken, crusted and bloody and squished at an angle painful to even gaze upon. Blood stained the upper neck of his tunic and soaked the material covering his chest.

A ragged squeak of disbelief passed Gallwin's lips.

"Who did this?" Morg asked, not offering a drop of firewater to ease the pain.

Gallwin started talking, struggling to make himself understood.

Seeing no need to linger, Corlak left them all and returned to the alehouse entrance. The enforcer rubbed his face and sighed mightily, hoping Morg would tell him to close the door at any moment, signaling the alehouse was done for the night. Corlak had a room upstairs, and he thought about his bed and sleeping past noon.

While that thought lingered, he noticed someone standing before a shuttered storefront, a score of strides away. A big outline of a man, edging into sight from the dark. Corlak blinked, as it was hard to see—the lamps were all but burned out for the night. He leaned over the alehouse railing and frowned at the figure, if only because it was so late, and not another person was to be seen.

The figure walked across the empty street in long, eager strides, twice those of anyone else. The head seemed barren and black, as if draped in leather, but the face and beard beneath gradually came into sight.

"What do you want?" Corlak asked as the stranger approached.

No answer as the stranger marched straight for the alehouse, getting bigger with every step. Concern flared within Corlak—enough for him to reach for his nearby club, waiting against a post.

"Looking for a morning drink, are you?" Corlak spoke as he straightened, reassured by the grip of the weapon. He positioned himself atop the steps, blocking the entrance while making a point to show that length of the exceptionally hard wood.

To his surprise, the big man stopped before him.

"We're closed," Corlak warned, looking *up* into the brute's narrowed eyes, and no longer feeling so confident.

The lightless street hid the big one's face, which studied Corlak for a moment, as if discovering something.

"Is that ink?" rumbled a voice. "On your neck?"

Corlak smiled and nodded. "Aye that, it is. You know what that means, don't you?"

Which was when the big man grabbed him by the throat.

Finishing his story, a sniffling Gallwin stopped for breath and rooted around the inside of his mouth with a finger.

"You understand all that?" Barrick asked while scratching at his beard.

A clatter from the entrance turned two of them around and lifted Morg's questioning face.

Although partially draped in shadows, a man stood outside the open door.

A big man.

That big man entered the alehouse, his boots heavy upon the floor. From one hand hung Corlak, stretched out by the neck—face-up, utterly limp, his knuckles and heels dragging.

The big man dropped him, and that jerked Gallwin from his silence.

"*Thash th'whon!*" he blubbered and pointed, spitting as he spoke. "*Him!*"

Barrick pulled a pair of knives from his belt, the hidden kind, where the short blades stuck out from between fingers. He rushed to meet the huge invader, who gathered up a chair and smashed it across the oncoming attacker's face. Spindly legs flew as the seat of solid wood exploded against Barrick's skull, dropping him in a heap.

The big man wasn't done, however. He closed in on the man on the floor, lifted his head, and punched him, one blow to the face.

Eyes wide and staring, Morg pushed himself up against the bar.

The big man strode forward with a face full of hate. When he was close enough, he grabbed the front of Gallwin's tunic. Fibers ripped as he lifted the bloodied man off the floor, high enough that Gallwin started squirming.

The big man growled a note of recognition as he studied the battered face before him—before he hurled Gallwin over the bar. Gallwin crashed face-first into the bright row of bottles. Clay fragments flew as Morg barely got out of the way. Gallwin fell to the floor, landing in a dappling pool of shards and drink.

Morg looked up as a massive fist clutched the front of his robes. The big man pulled Morg across the bar, his knees cracking off the hard edges.

Then their faces were very close.

Hot breath steamed Morg's features as the bearded brute studied him one way and then the other, inspecting his face, profile, and neck.

"No ink on you," the big man rumbled in disappointment.

That widened Morg's eyes.

"You with the Sons?"

"No . . ." Morg blurted, but the word was laced with fear thick enough for both men to know it.

"You lie . . ."

"He's with the Sons . . ." rumbled another, more familiar voice, one that almost brought tears of relief to Morg's eyes.

For his *third* enforcer, the mighty Sundro, wandered into view, back from the shite troughs where, at the end of every night, he would frequent for a long and welcome squat. Morg had often complained about the time Sundro took for a squat, but right at that moment, the barkeep could not have been happier to see him.

"Sundro," Morg squawked, before his captor violently shook him, shook him like a child's toy, up and down and all around.

Right into the solid girth of a nearby post.

Morg's head bounced off that dense pillar of wood, leaving a wet blot at the point of contact. His eyes crossed briefly before Gurga threw him aside, and he collided with and tumbled over the end of the bar.

Gurga faced Sundro and gauged the size of his new foe. He was a large one. Not nearly as towering as Gurga, perhaps a head shorter, but broad, with bulging shoulders and a fat midsection protected in bands of leather. In fact, Sundro was a potato-shaped barbarian of a man. A sleeveless tunic left his thick arms exposed, for all to see the ink upon them. A lattice of spearheads and something that resembled the ebony petals of flowers. A heavy beard concealed his neck, and the mop of hair had been cut perfectly across his forehead, some two fingers above his eyes.

In turn, Sundro examined the men scattered about the floor. His hands clenched and unclenched into fists as his anger rose, contorting his face.

"You killed them . . ." Sundro rasped.

"You with the Sons as well?" Gurga asked.

The enforcer glared and nodded, eager for what was to come.

"Then I'll kill you, too," Gurga said.

Absorbing that, Sundro brought up a pair of heavy fists, presenting a knobby ridge of knuckles, the skin white and scarred and toughened by years in the trade.

Gurga showed his own leatherbound fists, gloomy with iron bits and stained by the night's business.

On some unspoken signal, the two enforcers circled each other, sizing up the challenge before them. They kicked aside meddlesome furniture when needed, shattering the grim stillness of the situation. In short time a ring of overturned tables and chairs surrounded them. Despite his bulbous size, Sundro moved confidently, hinting at a deceptive speed. He even punched the air at times, loosening up the power in those heavy arms.

"I'll break your back across my knee," he whispered from behind his bobbing fists.

Gurga said nothing to that. He'd heard much the same many times before.

Then, as if tired of the dance, Sundro charged forward. He jabbed, two quick darts that came within a finger of Gurga's face before the larger man jerked himself back a step. Sundro swung his right fist, announcing it with a loud grunt, bringing it around like the bony battering ram it was.

Gurga blocked it off a bracer and circled to his left. He avoided a thick post and kicked away a chair.

Sundro came after him, swinging—three jabs and a looping right aimed for a chin—each strike punctuated with a piggish grunt. Gurga slapped away all three shots and absorbed the last on his left shoulder. He cocked his own fist for a counter, but Sundro ducked low and away, quickly getting out of range despite his mass. Not nearly as slow as his size might suggest—but then again, Gurga had fought his share of quick-stepping troublemakers.

Snarling, Sundro waded in again. He launched two probing lefts followed by a hammer of a right. Gurga blocked the left punches but the right landed—hard—above his hip. His leather absorbed most of the blow, but there was no doubt about the power behind it.

Gurga raised his fist again and Sundro ducked and bobbed, protecting his head as he got out of harm's way. Realizing the strike never fell, Sundro stepped one way before going back the other, at times lowering his guard and leaning forward, goading his opponent to take a swing.

Arm cocked like the weapon it was, Gurga extended his other arm as a guard, warning his opponent of what waited for him if he grew brave. All the while, Sundro's breathing increased, becoming a ragged, whistling bellows of a noise, interrupted by huge intakes of air.

It was during one of those big gulps that someone moved behind the bar, their elbows and knees crunching over the jagged slivers of broken bottles.

Sundro rushed forward again, swinging both arms. He pummeled Gurga's lower abdomen, landing several shots and buckling the bigger man. Four solid hits before Sundro struck with an uppercut, connecting with the enforcer's bearded jaw. The force cracked Gurga's head back, slamming him into a stout post. A chugging Sundro waded in, hammering his foe's armored midsection. Heavy shots they were, thrown from the hip with Sundro's full mass behind them, and each bone-jarring blow rattled Gurga against the wood.

Then, on some odd impulse, Sundro stopped punching and rammed a shoulder into the bigger man's guts.

The first one bent Gurga against the post.

The second shoulder actually hurt.

There was no third, however. Having enough, Gurga reached down and grabbed that cow kiss of hair, knotting his fingers deep. He got a great, greasy handful and uprooted the very head attached to it all.

Sundro's expression was one of surprise and pain as Gurga plowed an armored fist into his nose. Skin and bone burst apart in a soupy spray of matter. Sundro's eyes squeezed shut and his knees wobbled, but Gurga held on, refusing to let him fall.

Whereupon he reared back and struck him again.

And again.

Great, falling boulders of bone and metal crashed upon the smaller enforcer's face. Sundro's nose flattened in a splash of blood. A great slit popped open under an eye. A goose egg welled up over his other eye. Broken teeth sprayed across the floor. He faltered and flailed blindly for the hand holding him.

Gurga's last punch freed his opponent from his grip, leaving him a handful of hair. That blow smashed mostly forehead and splayed the enforcer flat across the floor, straight-legged and twitching.

Comfortably winded from the pounding and not wasting any time, Gurga rounded the stricken man. He placed a heavy bootheel upon the enforcer's throat. The contact causing a dazed Sundro's swelling eyes to crack open.

Gurga drove his bootheel down, repeatedly, until Sundro no longer moved.

Grimacing, aching from the short but meaningful combat, Gurga glanced about the place and saw no other threats. He focused on the bar and walked around it, flexing one shoulder and wincing at where Sundro had struck him.

As soon as he rounded the bar, Gallwin propped himself up on one shredded elbow, blackness dribbling from a multitude of fine cuts. His mashed and bleeding features knotted in puzzlement at who stood before him, before switching to one of pure terror.

"*Muh*," Gallwin got out before scrambling away on all fours.

Gurga grabbed an ankle, his grip as unforgiving as an iron shackle, and pulled his squealing rabbit back. Gallwin kicked, but Gurga had no patience for such foolishness. He caught the foot, seized it really, and yanked the criminal out from behind the bar—over that sharp rug of broken clay.

Gallwin screamed.

Gurga clutched an arm, then a shirt, and hauled the smaller man up before slamming him against a corner of shelves, the same shelves once decorated with many fancy bottles. Things trembled and crunched. Clearly in agony, Gallwin didn't have the strength to do anything more than allow it to happen.

"This it?" Gurga asked, over his fists knotted in a bloody shirt.

No response, so he shook the smaller man until his eyes opened.

"*What?*" Gallwin bawled.

"This all of you here? All of the Sons?"

"The Sons?" Gallwin repeated and smiled, the sight repulsing. "Of course not, you unfit *animal*. The Sons . . . are *everywhere*. They're every*thing*. They'll find you, and when they—"

Gurga shook him, ending that nonsense. "Where are they?"

Panting, a defeated Gallwin eyed his captor. "I'll tell you. If only to send you to them. So they can kill you."

Gurga truly jangled him about then, hard enough to bounce his chin off his chest, and for his remaining teeth to clap together. Gallwin shuddered, spat blood, and at times released little childlike squeals until the ride stopped.

He slumped in the bigger man's clutches, struggling for breath. "Oh," he whispered, his senses scrambled. "I wish . . . I could see . . . Linfur . . . when he kills you."

Linfur.

"Where is he?" Gurga demanded.

Gallwin told him, and the enforcer made him repeat the location of the place.

"In back of a butcher's store?"

"Aye that. Back of a butcher's store. There. You'll find. Your death."

Setting his jaw, Gurga pulled the smaller man off the shelves and turned him around. The bar's countertop was a solid length of wood, fashioned from half a log, and as sturdy and unmoveable as Sunja's walls. The edge of the bar was a dull thing, fashioned by hand but scratched and worn from the years.

Gurga gripped Gallwin by the back of his head and, with whatever strength he had, plowed the Son's throat into that iron-hard edge.

The night sky lifted, giving way to dawn as Gurga left the alehouse. He stopped on the outer porch, his boots scuffling, and studied the scene before him. Not a soul walked the streets and the oil lamps and odd torches had long since burned out.

Taking in a deep breath of morning air, he lumbered away. Here and there, a few lost lads lay along the edges of the cobblestone, sleeping off the night's drinking, but they were of no concern to Gurga.

Still, it took some time to determine where he was exactly. Took more time for him to find the alehouse where he had paid for a room. The door creaked when he pushed it open, and the floorboards rattled as he plodded into the place. A few folks slept on tables, heads cradled in folded arms. Some lay sprawled upon benches with their faces up, lips sputtering spit with every expulsion of breath.

Rolling his shoulder, Gurga went for the steps. A deep tiredness had seized him, and not a relieved one, where he knew his work was done for the night. There was more to do. Perhaps much more, but all he wanted right then was sleep. When he was rested and ready, he would go hunting for the one called Linfur.

And those unfortunate enough to keep his company.

14

Daylight bled through a pair of red curtains, soaking the room in a shade of deep-reckoning carmine. Entangled in a swirl of sweaty blankets, Linfur cracked open an eye and stared at the curtains. They were closed. Which was interesting because he thought he'd left them open. The nights had been insanely hot, bringing no relief at all from the ruthless summer. This morning promised to be the same, judging by how no wind rustled the curtains.

Linfur glared at them. Did he close them? Couldn't remember. He lifted his head and sighted the fat neck of a clay bottle. Firewater. Sunja's best, in his opinion. Far too good, and he'd been indulging in the best perhaps a touch too much lately. It was affecting his memory, or so he suspected.

Voices drifted into the room, crinkling Linfur's brow. He sampled morning air thick and heavy with moisture, enough to drink like soup. Groaning, he rolled onto his back and scratched his bare belly before kicking at the blanket sticking to him. The kicking became a thrashing as he strove to free himself. Once uncovered, Linfur sighed and considered the curtains again.

Dying Seddon, he cursed and pushed himself up, muscular arms rippling. Chains and entwined serpents covered those arms from wrists to shoulders. Another reason why he disliked the summer months, as it meant he had to wear long sleeves to hide such lovely art. Oh, he would flash the ink when he needed to, to grease the kogs or throw a thunderbolt of fear into a punce, but Jaro frowned on anyone displaying the ink all day. Only Strach managed to get away with that.

And Strach had long disappeared. Assumed dead.

Assumed dead, Linfur thought, hanging his head between his meaty shoulders. A lick of sandy hair spilled over his angular face. He pushed it back, but it again fell into his eyes.

Morning, he thought, and sprang from the bed.

With a hint of urgency, he threw open the curtains and ignored the wall of planks across the alley. He stuck his head out, holding back his hair, and grimaced at the overhead clouds.

Dying Seddon, he snarled. No way of knowing how early it was, but by the sights and sounds of the crowds wandering the nearby streets, it was well past dawn. So he rushed to a washbasin and poured water from a jug. A quick scrub followed, where he wiped out his pits and cracks before drying himself with the damp blanket from the night before. Then came a not-so-liberal sprinkle from a bottle of scented water, which he rubbed under his chin, around his neck, chest, and belly, and along his wrists. He then pulled on fine, gray pants and a belt, which concealed a knife sheathed at the back of his waist. A pair of scabbards, one above the other, held a short sword and a dagger off his left hip. He threw on a white shirt, which tumbled over his broad shoulders and reached his hips, hiding all of his ink. His boots went on last.

Thus dressed, Linfur slicked back his hair with both hands, took a snort of morning air, and regarded the bottle of firewater on the nearby table.

Shrugging, he picked it up and shook it. A few mouthfuls remained. He drank those, the gulps loud in his ears. After a violent shiver, he wiped his mouth and belched. He went to the bed and hauled out a pisspot, partially filled from the night before. That one he pushed aside, carefully, so as not to spill the contents. Wincing at the smell, he checked the *second* pisspot beneath the bed, located behind the first, and quickly pulled it out. That one had a lid, which Linfur flipped in a hurry to reveal a pair of small leather purses.

He plucked them both free and stuffed them into hidden pockets under his shirt. After that he hurried to the door and removed the two planks above and below. Out he went, past a few doors that blurred by and down a hallway, where it opened into a rather rustic upstairs overlooking the floor of a sizable alehouse. No open windows there, leaving the place resembling a square cave of sorts, where light seeped through the cracks and dust drifted along the beams. Linfur reached a wide staircase and thundered down it.

A pair of scraggly louts climbed to their feet upon hearing the noise. The barkeep turned at the commotion and watched him descend, giving a morning nod while wiping out a mug.

"Anyone perish last night?" Linfur yelled at him, tossing each brutish life-taker a leather purse.

The barkeep closed his eyes and solemnly shook his head.

Damn shame, thought Linfur and rushed out the door. Breath-stealing humidity greeted him as he glanced left then right. People walked by in numbers that suggested it was indeed morning. And he had matters to attend to.

The two throat cutters from the alehouse stopped behind him. One was called Chur. The other was Grohk. They were unsightly bastards, grizzled, intimidating, and hard to behold at any time. Neither man spoke and Linfur didn't bother talking to the asslickers. He started walking, plowing through the crowds, glaring at anyone coming toward him. Those that recognized him quickly got out of the way. The ones that didn't saw the two brutes flanking him and *then* got out of the way.

"Why didn't either one of you tits wake me?" Linfur grumbled as he marched through the tide of bodies.

"You said not to," protested Chur.

"Said you'd kill us," added Grohk in a gravelly voice.

"I always say that," Linfur grumped, which was true. He always did, and he meant it every unfit time. The two hellions tethered to his ass were smarter than they looked.

A food booth caught his eye, one with fancy pastries smelling of sweet spice. That smell hooked him hard. He charged the baker, a little old woman dressed in even older clothing and an apron. Her little button eyes widened at the sight of him as he stopped and studied the pastries ready for sale.

Without sparing her a look, he snatched up a cloth satchel and grabbed everything in sight. With every morsel he took, the woman's sallow face dropped a little more.

But she dared not stop him. And she dared not say a word.

Linfur left her without paying her a single coin, but not before stuffing half a pastry into his face. He chewed as quickly as he walked, glaring at the city, at times sputtering fragments while wiping his mouth. Not once did he offer the two dogs following him a bite. Not even a lick.

He entered a familiar narrow alley with his guards following. Piles of rubbish dressed the walls, mostly sticks and discarded crates, while a thin stream of gruel-like gravy marred the cobblestones right down the middle. Linfur marched through it all, avoiding the larger puddles, and soon spotted the figure he so wanted to see. There, amid the gurry, sat a beggar with his legs splayed before him. A pair of tattered pants covered those limbs, while a scraggly beard reached his waist. One eye was blue but the other had clouded over, and when he saw Linfur, he released a gasp of horror and struggled to his feet.

Linfur finished his pastry and, with a quick lick of his lips, slapped the miserable bastard across the frizzy jowls. Wasting no time, Linfur pinned him to the cobblestones with a knee. One hand flicked out a thin dagger with nearly magical dexterity, and he put the tip to the beggar's eye.

"Good morning, master," Linfur smiled with forced pleasantry. "Where is it?"

The beggar whimpered, very much aware of the blade at his eye. He pointed a shaking finger at the wall across from him. A small pile of garbage rested at the base of the stone foundation.

Linfur scowled. "Where? Underneath the gurry?"

The beggar nodded as much as he dared.

Linfur got off the man and went to the wall, where he immediately drew back. "You didn't squat around here, did you?"

The beggar rattled his head.

"Didn't empty the bull? Hm? Slap the dew off the sheep's head?"

Another hard shake.

"Because if you *did* piss a stream around here, and if any of your fluids stain *me*, I'll personally flay your bells from your crotch. But you know that, don't you?"

Another energetic nod.

"Shut up," Linfur warned him. "Grohk, get the coin would you?"

Not worried about any such fluids, Grohk sprang into action while Chur took up his companion's duty, on lookout at the mouth of the alley. Grohk kicked at the debris before kneeling and pawing at the ground. With a few questions posed by pointing a finger, he eventually upended a loose brick, tossed it aside, and picked at whatever lay underneath.

All the while, Linfur watched the fearful beggar, now sitting against the wall.

Until he grew impatient. "Well?"

"Seven coins," Grohk reported.

"Seven?"

"Aye that."

"Gold?"

"Silver."

Of course. Not like the rabble was going to get gold when they held out a hand, but Linfur was always hopeful. He fumed at the beggar. "Seven silver? You're not hiding a few coins for yourself, are you? Be a terrible, terrible shame if you did."

The old man shook his head as if he'd smashed his toe with a war hammer.

"So just the handful then?"

A terrified nod.

Linfur sighed. "I don't believe you're begging hard enough, lad. May I call you lad? Yes, of course I can. Look. This isn't hard work you're at. Not at all. All you need to do is . . . approach whoever looks like they have a bit of coin . . . and *ask*. Just ask. That's all you do. And look like you *need* the coin. I mean look wretched. *Deplorably* wretched. Even more wretched than you do *now*. Get them to pity you, like dogs with sad eyes and a missing leg looking for scraps. Hm? Like half-dead cats scratching at a door. Do you understand any of this? Does what I'm saying sound reasonable to you?"

The beggar nodded energetically.

"Here," Linfur said with a smile. "Let me help you."

Without warning, he punched the old man's face, bouncing the gray-haired head off the wall behind him. The old soul fell over with a shrill whimper while reaching for his bleeding nose. Linfur braced a forearm against the wall and kicked, driving his boot into a dirty midsection, crumpling his victim. He kicked three times before his shoulders slumped and he took in a breath of air.

"There," Linfur said, standing back while flicking his hair from his eyes. "Wait. No. You still don't look wretched enough. Like you don't really need the coin. Hold on . . ."

Three more kicks to the body—fast, hard blows—and the beggar stopped moving.

"Now then," Linfur huffed, toe scuffing a bit of gurry onto the motionless man. "That looks better. Don't wash that blood off. Leave it. Let it dry. Use that when you beg. Make sure they see it. You can wash it off tomorrow. Or the morning after. I'll expect to see triple what you have here today. At least triple. Understood?"

With his face mashed against the ground, the beggar managed the barest of nods.

"Excellent," Linfur said, and stomped on the last two fingers of the old man's hand.

That bit of savagery summoned a squeal, which Linfur silenced with yet another boot to the belly. "Apologies," Linfur explained without a shred of remorse. "Hard to stop once you get started. Here. Give me that."

Grohk held out the coin, stained and grimy, and Linfur frowned in distaste at the sight. "No, perhaps you keep hold of them. That one probably had his pisser in his hand before he hid it away."

Not bothered by the thought, Grohk stuffed the silver inside a pocket.

Linfur left the unconscious beggar bleeding upon the ground. He did not look back as he proceeded to his next stop.

"Seven silver pieces," he muttered as he walked. "I'll need a right big leather sack to hold it all if this continues. Seven. Seven *silver*. Oh my . . ."

Three young women walked toward him, and Linfur stopped at the sight, halting his guards with a lurch. Fair-haired and dressed in quality robes, belts cinched at their waists to flatter their curves. Linfur's lips puckered in appreciation while he wagged his eyebrows suggestively, believing it to be charming. It was, to some degree, as the women smiled as they walked on by, turning the Son of Cholla agent completely around to further admire them from behind.

Until Chur and Grohk came into view.

With a frown, Linfur tucked his charm away and got walking once again. With Chur and Grohk at his back, the gang leader moved about what he considered his underworld kingdom, paying each of his loathsome subjects a visit.

The beggars. From one miserable wretch to the next, Linfur and his hounds stalked the cobblestone maze comprising the backstreets of Sunja, treading through territory that was a little more familiar to him with each visit. This day was an important one, however, as it was a week since he'd last been about, gathering whatever bit of coin his filthy minions had managed to wring out of the populace.

So they moved along, visiting one woeful individual after another, melancholy expressions shifting to absolute terror upon seeing their approach. Linfur applied himself wholeheartedly to the role of right evil bastard. He grabbed necks and spat into faces, punched the ones slow to answer questions and put the boots to those who truly needed a lesson. All fine entertainment in Linfur's mind, and to think he scoffed for a day or two when he'd been given the task. Strach must have enjoyed every moment in such a role, as Linfur was enjoying it.

Morning rolled smoothly into afternoon, the rain holding off while he made his rounds. He visited nearly a score of beggars under his watch, snatching away every piece of silver or gold they had hidden away.

Don't pester the merchants, Brejo had warned. Well, Linfur *had* pestered a few. Seemed like it wouldn't be right if he didn't—to terrorize those who had practically nothing at all and then leave the fat ones alone? Foolishness, in his mind. Still, he was wary of whom he pressed, for fear of some wandering agent noticing his work and then reporting their findings to the kings.

By kings, he meant the Sons themselves.

One more stop, and he would visit them.

The storehouse stood in the poorer section of the city, a few streets over from the whispered Iron Games and the residence of the Sons. If the northern part of the city shone like a gemstone on the darkest nights, this part, this tiny hole, was the unwashed blossom one could smell a day away. Linfur knew the place. Jaro himself had given him directions, and Jaro had a way of making one remember details with a mere look.

Very few people wandered the area about the storehouse, knowing the reputation of the place. The street watch rarely patrolled here, due to payments made by the Sons to ensure that very thing. With so little traffic, Linfur and his boys quickly strode along a narrow lane. A few homes still stood down that dark strip, the owners old and feeble and all too trusting of the rusted spikes they'd installed in their stone walls for protection. Farther down the lane, however, the scenery grew dirtier and more decrepit. Weeds flourished between the cobblestones, rustling with the barest breeze. Abandoned homes and storefronts slouched in sagging ruin, while roof slats and clay tiling lay in crumbling piles along their sides. Doors lay flat across thresholds, hanging from rusty hinges or rotting strands of leather. Piss pools lay in abundance.

Shadows ducked out of sight upon seeing the three men. A number of black cats with humorless eyes and swishing tails crouched upon one roof and watched Linfur and his henchmen as they passed.

Linfur ignored the animals, avoided the piss pools, and picked at his earlobe. It was odd how quiet things were here, when life bustled only a few streets over. Here, however, a near-perfect silence held, not unlike a prisoner holding his breath until the jailors passed. Linfur regarded some of the darker windows as they walked along, feeling fearful eyes upon them. Without question, a number of beggars hid inside those places, scurrying at the sight of anyone. Especially him. Strach had ruled this area with a steely fist, and while news of his demise had circulated the streets, there was very little rejoicing.

His subjects were waiting for his replacement.

Now, admittedly, Linfur was a bit behind in his work. One day soon, however, he and a few hardy lads would go through this whole area and explore every crack, every hole, to see who was hiding from them.

The storehouse loomed ahead, as wide as a house and a full level higher than its nearest neighbor. It appeared narrow for its height, but once inside, its true size became evident. The storehouse was long, stretching all the way back, with the only entrance facing the street. Old but serviceable shutters covered the windows, suggesting there was still a grudging level of care in keeping it.

Linfur stopped before two large doors, one with its own wicket gate. Thick planks barricaded the nearby windows. Though it looked deplorable, closer inspection would change one's mind. It was a solid building, made of old but heavy timbers, kept together by sizable wooden pegs and rusting nails.

Linfur stepped aside and jerked his head at Chur, who hammered the door with the pommel of his dagger. The blows rang out, barely rattling the wood. No one answered so he pounded again.

They exchanged looks and waited. No one answered.

Growing impatient, Linfur shooed his henchman out of the way. He faced the door, listening for activity, wondering if he would have to return later in the day with more lads . . . He'd be right and proper annoyed if he had to do that.

Something thumped inside, followed by a faint scratching upon the wood.

The door opened just a crack, revealing a tall brute wearing a shirt of chainmail. The guardian widened the crack a little more, allowing a peek of a few other shadows inside. Just a peek before a familiar face filled the gap. Brown hair, eyes, and neatly trimmed beard.

"Ah, it's you lot," the bearded face smiled, while glancing left and right and over Linfur's shoulder.

Linfur bared a cold smile. "Just us, good . . ."

The bearded man returned the smile but didn't provide a name. Something Linfur appreciated and yet was annoyed by. "May we enter?" he asked, forcing the charm.

"Apologies, but no, good Linfur," the man said. "All manner of sorcery is being flung about inside." He stepped into the day, placing his back to the door.

"It is our property," Linfur reminded him.

"It is that, but for *my* sake, I cannot. Not because of you, for your reputation is well-known, but because my master wishes it to be so. Which is another reason why he pays extra, I believe."

"You have me there," Linfur admitted, rubbing his hands. "Well, then, do you have it?"

Glancing around once again, the bearded man handed over a small pouch, which Linfur immediately took. "What's this?"

"Payment for the month."

"I was expecting—"

"We are having difficulties with our deliveries," the bearded man said. "The border watches and city guards are proving to be more, ah, vigilant. The border patrols in particular. We haven't received anything in two weeks now."

That was a surprise. "In two weeks?" Linfur repeated, feigning a frown. "That's terrible."

"I know."

"The Sons enjoy their herbs."

"As many people do."

"It relaxes them."

"Believe me when I tell you, these delays are playing upon my master's mind. Very much so."

"As mine. As ours, as I'll speak on the Sons' behalf. You're not receiving any snow orchids at all?"

The bearded man shook his head.

"Damnation," Linfur said. "They very much enjoyed what you gave them."

"We're working on matters now, but . . . I'm afraid *that* is all I can offer."

Linfur untied the leather strings of the bag and peered inside. He blinked, surprised at the contents—a good handful of blue and green gemstones. "Well," he said, impressed at the sight. "I think the Sons will be happy with this as payment. Not what we were expecting or wanted, but . . ."

"My, ah, most profound apologies . . ."

That cocked Linfur's eyebrow. "Well . . . this will certainly do. And if it doesn't, I'll be back. For more."

"You'll get a good price for those stones."

We'll get a damn good price for these stones, Linfur thought, handing the payment off to Grohk, but what he *said* was, "Doubtful. Hard to sell gemstones in the city."

"I hope to have a gift for you next time," the bearded man said.

"We may have some people in places that might help," Linfur offered.

The bearded man shook his head. "Trust is a difficult thing in our business, good Linfur. We don't even trust you, entirely, but I have convinced my master to work with the Sons. He very much sees Sunja as an opportunity, and hopes he can maintain . . . secrecy over his own affairs. Certainly, you still have your share of the orchids?"

"But we wish for more," Linfur said, forcing another smile.

"As do our customers," the bearded man said. "But the agreement was payment in coin for permission to work our trade here. Not the orchids. That was a gift."

"A most generous gift," Linfur agreed. "Well then, thank you for this. I hope you solve your shipment problems. And I hope next time you'll have another gift for us."

"We will. I promise you."

Linfur continued smiling, even though he'd learned long ago never to trust anyone saying exactly those words.

They nodded their goodbyes and the bearded man disappeared inside the storehouse. The door closed followed by the usual clacking of wood, then all became quiet.

Linfur stood there, mulling matters over. He did have the coin, and a little extra, and the Osgarman bud had only been a gift in the beginning. He also knew the Sons enjoyed that gift, as it was superior to the herbs they were bringing into the city, and they'd already begun selling it without informing these mysterious merchants.

Not that the bearded man needed to know any of that.

"Onward, lads," Linfur muttered and walked away, replaying the conversation in his head. He had collected payment from the orchid people only once before, speaking with the same lad. Pleasant enough. Very well-spoken for one born in Sunja but raised in Mademia. Still . . . the words *My most profound apologies* had fish-hooked themselves in Linfur's mind.

He supposed he would have to visit Mademia one day.

15

That same morning, Prajus opened his eyes and stared at the bare ceiling timbers. He heard movement beyond the curtain of his sleeping quarters, from the other gladiators. Loud, wolfish yawns cut the air, as well as a few groans, sleepy curses, and foul whistles blown out from blossoms. Such was the quality of his neighbors, and Prajus sighed at the thought. After a few days of training, he had no doubt he was the best here . . . and yet he slept with the dogs, the pureblood gurry, despite their best attempt at looking or sounding otherwise. Prajus sighed again. He studied the little alcove assigned to him. Sparse, hard, and so very uninspiring. Straw bed with a single coarse blanket and a lumpy pillow. A hole cut into one corner for pissing and squatting. A short table at the foot of the bed. One wall had a few shelves for personal belongings, not that Prajus had any and, if he did, he certainly would not keep them there. Or anywhere in the quarters.

It occurred to him that only prisoners had it worse.

That annoyed him a little more, knowing he deserved better. It poisoned him, truth be known. Even angered him. He smiled coldly and suppressed the feeling, until it was needed.

Someone hammered at the post beyond his curtain. "Out of your hole, maggot," a voice shouted. "'Afore we come in there and drag you out."

Rigger. Prajus recognized his long tongue straightaway.

Interestingly enough, no one had bothered him since he killed Brontus. Even during yesterday's evening meal, when Prajus sat and ate alone, he had noticed a subtle change upon the air. The other fighters didn't cast harsh looks his way or openly mock him. No one bothered him for the entirety of the evening, and not once did he hear anyone talk about him loud enough to overhear.

No one had congratulated him either, he reminded himself, but there was a definite change afoot. Some wary ruminations. He sensed it.

Until that morning, that was.

"*Out*, I said," Rigger shouted again in a diminishing voice.

"Out, I said," Prajus whispered, considering a response, but decided against it.

With a huff he rose from his bed. He dressed, frowning at the mild stink from the nearby shite hole. He ignored the one tunic, pulled on a loincloth, and took his time leaving his cave. All the other curtains were pulled open, and for a moment he believed he was the last to leave, when he heard the barest groan.

He considered the open doorway leading outside, and chose to investigate the sound, some five alcoves down.

"Hold on," someone said. "Hold on, I said."

"It *hurts*," someone growled in reply.

"Aye that. Suppose it does."

Prajus halted beside the curtain and peered in. There, in his own sparsely furnished cave, was the carved-up carcass belonging to Ansut. The gladiator lay on his blanket, which was drenched in perspiration as if the lad had just risen from bathhouse waters. A healer tended to him, his back turned to Prajus as he worked upon a foot. At least Prajus thought it was the topper's foot. He couldn't rightly see. The rest of Ansut was visible, however, and it wasn't pretty. The left side of his face resembled a bruised plum, swollen and glossy from a layer of whatever ointments were smeared upon it. An assortment of bandages covered the pit fighter's torso and upper arms, marking each and every lick of the blade. Ansut arched his back and clenched his teeth, grimacing at some unseen prodding. In fact, the man hissed and flinched with every not-so-gentle touch. He lifted his hand—the one stomped on by his opponent—and waved it about, unable to do anything more with it. The healer had slapped a series of sticks to each finger, straightening them, before binding everything with bandages. The result was a fat flower of a hand, dangling white petals, and wooden tips.

The healer poked at something tender, drawing a hiss from the stricken man.

"What?" the healer asked. "That as well?"

"Aye that, that as well," Ansut winced.

"Damnation." The healer scratched at his forehead, thinking matters over, and moved aside somewhat. Enough to allow a peek at the bruised and bleeding wound to Ansut's calf. A long red slit, stitched from north to south, and very shiny from a lathering of ointment. The purpling of the meat around the wound indicated the blade had been twisted, perhaps more than once.

Sergur, Prajus thought, *you savage pisser you*. He approved, and glanced up to meet Ansut glaring at him. Pain crackled that hateful gaze, hard enough to shiver the suffering gladiator.

Sensing something amiss, the healer checked on his patient before twisting around in puzzlement.

Prajus left them both.

As usual, he ate his morning meal away from the other gladiators, absorbing a few hard looks while he did. It seemed that the goodwill from the day before was all but gone. Prajus ignored them all while eating, or appeared to, as he was very much aware of every fighter around him. Once finished, the trainer Rezzo commanded them to walk about the training grounds, to warm up their legs and work their food down in them. The pit fighters circled the grounds in stretched-out dribbles of twos and threes, with Prajus somewhere in the middle of it all, keeping his own company. Ahead of him was a series of lowered heads and bare torsos, some knotted with heavy muscle, others leaner. A few strides behind him, however, walked Rigger, Mison, and the one called Greygar.

Prajus knew they were back there, as every now and again Rigger whispered pure foulness. Just loud enough to be heard.

"Look at the swagger of him," the man muttered. "Look at it. At home in some proper court, I suppose. Thinks he's one of us now, he does. Puts one topper into the ground and he thinks he's one of us. Well, he's not. He's not one of us. Just a pile of swaggering gurry he is. I hope I get paired off with the pig bastard. I hope."

At that last request, Prajus turned around to walk backward, so that he faced all three. He smiled, for he knew there was no better way to annoy someone who hates you. A hard, knowing smile, aimed at each hateful face looking at him, sending a message of his own. Once done, he turned around again, before Rezzo or Bernd started shouting.

"Oh you're a brazen kog, aren't you?" Rigger started again. "A right unfit asslicker. You wait. You just wait . . . I'll have my chance at you. I'll have my—"

Prajus let him go on, committing every word to memory, saving it, for the grapes were sweeter the longer they hung on the vine.

Not long after, the trainers ordered them to gather up wooden swords. Prajus took his with a flicker of a smirk in Rigger's direction. Rigger answered with a ratty smile of his own, one that shifted into raw hatred. When practice lines were formed, however, Prajus found himself standing across from an imposing individual called Mokk.

And Mokk's narrowed eyes and posture suggested he was ready to crack open skulls.

Well, Prajus thought, wondering if today would be the day to make his presence known.

"*Half-strength only, maggots*," Bernd roared with Rezzo walking away from him. "No bloodletting this day, else whatever you give, you'll take in return but twice as hard. Now make ready. Lift your guards. Eyes on your foe. On my mark . . . *begin!*"

He shrieked that last word, and Mokk, nearly half a head taller than Prajus himself, jabbed a wooden sword at his chest.

Prajus parried with a frown, disappointed with his foe's poor execution. He stabbed back, twice—mere drops before the downpour—before releasing a well-practiced combination of thrusts and slashes that flowed from one to the next. Taken off guard, Mokk managed to stop three before being forced to give up ground.

Aye that, Prajus thought blackly, watching Mokk's angry confusion. *It's like that.*

He didn't bother pursuing but rather waited, weapon lowered to his waist, questioning his foe's retreat with a sly look.

Which Mokk did not care for. He charged in, swinging much harder. Splinters flew as Prajus parried the heavier blows. He stood firm, refusing to be driven back, and stabbed at times to keep his adversary away. In time, he defended only, twisting Mokk's clumsier thrusts and seeking to disarm his opponent. Mokk would have none of that and evaded most of those snares.

When the onslaught was over, Prajus nodded in approval. "You're a cut above the rest of this rabble, good Mokk," he said, loud enough to turn heads.

Not flattered in the least, Mokk attacked again, harder than before. So Prajus parried the blade to the outside and held it there for an instant. Long enough to lock his foe's elbow joint with his free arm.

Mokk grunted at the snare—just before Prajus pivoted to throw him face-first into the sand.

Mokk rolled onto his back in time to greet the wooden blade not half a finger from his nose.

"Be civil, good Mokk," Prajus warned.

Mokk tensed to rise, on the verge of becoming very *not* civil.

"*Mokk!*" Bernd warned, sucking the fight clear out of the gladiator in one breath. "*Prajus*," Bernd bawled next, turning heads. "Step out of line and go to Master Nexus."

The trainer pointed the way.

Puzzled by the command, Prajus did just that, leaving behind a glaring Mokk. As he left, he noticed the sinewy fragment hanging off his sword. The training drills continued while he approached the raised platform of Nexus. Old Tino the taskmaster sat beside the owner. A pitched canvas above their heads shielded them from the sun, but not the sweltering heat.

Nexus glared at him, waiting until the fighter drew close enough before speaking. "You're a punce, aren't you lad? A right and proper punce."

Prajus stopped and thought about it. "I might be, but I don't think so."

"Of course you don't think so. What was that about? Heaving the lad into the dirt?"

"That?" he held up his practice sword, drawing attention to the dangling splinters. "The lad was trying to split my head apart when the orders were half strength."

"Some lads are stronger than others," Nexus countered.

"Some are, Master Nexus. Agreed."

Nexus continued to glare, but not so viciously as before. Tino said not a word. After a few beats, with the noise of training resuming behind them, Nexus flexed his jaw as if it hurt to do so.

"You fight this day," he said. "The House of Ustda has taken exception to you killing their lad. The blood match is today . . ." Nexus locked gazes with his pit fighter. "So send them *another* message . . ."

Some time later, inside the private chamber belonging to the School of Nexus, Prajus sat alone on a bench. He sat with eyes closed and head lowered, armored in the same ill-fitting gear as before. Voices spoke around him, but he ignored most of them.

Except Nexus, who was swearing, and swearing *hard*.

"Dying *Seddon!*" the wine merchant barked. "Dying *Seddon! What was that?* What was *that?* Vorish, you fat bastard! I'll have you gutted! I'll have your leathered ass crack for my *boots!* Those pissers cost *coin*, you hanging berry of shite! Coin! Saimon *below*, take you and scorch you fire-red from head to prick! I'll have your toppers yet. I'll decimate that entire hovel of shite you call a *house!*"

The swearing opened Prajus's eyes just a little.

"What was that bastard's name again?" Nexus bawled at his trainers. "Trako, was it? *Trako?* I'll remember that name. I'll remember it. So I can take a hot sputtering squat over his carcass when he's dead!"

Nexus stopped to refill his goblet only to launch the thing at the wall, where it scattered the gladiators standing there. In the clatter of metal and the scuffling of feet, Nexus grabbed the bottle of wine and chugged several mouthfuls.

All the while, Rezzo signaled three of the men to go outside and collect whatever was left of the gladiator called Nillak. Nexus's other gladiator who fought that day.

"War's afoot," the owner carried on in a hot and phlegmy voice. "Make no mistake. War's afoot. This was planned. Organized, even. By all of *them*. Because of *him*. That one *there*."

Prajus lifted his head. He suspected if he didn't, the merchant would have every lout in that room with a blade cut him down.

"It is my *will* to have him here," Nexus blared, red-faced and spitting. "My will *alone*. *Mine*. And they don't approve? Well, I *do!*" he shouted and stomped. "No one orders me about. No one forces their unwritten rules upon me. That's the second gladiator of mine they've crippled! Crippled and removed from the games. Break his leg . . . ? I'll break their *necks*. They want a war? They want a *war?* Bernd! Issue the blood challenge!"

Grateful to get out of the storm, Bernd left.

Nexus paced, his rich robes swishing, until he reached a wall. He stopped only long enough to guzzle wine. "Kill them all," he seethed at the fighters within the room. "Anyone that faces you on the sands. *All* that face you. Slaughter them. *Massacre* them."

Prajus chanced adjusting his helmet. Such talk was odd to hear. Gastillo certainly didn't speak in such a manner.

The knock at the door turned Nexus about. Eyes blazing and face contorted, he strode across the floor like some terrible wraith and halted before Prajus. "*You.*"

Prajus dared not move.

"Don't you simply kill the next one," Nexus ordered, wine lacing his breath. "Make an example of him. You hear me, *Prajus?* I brought you here for one reason, and one reason only, and that's to *gut* any unfortunate bastard that displeases me! Well, I'm right displeased this day! Right and proper displeased. They broke Nillak's leg. That's it for him. His games are done. You take a life in return. Show them we have no fear of them. Understand me? This is their blood match, but you? You bring me back a *head*."

Hot breath washed over Prajus's eyes, followed by the barest flicker of spittle across his cheeks.

". . . As you wish," he said.

Underneath a sweltering rug of clouds, annoying sweat slid into Prajus's ass crack as he entered the arena. An angry deluge of jeers and curses poured over him, drowning any introduction the Orator might have prepared, which was a shame. Prajus rather enjoyed those. The audience, however, clearly did not, and once the Orator said his name, well, nothing could be heard after that except the barrage of hateful noise.

The whole arena knew of him, of what he'd done.

And they didn't like him in the least.

Curses and only partially heard insults sizzled the air in a wellspring of hot, frothing loathing, the likes Prajus had never heard tell of before. Gurry pelted him—half-eaten apples and other fruit. Things bounced off his armored shoulders. Something hit the side of his helmet, hard enough for him to flinch, and that set off a boisterous roar of approval across the gathered multitudes. Prajus searched the audience for the person who had thrown the thing, but they were all lobbing gurry at him. Livid faces screamed and shook fists. Those along the lip of the arena wall leaned out and cursed him. Even more surprising were the Skarrs standing guard upon the stairways, doing nothing to prevent any of that onslaught.

That was a bit annoying, truth be known.

Still, Prajus didn't react, choosing to ignore it all. He strolled to the center of the arena where Wocello waited. Imposing Wocello, from the House of Ustda, intent on revenge for the death of his fallen companion. A shirt of black chainmail protected the big man, while leather greaves and bracers covered his limbs. He wore an equally dark helm, fixed with a broad bib over the eyes, and three fins sprouting from the crown. That piece of armor hid his face behind a visor decorated with steely lines, making him appear as grim as the greatsword he held, tip first in the sands. Gray bandages peeked out from underneath the short sleeves covering his upper biceps.

Wocello's faceless helmet tracked Prajus as he drew closer, and the cursing of the crowd simmered down to a growl, anticipating the violence to come.

"You're not that big, are you?" Prajus asked, stopping a short distance from his opponent.

Wocello's fabricated face did not reply, but the eyes beneath that broad bib of metal watched him.

"No?" Prajus asked. "No words before the butchery?"

Wocello cocked a head. "Brontus was my friend," came the metallic reply.

"Punce. There are no friends in these games. I saved you from fighting him in the later rounds."

"If so, it would not have been to the death."

"So you say *now*," Prajus scoffed, growing impatient. "All right then. I'm bored already."

"I mean to take you apart," Wocello declared, whipping the greatsword up in an arc of sand.

So do many others, Prajus supposed.

The onlookers released a booming swell of cheers as Wocello leaped to the attack, swinging that length of monstrous steel, seeking to separate his adversary's head from his neck in one fell swoop.

Except Prajus ducked under that tree-felling cut and slashed Wocello's closest leg, splitting leather and meat to the bone.

The stricken gladiator crumpled, greatsword falling, his momentum plying the huge blade from his hand. He landed in a cloud of dust, where he clutched at his lower leg. Blood spurted between fingers as Wocello attempted to stand and failed, collapsing once again.

Prajus kicked him from behind, planting his boot squarely into his foe's lower back. Wocello pitched forward and his armored face scrubbed sand as he let go his ruined leg. That released a great gout of blood, and when Wocello tried to pull the leg in, everything below the knee stretched apart in a red flowering of severed muscle.

And dragged.

The audience screamed at Prajus, hard and loud enough for him to pause.

"Oh, I haven't forgotten *you*," he smiled at Wocello, barely hearing his own voice. "But I have my orders."

With that, Prajus tossed his shield away and gripped his sword with both hands.

More screams, loud and piercing, alerted the crippled man of what was about to happen. Wocello glanced about, reaching for his greatsword while attempting to rise—but Prajus quickly closed the distance. Without mercy, he chopped into the fallen gladiator's neck, barely hearing the crunch.

Wocello collapsed onto his side, slapping a hand to his fountaining neck.

"Sturdy mail you have there," Prajus muttered and realized he could not hear himself over the screaming audience. His cut had been a powerful one, but awkward, landing just below his foe's neckline and biting several links, but missing that prized gap between helm and collar.

Unarmed and barely moving, Wocello kept a shaking hand to his neck.

Prajus set his legs as if about to split a stubborn block of wood. When he lifted the blade, he held it for a beat over his head, before hacking into that neck a second time.

Then a third.

Severed fingers jumped at the connection, and the crowds released a devastated moan.

Prajus finished his work a short time later and stepped back to inspect his work. He nudged the decapitated head, to clear it from the rest of the body. The moans continued, turning into curses and insults, but Prajus paid them no mind. He examined the helmet before picking it up and shaking loose the hairy bits inside. Wocello's head fell with a thud onto the ground, producing more outrage from the audience. A chunk of skin was missing from the dead man's nose, beneath a low brow and a mouth filled with red teeth.

Lords above, Prajus thought, studying the face. *You certainly weren't a pretty one.*

He remembered his orders then.

With one fist, Prajus lifted his trophy high into the air. He strolled in a wide circle, taking his time, ensuring the entire arena saw him. They did, and they let it be known they would have preferred to see Prajus's head on display. Disappointing them pleased Prajus all the more. He spied Nexus and his trainers, standing at their window, their chests pressed against the sill. A delighted Nexus screamed at him, shaking one fist while holding a bottle in the other.

The sight widened Prajus's smile all the more.

Finally . . . he thought and rattled the trophy head before letting it drop to the sand.

From the depths of his private chambers, a stunned Burco Ustda watched the unfolding events. His mouth hung open as his eternal optimism had been badly shaken. Grisholt's lot had been bad enough, but this? Never had he seen a gladiator parade around the arena while holding the head of his fallen opponent. *History*, the words rang out in his head, reminding himself he'd said it so many times before. *This is history, you know.*

He traded worried looks with Torgul, his taskmaster, before returning to watch Prajus leave the arena. The gladiator held up a hand as he went, saluting the hateful crowd. A shower of gurry rained down upon him as he neared the opening portcullis, but he didn't hurry from it.

Then he was gone, into the tunnel.

As Burco watched the departing pit fighter, his shock receded, replaced by a swelling anger. The word had been to cripple Nexus's gladiators. Incapacitate them enough to remove them from competition. Now, however, with a pair of his best men killed by one of the wine merchant's, the latest being *flaunted* about the arena, Curge's words meant nothing.

Burco wanted bloody revenge.

He held his chin as he watched the man leave. "Who else do we have?" he heatedly asked his taskmaster.

High above the arena, Curge frowned.

The day's matches had gotten off to a grand start, with Trako from the School of Vorish breaking Nillak's leg, eliminating yet another of Nexus's dogs from the games. Even better, the victory no doubt cut a line across the wine merchant's pride and his purse. The very notion greatly pleased Curge, and he drank to Nexus's continued misery.

The last fight, however, worried the one-armed owner. Wocello was something of an experienced sword of the games. A recognized name with a long fighting history within the season. Though he wasn't champion material, he was a solid test for anyone challenging for the prized title. Prajus had dispatched him easily. Worse, he had flaunted the man's head, heedless of arena superstitions, goading audience and owners alike.

The owners had sent their message, and Nexus had sent one back.

Fuming, Curge wondered just how bad things had become . . .

16

With the run of visitations ended, Linfur returned to his own nest at the back of a butcher's store. There he collected more coin from three other henchmen. His collectors were heartless, ruthless men. Cold, soulless bastards who would shatter fingers or pluck out eyes to motivate the wretched to gather more coin. Once that bit of business had been done and Linfur sent the lads on their way again, he took whatever had been gathered and went to see the Sons.

The Sons' secret stronghold wasn't far from the storehouse of the orchid merchants. It was a two-story building, located off a side street and down the throat of another, cluttered with piles of roof slats and clay tiling. Tall and without any notable features, it was one of several seemingly abandoned storehouses. Planks boarded up windows that were cut unevenly into the second floor, while a few ribbons hung like dead strands of hair from its peak. Red bricks and thick timbers marked the front, with a pair of doors set in the middle. One door was closed and nailed shut with wood pried from neighboring structures, while the other door sported a man-sized oval hole through its lower half, as if rats had chewed through.

Those not belonging to the Sons would worm their way through that hole if they wanted to enter. Linfur glanced around and went to the next storehouse over. High above the ground and spanning the alley between the two structures was a plank that connected the two structures. Linfur spared it only a glance before moving onto the next building, and the next alley over. There, he checked about before darting in (a matter of habit rather than caution) and walked a few paces before stopping. He rapped out a tune upon the planks. A tune answered, and he responded with another series of knocks.

The door opened, pulled by a guard posted just inside, who bade Linfur and his lads to enter. There, in an ordinary room not at all pleasing to the eye, Linfur left his henchmen with a handful of the Sons' own guards and proceeded upstairs. The steps creaked with every footfall, sparking an urge to find and strangle the punce who had built them.

The Sons wanted the stairs that way, however, to better hear anyone climbing them. *The Sons*, Linfur thought, the bag of pastries thumping against his lower leg. *The kings*, he smirked, knowing they would not appreciate being called such. Brejo especially would hate the name. He was the leader of the three brothers who ruled the street clan, being the eldest of long-dead Cholla. Brejo had the sleepy menace of an overfed ogre, who might kill you just for a moment's distraction. Linfur doubted the man would do any killing himself, preferring to order Jaro to do it. Jaro was the middle brother and the appointed enforcer and executioner for the clan. It was Jaro who persuaded Brejo and Calagu—the third and youngest brother—to bring Linfur into the organization, and later tasked him with managing Strach's territory. To work it, terrorize it, and scratch every last coin out of the streets for the Sons' coffers.

Linfur thumped onto a landing and faced a door. He carried the bag of pastries in one hand and cradled a satchel heavy with coin in the other. Seeing his dilemma, he tapped the base with one booted toe, as softly as possible.

"Enter," said a voice from within.

Calagu. Linfur frowned, feeling the weight of the goods he carried. The kings did not open doors, unless it led to their private shite hole.

Sighing, he dropped the bag of food to open the door.

A puff of gauzy smoke enveloped him, the exotic smell as soothing as it was blinding. Jaro leaned into sight, splitting the gray puffs into lazy twirls. Dark eyes. Thick gray beard, pointed from years of stroking. The Son wore no shirt, revealing a glorious flying dragon inked upon his muscular chest, its wings spread wide. Ink serpents and heavy chains covered the enforcer's muscular arms as well, all the way to his wrists. The dragon, however, was the most eye-catching. The most intimidating.

"Master Jaro," Linfur greeted, dipping his head. "Permission to step inside, if it pleases you."

If it pleases you, Linfur's mind snarled in contempt, loathing himself for uttering such buttery nonsense. He forced that down, reminding himself where he was. The Sons would butcher him if they detected a hint of scorn in his voice.

Jaro eyed him for a nerve-tingling moment, before inspecting what Linfur carried.

Thank the Lords for that, Linfur thought. "I bring gifts," he said. "The spoils of the day."

Jaro waved him inside, deeper into that fog bank, where his other brothers lounged in decadent luxury. A heavy warmth filled the room, dense and oppressive in the smoky chamber. Rich furniture lay about—couches, chairs, and tables—all spread out with surprising thought. A well-used brazier marked the middle of the floor, floating as if on clouds. The smell of incense wafted from it, spicing the interior. *Osgarman bud*, Linfur thought, *the last of it perhaps only just burned*. He was grateful for the scent when visiting the Sons. Especially when he had bad news.

The herbs relaxed the brutes.

Within the foggy swirls of smoke, Calagu struggled to rise from nests of piled cushions. His wild bush of hair seemed longer this day for some reason, and the man raked fingers through the jungle atop his head, rooting out whatever was itching.

Brejo, however, the undisputed leader, remained upon his cushions and watched Linfur's every move. Like his brother, Brejo did not wear a shirt, exposing a gray mat of wiry hair.

Inked tattoos of chains and lightning flared up his arms. Deep warlike grooves lined the face of the oldest son, as if his head was forcefully pinched while he slept. A tuft of ashy hair topped his head. Brejo said nothing, content to stare at the visitor.

An overfed ogre, indeed, Linfur thought and remembered what he carried. "Gifts," he said, holding out the bag of pastries. "And gifts," he said, offering the satchel.

Jaro took both, hefting each before tossing one at Calagu, who flinched as he caught it.

"What's this?" the Son asked and opened it without waiting for an answer. "Oh-ho! Sweet pastries!" he pulled one out and admired its plump shape. "Well done, Linfur. Well done. You're learning fast."

He bit into the baked treat and rolled his eyes before falling back on his cushions.

In the weakening haze, Brejo continued to study Linfur, one eye twitching. The clan leader relented when Jaro jingled the contents of the second bag. The enforcer opened it and peered inside, nodding in approval. He delivered it to his brother, moving slower than usual, holding it out so Brejo could see.

Brejo did, in his own good time.

"Good," the leader said, black eyes shifting to Linfur. Things grew quiet then, except for the sounds of Calagu eating.

"All goes well with you?" Brejo finally asked, his other eye now twitching.

"Well enough," Linfur admitted, forcing himself not to dwell on that unnerving gaze. "The work isn't as, ah, deplorable as I thought. The locals are motivated, as you can see. Ah, here you are."

He handed over the bag of fancy stones. Jaro again delivered it to Brejo. The oldest brother emptied the sparkling contents into his hand.

"Is this all?" he asked.

Linfur tore his attention off the riches in Brejo's hand. "Apologies. It is. There was no gift of orchids."

"No?"

Linfur shook his head, and that little bit of motion tipped him just a little. He straightened. "Apparently they've had trouble with getting it here, so . . ." he pointed at the stones. "You get a little extra there."

A frowning Brejo didn't say anything to that, which jangled Linfur's nerves just a bit. Not as much, however, as he realized with numb alarm that he was breathing in the same smoke the Sons were enjoying.

"Trouble getting it here?" Calagu repeated, the haze wafting about his middle as if he rode upon a dream. "We've heard no such thing from our sources. We're getting our shipments."

"Obviously a different source," Linfur said, steadying himself.

"Obviously. Well . . . a bit of bad luck for them. More fortune for us."

"They are still paying us for the storehouse. Warehouse. Whatever you call it."

"Both are fine," Calagu said.

"And there's this . . ." Linfur said, remembering. He pulled a piece of parchment from his pocket. "From the Grisholt fight."

Jaro and Brejo exchanged looks before the enforcer walked over and gently plucked it from Linfur's fingers. That little bit of motion alone seemed like a flutter of wings.

Jaro unfolded the parchment. His brow arched at the sum scrawled upon it.

"It's waiting for you with the Domis," Linfur explained. "I felt you would prefer if one of your own collected that amount. With guards, of course. Handpicked guards since the sum is so . . . considerable."

Jaro handed the number off to Brejo, whose dour expression brightened with surprise at the sight. "Well done," he said, actually smiling when he spoke. "Very well done."

Linfur held up his hands. "I only place the wager with your coin, Master Brejo. That's all. I'm merely an extension of your own hand. And no word on when one of Grisholt's lads will fight again. He did lose a man that day. A blood match will be issued sooner or later. Grisholt strikes me as a delightfully *spiteful* individual."

"One of many," Brejo grumbled and held out the slip to a chewing Calagu.

"Blessed Lords," the youngest man blurted, sending crumbs flying. He took the parchment while picking at his teeth, eyes fixed on the number. "We're rich," he whispered to his brothers.

No one argued the point.

His senses dulled, Linfur regarded each of the Sons, as he no longer felt any anxiety in their presence. In fact, he felt oddly at ease, and wondered why that was odd at all. The snow orchids clearly had a hand in his relaxed state. He sighed, watching Calagu check on the sack of coin.

As vicious as the Sons were, they were, in fact, exceptionally prompt when it came to paying their own.

Careful to keep a pleasant and, above all, obedient smile upon his face, Linfur watched and listened as Calagu counted out his share. Brejo started talking to Calagu then, ordering him to make arrangements to visit the Domis. To Linfur, his words had the barest echo upon them.

My most profound apologies.

The words flared in the gathering haze of Linfur's mind. *Mademia*, the bearded lad once said. Born to Sunjan parents. Curious.

"Something bothers you, Linfur?" Calagu asked.

Linfur blinked as if surfacing from a dream. "Apologies. What?"

"He asked if something bothers you," Brejo repeated gruffly.

Even Jaro watched him.

Linfur blinked again. "Nothing," he replied, sounding natural enough to his ears, but dread surged within him. These were the Sons, after all, and detecting falsehoods and rooting out lies was a favorite pastime for these men. "Just thinking about the snow orchids. Wondering what might be causing them trouble."

"The orchids might be causing *you* trouble," Brejo declared in a menacing tone, as if he were thinking about stabbing a length of steel through Linfur's head. But then the clan leader smiled broadly and waved it away as if it were nothing.

"Not our concern," Calagu said, holding out a purse of leather stuffed with coin.

Feeling spared, Linfur accepted it with both hands. "My thanks, Master Calagu."

"You've trained this one well," Calagu said to Jaro, who nodded in agreement.

"Go on," the youngest Son said, but with a hint of humor in his eyes. "Leave us. Bring us more when you're able."

"I will," Linfur said, feeling quite relaxed. "Until next time, then, Masters Calagu, Jaro, and Brejo. Enjoy the rest of the evening."

He left, careful not to hurry, to appear too anxious to leave, and staggered through the door. Not even that little stumble bothered him. If they were going to kill him, it would be Jaro to do it, and from behind. Perhaps a blade across the throat. Or simply a powerful arm wrapped around his neck and the relentless squeeze before . . . blackness.

Linfur quickened his stride and thought he heard laughter behind him as he descended the stairs.

Snow orchids. He understood why the Sons wanted the stuff.

Leaving the storehouse seemed a dreamy blur of time. One instant he was in the guardroom at the bottom of the steps, and then he was outside, with Chur and Grohk following him.

"Something to eat, lads?" he asked the pair guarding his flanks. "Morg's place is close by. He might have something cooking. That man can roast a pig. Or beef. Or even chicken, if he has them. And while I'm there, we can collect what he owes me."

By Linfur's hazy recollections, Morg owed him about a week's worth of coin taken from the business. With that thought and his purse jingling merrily, he and his two killers proceeded at a leisurely stride to Morg's place.

The trouble with the Osgarman snow orchid, Linfur discovered, was that you only remained pleasantly pickled while you breathed the herbal smoke. When you were out of its billowing clutches, you quickly regained your senses.

With every step, Linfur's pleasant mood lessened and his eyes widened as he shook off the smoke's effects. At one point he patted his pockets to check on the purse still there. At least he didn't imagine that. *Damnation*, he thought, feeling an achy twinge behind his eye. *Quick to soothe and quick to pain.* He vowed to stay with his firewater. At least with that he knew what to expect.

After a sobering walk, Morg's alehouse came into view. With Chur and Grohk on his heels, Linfur hurried along a bustling street, the sun a third of the way through its evening descent. He weaved around the slower traffic, even shoved a few when needed. Oh, there were some hard looks when he did give someone a push, but those looks quickly softened into recognition and then fear.

Power. Linfur wasn't a king yet, but it felt damn good to be a prince.

A dozen strides from the alehouse's front porch, he realized something was wrong.

The enforcers were nowhere in sight.

Even stranger was the closed door and all the shuttered windows. None of that was right, since Morg's alehouse earned directly for the Sons, and to a lesser extent, Linfur. It was practically evening, after all, and the streets were thick with thirsty people. The place should be ready for a busy night.

Annoyed, Linfur stomped up the steps, glancing about for the two glowering dogs Morg employed. Lying on the porch was a discarded club, with its worn binding wrapped around the lower end. The sight of that skull cracker stopped Linfur, sharply enough that Grohk bumped him from behind. Linfur glared at his henchman before eyeing the abandoned weapon. He'd seen it before, belonging to one of the enforcers.

"Who owns that?" he asked.

"Corlak," Grohk supplied as they all piled onto the porch.

"Is he one for leaving it lying about?"

"No, not him."

"He loves the thing," Chur added in a wary tone.

"Yes," Linfur agreed, sizing up the door. "He did enjoy his stick."

On impulse, he picked up the hard club and slapped it to his palm. Thus armed, he opened the door a crack. A beam of light widened across the floor. Darkness ruled beyond that, however, and a surprising smell greeted him, one very different from that of spent snow orchid.

A trapped mass of warm, fetid air wafted past, carrying the unmistakable taint of blood, wrinkling Linfur's face. And as the door opened farther, the stink grew stronger.

"Harsh night last night, Morg?" he called out, scowling. Hinges groaned as he pressed through, easing the door open with the club.

"Saimon below," Linfur muttered, going farther inside, very much aware of Chur and Grohk behind him, and sensing he might need them.

"Close that," he ordered, and the door was closed.

A choking, gut-twisting stench enveloped them, of blood and other juices best kept inside a body. Chur broke first with a groan and earned a dark look from Grohk. A wincing Linfur stared as his eyes gradually adjusted to the gloomy interior. Someone had visited Morg, either during the day or last night, and that someone had delivered a right and proper thrashing to the alehouse owner and his enforcers. A few scant rays of light leaked into the room from shuttered windows, but it was enough to see by.

Corlak lay on his back not a stride away, stretched across the bare floorboards, his lifeless eyes staring at the ceiling.

The unmoving husk of Barrick wasn't far from him, sprawled out in a heap of smashed furniture and sprinkled with the shattered bits of a chair. One eye was closed, but the other was open a crack. A dull pool of soup surrounded his head, stemming from his nose and mouth. Whole teeth and fragments lay scattered before Barrick's face, resembling jagged corn kernels.

"Saimon below," Linfur whispered a second time, examining the grisly details.

"That's Sundro," Chur said, pointing at the barrel-shaped enforcer on the floor, the head turned away. Grohk moved to the dead man's side, stepping around the big body and cringing upon seeing the face. He shook his head.

Jaw clenched in contempt, Linfur looked around that shadowy interior. "Morg?"

No answer.

Hating the next bit, he crept toward the bar, watchful of blood upon the floor. A few flies buzzed, eerily loud in the empty interior. Linfur rounded the corner and a pair of sandals came into view, still attached to feet, the toes spread outward. Then the legs and the rest of the corpse, face down at the end of the counter. At least Linfur assumed it was a corpse, as it was dark behind the bar. He'd be surprised if the lad was still alive.

Morg. Without question it was him. Mindful of blood and shattered clay underfoot, Linfur slid along the counter, when he stopped and inspected his suddenly dewy hand.

"Unfit," he sighed, seeing how a good amount of gore had spattered the counter as well. And he'd slipped his palm straight through the worst of it. Unimpressed, he held out his hand as he examined the dead man underfoot. Linfur kicked a leg. No response, so he hunkered down and wiped himself clean on Morg's clothing. As an afterthought, he squeezed a knee and then a thigh.

"You're quite dead, aren't you, Morg?" Linfur asked softly. "Perished and long gone, aren't you?"

Nothing from the alehouse owner.

Hesitant about grabbing the man's hair, Linfur shuffled over until Morg's deathly features came into better view. Smashed and bloodied. Horribly wrecked and swollen.

"Aye that, long dead," Linfur sighed and stood. On impulse he nudged the head of the corpse with his boot, whereupon he noticed another set of feet, sandals up, farther behind the bar.

"Sweet Seddon, there's been a massacre here," he released, turning Chur and Grohk around.

"Another one?" Chur asked.

"Aye that, another one. No idea who he is, but . . ." Linfur stopped when the floor became sticky and increasingly crunchy, and that soured his mood even more. Then he saw the reason for the man's death. The corpse was sitting, his fat tongue protruding, while his throat resembled a squashed plum.

Linfur ran his tongue over his teeth and glanced at Grohk. "Go upstairs, would you," he said quietly. "See if there's anyone up there. Mind the corners, although I don't think there is any danger. Not anymore. You can hear anyone plod across the floor up there, and all I've heard since coming into this place is my own breathing. And yours. And the buzzing of shite flies."

"You think they're gone?" Chur asked, dagger pulled and at the ready.

Linfur nodded *Most certainly* and looked about the bar again. Something interesting caught his eye. The strongbox remained untouched beneath the counter. "Toppers didn't even take the coin box," he said in disdain and pulled it out. Riches shifted noisily as he carried it past the dead men.

"All there?" Chur asked.

"I suppose," Linfur reported, dropping the lidless box upon the nearest table still standing. "Certainly feels like it. What was there." Linfur stirred the contents with a finger. "Not a bad night either. And they left it all."

"So . . . not thieves?"

Linfur frowned. "No, not thieves. This was something else." His upper lip grew itchy, so he scratched it with his lower teeth and indicated the other dead man behind the bar. "See who that one is."

Chur did so as Grohk thumped his way overhead, searching room to room and sounding twice as heavy as he was. With no fear of mucking through blood, broken bottles, or any other slop for that matter, Chur went behind the bar and flipped the carcass over. He bent and studied the face.

"Hard to see," he said. "Not enough light."

"Light a torch then."

"Hold on," Chur grabbed a fistful of hair and lifted the head. "Ah, yes. It's Gallwin. Lords above."

"Gallwin?"

"Aye that, little shagger runs errands and messages for the ones over at the storehouse there. The one with the bud."

That stilled Linfur. "The bud? The Osgarman snow orchids? *Our* snow orchids?"

Sensing alarm, Chur released the head. The resulting thump stopped Grohk in his tracks overhead.

"Saimon's rosy ass," Linfur hissed. "Come on . . ."

A short energetic rush later, through that twisted puzzle of back alleyways and forgotten crevices, Linfur and his killers reached the orchid merchants' storehouse belonging to the Sons. There they discovered the first corpse, in the little room beyond, his face a savage red smear.

A lump of unease bobbed in Linfur's throat as Grohk pulled the stiffening body out of the way. Chur went inside and fumbled about the dark, until he managed to light a torch. Linfur entered after that, pulling his short sword as he did.

"Oh, you . . . *bastard*," Linfur whispered upon seeing a second corpse sprawled upon the stairs. Torchlight cast an orange hue over the dead man's face and his crushed throat. A line of broken skin stretched across the forehead, stamped deep and crusted with blood. Linfur noticed the unlit lamp and motioned Chur to get behind him. With his dogs on his heels, Linfur led them up the steps, cringing at every infuriating squeak.

By the time he peeked into the room above, he was well-prepared for what he expected to see.

Another massacre, with the remaining guards slung about the room. They looked right and proper *beaten* to death, in the same manner as the lads back at the alehouse. Not a slash, chop, or stab wound to be found. The boys had been thrashed and left to rot. Even the little bit of furniture scattered about the place had suffered, either broken or upended. Shards of shattered bottles crinkled underfoot. Grohk nearly fell when he stepped on some dice. He caught himself and scattered the pieces with an angry kick.

He wasn't the only one angry. Or worried. Linfur's concern doubled as he spotted the stairs to the lower level. With his short sword at the ready, he moved to the landing and gazed down.

Darkness, deep and foreboding.

"I can toss the torch down there," Chur offered.

"Toss the torch down there?" Linfur scoffed. "Are you mad? You remember what's down there?"

Scalded, Chur nodded.

"I mean," Linfur continued, "I *could* let you toss a torch down there, but truth be known, the Sons wouldn't care who tossed the torch in the end. They'd butcher all of us for it. Especially me, for allowing you to do so in the first place. *Toss a torch down there,*" he finished with contempt. Rubbing his chin, Linfur motioned for Grohk, who held a blade in one hand while attempting to light an oil lamp. He got the thing going and handed it to Linfur.

"You think anyone's down there?" Chur asked.

Linfur didn't think so. He descended, the orange light pushing back the dark step by step. Wood creaked three stairs down, freezing him. Waiting for a reaction and detecting none, he took another step, resulting in another flat note. Every step that followed summoned a warbled squeak, rotting him to his core.

"I'll murder the first woodworker I see," he whispered.

At the bottom, Linfur peeked into the room, blade at the ready. The thumping in his chest was so hard, he would have swung the lamp at shadows if he saw any. As it was, his worry lessened as he gazed upon a brightened interior filled with bales of hay. Linfur went to the nearest stack and took in a great whiff.

There. Oh, yes. That was the stuff. Mild but untouched, and more importantly, *unmoved.* With a nod at the hopeful faces behind him, he checked on the rest. *Nothing.* The orchids lay exactly where they had been stored.

Linfur pointed with his sword. "All right, upstairs now."

And back they went, to the sleeping quarters, which was all but as it should have been, except for a faint stink of pissy blankets and some other foul odor.

With the storehouse deemed empty of lingering killers, Linfur retraced his steps to the slaughter on the main floor. There, he wandered over to the exit stairway and stared at the entrance below.

"You didn't close the door," he informed them both.

Neither man said anything, but Grohk moved to do that.

"Leave it," Linfur told him. "If we were followed, they would have been on us by now."

"They could be in the alley," Chur suggested.

Linfur scowled. "Shut up, you punce. *They could be in the alley.* For that? You can go down there and find out. Oh and scream if they are. Go on . . ."

Glowering, Chur plodded downward, the stairs squawking.

A short time later, he hurried back up.

"Well?" Linfur asked.

"No one. Not a soul. It's full dark out there."

"Suppose so. Well, I have unfortunate news, lads. Someone is killing off our boys. Someone who isn't rightly interested in coin. They left the bud down below because, well, they clearly didn't know it was there. But they know this hideaway. They could return, and next time they could find it. I'll stay guard here. Go on back to our place and gather up whoever is nearby. Whoever is still alive, that is. I dread to think what might await you there. Regardless, if anyone's still alive—if *you're* still alive, then bring them here. We have work to do."

Chur and Grohk exchanged looks. "We're going to move the snow orchids?"

"Well of *course* we are. Unless you simply want to leave it here for that next time? Hm? And then explain *losing* it to the Sons? I can guarantee you, I'll fight to the death guarding it. Better that than the Sons' punishment for *losing* it."

"You mean Jaro's punishment," Grohk said in a low voice.

"Yes, I mean Jaro's punishment. Jaro's *torturing* punishment. So get moving, asslickers. Bring back a few extra hands and we'll move all that below to a new spot. I know just the place. And lads?"

That lifted chins.

"Make no mistake, our necks are on the executioner's block this night, but the axe hasn't fallen. We move this and never talk of it? We're fine. The Sons will never know what happened here."

Grohk and Chur fidgeted and scratched at themselves.

"Six men died here," Chur finally said.

Grohk nodded. "They'll find out eventually."

"By that time, we'll have found out who did all this," Linfur said, "and we'll offer their heads to the Sons. Then we'll let them know, when all is over and done, when the problem has been solved. Until then, no one from our pack says a blessed word *to anyone*. Understood?"

Nods from them both.

"Good," Linfur said. "Now, on your guards . . . and get going . . ."

17

Sunlight shone through the barred window above Pig Knot's unmoving head. He lay splayed out upon the floor, but when the heat started to cook him, he shifted and groaned. His nose itched, so he rubbed it carefully, and even that little bit of movement hurt. When the pain receded to merely a grimacing ache, he lowered his hand and thought about his *other* hand.

A miserable sigh left him as he examined that mutilated paw of meat and bones. Seemed like he was doing that a lot . . . when he was conscious. He stared at the charred and blistered stumps of his poor fingers, all three cooked just above the knuckles. The fire they'd used to cauterize the open wounds had licked the rest of his hand as well, turning skin from a harsh red to a leathery brown. Raised blisters with watery heads the size of fingernails spotted the flesh. Pig Knot frowned at the damage, noticing the skin just beyond the worst of the afflicted area hurt the most.

When Kelmo had cut his fingers off, he'd gathered them up from the floor and dumped them into the shite hole in the corner of the cell. He'd done so with a haughty smirk and a twinkle in his eyes.

That brought a wincing smile to Pig Knot's battered features. He had to congratulate himself on not begging for mercy when the knife crunched through finger after finger. Oh, Kelmo could easily have taken them all off at once, but why do that when he could prolong the agony for long, torturous moments? Even then, Pig Knot didn't break. Didn't scream at Kelmo to stop. Not when the unfit killer called Odusk loomed over him, with a blade ready to cut out an eye. Oh, he *wanted* to scream, wanted to scream quite badly, but he did not. He might've clamped down and bucked when he felt the awful bite of the knife.

But he didn't scream.

Small victory, but he still gave himself a mental pat on the shoulder. For that part, anyway. For when Slok stepped in and put the torch to Pig Knot's hand all at once, well . . . whatever willpower Pig Knot had left, whatever stout *defiance* might have remained in him . . . it had all fled. Fled in one great, mind-blowing blast of searing heat. One so intense, it had robbed him of his voice. His mouth had opened all the way, threatening to pop at the hinges, but no sound came forth. He had bucked then as well. Thrashed, really, like anyone else who'd had their fingers chopped off and seared with an open flame.

And for once, Pig Knot swore on his tolerance for pain, because the fire did not leave him unconscious. Not at all. He'd probably never been so awake in all his days.

Oddly enough, Odusk hadn't cut out his eye, not even during the worst of it.

Pig Knot hissed and gently lowered his tortured hand.

"Unfit," he whispered and considered his situation, mindful of everything that hurt. He lowered himself onto his left side and held his mangled hand upright like a charred flag post. On wicked impulse, he dared to move his remaining fingers and groaned at the tightness.

That was as good as he would ever have it, he figured. So he let his head thump against the floor and regarded the cell door.

"Zepedos," he said.

No answer.

"Zepedos?"

". . . Yes?"

"Were you sleeping?"

"Aye that."

"Apologies."

"None needed. Are you well over there?"

"As well as can be expected," Pig Knot said, closing his eyes.

"How are your fingers?" the thief asked.

"Cooked. As is most of my hand."

"Blisters?"

"Aye that. How did you know?"

"I've seen one or two others touched by fire. One badly. One not so badly. The badly one perished. The other one . . . didn't."

Pig Knot thought on that. "Any words then? That might have come to you during the night."

"Sadly, Pig Knot, after your screaming, no. I laid my head down and, well, slept. As I've said, watch the blisters."

Watch the blisters, Pig Knot thought. "The one that died from the fire . . ."

"Yes?"

"He was badly burned?"

"He was badly burned," Zepedos said. "Fell asleep after a night of drinking. Rolled over onto his cooking fire, which did its work. He put it out himself, but . . ."

Pig Knot waited.

"But the damage was done."

"They only burned my hand."

"You should live."

Pig Knot's brow arched. He supposed he would, but he wondered if Kelmo intended to cut a few more pieces off him. The sum of his many hurts nagged at him, pulsating without end, but the burns wailed the most—the *loudest*.

Zepedos ceased talking and Pig Knot was grateful for the silence. He lay there in sharp discomfort, waiting for the aching to end or even lessen. It did not. After a time, he turned onto his back and propped his hand up on his hip.

Outside, he could hear the rush of city folk going about their day. Pig Knot could shout to them, but doing so would bring the Skarrs, so he kept his mouth shut. At one point he sat up, covered in a sheen of perspiration, and crawled to his water bucket waiting against the wall. He peered inside and was met with dark, unrecognizable bits floating about. Sighing, he eased his hand into the water and kept it there, wondering if healers earned a good amount of coin. They had to, else why stay with the trade? He wouldn't be at it. Not even if he managed to escape here. Not that he expected to. He didn't. His fate was clear. One of these days, Kelmo would tire of keeping him and that would be that. The sooner the better, but Kelmo plainly wasn't in any hurry to finish him off.

Pig Knot once again studied his cell and wondered just how great the officer's wrath might be.

Sharo fed the prisoners later in the morning, throwing scraps of bread and a few slivers of cooked meat into their cells. Pig Knot at least knew the meat wasn't his missing fingers—those were long gone down the squatter. Sharo fed them again in the evening and refilled their water buckets. When he did, the jailor did not speak to Pig Knot but offered him a genuine look of pity.

Neither Kelmo nor his hellions paid him a visit.

A day later, Pig Knot's aching hand woke him, insisting he look at it. A sickly yellow seepage leaked from the edges of the burns. The blisters looked to have deflated, at least to his eye, but he wasn't sure. Going against his better instinct, he dabbed at the more tender spots, hissing at the contact, while slowly flexing his hand. Not wanting to sully his supply of water, he scooped out some and poured it onto the worst bits.

"Zepedos," he said.

"Yes?"

"My hand. Around the burns. There's . . . some gurry leaking from them."

"Pus, perhaps?"

"I don't know."

"Show Sharo then, when he appears."

Later in the evening, when Sharo came to feed them, Pig Knot did just that.

Wrinkling his face, the jailor leaned in as much as he dared and shook his head. "Don't know, lad," he said and stepped out of the cell. "Not a healer." With that, Sharo closed the door and peered at him through the bars. "Truth be known, I'm surprised you lived this long. What's a little slop on your hand?"

"I worry about it."

That hitched up Sharo's face in a question. "Worry about it?" he checked on who was listening before he leaned into the bars. "Lad, I hear how they talk about you out there. I hear what they want to do to you. Kelmo is keeping you here, and believe when I say Kelmo is keeping you alive."

"Keeping me alive?"

Sharo nodded and then left.

The following morning, the hand had not improved—rather, it looked a touch worse. Slop continued to ooze from his cuts, drying into a sickly crust he washed away with a little water.

"You awake?" Zepedos asked from his cell.

"I'm awake," Pig Knot answered, occupied with his hand and the constant aching from the rest of him.

"Your hand improving?"

Pig Knot shook his head and remembered the thief couldn't see him. "No."

"Feel like you're dying?"

"Every day. Slowly."

"Really?"

That time Pig Knot didn't answer. "It's all red and black and such. Bleeding around the edges. Looks unfit."

"And you feel you're dying?"

Dying. Was he? He was in miserable condition, but was he dying? "No . . . only wishing for it."

"Careful with that. It just might happen."

Regarding the stone walls and bars of the cell, Pig Knot could only wish.

"Keep putting water on it," Zepedos advised.

"Many thanks, good healer."

"You're welcome."

The conversation ended and Pig Knot lay on his side again, tucking his hand under his armpit and letting it hang over him like a burnt flag of conquest. He rested his temple against the stone, aware of the bustling activity beyond his window, the distant voices melding into an oddly comforting murmur.

The squeal of metal roused him, and he realized with a start that he'd been sleeping.

Men stood at the cell door and worked the lock. Slok and Odusk, along with a third man. An older soul, middle-aged and dark of complexion, with a thick tuft of graying hair upon a narrow head. Two leather satchels hung at his hips, the shoulder straps crossing on his chest. The new face stood beyond the swing of the opening cell door, where the two guards stepped aside and bade him to enter. He didn't, however, not right away. Instead, he moved to the threshold and gazed upon the smashed carcass of the sole occupant.

"Dying Seddon," he whispered.

"There he is," Slok said.

That was met with a stark look of disbelief from the man.

Which didn't go unnoticed by the Skarr. "Just saying, there he is."

Keeping silent, the man with the satchels regarded Pig Knot once again. He took a deep breath and studied the cell, his disbelief blooming into disgust.

"You don't wash this place?" he asked the Skarrs.

Odusk shook his head while Slok said, "Not really, no."

"Not even a bucket of water? Thrown across the floor?"

"Oh, we do that when it's empty," Odusk said.

"So I smell. And see."

"If they're in there," Slok said with a righteous air while pointing a finger, "they deserve it. They're animals. No better than pigs. Or the rats in shite troughs."

The new man grimaced and entered the cell. He stopped before Pig Knot and took another long, considering moment, studying the battered prisoner from head to stumps and everything in between.

"Dying Seddon," he repeated with a touch more disbelief. "Who did this to him?"

The two jailors exchanged looks.

"We did," said Odusk with satisfaction.

"Most of it," Slok added. "Following orders, of course. But we do enjoy our work."

"Dying Seddon," the man whispered and remembered his purpose. He inhaled sharply, examined the task before him, and stripped off one satchel before studying the floor. Not impressed with what he saw, he looked around, fuming all the while.

"You have any mats?" he asked impatiently. "Clean ones without the blood and filth."

"We do," Slok said.

"Bring me whatever you have."

Slok nodded at Odusk, who dutifully went off.

"You have a name?" the man asked of Pig Knot.

"We call him 'Pig,'" Slok provided.

"I'm asking him."

"He'll only say the same."

"I'm certain he will with you there looking to kill him."

"Only if I get the word," Slok smirked.

That earned him another look of disbelief. "Keepers of the peace," the man muttered.

"Keepers of the peace," Slok repeated. "And the streets are safer for it. Now then, are you going to just stand there and look at him, or . . . ?"

"Not until I get those mats."

"Thought a healer wouldn't mind a little bit of blood and filth."

That earned him another look, plus a weary shake of the head.

"You a healer?" Pig Knot asked.

The man regarded him and, after a moment, sadly nodded.

"You any good?"

"For all this?" the healer asked. "I better be."

"Why?" Pig Knot asked.

The healer shrugged. "Someone doesn't want you to die just yet. Though I don't understand why."

"Better to kill him a little at a time," Slok explained while pinching at the air.

"I can see that."

"We didn't take his legs," the Skarr pointed out as Odusk returned. "That wasn't us. That was someone else."

The healer didn't comment and instead waved to where the mats should be placed. Odusk obliged, but Slok plainly didn't like being ignored. "Just make certain he stays alive a little while longer, good Granik," he said. "That's all we require of you."

Odusk finished laying down the mats and backed away with a nod. Granik the healer watched him leave the cell, and only when the guard was outside, did he turn his attention back to his patient. Frowning, he bent over and pulled a mat closer to Pig Knot. When he had it where he wanted, he knelt beside his patient and dropped his satchels. Shaking his head, he took a moment to peer into the nearby water bucket and hissed at the sight.

"One of you bring me some fresh water. Fresh, *clean* water. And a bucket of hot if you have it."

The Skarr jailors exchanged looks again. "Hot water?" Slok asked. "For him? Can't you do with the cold?"

"You want him to live?" Granik asked.

"Well, aye that, for a while longer, at least."

"Then bring some hot if you have it. Heat it if you don't."

Slok frowned and rubbed his chin, thinking matters over. In the end, he nodded at Odusk to do as asked.

"Dying Seddon," Granik said as he searched for the best place to start.

"Looks bad?" Pig Knot asked.

"Bad? Dead men look bad. This . . . this is . . . well . . . before I do anything I have to clean you. To a workable state at least. What pains you the most?"

Pig Knot held up his butchered hand.

Granik sighed. "They do that?"

Pig Knot gave a little nod.

If the healer had been horrified before, he was clearly disgusted as he examined the wounds. "Unfit," he muttered. "Unfit."

"What was that?" Slok asked, suddenly attentive.

"I'm talking to him," Granik said without turning his head.

Slok backed off with a dismissive wave.

Odusk came back with two buckets of water and what looked like a wad of thick rags under one arm. He laid everything right where Granik wanted it.

"My thanks," the healer said in a distracted voice. "I'm going to clean you now, Pig. As well as I can, without hurting you any more than needed. If I touch a tender place, please tell me. Understood?"

Pig Knot did.

So Granik washed him down. He dabbed and pressed, careful not to scrub, gradually restoring Pig Knot to a state of cleanliness. The warm water, applied by cloth and a gentle hand, widened Pig Knot's eyes upon contact. Despite the nagging aches, the bath felt good. He'd forgotten how good, and it stirred memories of better times with attractive women.

Granik worked slowly, but every passing moment brought Pig Knot a little more back to life.

Once done, the healer discarded the wet cloths and opened his satchels. A number of clay jars appeared, one after another, lined up beside the patient. Then came several neat rolls of cloth bandages. Granik leaned over one satchel and pulled out a fold of leather, which he flipped open on the mat.

Metal gleamed and Pig Knot's eyes narrowed.

Long instruments of bone and steel. Rods ending in flat heads and others in hooks. One or two that ended in very small blades that looked exceptionally sharp indeed. Pinchers and knobs of iron, and everything held in place by little straps. And that was only the first fold. Granik flipped open three more, each landing with a thud, filled with healer tools that went from curious to frightening. Near the end, he extracted coils of leather string and cloth balls stuck with shiny needles.

Uncertainty swelled within Pig Knot.

Granik noticed, cocking an eyebrow. "Don't worry, good . . . lad," he said while arranging the items the way he liked. "I won't do any worse to you. And if you're fortunate—or unfortunate—I just might save your life."

"Do what you will," Pig Knot whispered.

The healer considered that. "No," he muttered. "I suppose I wouldn't be overly happy about that either."

When he was ready, he plied back Pig Knot's head and studied one swollen eye and then the other. He stretched apart eyelids to their fullest, pulled down lips, and peered inside his mouth. Even checked ears. Granik frowned at the worst of it, hiding his feelings at the marginal best. He inspected the bruises and cuts, and upon completing his examination, he sat back and sighed. Just a short release of air, understanding the task before him and collecting his thoughts about what needed to be done next. The healer then cracked open one jar and then another. Gobs of different ointments were applied, some smelling of overly ripe onions, others smelling of wet soil. Granik applied them to the various crusted-over cuts and bruises, taking care to either rub them in gently or merely dab. Once done with that, he cleaned off his fingers, tossed the rag away, and cracked open another jar. He fished out a pinch of shrubs and held them before Pig Knot's face.

"Eat this . . ." he said sternly. "And don't bite my fingers."

"If he bites you, Granik, I'll make him regret doing so," Odusk vowed.

Granik said nothing to that, and Pig Knot ate what was given him. Pleasant. Sweet, even. Full of flavor and, dare he imagine it, tasting of spring. Perhaps the finest of the seasons.

"What is this?" he asked mid-chew.

"Cormidus," the healer replied while applying a dollop of ointment to a crusty gash above Pig Knot's brow. "For your pain."

"You don't have to give him anything for the pain, Granik," Slok advised from beyond the cell. "We prefer him to suffer."

That stopped the healer. "Then why am I here at all?"

"We just don't want him to *perish*, is all," Slok clarified with a smirk. "Not just yet, anyway."

"Unfit," Granik muttered. "That's something a Dezer would say. The effects last only a day, if that, so he'll be in misery again this time tomorrow."

"That's fine enough," Slok said.

That heartless assessment stopped the healer again, and he shook his head before continuing to rub in the medicine. "You chew that slowly," he told Pig Knot.

"Too late."

Unbothered, Granik tended to the other cuts. When he finished, he prodded and pressed areas of interest, avoiding the worst bruises. He asked questions while he worked, if things hurt, and Pig Knot answered that things did indeed hurt. In some cases, things right and proper pained him. Granik applied more salves to the red and sepia-colored patches, and covered everything with bandages, which he wrapped where he could.

When all that was done, he motioned for the mangled hand, which Pig Knot obligingly offered.

"Dying Seddon," Granik whispered, studying the thing. He helped Pig Knot sit up for the next part, and dipped the hand into the bucket filled with warm water. There, the healer let it soak while they both sat and took a rest. No one spoke during that time, and Pig Knot concerned himself with the pair of unfit bastards standing outside the cell . . . both of whom watched the healer's and the prisoner's every move.

When he was ready, Granik pulled out an empty bowl. He then opened three more jars and, sizing up the damaged hand, scooped out small amounts of salve from each. Once he had what he wanted, he started mixing with a finger. When the final blend was ready, he dabbed it on the three stumps.

"This," Granik explained in a low voice, "will battle the infection."

"Infection?" Pig Knot asked softly.

"Aye that. But this will help. You can expect a fever, however. And a fierce one. Are you feeling any pain right now?"

And like sorcery, Pig Knot discovered, in that precise moment, all his nagging wounds had gone from screams to whimpers. "A little," he whispered.

Granik nodded and began packing his items. "It'll stay that way until this time tomorrow. Then it will return. Unless you take this." From a jar, he sprinkled a small mound of shrubs into his hand. At least two perhaps three days' worth of pain relief, considering what Pig Knot had consumed earlier.

"What's that?" Slok asked, coming forward, eyeing the handful.

"For his pain," Granik said.

"Give it here."

At first Granik hesitated, but he relented and passed it along. "That's costly, I'll have you know."

"It is?"

"Aye that."

"Then you take it back and keep it," Slok said, holding out his hand.

"You're only supposed to heal our Pig," said Kelmo, appearing at the entrance of the cell and turning heads. "Just a little."

The Koor frowned at the healer and gestured for him to take back his medicine.

Which Granik did, with a shrug. "I can leave you some of the mixtures. For the burns."

"Will I have to pay for that?" Kelmo asked.

"You will."

"Then thank you but no, good healer."

"Why heal him at all?" Granik wanted to know.

Kelmo did not answer and held out a few coins instead. The two men locked gazes, and when it was clear the officer would not answer, the healer huffed and took his payment.

"So he'll live?" Kelmo asked.

"He should have perished long ago, truth be known," Granik answered. "He'll live. Until the fever takes him. It won't be pleasant, but he should survive that as well."

"We'll place wagers," Slok said from the side.

Granik regarded him before facing Kelmo. "Are we done then?"

Kelmo nodded. "Slok?"

Hearing his name, Slok gestured for the healer to follow him out of the cell, which he did. Pig Knot watched him leave, suspecting if Granik didn't leave, then there was a certain chance he may never leave at all. *Smart*, he decided. But then the man was a healer. Healers were a smart lot. Even that one with the House of Ten, whose name Pig Knot struggled to remember. *Shan*. That was it. Smart lad.

"So you should live," Kelmo said drily.

"Apologies," Pig Knot said and winced, not in pain, but at his constant inability to keep his mouth shut.

Kelmo seemed unbothered by the remark. "You're probably wondering why I had a healer work on you."

"No, I'm not," he said, though he very much was.

"I have a secret, Pig," Kelmo leered. "I *enjoy* having you here. You're very good entertainment. Can't kill you all at once."

With that, the officer nodded at Odusk. The henchman slammed the cell door shut and locked it.

"Can't kill you all at once," Kelmo said again with a smile. He turned and left, releasing a little chuckle as he went. Odusk regarded Pig Knot, sneered in agreement, and followed his commander.

The door to the cellblock slammed shut. All became quiet.

Pig Knot sat, his back to the wall, hearing the distant sounds of civilization pass him by. He sighed, a great and heavy thing, and a great wave of sleepiness swept over him. The medicine Granik had given him was producing one last bit of sorcery.

"Rest, lad," Zepedos whispered, at the very edge of consciousness.

Pig Knot closed his eyes, only just aware of the brick rubbing his back as he slid onto his side.

18

The wind grew louder outside, gathering strength and chilling Pig Knot's bare feet. That freezing contact roused him from a hazy stupor, and he wiggled his toes, just a little, before resting. *Hot*, he thought, so very hot. Too hot really, so he pushed through the folds of old clothing, tattered traveling cloaks, and filth-crusted blankets. Those stuffy layers fought back, sapping his strength until, finally, with a sickly gasp, he freed himself. Pig Knot lay on his back in damp clothes and slapped his forearm across his brow. An unfit dew of perspiration covered his young features of only ten years. Or maybe it was eleven. Or nine. He wasn't entirely sure, truth be known, but he wasn't a young man yet and had the hairless chest to remind him he wasn't.

He had plenty of sweat, however, which was puzzling.

It was *winter*, for Seddon's sake.

Feeling weak, he elbowed his way through the heavy cocoon of old fabric feathering his nest. Musty riding cloaks. Shirts. Anything he could steal or scavenge to keep warm. The thickest of the cloaks hung over the entrance to his home—an old beer barrel turned onto its side. Slivers of broken planks, their lengths cracked from hard blows, hung a little more than halfway down from the top. The boards across the bottom had been smashed and pulled away, allowing a narrow entrance into the heavy barrel. Pig Knot could have made the hole bigger, but that would have allowed the elements inside and drawn unwanted attention. This way, with an old lancer cloak nailed across the opening, his little home blended in with the rest of the gurry in the alley. So he left the hole as it was, and took care when entering and leaving, to avoid any unpleasant scratches and splinters from the broken bits.

Lying there, facing the covered entrance, he noticed his freezing feet disappeared underneath the hanging cloak. Pig Knot rolled over, his home gently rocking as he did so. Mounds of garbage on either side of the barrel braced its sizable girth and kept it mostly in place. He squirmed around, taking frequent rests, until he reached the cloak and pulled it back.

And squinted at the blast of cold.

Still winter. No surprise there. A light dusting of snow clung to the cobblestones and whitened their seams. More snow was just starting to fall. Great feathery tufts driven by winds that slashed at Pig Knot's pinched face. Above all that, over the looming edges and peaks of the surrounding buildings, dark clouds gathered.

A violent shiver forced him to retreat and the cloak fell back into place. He lay upon a mound of clothing, no longer so comfortable, but cold and clammy to the touch. *Winter*, he thought in miserable wonder. And here he was, without a crumb to eat. Not a drop to drink. If the snow eased off, he might crawl out again and have a look about. Maybe one of his younger friends would be able to help him. That troubled him. His friends . . . did he have friends? He believed he did but he couldn't think of any names. There were faces, but they were featureless and topped off with full heads of hair. That wasn't right, however, and he thought harder, trying to remember, and a face did come to him. Not a youthful one, but an older man, in the prime of adulthood. Dark of eyes, beard, and complexion. And this scraggly individual glowered at Pig Knot, as if both disappointed and concerned, in a fatherly way. The face drew breath to speak, but all Pig Knot heard was . . .

Fever.

The fever had him.

That hot thought flared before fading, as quickly as a fiery ember on a breeze. He rubbed his nose with a finger. That widened his eyes. His hand was that of a much older man, with three shining stumps.

"What was that?" a voice asked.

If his aged hand and missing fingers hadn't woken him, the voice did. Pig Knot stared in disbelief at his ceiling, which was now brick and wood instead of curved planks smelling of old beer. The damp clothing padding his nest had disappeared as well, leaving him on a stone floor darkly stained with his own perspiration.

"What?" Pig Knot asked as a freezing chill pricked his skin.

"I asked what that was?" the voice repeated. "You said something."

". . . I did?"

"Are you all right?"

Shivering, Pig Knot crossed his arms for warmth. "No. Fever's . . . got me."

"Ah, thought as much. You were talking all through the day."

"I was?"

"You were. Nonsense mostly. I didn't understand a word."

"Cold, now," Pig Knot said and remembered a name. *Zepedos.*

"Cold?" Zepedos asked. "Here?"

"Very . . . cold."

"The fever."

Oh yes, Pig Knot thought, bringing up his knees.

"It'll pass."

But the chills did not pass. The chills intensified, until it felt like Pig Knot was no longer on a stone floor but rather the snow-blasted plains of the distant Ice Kingdoms, where a single gust could freeze a person in midstride if they were caught in a storm.

The voice spoke again, but Pig Knot didn't rightly hear it, and he couldn't remember who it was. Instead, he lowered his chin into the crook of his arms and set his quivering jaw. Some time later, Pig Knot slipped away into darkness. An icy darkness that lasted a long period before easing off into a terrible inner heat. One that squeezed the sweat from every pore and left him gasping. At times he woke, for no reason it seemed, only to flop onto his back and lay there, suffering from heat that baked him from within. The shivers returned every now and again, clutching him in a freezing grasp, holding him for the next round of heat.

Vicious shivers. Sweltering heat. Wave after relentless wave, one ending in time for the other to begin. He lost all distinction of night and day. Heard voices over what seemed like the passing of years. At one point he pissed himself in what felt like a flow of hot tea, but he didn't have the strength to do anything about it. He shuddered and felt a great loosening below his waist. Then he was taken by the elemental dark again, until a slap of water awakened him with a sputter.

A wicked face chortled and leered. "You're sleeping in your own shite, Pig. Hear me? You're sleeping in your own shite."

Slok. His name was Slok, but the shivers were so fierce that Pig Knot couldn't speak.

A hand grabbed his dripping chin. "When you feel like dying, lad, you go right on and do it. Save us the trouble of feeding you, 'eh."

Slok shoved Pig Knot's face away, and that was that. He went back to suffering, time passing in hot and cold waves.

"He's not eating," another voice said. Odusk. It belonged to Odusk.

"How can he eat?" asked another. "The lad's cooking there."

"How long's he been this way now?"

"Two days," Odusk said.

Pig Knot cracked open his eyes. Jana's husband. What was his name? He could not remember.

"Two days. And he's still like this." *Kelmo.* That was his name. He remembered.

"The healer didn't say it would last this long," Odusk pointed out.

"Healers," Kelmo scoffed and loomed over his prisoner. "Don't perish just yet, Pig. Don't. I have plans for you."

With that, Kelmo straightened.

"What if he does die?" Odusk asked.

"So what if he does?" Kelmo repeated, the words echoing as Pig Knot lost consciousness.

The heat intensified, so much so that Pig Knot hissed upon drawing breath. He opened his eyes and realized he was no longer in his cell but hanging by his wrists. A rope went straight up and over his head, into the darkness above, disappearing in the gloom. Pig Knot felt the terrible ache in his wrists but he could still move his fingers. He scratched at the knots, which did nothing. Whoever had tied him had done a masterful job.

Things grew hotter still, and Pig Knot looked down . . . and gasped in disbelief.

The heat emanated from a vat of fire, the surface popping and spurting as it boiled from within. His feet, his bare *toes*, in fact, well-illuminated by that bubbling inferno, dangled not a stride from its glowing depths.

Pig Knot screamed.

He twisted one way and then the other. He picked frantically at the knotted rope overhead. There were no walls, only the pool of fire below him, into which he was being slowly lowered.

So what if he does, Kelmo whispered at his ear, twisting the once-gladiator around. *What if he does.*

Pig Knot screamed again and realized he had *legs*. Both legs. That blunt realization silenced his wailing and he peered down at his dangling limbs. Even kicked them this way and that before ending in a short-lived jig. During that time, the rope lowered him to within half a stride of the fiery surface below. The fearsome heat steamed the bottoms of his feet.

But he had his legs back. And that was reason for him to smile in wonder. *Sorcery.*

Or the delusions of a dying man.

At the rate he was being lowered, he figured—

The rope snapped.

Pig Knot plunged feetfirst into searing oblivion with nary a scream. The shock broke something inside him, not unlike a bone snapping under wads of cloth. And the heat, as surprising and terrible as it was, enveloped him entirely, cooking him, melting his very skin from the bones . . .

Before a strange thing happened.

Well . . . strange for Pig Knot anyway.

All that roasting agony dissipated all at once.

And instead of the next wave of frigid cold, an odd sense of well-being flowed into him. An exquisite warmth and feeling of wholeness, ever strengthening, one that was as surprising and yet familiar, as if he'd felt it all his life. A comforting sensation of being healed from deep inside, as welcoming and loving as a mother cradling her child in her arms to ward off bad dreams.

But this was no dream.

That feeling of being so wholly comforted and at ease spread from within his chest and into his limbs and extremities. It held him in a snug sheath of warmth and peace and did not relent. Where once he had shivered to the point of biting off his tongue, or nearly been charred to death, a deep and resounding feeling of . . . wellness held him.

Other feelings surrounded him. Presences which were unknown to him yet oddly familiar . . . radiating goodness, filling him with an even stronger sense of well-being and, dare he admit it, affection. Whispers of comfort filled his ears, and though he understood not a word the sounds relaxed him even more. Pig Knot knew no fear. No pain. He wanted for naught and merely . . . basked in that lovely sensation.

In time, the presences lessened, one by one, like ghosts leaving the room, leaving Pig Knot with a lingering sense of ease. The last one departed, and he knew it was the last one, but there was no sadness. No misery. And before the last presence did leave, it left him a gift. A fleeting gift, but one all the same.

A warm hand caressed his forehead . . . and Pig Knot smiled at the touch.

Something brushed along his face then tickled his nose.

He puffed and pawed at his face, only half conscious of doing so. Then he sniffed and scowled, becoming aware of his own stink.

The grand feeling left him entirely.

He cautiously opened his eyes to darkness.

What felt like a length of stringy fur brushed past his lower thigh, and he flinched at the contact. He squirmed onto his side and looked down that way, noticing the square window lashed by iron bars. It was night outside, and darker yet in his cell.

A murmur of movement then, and Pig Knot strove to find a wall. Finding one, he sat up, glaring at the dark.

Something was inside his cell, *with* him.

"Who's there?" he croaked, the sound shocking. He cleared his throat and discovered he had a powerful thirst. His water bucket lay about somewhere, and it took him a moment to locate the shape. When he did, he pulled it close, gladdened by the slosh of liquid within.

When he had had his fill, he plopped the bucket down and listened. Zepedos snored softly in the next cell. The clap of the bucket hitting the floor failed to wake him. Pig Knot continued to listen, wiping his face, and, after a time, decided he was alone. Whatever had tickled his face was the tail of his dream, one which he struggled to remember. Fire. Then . . . being a boy, shivering, in a barrel smelling of beer.

Then he was back here, in Kelmo's jail.

The fever had left him, that much was clear. He felt better, much better, but filthy, feeling the residual grime of a terrible sickness still clinging to his skin. Even worse, he was certain he'd pissed himself. The smell informed him he'd had a bout of the scutters as well, and not just the one fluttering discharge. Horrified realization rushed through him. Sick, lying in his own shite, and delirious from the fever. Seddon above, why had the Lords taken a special interest in torturing him?

"Just end it, will you?" Pig Knot implored quietly.

No reply, except for Zepedos's snoring.

"No," he whispered, flexing his healing hand. "I suppose not."

Knowing he'd at least recovered from the fever, he rattled the water bucket again and believed he had just a few fingers left in it. Not nearly enough to clean himself, but he would try.

The approaching dawn revealed the cell bit by bit, and the lighter it became, the more Pig Knot gawked at himself. The fever had not only stolen his senses for a time, but it had ravaged him. His flat stomach and ribs were even more noticeably pronounced. Even his arms and thighs looked thinner.

Later that morning, Zepedos stopped snoring, and Pig Knot waited a few moments before he cleared his throat. "You awake?"

"Aye that. Awake. You alive?"

"Aye that. Still alive."

Silence then. "I wager you're wishing you never left that gladiator house of yours . . ."

Pig Knot smiled weakly, conceding defeat, when the outer door to the cellblock swung open with a clatter. A scuffling of movement, followed by a grunt and a mutter of discontent. Sharo appeared, a bucket in hand, and Slok moved behind him. The Skarr held a key and inserted it into the lock. When he pulled the door open, both Sharo and Slok stopped and stared at Pig Knot.

"You're alive," Slok whispered.

Not interested in saying anything, Pig Knot instead scratched at his chest before moving on to his shoulder.

Scowling, Slok motioned for Sharo to get to work. The jailor entered and winced at the stink. He dropped a bucket of water next to the prisoner. Half an apple then, cleanly cut down the middle, followed by a handful of dried meats and a few nuts.

Sharo gave it all to Pig Knot, who marveled at the feast.

"Enjoy it, Pig," Slok said from the entrance. "Chew it slow."

"Can I get him a cloth?" Sharo asked.

"Why?"

"So he can clean himself."

"Clean himself?" Slok asked, as if it was an unfit thought.

"The lad stinks," Sharo said. "Even you can smell that."

Mulling that bit over, Slok nodded and the jailor went off.

Pig Knot nibbled at the meat, taking care to eat it. *Lords above.* It was seasoned with spices, tender, and easy to chew. So he stuffed the food into his face, gobbling it down in case the unsightly bastard at the door decided to take it away.

Slok did no such thing, however. Instead, the man locked the cell, took a step back, and waited. At times he checked on Zepedos. Sharo returned a few beats later and tossed a handful of washcloths at Pig Knot.

"Use them," the jailor said, placing another bucket outside the cell. "When you're done, leave them in the bucket here. I'll get them later."

Sharo fed Zepedos in the next cell and, once done, he left with Slok on his heels. The Skarr kept one hand on his sword the whole time, as if expecting Pig Knot to come at him through the bars. The very thought almost got him smiling, which he forced down until the guard was gone, slamming the cellblock door behind him. After eating his slice of apple, Pig Knot studied the rags. Sharo had brought a good handful and they even looked clean. He gathered them together and pulled the water bucket close.

"I don't understand," Zepedos said after a time. "They smash you, to where you're nearly done. And then they bring in a healer, who gives you . . . medicine for your hurts. *Then* they . . . give you water and washcloths so that you may clean yourself."

"And a decent meal," Pig Knot said.

"They're planning something."

Without question Kelmo and his torturers were planning something. Pig Knot didn't think they were about to kill him, and yet he knew they didn't care in the least if he died.

So what were they planning?

Nothing good, he decided and dipped one of the washcloths into the water.

19

A day of rest became three.

Clavellus would have enjoyed it better, however, if he had *known* that one day would stretch into three more.

And on the morning of the fourth day, he woke to discover his missus had once again slipped from their bed, leaving a cooling absence that he very much disliked. With streaks of shadow playing across his face, Clavellus stroked the spot where she'd slept, clutching at the soft blankets. He smacked his lips, rolled onto his back, and scratched at his plums. *Three days*, he reminded himself. The house had been waiting for word of their next fight for three days.

He would wager a strongbox of coin they would receive word *today*. Guaranteed.

The balcony beckoned brightly, so he rubbed at his hairless head and swung his legs out over the bed. A sharp tightness lanced up his back, as stiff as a dagger to the spine. That left him flat for a moment, gauging how bad his back might be, when he rolled onto his side. Taking his time, he pushed himself to a sitting position and lowered himself to his knees. He located his pisspot and removed the lid, wincing at the smell. He got around to doing his business. Once done, he stood, carefully, hearing and feeling the cracking in his knees.

"Lords above," he whispered, placing his hands to the small of his back and wondering where his youth might have gone. "Maybe the same place as the missus," he whispered with a look at the balcony. Moments later he dressed in fresh clothing, wearing a thin summer shirt with sleeves that reached his elbows. It was still hot for such, but he liked the sleeves since they covered his upper arms and hid just how skinny they'd become.

"Lords above," he repeated and stretched his back. No pain, which was excellent, but a wary stiffness near his waist. Stiffness from how he'd slept, perhaps, and he played with the idea of talking to Shan about it. Scratching at his beard, he wandered over to the balcony, the brightness of the day narrowing his eyes. He stopped at the railing and bent over to rest on his elbows. On the training grounds, two figures strolled about the outer edges of the sand. One of them was the Perician, Junger, and the other was—no surprise—his wife. They chatted, or rather Nala chatted, in a low voice respectful of the morning. She wore a summer robe, a pretty green one with bands of white, and Clavellus took a moment to simply watch her, all thoughts of his back and a healer forgotten.

The pair rounded one corner, Nala now listening to Junger as they walked. Clavellus rubbed his nose and checked the sun. There was no wind. A breathless morning if there ever was one, with good, clear skies. To the northwest, however, toward Sunja itself, a worrisome bank of clouds had gathered.

"Good morning," Nala greeted him, distracting his thoughts from the weather. The pair were now walking toward the balcony.

"Good morning," he smiled wistfully, loving the very sound of her voice. "Is she boring you, Perician?"

"Not at all, Master Clavellus. I'm enjoying her company very much so. She's been telling me about the town she's envisioned."

"Ah yes, that."

"I have to tell someone," Nala said.

"Quite the plan," Junger said.

"Aye that," Clavellus agreed and muttered. "Quite the something."

Nala glared at him, as if hearing, and perhaps she did.

"Has she mentioned the marketplace?" Clavellus asked.

"She has."

"Lords help us all," the taskmaster mumbled, lowering his head and scratching at his crown.

"He's a very good listener, this one," Nala said sweetly as they stopped beneath the balcony. "Are you training this day?"

Clavellus thought about it. "Probably will. Light drills only."

"See to it you don't give this one too hard a time," Nala warned.

"Light drills only, Master Clavellus?" Junger asked.

"Aye that. I expect to hear word about your next fight this day. Sometime soon."

"They left you alone for a full three days," Nala said, shielding her eyes with a hand. "Might they do it for another?"

"Perhaps, but I'll wager we'll be back on the sands tomorrow."

"Why so long do you think?" she asked.

"Nature of it all. Ten houses are competing. All with a full roster of fighters. With the Free Trained and the prisoners now thrown into the Pit, things will take longer. To a point. Until all the carnage is over and done and there's no one left to fight."

"Dreadful thing, these games," Nala sighed and regarded Junger. "Thank you again for your company on my morning walk. I'll miss you when you're gone."

"Only for a day if that, I figure," Clavellus said. "Unless the Madea has other ideas." *And he just might*, he thought, but kept that to himself.

"Thank you for a lovely walk, Lady Nala," Junger said, smiling warmly in return.

Pleased, Nala walked toward her front door and flashed a look in her husband's direction. "I like this one," she warned.

Clavellus frowned as she entered the house. Then he looked at Junger. "I like you too, but I'm not sure Machlann does."

Junger's smile faltered.

As the morning progressed, the rest of the inhabitants woke and went about their routines. A warm breakfast was served, consisting of porridge sweetened with blackberries, hard-boiled eggs, and a choice of sliced apples or quartered oranges. Clavellus ate what he wanted, drank a mug of herbal tea and then some warm water, and let it all settle before moving on to the next part of the day. He avoided the others, wanting to be alone for a bit, but eventually wandered into the training area and sat under the same shaded table put up days earlier.

His silver mug was there, magically cleaned from the day before. A few other cups were present, along with a jug filled with water. Clavellus frowned upon the jug's contents, checking on the sun to best determine when he could get at the good stuff. He then glanced around to see where the servants had gone without him noticing. Only the usual household guards were around, however, roaming the walls above. Below them, recovering gladiators sat in the shade.

All except Goll, who stalked a wooden practice man, swishing a wooden sword about as he closed in on the figure. Over the past three days, most of the cuts and swelling he'd sustained had diminished. Shan had done that, and Clavellus remembered the healer yelling hotly at the gladiator, warning him to follow his instructions, else he'd leave and return to his wife in Sunja.

The very notion bothered Clavellus, truth be known. He thought he'd offered the healer a private room for his wife at the villa. He would offer it again.

"Goll," Clavellus called and got the Kree's attention. "A quarter-strength when you're swinging that stick, and a quarter *only*."

Goll looked away, closing in on the target's outstretched limbs.

"*Goll*, you unfit *punce!*" Machlann blasted, standing before the barracks and unimpressed with the lack of respect shown. "You acknowledge your taskmaster *now*, or by Saimon's fiery hole I'll *punish* you this day, *eeeee . . .*"

That straightened the pit fighter, and he testily saluted Clavellus with his sword. Once done, he resumed clattering combinations off the practice man.

The taskmaster watched as Machlann strolled angrily over to join him at the shaded table. There he sat with a thump and glared at the Kree gladiator.

"Probably wants to be punished," Clavellus muttered, squinting at the sun. "You know he's a hard one."

"*Eeee*, be as hard as a granite *kog* for all I care," Machlann said. "He knows rank and rule. I'm not too old to crack him about the ears to remind him. Unfit pisser."

Fuming, the trainer noticed the jug. He pulled it over and scowled at the contents. "Too early for you, is it?" he asked.

"I didn't fill it."

"Suppose not."

Timbers shivered under Goll's onslaught. Splinters flew. At one point he cranked out a dozen strikes in rapid succession, just as Shan the healer came out of the living quarters. The sight of Goll stopped the healer and he glared, wavering upon what to do.

"The healer's about to burst," Clavellus noted, pouring himself some water.

"He's a sensitive one," Machlann said with disdain. "Far too sensitive for this business. What did he think we'd be doing here, anyway?"

"I don't think he rightly knew, truth be known."

"What?"

"Not the full extent of it," Clavellus clarified, offering the jug.

"He knows now," Machlann growled and poured himself a drink. "Should go on back to treating fevers and cut fingers."

"Don't say that to him."

"Why not?"

"He just might. As you've said he's a sensitive one, but he's not stupid. Once he's had enough, he'll leave but, truth be known, he's a *good* healer. There aren't many good ones around. He looks after the lads, tends to their wounds, and does their condition worsen? No, they recover. Quickly even. That's a healer who knows what's what. I'm not surprised he's becoming a bit sour but . . . he's too valuable to us. I'll make certain he stays."

"Coin?" Machlann asked, taking a drink.

Clavellus nodded. "And other enticements. Good living quarters for him. Move his missus out here. We'll make it right. Make it more tolerable. At least a little."

"For only a few weeks more."

"Any other season. This time? Who knows how long the season will be. Hopefully he'll have grown used to it all when it's over."

"Used to it all," Machlann grumbled while watching the Kree break into another combination. "*Eeeee!* Your *taskmaster* called for a quarter-strength *only*, my missus! A *quarter-strength!* Stop trying to *limb* that piece of timber!"

Goll broke off with a puff, waved, and stomped to the other end of the training grounds.

Simmering, Machlann leaned back, chewing with vigor on the inside of one cheek. "How long do you think it'll go on?" he asked in a much lower tone.

"The season?"

"Aye that, the season."

Clavellus shrugged. "For however long King Juhn wishes it. Or until there's no one left standing. By which I mean we're all too bruised or broken to continue."

"Or dead."

Clavellus saluted that thought with a raised mug. He finished his water, sulked at the taste, and looked about. "Getting close to that time."

Koba appeared, as did Junger, coming out of the barracks with the recovering Brozz. Brozz limped to the shade and carefully sat, easing his back to the wall. Junger continued to the rack of practice swords and selected one.

A glaring Machlann directed Koba to observe both pit fighters.

Junger took a moment to salute the taskmaster and senior trainer and received nods in return. The Perician then saluted Goll who turned away without acknowledging the gesture. Unbothered, Junger went to a practice man.

Machlann waved Koba over. "See to it they both get their exercise. Strengthen their legs for both. Arms and shoulders for the Perician only. Nothing overly strenuous for the Kree. The man might split apart, and the healer's screaming would be unfit. Just enough to keep things warm."

Orders received, the younger trainer went back to work.

Junger struck a head, the impact frighteningly loud. He sized matters up and struck an arm with similar results. Then he tapped the other arm and, when it looked like he would continue the pattern, he ripped into the target, striking everything. Up, down, right side, left side, and on and on, and never in a similar pattern. He darted out only to lunge back into the one-sided fray, attacking from one angle and then another. Splinters flew. The frame shivered from the pounding while the spectators couldn't look away from the display. The constant barrage of what surely would be limb-severing blows or outright decapitations attracted more onlookers, wondering about the commotion. A black-bearded Muluk lumbered into view, scratching at an armpit and looking as if he'd only just risen. One-legged Garl limped out of the living quarters, followed by Torello, who scowled at the noise. Even Ajik stood beside his bellows, hammer in hand, watching the swordplay.

After a few moments of battering the target, the Perician abruptly stopped, exhaled, and nodded as if all was well and done. And in the calm that followed, in that spent charge of a storm, a respectful silence fell upon all who witnessed it.

Goll was the first to move, milling around the outer edges of the sands. That broke the stunned stillness, and a return to regular activities filled the compound.

"The lad's fast," Machlann said under his breath.

"Fast?" Clavellus asked. "*Lightning* is fast. That was sheer sorcery, man."

The old trainer scrunched up one jowl, suggesting he wasn't overly impressed.

"Name one hellpup that's faster," Clavellus said.

Machlann waved him off, not inclined to do anything of the sort.

With a victorious frown of *Thought so*, Clavellus considered the water jug and scowled in earnest. "Enough of this. Clurik!" He lifted his mug at the villa's cook and winemaker and pointed at the jug upon the table. Clurik waved and waddled off.

Machlann grunted approval.

"He's *dying* to put on a similar show," Clavellus whispered, indicating a stoic Goll.

The old trainer nodded.

Muluk shuffled over, his limp improved but still not quite a smooth walk. A great yellow smile spread across his woolly face as he neared the table.

"Wine in the jug, lads?" he asked.

Machlann grimaced at the question.

"It's coming," Clavellus answered, indicating for the house master to sit at the nearest chair.

"Master Koba," Goll suddenly called out, distracting all. "What say you to a little friendly competition? Junger there is quite good at pummeling a wooden man, so why not sharpen our skills against each other?"

Clavellus and Machlann stiffened at the request. Koba waited for direction while the training ground grew silent. Goll and Junger eyed each other.

"We'll have none of that gurry," Clavellus yelled, examining his fingers.

Goll looked over at them. "I'm offering—"

"*Eeee* you're stirring up a pot of *shite* is what you're doing!" Machlann interrupted. "There'll be no damn contest between *you* two, and that's the end of it!"

"Master Goll," Clavellus said, a touch softer. "You're barely all there. Still on the mend. You two are the only fighters we have remaining in this competition. If one of you injures the other, especially *you*, Master Goll, your games could quite possibly be finished. Not even Shan's unfit skills at putting a person back together will be enough. Not that it will come to that."

"Because you tits aren't fighting," Machlann snapped.

Clavellus lifted his hand, agreeing with the trainer.

"Other houses have sparring matches between their own," Goll countered. "I see no reason not to do the same."

"Different houses have different thoughts on training," the taskmaster said. "And they have a full roster competing. We do not. We do *not*. There is only you. And him. And no one else. If one of you should fall here today, then there is only one. And the burning glee of the other houses when they learn of it."

"And they will," Machlann added.

"I'd rather have you face each other in the last fight of the season than here today," Clavellus continued. "Understood?"

Plainly not happy with the judgment, Goll glanced at Junger before turning away.

"Good," Clavellus said to himself, hiding his relief.

"Continue with the torture, Master Koba," Machlann said, which the trainer immediately did.

"Lords above," Muluk said as he sat. "He meant to fight him."

Clavellus nodded. "What I said is true," he explained in a low voice. "It's just . . . that man is angry."

"And prideful," Machlann said.

"And determined," Muluk added.

"Aye that," Clavellus agreed. "All that. Talk to him when you can, Muluk. Those two? I believe they are two of the best hellpups competing this season, unless there is someone else we haven't yet seen or heard tell of. It would be foolishness to have them hack away at each other right now. Especially when *that* one is on the mend." He chopped a hand at Goll. "If they continue putting down their opponents, if they make it to the final eight . . . well . . . there's every chance to believe they'll be facing each other at the very end. If Goll wants it, wants it badly enough, it will happen. And it'll happen before a bigger audience than this one. But until then . . ."

Muluk nodded. "Keep the peace."

"Keep the peace," Clavellus warned. "Keep ranks. And keep them *apart*. They belong to the same house. We have far too many enemies out *there* to be making new ones in *here*."

"I'll do what I can."

"Please do. Ah . . ."

Clurik arrived with two bottles in hand. The servant was a round individual, heavy of jowl and belly, with bushy eyebrows that tapered off into fine points. Weathered and rough, he made a show of smiling briefly while presenting the bottles by the neck.

"Here you are, your majesty," he said in a phlegmy voice.

"Only the two?" Clavellus asked innocently enough and nodded at Muluk. "Our friend is here."

"I know of your friend," Clurik said with wary side eyes. "Should I roll out a barrel or three?"

Clavellus frowned at the jab. "That the Black?"

Clurik nodded in defeat.

"Bring us two more."

"At once, sire," his cook rumbled and placed the bottles down. With a tired look he returned to his kitchen.

"Good man," Clavellus confided to Muluk while popping a cork. "Bit saucy at times. Bit brazen. But no one makes the drink like he does."

"He does make good drink," Muluk said.

"Oh, the *best*. And he knows it. We all know it. Here . . ." The taskmaster poured for the Kree. "Don't mind the gurry he spouts," Clavellus explained as he poured a drink for Machlann. "He's been here so long I barely hear him."

"How long then?" Muluk wanted to know.

"Long. Come now, good Muluk. Enough of that. Let's enjoy the show . . ."

So the three of them sat back and watched the morning drills. As instructed, Koba directed an unhappy Goll to march circles around the grounds. Then he turned his attention to Junger and had him lift a heavy timber. The exercise timbers were a collection of weighted wood beams, perhaps two strides long and carefully crafted with handholds. Junger selected an older, well-used piece and bent over the thing. He gripped it and took a few breaths to ready himself. From there he straightened, puffing as he did, lifting the thing to his waist. Then he curled it to his collarbone. Another pause before he pushed the weight over his head, extending his arms but not locking them. He held it for a beat before he lowered the wood to the ground and started again.

Twenty times Junger lifted that timber, his sneer becoming more pronounced the deeper into the repetitions. Twenty times he grunted, ending each movement with a forceful puff of breath, but not once did he look overly winded. At the end of the last lift, Koba instructed the fighter to take a walk around the sands.

While Junger strolled, the trainer turned to Goll and pointed him to the practice man. There, under Koba's watchful eye, the Kree fighter battered the target for several combinations. The strikes rang out, but they were not heavy blows, not with so many watching him.

After a time, Koba ordered him to cease pummeling the target and take a walk, following the same path as the Perician. Stripped down as pit fighters usually were, the sweat fell from them with every step. Both men ignored the other, but Goll started to gain ground.

Which was about when Koba ordered Junger to return to the heavy timbers.

"Blessed Lords," Muluk moaned softly over the lip of his mug. "How many times will you have him lift that gurry?"

"Five rounds of twenty," Machlann said offhandedly, still watching the proceedings.

"Why five?"

"Because I said so, punce."

A troubled Muluk traded looks with Clavellus.

"Ten rounds is the usual number," the taskmaster explained. "Those timbers all have different weights. From the lightest to the heaviest. Our Perician is lifting a lighter one this time, isn't that right, Machlann?"

The trainer nodded.

"But by the time he's finished," Clavellus said, "the very end of the fifth round—that weight will feel much heavier. Not as heavy as ten rounds, mind you, but heavy. Enough to warm the blood."

"And just the practice sword for Goll?" Muluk asked.

"Just the sword for Goll. Light practice at that."

Muluk ran a hand over his beard and glanced toward the smithy. Ajik was over there, fashioning something from a length of leather.

"Well, I'll have my own work this day," the Kree said. "I'm going to have a talk with that one over there."

Clavellus looked. "That one?"

"Aye that."

"He can't speak the language."

"Not a word," Muluk said. "I was wondering, could you spare one or two of those bottles?"

"The Black?"

"Aye that."

"What about wine?" Clavellus asked. "Or even mead. I ask because I prefer the Black."

"Whatever you have the most of."

"I'll have Clurik get you a few bottles."

Machlann pointed at the wall where two guards stood. One faced what lay beyond the battlements, while the other waved for the taskmaster's attention.

"We have visitors," Clavellus said, taking a drink.

Sometime later, the messenger called Naulis rode into the villa. He left his horse with a guard and walked with purpose to the men gathered around the table. A perspiring Goll waited there as well, hands on hips, impatient for news from the arena.

"Greetings all," Naulis said, bobbing his head.

"Good Naulis," Clavellus said. "What's the word from the city?"

The small man stopped before them, tonguing what was left of his teeth. While Naulis wasn't a fair-looking fellow, that little bit of probing didn't improve matters much. Deeply sun-browned, Naulis flicked away a few strands of matted hair from his eyes and took a deep breath.

"I found Borchus," he announced with a frown. "The lad's dead."

The news wasn't surprising but hearing it summoned a few scowls to the assembled faces.

"Borchus is dead?" Muluk whispered with a dazed look.

"Where did you find him?" Clavellus asked in a somber tone.

"Last place I figured to look," Naulis reported. "Temple of the Salish. There was no sign of Borchus in the city, so I figured where he might be if he had perished."

"He was there?" Goll asked.

Naulis shook his head. "His ashes were. The Salish burn their dead. Not much land for burials in the city so . . . anyway. I checked the records the Salish kept, of the recent dead, and there was his name. Asked the Salish who cooked him that day and he gave a good description. It was Borchus. He's dead and gone."

A collective silence met that, as they each took a moment to remember the agent and all he'd done for the house.

"Any idea who killed him?" Clavellus asked, breaking the quiet.

Naulis closed his tired eyes and shook his head.

"You'll find out," Goll ordered sternly.

"I will?"

"Aye that, you will."

Naulis was suddenly awake. "That sounds like a bit more work . . ."

"Muluk will pay you for your efforts."

"A bit more *dangerous* work. Borchus clearly had a few enemies. The Salish said a group of people brought his carcass into the temple along with that of a woman. Both were cut up. Right nasty it was, or so said the Salish. There was talk of it being the work of a street clan."

"Street clan?" Clavellus blurted.

"Aye that. The Sons of Cholla."

"Cholla had sons?"

"Three or four of them, apparently. I don't rightly know how many. Enough to fill a shite trough, anyway."

"Find out who killed him," Goll repeated.

"Look, Master Goll," Naulis started. "I'm just a spy. Just a spy. And a reluctant one at that. I don't mind running messages to and from the city but . . . asking people about the Sons of Cholla? Not something I want to do. They kill people. Often for very little reason. Or none at all."

"As I've said, Muluk will pay you."

A downcast Muluk, somewhat pickled and remembering the fallen agent, nodded that he would indeed pay coin.

"Dangerous work for a spy," Naulis said.

"You're no longer a spy," Goll declared. "Now you're an agent."

That froze the unpleasant expression upon Naulis's face. "Oh I don't think I want to do that."

"There's more coin for you. Muluk."

Muluk got up, intent on heading for the underground store-rooms holding the house finances.

Naulis rubbed his nearly nonexistent chin as if he'd been struck by a mace. "Hold on, now. It's not worth it. Not if the Sons are involved."

"Then just keep listening . . ." Goll insisted. "And if you hear tell of these Sons, perhaps even where they are located, let me know."

"And you'll do what?" Clavellus asked him. "Root out a street clan? I don't think so."

"I'll leave a mark."

"You'll leave them *alone*, is what you'll do. Whether they're responsible for Borchus or not. Cholla was a right and proper pig bastard back in the day. Any sons of his will be trouble we can't deal with at this time. Not until the season is done. *When* the season's done . . . we'll have a sit-down and discuss these Sons. And what to do about them. If they did kill Borchus," Clavellus locked gazes with the Kree, "we'll have our revenge. And I mean killing the whole nest of them. But not until the season is done. Agreed?"

Goll didn't answer.

"Look, I knew the lad longer than you. Borchus knew the dangers of his work. He would say the same thing, choosing the smart path over the emotional one. And when we've exacted our revenge, when we've wiped all those punces off the streets with the heels of our boots, I guarantee you he'll be smiling from wherever in Saimon's hole he might be."

A simmering Goll reluctantly nodded.

"All right then," a relieved Clavellus said and motioned at Naulis. "Anything else?"

The newly appointed agent nodded. "About your next fight . . ."

Garl stood in the shade and stared out over the house grounds. At his foot sat Torello and the ever-quiet Brozz, both men resting in the sand, recovering with their backs to the walls of the barracks. The past few days, when he was able enough, Garl would go outside and hobble from one spot to the next, following the shade as it made its way across the house grounds. He really liked the spots with benches. But there was no bench here. All that was here was sand, and it stuck to the fleshy bits of the men seated. It didn't stick to Garl's fleshy bits so much because he stood with his crutches under his arms.

Garl sighed, staring at his missing leg. At times he glanced over at Torello—just a glance—as the lad wasn't pleasant to look upon for very long. That thought almost put a smile on Garl's weathered face, but then he took a look at Brozz. The Sarlander didn't appear much better. Stitches lined his torso, making him even more intimidating, and a fresh bandage covered the once-infected wound to his belly. He gazed at the training area with a stoic expression, his huge drooping mustache nearly hiding his mouth. The healer had removed the wads from the man's broken nose, and though the swelling had lessened, it still had not come down like the rest of the bruising on his face. Garl looked away before Brozz felt the stare. The Sarlander was a pleasant enough sort, but you could barely get a word out of him. At least he'd hung that dreadful necklace of crow heads off a peg inside, so that was something, but still . . .

"What's happening over there?" Torello asked, nodding at Clavellus and the others gathered around the table. He scratched at the black stubble upon his face and then picked at his nose.

"They're having a talk, is all," Garl said, lifting his head and squinting at the group.

"A right serious talk, then."

"Men talk," Garl said. "We're talking right now."

"That one from the city, Naulis, is over there now."

"Who?"

"That one . . ." Torello said pointedly. "The one without a chin. Looks like he's biting into a bun except he's not."

"Bit harsh."

"Well he does. You can't see him?"

Garl peered again, baring teeth as he did, long enough for both Torello and Brozz to give him curious looks.

"You can't see him, can you?" Torello asked.

"'Course I can, you knob. He's right over there."

"What's he wearing then?"

Garl cleared his throat. "Clothing."

Torello shook his head before sharing a look with Brozz. "You hear that?"

Brozz went back to watching the men at the other end have their talk.

"Well, I heard it," Torello continued. "Go on then. Have your look."

"I'd see him better if we were sitting over on the bench there," Garl said.

"Oh, aye that you would. But for some reason, it's cooler here than over there. Why is that?"

"Don't be a saucy tit."

Torello gestured at the bench. "No, really. Go on over there and sit in the sun. You'll truly enjoy all that heat. Go on. I'll keep this brute company in the meanwhile."

Brozz didn't acknowledge that.

"Well, you are a brute," Torello rumbled on and glanced at him. "Lords above, wouldn't kill you to participate in the conversation every now and again. Just a little more than an unfit grunt or that black-eyed stare of yours. Since we've accepted you into our little circle."

"What little circle is that?" Garl asked, scratching at his neck with his hand missing two fingers.

"Our little circle."

"Hardly a circle."

"Our group then."

"Not even that."

"With him it is."

"Oh that," Garl muttered and went back to watching the house masters talk. "He hasn't said he's anything to us."

"Well, he is," Torello said. "He's sitting with us here now. Like it or not, Sarlander, you're with the two of us now. You with the healing hole in your belly. Me with the unfit ankle. And him," he gestured at Garl.

"I'm not with him," Garl said to Brozz. He noticed the gathering across the way. "Something's happening over there."

And it was. They were still clustered around the table over there, except for Muluk who lumbered toward the three men. He carried a bottle and looked unusually downcast, which wasn't quite right, not when Muluk had a bottle in his hand. Then he pointed at Garl and approached him.

"What did I do?" the older man asked.

Muluk huffed sadly and shook his head. "Just got word that Borchus is gone."

That stunned the one-legged man.

"Perished," Muluk said and handed the bottle over to him. "Naulis doesn't know how, but . . . seems the Salish burned his remains."

"The Salish burned him," Garl whispered.

"We don't know anything beyond that," Muluk said. "Anyway . . . we . . . aye that. There. Drink that. Give a shout if you need more."

With that Muluk nodded at all three and walked away.

A stunned Garl handed the bottle to Torello, who took it without a word. Torello knew what Borchus had done for the once-gladiator and once-beggar, how he had saved him from the Sons of Cholla. Garl knew it as well. Knew it to his very core.

And was eternally grateful for it.

Without a word, Garl dropped one crutch and lowered himself to the ground with the others. He sighed, stared ahead, and said not a word.

After a moment, something tapped him on the arm.

Torello. With Brozz watching over his head.

Torello held out the uncorked bottle.

And Garl gratefully took it.

20

A thickening rug of clouds hung over the city of Sunja, promising rain.

Just outside of Shan's house of healing, the men of the House of Ten waited in a pair of covered wagons. After a long and hurried journey from the villa to the city, Goll decided to get out and stretch his legs for a bit. He strolled about the wagons, ignoring looks from passersby, and glanced at the front door of the healer's house. On one pass, however, a pebble lodged itself between his toes, and no matter how much he fussed he couldn't seem to rid himself of the thing. Growing annoyed, he held on to the wagon and went about removing his sandal.

"What's wrong?" Clavellus asked from within, sitting with his elbows resting on knees.

"Pebble between my toes," Goll replied.

"That's all?"

"What else might it be?"

Clavellus smiled. "The mighty Goll. Stricken by a pebble. They'll write songs about you."

"They best get them right," Goll muttered, digging between the digits and flicking the irritant away. Once done, he put the sandal back on, adjusted it, and looked at the front door of the house again.

"They'll write songs about both of you," Clavellus said, including Junger, who sat farther back in the same wagon, well-concealed from prying eyes. Remembering the previous reactions he'd gotten on the street, it seemed a wise location. If they chanced walking to the arena, they would have been mobbed by appreciative crowds.

Not that Goll shared that sentiment.

"He'll be along when he's done," Clavellus said, changing the subject.

"He's taking a long time," Goll said.

"Well, it's his missus. Their home. And their livelihood. He's going to have to convince her to leave. Then they'll need time to gather their belongings."

"More time than you figure on," Machlann said, sitting across from the taskmaster.

"All the more reason to stop now . . ." Clavellus added. "Have them talk and see what she thinks of it all."

"Should have done this on the way back," Goll said, straightening his back.

"Well, perhaps," Clavellus said when the shouting reached their ears and lifted faces. The house could not contain those harsh notes.

Wearing a pack he didn't have when he went inside, Shan exited the house and closed the door, muffling another angry outburst. The healer grimaced and scratched vigorously at his thinning, sandy hair. Ignoring the stares, he hauled himself into the rear of Clavellus's wagon. Once aboard, the healer sat beside Machlann and exhaled mightily.

"She'll consider it," he said in a pensive tone and rubbed his chin.

Some time later, the men of the House of Ten entered their private chambers beneath Sunja's Pit. A gust of humid air greeted them as they opened the door. Weak shadows draped the walls and the bare benches lining them. Daylight filled the arched window at the back of the room and a heavy curl of sand had collected on the lower sill.

With the rest of his lads behind him, Clavellus wandered toward that window, passing underneath crossbeams of wood and stone.

"Oh my," he whispered, gazing upon the Pit. Nodding approval, he swept away the gathered sand upon the brick. "It's a fine day," he said, patting the sill. "A fine, fine day."

Goll and Muluk stopped beside him. Muluk squinted at the dismal clouds blocking the sky. "Looks like shite to me," he said. "Could piss rain at any time."

"We're here now," Clavellus said, turning about. "Rain won't stop anything."

Metal clattered when Goll dropped a sack filled with bits of armor onto a nearby bench. The once Sujin called Valka nudged it with a second sack.

"My thanks," Goll said and opened the first.

Junger sat heavily upon the opposite bench, closer to the door. He placed his sword and scabbard across his lap and nodded at Clavellus. The taskmaster smiled back before turning to Goll. Muluk stopped beside his countryman and started picking through the second sack. Koba stood near the door, tall and imposing, and barring entry to anyone not belonging to the House. Valka joined him.

Shan stopped beside Goll and watched the Kree pull piece after piece from the sack. The healer then unslung his own pack and placed it near Goll's armor. Without a word, Shan went about extracting the contents, examining each briefly before laying them down with a thought to organization. Needles. Spools of thread. Thin and thick leather straps the length of one's arm. Oddly shaped clamps. Sealed jars containing various ointments. A small set of scissors. Compresses both dense and thin. Rolls of cloth bandages.

Many rolls of bandages.

So many, in fact, that it drew the puzzled ire of Goll nearby as he watched the healer unload the goods. "What's all that for?"

"Wounds, of course," Shan replied simply. "I have a feeling it'll be a particularly bloody day. And after last time? I'd rather have it before me and ready to use than not."

"There are only two of us fighting this day."

"I know. And one of you won't get so much as a scratch." Shan met his eyes.

Burned by that, Goll resumed unpacking his armor, and the healer continued with his own preparations.

Overhearing the exchange, Clavellus faced the window to hide his smile from the prideful Kree. He scratched his nose while fans filled the stands. The clouds thickened while the humid air felt close to bursting with rain.

Machlann stopped beside him, and the old trainer had a rare half smile on his bearded face.

"Lords above," Clavellus said. "I so love this. The quiet moments before the mayhem. The anticipation of what's to come."

Machlann nodded, inspecting the arena and the dismal clouds above it all.

"Is there something wrong with me?"

The old trainer shook his head.

"Here we are . . ." Clavellus said, pointing at the Orator climbing the steps of his podium.

The initial fights were a sordid affair, despite the Orator's best attempts at putting a bit of color into an otherwise drab bit of dressing. The first contest matched prisoner against prisoner, and their lack of training showed as soon as the portcullis dropped behind them. Their names were forgettable, their physical condition sorely lacking, and their fighting ability poor. Armed with only short swords and without any armor at all, they hacked and hewed at each other, often missing, and quickly tiring. Red-faced and panting, they spent as much time struggling for breath as they did flailing at each other. The audience didn't care for the showing either, and discontent grew with every passing moment.

The prisoners fought on, each swing slower than the one before, each parry a last instant thing of desperation. As their exhaustion worsened, they stumbled out of the other's way, until even that became too much. Gasping, they put fists to knees while eyeing the other.

A few pieces of fruit fell around them.

One prisoner recovered sooner and dragged himself forward, while the other man staggered back, looking to escape. When the hunter reared back his blade, his opponent—not so exhausted after all—lunged forth and stabbed his attacker's midsection in a spurt of ink.

The audience cheered for that first death of the day, but Clavellus knew they really applauded the end of the contest rather than the finish itself.

The next two fights were no better. Pairs of prisoners were marched out onto the sands. Names and histories were given and soon forgotten, and what followed was more unskilled carnage ending in death. Such distasteful showings urged Clavellus to crack open a bottle of Sunjan Black.

Then it was time for the Free Trained.

Unlike the prisoners, the houseless warriors that composed the bulk of the usual arena scroff possessed some skill, admittedly to varying degrees. The men of the Free Trained had their own reasons for competing—usually coin—but a handful hoped to attract the attention of watching house owners, taskmasters, and trainers. Clavellus reminded himself that two of the men behind him came from that same rusty rabble, and those two might very well possess the skill and fortitude to go deep into the games. The thought caused him to hide his smile behind the rim of his cup.

Unfortunately, the Free Trained chosen to fight this day were only a few notches better than the previous gurry. The first match ended far too soon, with one warrior clutching at a gushing wound to his leg. The next fight almost put Clavellus to sleep. Both men appeared content to clang swords together for a bit before retreating out of reach and circling. And circling. And then even more circling. Left and right and left again in a dreary shuffle. Worse still, they both used an unfit amount of feinting to no great effect, even feinting when their opponent was clearly nowhere within striking range.

At one point, Machlann went off to look for a public pisspot. He returned some time later to find only Clavellus, Koba, and an armored Goll watching the fight, their elbows resting on the brick. Outside, the audience's annoyance came to a dangerous boil.

"They still at it?" the old trainer asked.

"They never really started," Goll answered, scratching at an ear.

"Nor do they look ready to stop," Clavellus said.

Not long after, however, one lad rushed his opponent and rammed him. Both fell over in a spray of grit. The attacker rose first and planted a knee upon the armored chest of his adversary—who released both a shriek and his sword, practically flinging the weapon away before waving in surrender.

Which was granted.

The two fighters later left the Pit, much to the delight of the audience.

"Well, that was nothing," Goll remarked, easing away from the window.

"Thank the Lords," Clavellus muttered.

"Free Trained," Machlann grumbled and looked at Goll. "You understand now?"

Goll nodded.

"Seddon above," Clavellus muttered, rubbing his nose as if smelling an overfilled shite trough. "I don't know what might be worse."

"I wonder why anyone watched that at all," Shan said from behind them. "The stands are full."

"They're not here to watch that gurry," Clavellus corrected. "I can tell you that. They arrive early for the most favorable seats and then wait, enduring the slop, for what comes next."

"And that's us?"

"That is us, dear healer. That is us."

With that, Clavellus turned from the window and walked past them all, as the first cheers rumbled around the arena.

The people knew full well who was fighting next.

They *all* knew.

In their chambers, taskmasters and trainers lined the windows, some even shoving for position. They eagerly leaned over the brickwork as if fearful of missing the slightest movement. Old warriors and venerable tacticians all, they pulled on beards, rubbed at eyes, and gnashed whatever teeth they had left. They cleared their minds and readied themselves for what was coming. A tremendous rumbling filled the Pit, much like summer thunder. The air thrummed with a building energy, and if anyone did *not* know the reason for the rising excitement, they were quickly informed.

Razi, of the House of Razi, heard that noise as it spilled over the arena's ancient heights, and it set his frosty jowls trembling. His head sank between his shoulders as he shoved aside his taskmaster and trainer to reach the window. Color gushed into his fat face and he craned his neck, looking this way and that, the excitement palpably spreading, nearly powerful enough to flatten the hair on his head. Grimacing, exposing widely spaced teeth, he scratched at his brown robes and pulled his neckline open a little more, exposing a feral nest of hair.

"Brazen he-bitches, *all*," Razi swore, anger scalding his throat. Slapping the bricks hard enough to sting, he whirled around, robes swishing and belly bouncing as he did. He marched back, past the badly bruised Habol who was still on the mend after a beating from Trako, of the School of Vorish. He marched past Rune and a handful of other fighters not battling that day, until he stood before the one who was fighting.

Korzo.

Taller than most and armored in black leather resembling a set of thick ribs, Korzo cut an intimidating figure. A pair of bull horns decorated his iron helm, set above the narrow slits of the visor. His bare, heavily muscled arms ended in a set of spiked bracers. One hand gripped a small, rounded shield. The other held a long-shafted war hammer, with a brick-shaped head of immense size. Spiked greaves covered his lower legs.

Korzo faced his house owner.

"You listen to that," Razi ordered, spittle flying with the words. "You *listen*. Hear it? *Hear it?* That's what they think of you. They think you've already *lost* to this hellpup. Already lost and the fight's not even *started!* You show them different. You show *them*. Show them they were wrong to doubt Korzo. Show them they were so dearly wrong to doubt the House of Razi! You put *down* this upstart wonder. Put him down and bring me his *head*. On that *shield*."

Within his helmet, Korzo's eyes narrowed into slits. He nodded.

Just before the familiar knock upon the chamber's door.

Any other time, Curge would lean back in his chair, crack open a bottle of his favorite swill, and enjoy the privacy of his viewing box while watching the games.

Not this day, however.

When his agent, Bezange, reported that Junger of the House of Ten would be fighting this day, Curge made certain that not only would *he* be watching, but every butcher fighting under his banner would be watching as well. In fact, he commanded them to, granting them leave for the day to take in the games so that they could witness the one called the Perician Wonder. He'd even brought Baris his taskmaster up into the box with him, to better see—what Curge believed—was the man *someone* had to defeat this season.

"Baris," Curge called, turning the thick taskmaster around from the table of bottles. Short, perhaps even squat, with a stern face that might have been smashed by a log, Baris the taskmaster had the quiet demeanor of a sleeping bull and a deep, nearly mystical knowledge of the combat arts. He had been a trainer when Dark Curge had been a gladiator, and Curge made certain his house retained the man after the passing of his father.

Curge moved his own chair closer to the wall, urging Demasta to do the same for the taskmaster.

Old Baris waddled over as if hindered by a troubled leg, and Demasta got out of the way of the shorter man. The taskmaster gruffly nodded thanks and sat, jerking the chair a little closer without spilling a sip of his wine.

"Where is he?" he asked, peering into the arena.

"Not yet, but he's coming. Listen to them . . ."

Baris cocked an ear, and the increasing noise narrowed his eyes.

"See?" Curge said, leaning over. "And the dog blossom isn't even on the sands yet . . ."

The cheering dropped to a low rumble as the Orator appeared at the eastern end of the Pit. White-haired and robed, and as thin as a starving sapling, he energetically climbed the steps to his podium, where banners of green, yellow, and white adorned the wood. Behind him and situated much higher were a pair of booths of polished hardwood, festooned with even more banners of the season. Members of the Gladiatorial Chamber filled one of those boxes. The other one, built strides higher, belonged to the king—and was noticeably empty.

Yet again, Curge thought, unable to remember exactly when the ruler had last graced the games with his presence. A thought quickly forgotten as the Orator lifted a pair of thin arms, gesturing for silence.

To the surprise of no one, the old man got it.

With the voices of the audience restrained to a murmuring hiss, the hunched Orator gripped the edges of the podium as if bracing himself. He took a moment to gather his wind, eyeing all those in attendance.

The people waited for him.

"Men and women of the Pit," he began, his voice crackling loud and carrying. "I am so happy to have you with me on this day. On this day, under clouds that might drown us at any moment. Fear not the weather above, however, as I have good news. Very good news. Good enough to make you forget about the stormy heavens above our collective heads. News that will . . . make you forget the deluge of gurry we witnessed earlier this day. The next match . . . will *restore* your excitement for these glorious games. Dare I say, the next match will leave you speaking of it in the days to come. And when I say speaking, I mean *babbling* . . . at a pace that will confuse your companion and leave them startled and staring. For the next match . . . has a swordsman fighting in it. A right and proper swordsman . . . the likes of which we have only just begun to realize. We've seen swordsmen upon these sands before, but I dare say not like this one. No, not at all like this one. This one is special. Extraordinary, even. We have witnessed . . . truly great feats of skill from this swordsman I'm about to introduce. Some grand feats. *Wondrous* feats . . ."

A noticeable buzz rippled throughout the arena. Just a rumble, but it swept from one end to the other, and the skin of all who heard it prickled at the sound. That powerful vibe even washed over Dark Curge, and, unknown to him, he'd pressed his stump against his chest. With a huff, he glanced at Baris, but the narrow-eyed taskmaster showed no emotion at all.

The Orator held up one arm, and when that failed to calm the crowd, he held up the other.

The rumbling lessened just a touch, but it was enough for the Orator. "He is a man that, to this day, has yet to pull steel upon our sand-swept stage. From nowhere he came, brought in by the upstart House of Ten. A house that has only just established itself this very season, *after* the season had begun. A house that has only a pair of gladiators still fighting for it. One of those pit fighters is the swordsman I've spoken of. A *true* swordsman . . . as was revealed when he defeated *three* gladiators in a single day . . ."

The excited bubbling spiked as the audience remembered. The Orator waited for the noise to subside before continuing. "Think of the stories he's given us already . . . and he will no doubt give us another story this day. A story? Apologies. A *spectacle*, I say."

The Orator turned, taking in the sheer scope of the audience. Curge did the same, and he believed the place would soon collapse.

"He hails from Pericia . . ." the Orator announced.

The cheers spiked again.

". . . He is *Junger* . . . *The*—"

But the rest of his words couldn't be heard, because, like some grumbling volcano threatening eruption for years, the Pit exploded with excitement.

The force of that blast caused several people to grab at their ears. Some hunched their heads into their shoulders in wonder. Those screaming flayed their throats raw. And it wasn't just an overpowering burst of sound—the audience grew wildly animated, waving arms and pumping fists. A scattering of unknown debris flew up from the masses, peppering the air. Bottles and cups were raised and held in a sloppy salute while a few voices shrieked to be heard above all, on the verge of ruining their kinkhorns.

And it went on and on . . .

Curge looked over at Baris once again. The uncorked energy from that rolling, positively stunning blast crinkled the taskmaster's forehead, and he covered one ear as if shielding it. Nearby, Demasta's usually fearsome face slackened, visibly shocked by the force.

Curge might have said something then to explain the outburst, but he didn't.

He *couldn't*.

No one would have been able to hear him anyway.

The portcullis rose in a smooth motion, suggesting a fresh gob of grease. The ear-rupturing cheers continued and when Junger emerged from the yawning entrance, the level of noise surged yet again, impossibly so. If the arena had had a roof of any kind, the intensity of that blast would have robbed hundreds of their hearing. And into this hot pot of adoration Junger strode, out of the shadows and onto the sands. Without armor, without even a shirt, he strolled into dull daylight. He carried his sheathed sword in one hand and acknowledged the crowds with the other. He charmed thousands with a confused smile and a shake of his head, as if genuinely puzzled by such an overwhelming reception.

They stood and applauded him, shouted at him, and waved at him, with hopes of catching his attention. There were far too many to acknowledge, however, and Junger realized it. So he walked a few steps more, not dwelling on any one section of the adulating crowd. Until he straightened and faced the opposing portcullis, and the man already walking away from its closing maw.

If the Orator had introduced him, no one had heard.

But the Perician knew who he faced . . .

Korzo. From the House of Razi.

Thick as a bull and with the horns to match. Armored in ribbed leather, with spiked bracers about his forearms and spiked greaves about his legs. The ponderous hammer drew the eye, however. It was as big as an anvil and looked about as heavy. Judging by the powerful arms on Korzo, however, the man had little difficulty using the weapon.

The reputation of his opponent didn't seem to have any effect on Korzo's swagger as he confidently strode toward Junger. So confident, in fact, that he tossed his shield away after a few strides, as if letting the world know he didn't need it for his opponent.

Junger held his sheathed sword in both hands and pointed it at his adversary.

Korzo did not slow.

"Greetings," the Perician said, as the big man got closer.

The pit fighter did not appear to hear him. Not that that surprised Junger. He barely heard himself. Lowering his head, Korzo slapped that long-shafted hammer from one hand to the other, until he caught it with both. And since it was so loud, Korzo forwent the usual greetings and lurched ahead, whipping the heavy hammer at Junger's head.

Who ducked.

With all the grace and speed of a barn swallow flittering through space and time, Junger slipped under that swooping brick of iron, avoiding it entirely. He sprang up behind Korzo and backpedaled a couple of strides before digging in his heels.

Feeling nothing but air, Korzo stomped to a stop and spun, swinging his hammer around for the expected counter. The crowds *ooohed* at the effort and did so again when Korzo discovered he was nowhere near his foe. Realizing where Junger stood, he steadied himself and plodded forward again.

Junger retreated in two broad strides, his knees bent and ready, swishing his sword in an impressive pattern that Korzo ignored. The pit fighter from the House of Razi charged and swung for Junger's profile.

Again, the Perician ducked harmlessly under those muscular arms—and struck—*bashing* the armored midsection of the bigger man. The impact buckled Korzo as his momentum carried him forward. He clutched at his guts with one hand, his hammer dropping to his side but not to the ground.

Junger did not press the attack and waited for his adversary to fall.

Korzo did not, however.

Instead, Korzo shook off the blow. He straightened slowly, and turned around with lethal purpose. His black helmet glared at the challenge before him.

The audience, used to seeing Junger dispatch his opponents quickly and with ease, held their collective breaths.

Far from done, Korzo hefted his war hammer with both hands.

He lumbered into a run and swung for Junger's head.

Junger ducked again under the blurring arm. He whirled and whipped that leatherbound blade across the bare bicep of the fighter. Korzo flinched and staggered, as if taking a lance through the chest. Though his arm hung at his side, he held on to his hammer with his other.

Junger did not wait a second time. He struck his opponent from top to bottom, battering him in a devastating patter. He cracked Korzo's helmet left to right before bringing his sword down upon a shoulder. That downward chop hit hard. Korzo lurched and presented his neck.

The Perician smashed the pit fighter's armored head, the impact silencing the crowd.

Like the mighty timber he was, Korzo pitched face-forward, crashing in a spray of dust. There he lay, with his heavy arms splayed on either side of him.

Without pause, Junger drove a knee into the fallen man's lower spine, pinning him. He then grabbed one of those bull horns and pulled the head off the ground.

Korzo did not resist.

Done as he was, Korzo did not do much of anything.

Holding him, Junger inspected the unconscious form before lowering him to the ground. He removed his knee and stood, backed away a few strides, and waited.

Regaining something of his wits and perhaps sensing something amiss, Korzo drew in one arm. Then the other. He lifted his dusty head and attempted to prop himself up on one shaky elbow.

Whereupon he collapsed and did not move.

The Orator's skinny arms flashed against the overcast sky as the whole arena roared once more.

Amid that flurry of wildly cheering individuals, one man stood to see over the bobbing heads and shoulders. Gair, from the House of Curge, struggled to see Junger walk off the sands. When he couldn't see the Perician, he turned his attention to the defeated Korzo. The fallen gladiator stirred, weakly, as a handful of attendants emerged from an opened gate and hurried to his side.

Korzo held no interest for Gair. The pit fighter was capable enough but his refusal to toss aside that boulder of a hammer had cost him the match. The heavy weapon had slowed him down far too much compared to the Perician. That left Korzo face down and boneless upon the ground.

Master Curge had allowed all his gladiators to watch the games this day, to specifically witness the Perician contest. Gair understood why. The man was shockingly fast, and when he struck, well, Gair had heard the gasps from those around him. If the sword Junger used had been bare-edged steel, he could have easily taken off any of Korzo's limbs. Or his head.

A few men bumped into Gair, yelling happily while waving spilling cups over their heads. They shouted and jumped, paying little heed to the gladiator or anyone else around. Gair let them be, deciding it was time to leave. Skarrs patrolled the stands, and they would not hesitate to arrest a gladiator striking any commoner enjoying the games, as much as the commoner might deserve it. Worse, Dark Curge would punish anyone confronting one of Sunja's citizens.

So Gair got clear of the celebrating rabble. He shuffled through the masses toward the stairway, intent on returning to the private chambers belonging to the House of Curge. All the while, he replayed the Perician's fight in his head.

"What did you think of that?" Dark Curge asked his taskmaster when the cheering had died away.

Baris, who watched a handful of attendants help a rattled Korzo to his feet, slowly cocked his head.

"Nothing to say?" Curge asked.

The taskmaster faced the one-armed owner. "He's fast. Agile. Accurate. When he strikes, he strikes hard. Doesn't miss. He's patient . . . to a point. Waiting no longer than he has to. Perhaps a touch overconfident. When he sees his target, however . . . he hits it."

Baris remembered his cup then. He drank, gulping down the contents. When he finished, he glared into the depths of the arena. "I'll need to see more of him. To better conceive a way to defeat the man."

Curge sighed. "Anything else?"

His taskmaster regarded him. "No."

At that, Curge took a long drink himself.

21

The thunderous cheering reached the corridors of the lower arena, causing a few sprinkles of dust to spill from the ceiling and mist the torchlit air. The rumbling followed Junger as he made his way back to the House of Ten's quarters. Smiling faces and cheers from a much smaller audience greeted his return. They surrounded him. A grinning Muluk was clapping, while Valka slapped the returning pit fighter upon the shoulder.

"Ho, Perician," Clavellus said, walking up to him. "That was a proper *spectacle* you gave everyone out there. A right and proper spectacle. I can say with no doubt that Razi, the *owner* of the House of Razi, is pacing and sputtering curses this very moment at what you did to his man."

"Who was he, anyway?" Junger asked.

"Who? Korzo?"

"Aye that, Korzo."

"No idea," Clavellus admitted. "One of Razi's breakers of bones. With a hammer like that, the lad's whole strategy was to connect just once. He wore *horns* of all things. I understand the idea of drama within the games, but *horns?* Unfit, I tell you. One question now . . . your previous fights were so much more . . . one-sided. Shorter, I mean. Why did you take so long with this one?"

"That lad was a tough one," Junger admitted. "Much stronger than the others."

"You usually overwhelm them," Clavellus agreed and composed himself. "Ah, your contests are over far too fast, anyway. I'm not complaining, mind you. You keep doing what you do. We'll keep watching. Muluk, did you place the wagers?"

"On him?" the hairy Kree scoffed. "The whole arena knew he was going to win. There's no coin in that. More coin to be won on whether or not he'll pull steel while he's out there."

"Did you place coin on that then?"

Frowning, Muluk shook his head.

"Well," Clavellus chuckled and gripped Junger's shoulder. "Regardless, you won a small purse, so no worries there. Just . . . relax now, all right? We'll head back to Shan's place later on. Allow yourself to rest before the next throttling. And we'll count the days until then. Did you hear them? The people? I mean, they *adore* you, you savage. The arena simply *adores* you. I can't remember when the entirety of the Pit cheered for one man. Machlann? Can you remember such a— an outpouring?"

A ruddy-cheeked Machlann rattled his head, his great mustache barely hiding his smile.

"I certainly can't remember," Clavellus resumed. "Of course, there were those years I was away from the games here. Even then, I heard of what was happening. No one has won over the whole audience like you have. No one."

"Yes, well," Junger smiled and moved to the bench. "Perhaps there might be a bottle of something later on?"

"A bottle?" the taskmaster repeated and dismissed that with a wave. "*Pahhh.*"

"Daresay he'll buy you a barrel," Muluk said. "Of whatever you want. Wherever you want it."

Supposing that might be the case, Junger sat and said no more on the matter.

Goll, dressed in full armor, stopped before him. The Kree house master held the other's gaze for a moment before offering his fist. "Well done, Perician. Well done."

Junger pressed his own against Goll's, and for a beat of time—just a beat—the two shared a moment's peace.

"All right, boys," Clavellus said, returning to the arched window. "The day still has a few more fights. Gather around if you like. Including you, Shan, if you can keep from emptying your guts."

That didn't amuse the healer.

"Just a jab, good Shan. A friendly jab. Apologies. After all the time you've spent on Goll, I doubt you'll see anything that will upend your gullet."

That turned Goll's head.

Clavellus chuckled and turned to the window.

Three other fights preceded Goll's appearance in the Pit.

Zilos, of the House of Tilo, faced Bozzen, from the House of Vandu. Zilos was Sunjan-born, wielded a short spear with dastardly skill, and had once fought Brozz several days back. Zilos wasn't a very tall man, but he was well-built with an impressive endurance. He entered the arena wearing breeches and a cowl of red over his face. Other than his spear, which sported a jagged head resembling a shot of lightning, Zilos possessed a frightening speed which he used to great effect in his battle with Bozzen.

Bozzen appeared overmatched from the start of the fight, and was quickly dripping blood from a few quick thrusts of Zilos's spear. A few more thrusts and Zilos stood over his defeated foe.

Then it was Punder, from the Stable of Slavol, facing Morric, from the School of Vorish. Punder was a big Sunjan who had received guidance from the deceased Sorban of the same stable. With the death of Sorban, the crippling of Blacktooth, and the decimation of several hopefuls by none other than Goll himself, Punder was perhaps the last hope for the besieged Stable of Slavol in an otherwise disastrous season. Such was not to be, however, as Morric, a heavy-handed Vathian who employed hooked flails in each hand, used a lethal combination of strikes to first yank Punder off his feet and then lash him repeatedly with those wicked lengths of chains. A boot to the head ended the fight, and Punder had to be carried to the infirmary.

The School of Vorish gained a victory in that match, but it would not earn another in its second fight of the afternoon. Horvo, who sought to pull his own season out of the pisspot, was worn down and finally forced to yield by Trydas of the House of Ustda.

It was during that fight when Clavellus approached a pacing Goll. The Kree had long since donned his usual vest of hardened leather. Metal bracers protected his forearms, while bronze greaves shielded his lower legs. A rounded shield and sword lay nearby.

The healer loomed about, plainly nervous about the approaching contest, and powerless to do anything but wait until the end.

"Good Shan," Clavellus said as a startling roar erupted from the spectators, distracting them all. The taskmaster waited for the noise to lessen. "That was the end of it. May I have a moment with our house master?"

Shan busied himself with inspecting his medical supplies once more, long since laid out and waiting.

Clavellus faced the armored Kree. "Are you ready?"

Annoyed, Goll cocked his head at the question.

"Got enough grease on and all that?" Clavellus pressed.

Eyes narrowed and stared from within the depths of the helmet.

"How's the pot feel?"

"Good."

"Good. Try not to get smashed about the melon this time."

"Did you have something else to say? A word of encouragement, perhaps?"

A lurking presence caused Clavellus to turn. Muluk, his hairy face pensive, nodded with the taskmaster's every word.

Unbothered at being discovered, the bearded Kree urged him to continue.

So he did. "A few words. This Vonomir . . . as I've told you earlier, we don't know anything about him. Except he fights for the House of Tilo. Tilo is a very old, very decorated owner. His house ranks only a notch below that of Curge's. His taskmaster and trainers are all well-experienced. Anyone they send onto the sands will be a challenge. A great challenge. And this Vonomir? He has six victories this season. But he *also* has two losses. You have your aches. Your bruises. Your cuts. I can tell you . . . he will have his own. Watch him. Be careful of feints. Of traps. Take no risks, unless you are positive you can strike a blow. You are undefeated as of this day, Master Goll. *Un*defeated. Other than Baylus the Butcher, this day will offer you your most telling competition. But I believe . . . I *know* . . . you will do . . . as you have always done."

Clavellus felt warm breath on his shoulder and frowned at Muluk. Understanding the look, the Kree backed off a step.

The taskmaster regarded his gladiator once again. "Good fortune to you."

With that, Koba stepped in and offered Goll a sword and shield.

In the private chamber belonging to the House of Tilo, the sound of cheering died away. Old Tilo sat on a chair fashioned solely for him, before the arched window, where he could watch the fights in relative comfort. When the noise of the last contest lessened to a low rumble, the old owner leaned back and smoothed out his brown robes. He regarded his taskmaster, a man called Proxo, and nodded at him.

Proxo stood taller than most. A former gladiator himself, he had enjoyed some success without ever winning the tournament. As he liked to tell anyone who listened, he'd survived it all, which was victory in itself. At fifty-six years of age, he was lean with a head full of cropped silver hair and an icy stare. Scars marked his shaven cheeks, and several more scrolled down his neck and along his forearms.

Nodding back at the owner, Proxo strode away, the whispery rush of the crowd filling his ears. In slow, deliberate strides, he made his way to the rear of the room. Armored men wearing faces of steel lined both walls. Those men straightened as the taskmaster strode by and kept their eyes lowered. Proxo passed the recovering Zilos, still wearing his own mask, while the healer tending to the pit fighter paused with a handful of bandages. Both men lowered their heads as the taskmaster passed.

Proxo stopped before the one called Vonomir.

A tight vest of leather molded into a chiseled physique protected the gladiator's torso. Featureless bronze greaves and spiked bracers covered his limbs. With a calmness that benefited anyone in the sport, Vonomir met that harsh stare of his taskmaster.

"It's nearly time," Proxo said in a deep voice, revealing a few missing teeth.

Vonomir nodded.

"You belong to Master Tilo," Proxo said without blinking. "You've been taken in by the best. Trained by the best. To *be* the best. This day . . . you fight the one called Goll. You know of him."

Vonomir nodded again.

"You know he comes from the ranks of the Free Trained."

Another tempered nod.

"You know that despite his gurry beginnings, the man's had proper training. As shown with his victories in the Pit. He's Kree. Probably has trained with the Weapon Masters of that place. Make no mistake. He'll be a handful. He's undefeated thus far, but he's been struck. Been hurt. Been *cut*."

Vonomir listened, his eyes hooded and relaxed, his breathing damn near nonexistent.

"Today, you defeat this man from the House of Ten. Today, you break him. And it would greatly please Master Tilo if you remove the Kree's head from his neck. Do you understand?"

"Clearly," replied the pit fighter.

Proxo arched his head. "Show me your face."

Vonomir donned his helmet, stirring up a faint smell of metal and leather. The dim light in the room cast shadows across the hellion's grinning faceplate, coloring it evil. A nearby warrior offered him a sword, while another held out a shield. Vonomir took them both when someone knocked upon the door.

No one dared to answer it, however.

"Master Tilo," Proxo spoke, not taking his eyes off that sinister mask. "He's ready."

From where he sat, Tilo still faced the arena. He held up a hand, showing he heard, and feebly waved it as if whisking away a fly.

Dreary daylight checkered the stone steps as the portcullis rose above him. Tools of the trade swinging at his side, Goll climbed the stairs to the yawning portal, hearing the Orator already talking about him. He couldn't rightly understand, but as he drew closer the words grew sharper and lifted over the soft rumbles of the audience.

"You know this one as well," the Orator boomed. "This is a man on his own determined quest. In the very first battle of the games, he nearly perished at the hands of Baylus the Butcher, spilling blood with every step. Since then he's returned, harder than before. Taking both heads and lives in bloody fashion. Kree by birth, trained by masters of the arts, this man has shown us, time and time again, that he belongs in our games. That he may even belong . . . in the records of our history."

A smattering of groans disagreed with him.

The Orator pushed on. "And yet, not only has he shown us the skilled killer within him, but he's also shown a touch of mercy. Perhaps he will show us something else this day. And to end a glorious day of butchery, I present to you *Goll*, from the House of *Ten* . . ."

The heavy breath of a midsummer heat enveloped him as he trod onto the sands. The very air felt swollen, bloated with moisture, and begging for release. Warm applause from the spectators followed him, their welcome marred by a few shouted insults and jeers. Still, considering how far he had come—and how much farther he had to go—the greeting was something unexpected. He didn't fight for the crowds. Far from it. He fought for himself. And yet, like his last contest, he discovered it wasn't a bad thing to have the approval of the audience. It was better than being sworn at.

The Orator shouted for the fight to begin.

Goll walked toward his opponent who'd been introduced before him.

Vonomir advanced, the features of his helmet becoming clearer across boot-scuffed sand. His sword and shield swung casually at his sides, suggesting a calmness not usually present in most fighters. *Confidence*, Goll recognized. The man had only been beaten twice this season, so that confidence was perhaps deeply rooted.

Goll reminded himself that he hadn't lost at all.

As they drew closer, a grinning hellion face taunted him.

Goll intended to yank that sinister mask from the pit fighter's head.

When they were no more than a few strides apart, Vonomir abruptly dug in his heels and brandished his sword and shield.

Goll did the same, and they circled each other, to the rising shouts of onlookers. Goll focused on his foe, matching Vonomir whenever he changed direction. The pit fighter from the House of Tilo didn't speak. The hellion mask, at times half concealed behind his shield, studied the Kree as he moved left to right and back again.

Slowly, the distance between the two gladiators shrank.

Goll opened with a series of slashes and cuts aimed at his foe's head and shoulders.

Vonomir stopped them all, sparks flashing with each harsh connection, before circling and breaking off.

Goll pursued, stabbing for a gut, once, twice, before spinning and swinging his shield's edge at that armored head. Vonomir parried both strikes, ducked under that looping barrier, and countered with his own combination of cuts and thrusts.

Goll slapped away one thrust with his shield and quickly backed away from the rest.

Vonomir did not pursue, and Goll stopped retreating. They resumed circling, warily, gauging the other, while the distance shrank again.

Vonomir feinted twice from the shoulders—twitchy flexes seeking to bait Goll into committing a mistake. The Kree did nothing of the sort, however. He held back, and when Vonomir hinted at moving left, Goll pounced.

Except Vonomir was already moving out of the way.

Feinted, Goll's mind screamed as he twisted, kicking up sand as he ducked and weaved. Vonomir slashed repeatedly for his foe's sword arm, seeking to slice it off at the shoulder. Shield and sword flashing, Goll stopped every strike, the connections jarring. The Kree backpedaled, fending off blows aimed for his head. Until Vonomir stabbed for his guts, looking to pierce him through the middle. Goll parried with his shield and sprawled, slashing for legs as he fell.

He missed.

The roar of thousands filled his ears as he landed face down. With an energy fired by desperation, he twisted and hacked at ankles.

Vonomir retreated, backing off to his left.

Which a frantic Goll matched, kicking up dust as he struggled to get his legs under him.

Then came the surprise of the day.

Vonomir motioned for him to rise, much to the sour dismay of some onlookers.

Goll did so hurriedly, watching his opponent as the grinning hellion mask in turn watched him. Goll crouched, his blade poised at the lower rim of his shield, gleaming like a ready stinger.

Vonomir attacked and the pair traded strikes and parries at the center of the Pit. Until one low cut forced Goll to block it with his blade, and the edge of Vonomir's shield crashed into his face.

Dazed, Goll staggered back as Vonomir pressed forward. Vonomir hacked at a shoulder and struck armor, driving Goll to a knee. With a grunt of effort, Vonomir smashed his shield across the Kree's face, throwing him onto his back. From there, Vonomir hammered at the downed man's head. Goll flailed with his shield, blocking several of those downward cuts . . .

Until Vonomir stabbed for his foe's chest.

Fright gave Goll a jolt of strength and speed as he swung his shield into that blow. The sword pierced the barrier in a squawk of wood, the blade stropping the very bracer protecting Goll's forearm.

A chorus of pained *ohhhhs* flew up from the audience.

Half a sword penetrated the shield, and its edge pressed hard against Goll's bracer, but it failed to find meat. He twisted and ripped the weapon free of Vonomir's grip, nearly taking the taller man down. Goll kicked for a leg but failed to topple his adversary.

They broke away, dust misting the air, while between them lay the ruined shield and protruding blade.

Goll held his sword at arm's length.

The hellion-masked Vonomir eyed him over the rim of his shield, brandishing a hardened fist behind it.

They wavered, adjusting to their remaining tools, and circled each other again. Goll watched his opponent, expecting a head-long attack, when a warm wetness seeped into his right eye . . .

Vonomir charged and crashed into him. He discarded his shield and grabbed for the only blade between them. An iron vise of a hand gripped Goll's wrist, and for a brief instant they grappled toe-to-toe.

Until the stronger Vonomir forced the hand down and pro-ceeded to punch Goll's armored head.

The first three blows bounced his skull about inside his hel-met. The final one sent him reeling backward, his free hand reach-ing for the ground—when the bloodied tip of Vonomir's sword ran through his unprotected palm. The weapon slid through with all the grace and sureness of a needle slipping through cloth, lighting up Goll's entire arm from fingertip to shoulder.

He screamed.

The audience drowned him out with their own screams.

Wasting no time, Vonomir aimed low and smashed Goll's head to one side. He punched it to the right, held the top, and plowed a fist straight into the armored face.

Goll collapsed onto his back.

Vonomir edged closer until he loomed over the fallen gladia-tor, fist at the ready but looking to see if the man was unconscious.

In that lull, Goll ripped his hand from that steely thorn. A thin arc of scarlet laced the air as he slapped the same palm over the hellion's face.

Blinding him for an instant.

In that rushed heartbeat, Goll, with everything he had, bashed his sword across his foe's armored head.

Vonomir staggered a drunken two-step before crumpling to his hands and knees. Goll climbed to his feet. Half blinded and arm buzzing, the Kree swayed and appraised his dazed foe. His left-hand dripping blood, Goll lurched toward Vonomir, reared back, and brought his heavy blade down squarely across Vonomir's helmet.

The force rocked the gladiator.

Goll struck again and again, tapping into a furious inner strength. The hellion mask rocked left to right, the metal crinkling. Vonomir finally fell over, head planted to the sands, and Goll stood over him. The Kree jammed a foot underneath his opponent and forced him onto his back. Huffing, grunting, Goll favored the wrecked claw of his one hand before he dropped a knee onto Vonomir's chest.

From there, he fixed the tip of the blade to an eye slit and waited.

And waited a little more.

Slowly, Vonomir lifted a hand into the air and held it for a beat . . . before he dropped it.

Goll pulled his sword away as the arena exploded with approval. Ignoring them, he struggled to stand and did so. Shrugging, he cupped his bleeding hand close to his chest and examined the damage.

At his feet, Vonomir stirred but made no effort to rise.

Goll left him, dripping blood as he made the long walk for the rising portcullis.

Above it all, Dark Curge leaned forward, drink in hand, and watched Goll leave the sands.

22

Blood dappled the flagstones as an angry Goll trudged through a corridor lined with watchful Skarrs. He met Muluk and Koba at the halfway point, and Muluk offered to take his sword. Goll gave it with a red-faced scowl and marched on without a word. Once behind closed doors, he plopped down on the bench next to where Shan had laid out his medicinal instruments and bandages.

The healer immediately went to work while Koba motioned the others to stand clear.

Which Clavellus ignored.

"Victorious!" the taskmaster announced happily, looming over Shan's bobbing head and shoulders.

Goll ignored him and jerked his bleeding fist away from the healer.

That infuriated Shan, who pointed a finger at the Kree's helmet. "Don't try me, not this day. Now give me that hand."

With a defeated hiss, Goll did as told. He thumped his head against the wall as he uncurled red-stained fingers. Thick droplets pattered the floor, stemming from a gash through the middle of the hand, splitting the meat between the fingers there. Shan cringed while studying the damage. The healer snatched up a wad of cloth and placed it over the wound. "Hold this," he instructed.

"I can't," Goll said through clenched teeth.

"You can't hold it? Why can't you hold it?"

"Because it hurts."

"Can you move your fingers?"

"Aye that," and he did, just a little.

"All right then," Shan said and put pressure on the cloth, turning it red.

Goll huffed and sighed and did not flinch at the damage.

"Perhaps you should cook that?" a nearby Machlann suggested, meaning the wound.

"Not needed," Shan said. "Muluk. When that cloth becomes soaked, replace it with another."

The bearded Kree moved into place while Shan examined Goll's armored face. "You're bleeding about the neck."

"He struck me upside the head," Goll said.

Annoyed, Shan stood and dragged a hand down his face, thinking matters over. "I'm going to remove your helm. Same as before. Up and over."

"Use the grease, then."

"There's little time for that," Shan said as he took the edges. "On the count of—"

He yanked, hauling that cursed thing up, releasing a stream of darkness that drenched Goll's profile. Goll grunted, winced, his right eye tightly shut. Above it, marking the curvature of his forehead and stretching to his hairline, was a lipless mouth the length of a child's finger. The cut bled relentlessly, painting that side of his face.

"Hate you for that," Goll groaned.

Shan ignored him. He worked on the gash, where dewy bone peeked through. A little grunt left him as he closed the cut and slapped a thick bandage against it.

"Muluk, hold this here."

Muluk moved closer, occupied with two tasks.

His hands free, Shan quickly bound the head wound with a length of cloth, pausing only long enough for Muluk to pull his fingers away. Once tied off, Shan returned to working on the hand.

"Well?" Goll asked.

"Well what?" Shan asked back, inspecting the appendage.

"Am I done?"

"No."

"No?"

Shan put himself before Goll's bloody features. "Stop *distracting* me with questions you can ask *later*."

Message delivered, he returned to work.

A grimacing Goll sighed and regarded the concerned faces. Before long, he settled back and stole peeks at what the healer was doing.

"He's stitching you together," Muluk described while tossing away saturated wads of cloth. "Pinching things before pulling—"

"I *know*," Goll grated and spat a red gob onto the floor.

"You'll be fine," Clavellus said with confidence. "I've seen worse. Machlann's certainly seen worse. You'll be fine. And think of it. You did it. You won again. Another gladiator put down. Well done, lad."

"Well done, my son," a pleased Machlann said.

Muluk hurriedly patted down Goll's face with a cloth, turning the material red.

"Did you wager anything?" Goll asked.

Muluk nodded eagerly.

A heavy knocking at the door turned heads. Valka stood guard back there, cocking an eyebrow at the others.

"Open it," Clavellus said.

So the old soldier did.

An imposing brute of a man stood there. Black-bearded and narrowed eyes, with slabs of leather armor strapped across his powerful-looking torso. A heavy broadsword hung off one hip. He sized up Valka before eyeing the others in the room.

Though no one pulled steel, Koba's hands gripped his belt, close to his broadsword.

"Master Curge wishes to talk with you," the bearded visitor rumbled.

Valka did not move.

"Step aside, Demasta," Curge ordered, and the guard did so, allowing those inside to glimpse several more guards in the corridor.

Valka still did not move, and Koba joined him.

Sighing, Clavellus gnawed on his lip before waving a hand. "Let him in, lads."

The pair reluctantly backed away, wary of the one called Demasta.

Only Dark Curge ambled into the room, however, stooping just a touch as he passed through. He stopped a pace inside, his barren head glistening while a bead of moisture slid down his face. The dribble annoyed him and he swiped it away with his stump. He spotted Goll while wiping his arm in his robes and studied the man.

Goll glared back, but Curge turned his attention to the healer working upon the gladiator.

"Curge," Clavellus greeted warily, facing the owner. "Offering your congratulations, are you?"

The question turned Curge's head, and he considered the taskmaster for several beats of time before returning to Goll's hard gaze. Neither man flinched, and once Curge had his fill, he regarded the others in the room until he met Junger's stare. There he paused, for one acknowledging moment, before facing Goll again.

"You did well this day," Curge said quietly. "Very well. Vonomir is . . . a hellion. As are most of Tilo's fighters. There are no easy victories there. It's not by chance you defeated him."

"Many thanks," Goll said through a clenched jaw.

"You also did well, Perician," Curge continued. "I can say without a drop of doubt, there aren't many participating in these games who were *not* watching you this day. I even ordered my own lads to come watch you. Very well done. You have . . . the full attention of the owners. Their training staff. Gladiators. And anyone looking to make a name for themselves." He nodded then, agreeing with his own assessment. "Seddon above will not save you now."

"What do you want, Master Curge?" Clavellus demanded. "Besides making threats to my boys."

"Wasn't a threat," Curge growled back. "You know this. Every boulder falling from this side of the mountain will look to flatten him. It's the way of the games."

A bemused Junger blinked at that.

"I said what do you want?" Clavellus repeated sternly. "With a pack of butchers on your heels?"

Curge checked on Demasta, who had locked stares with the much larger Koba. Seeing nothing amiss, Curge turned back. "Only as I've just said. The contest between the Perician and . . . what was his name? Korzo? Probably one of the best under Razi's roof . . . but certainly not the best fighting this season. No one questioned the outcome there. No one. Well, perhaps Razi, but that's Razi. I did question *your* outcome, however." He directed that at Goll. "Although I suspected you would win in the end . . . Narrowly. How is your hand?"

That lifted Shan's head, but he positioned himself to conceal his work.

"Just a cut, nothing more," Clavellus answered for him. "Our man is working on him."

Curge's fiercely blue eyes narrowed, watching the healer.

"Well," Clavellus announced. "Thank you for your visit, Master Curge. Very much appreciated. I think we've shown the respect due, as custom demands, but we both know you're only here for your own devious ends. You may leave now, and don't bother visiting us in the future."

If Curge heard, he didn't show it. In fact, the big owner didn't move. Didn't budge. After a beat of time, half his face hitched in a smile as he met the old taskmaster's stare. "Respect? Clavellus? From you? *That*, I doubt . . . I *have* seen enough, however . . ." Curge considered Goll for just a moment more.

Then he met the taskmaster's gaze. "To the end," the big owner said and walked out the door.

An expressionless Demasta backed into the corridor. From there, he and the rest of the guards followed their employer.

Hand on his sword, Valka stepped outside and watched them leave. He craned his neck for moments before he stepped back inside and closed the door. "They're gone," he reported.

Annoyed by the brazen visitation, Clavellus struggled to keep his voice even. "Apologies, all. My mistake. I shouldn't have allowed him in."

"We should post guards outside," Muluk said. "To watch for those shaggers."

That took some heat out of the taskmaster's face.

"He's a bold one," Muluk added.

"He's *Curge*," Clavellus flared. "*Dark* Curge. And he's not to be taken lightly. At *any* time. That one . . . oh, he knows what he's doing. What he just *did*. This is *his* realm. His domain, and he's aware of all within it."

"Brazen spying," Machlann said plainly.

"Brazen spying," Clavellus agreed and raked his fingers through his beard. "Damn him. And damn *me*. A slip of the mind. Are you finished with his hand, good Shan?"

"Almost. What I can do, anyway."

"Then don't delay. We'll leave the moment he's able to walk without bleeding a drop. This day is done."

23

Well-rested and recovered from his encounter with the Sons, Gurga slapped on his armor and gathered his weapons. He concealed what he could and left the alehouse a little after noon. Having not eaten since yesterday, he bought a few pastries and chanced eating while walking, as eating while walking could upset his guts. Memories of the previous night remained fresh in his mind, however, and he wanted to be quick with his business, for fear of forgetting important details.

Linfur was the name he remembered. Gurga also remembered the location, a butcher's store, where Linfur held court someplace in the back. Munching on cooling pastries and flicking flakes from his beard, the enforcer made his way through the city, searching for the butcher's store.

And searched.

And searched.

Until he found one such place, but it wasn't really a store. Or so a glaring Gurga thought, stuffing the last of his meal into his mouth and puffing out both cheeks. He gazed upon a pavilion of sorts, where four thick logs held up a roof slathered in uneven slats of stone. Under that roof, flies buzzed around red haunches of meat hanging from a rafter, over a hay-covered floor. Two men, their hands and arms stained to their elbows, hacked into a grisly chunk on a chopping block. Neither man wore aprons, so blood spattered their clothes with every chop. Behind them was a table covered in smaller roasts and thin skewers of meat. A third man stood with his back to them all, speaking with potential customers.

Gurga watched, chewing and mulling things over. The lad he had pulled the information from had said Linfur held court in a room *behind* the butcher's store. This place had no such back room, and no walls to speak of. Yet, this was the only place where they were openly plying a butcher's trade. The mystery creased his forehead and his expression grew even more thoughtful.

The man with a stained cleaver straightened and wiped at his forehead, leaving a streak. He spotted Gurga and his once-honest-working face grew worried.

The one helping him noticed his partner and followed his gaze. He faltered upon beholding Gurga.

The enforcer, however, went right on watching. And thinking . . . and chewing.

The two butchers traded looks before one scratched at his chin. He muttered something, and the one speaking with the customers turned, his smile wilting as he laid eyes upon Gurga. The two customers—a pair of ladies—also eyed the big man, their smiles vanishing.

The merchant doing the selling excused himself and approached Gurga. Unlike his two companions, this one kept himself clean of the butchery. He stuck out his jaw, scratched at it, and stopped just under the edge of that stony roof. There he nodded greetings, attempting to put some cheer into his face.

Unblinking, Gurga swallowed his last bite and felt around his mouth with his tongue.

The merchant stopped scratching and shrugged a question at the intimidating man.

After years of standing guard for Sindra, Gurga had developed a sense for troublemaking maggots. The merchant before him would not be trouble. Nor would the two lads behind him. Deciding all was well, Gurga turned away from the questioning looks. He brushed at his beard one last time, sprinkling flakes onto the cobblestones, and lurched into a walk. Disappointed and without direction, he sought merchant squares or stables or little shacks where a bit of dishonest butchering might be happening.

Worse, his guts grumbled at him while he walked.

By midafternoon, he found himself back at Sunja's Pit. Citizens had gathered outside of that magnificent structure. A good many hung around the food stalls, enjoying spits of roast chicken or beef before proceeding inside to watch the day's games. Some stood about in broken clumps, talking or perhaps even wagering among themselves. A ring of carefully placed bricks and mortar formed the public fountain, directly south of the Gate of the Sea. The pool looked about a dozen strides across, with a stone dais at the center. A sculpted figure of a poised and ready spearman rose from that platform. Opaque eyes peered into those shallow depths, and the barest furrow of concern creased his unseeing face. Several loiterers sat upon the edge of the pool with their backs to the statue, and they watched Gurga's every moment.

Not wanting to scatter them, he moved away and located the familiar foundation of a two-story building. So there he sat, shoulders slouched in frustration, hands to his knees and back to the wall. Not a breeze blew, and the wretched humidity sought to steam him while he watched the arena and its gathering crowds.

Linfur. The thought deepened his scowl. He hadn't even had the sense to ask what the man looked like. Or what he usually wore. Poor thinking on his part, and the mistake steamed him even more. The only choice he had now was to continue his search around the alehouses, the more villainous ones, in hopes of catching a glimpse of someone wearing ink.

A fly zipped past his face. Gurga ignored it, knowing he wasn't fast enough to slap the thing. His thoughts wandered, contemplating a search in another part of the city. As he sat and mused on matters, a foul smell reached him.

"Ah, greetings," someone muttered from his left.

The louse. Same nearly toothless smile, same dark eyes that crinkled at the corners, and same filthy rags he'd worn not two days ago. Perhaps the only thing different was the grubby bastard's overall color, which seemed a touch muddier, as if he'd slept in a watery shite trough. And he *reeked*, as if washing would destroy him entirely. The wretch held up his hands and even those were stained.

Gurga scowled at him.

"Don't hurt me," the louse said, ready to bolt. "Look . . . I had to run the other night. I had to. You're just one fellow. One big fellow but you must understand, there are more of them than you. And I figured one of them would stick a knife in your back or wherever and that would be that. Imagine my surprise to see you shambling about like the great tree you are . . . alive and well and back here, where I first saw you." He faltered, coughed, hoarked a substantial load by the sound of it, and gulped it back down.

Gurga stared at the little man. *Darsho*. His name was Darsho.

A crippling itch distracted the beggar, prompting him to claw at his ribs.

Gurga reached out and grabbed him by the rat's nest of a beard concealing most of his face. He clutched a fistful of hair, feeling the stiff resistance of unwashed whiskers. The grip silenced Darsho. The old man grimaced, his attention darting between the hand that held him and the face above it.

"I forgot . . ." he winced a smile, "you have a lengthy arm."

Gurga pulled him closer when something crawled over his fingers knotted in that filthy beard.

"I had to run," Darsho blurted, his eyes wide with dread. "They knew me. The one that—that was slapping the other one? He knew me."

"That one stabbed me."

"What?"

"In the back."

"*Stabbed* you in the *back?*"

"Right here," he nodded and tapped the very spot. "Same one I thought I was saving."

Darsho's expression of fear shifted to disdain. "That's *unfit*," he squawked, as if it were the lowest thing to do. "Well, he only did it because, well, it was Gallwin you were striking. Gallwin's a right vengeful pig bastard. Unfit dangerous. I mean, you don't know. That lad terrorized us—"

Gurga pulled on the beard, opening Darsho's mouth and releasing a pungent fume that was positively foul.

"*Terrorized* us, I tell you," Darsho managed.

"I killed him."

That silenced the little man, who blinked and stared as if he hadn't heard correctly. "You killed him."

Gurga nodded.

". . . Lords above."

The enforcer released him and rubbed his hands, hoping to dislodge whatever had crawled onto them.

Darsho straightened and didn't run away. Instead, he smoothed down the ruinous tangle of facial hair which reached his chest. "Many thanks for that. For killing Gallwin and for releasing me. You have a powerful grip, but I suppose you know that."

Gurga supposed he did.

"Ah, did you happen to kill the one Gallwin was slapping? At the time? The one that . . ."

The enforcer nodded.

Darsho gawked before scratching at his armpit and then an elbow. "You killed them both. And the ones in the storehouse. You are a brute."

Gurga said nothing to that.

"Might I ask, sar, *why* you're looking for the Sons of Cholla?"

Fair enough question, the enforcer thought. "They killed . . . my employer."

"Ah. I see. They kill a good many people, I'll have you know. Beggars. Cripples. All lost, unfortunate souls. The Sons aren't particular about whose throat they're cutting. Or the reason why. I suppose it all serves a purpose one way or another. Let me finish what I was saying. The one Gallwin was smashing? The one who . . . stabbed you in the back? I believe he only did so to gain approval from Gallwin. I'm certain that's the only reason he did such a thing. I know. We would all do it. Stab whoever was smashing the Sons, I mean. When you've been . . . throttled for so long, so . . . without mercy . . . as we have—by the Sons—well . . . if you can gain favor in their eyes, you might escape the *next* throttling. If that makes any sense . . ."

Gurga supposed it did.

"He didn't know who you were," Darsho went on. "Or what you were doing. All he knew was, if you failed . . . Gallwin would have fish-hooked him. Hm? That's why he stabbed you." He finished with a stern look. "Not apologizing for the man, you understand. Not me. But . . . just explaining why is all."

"Fair enough."

"Ah . . . you killed them all, didn't you?" Darsho asked, pinching at the edge of one nostril before scattering the results away.

Gurga nodded.

"I . . . followed you, you see. That night. When you had Gallwin. Figured I . . . might help him. For reasons I just explained. And because I led you to him. I had to. I ran off screaming into the night. Gallwin would have recognized my voice. So I had to come back. When I did, well . . . you surprised me. I found the storehouse. Saw the dead . . . all except Gallwin. So I went to the alehouse that he likes, to see if he was about. Well . . . you killed them all there as well, didn't you?"

Gurga nodded again.

That straightened Darsho. "You sar, are a *brute*. I have a question, however . . ." He glanced around before leaning closer. "Do you mean to kill them all?" he whispered. "All the Sons of Cholla? Or just that handful?"

Gurga squinted at the beggar.

"Because if you are going to kill them all . . ." Darsho glanced around before his voice dropped to a whisper. "I'll help you do it."

That raised the enforcer's knobby brow.

"I mean, I won't help you *with* the killing, of course. Clearly, boy, you can do that on your own. But I'll lead you to the ones terrorizing me and others. Using us. Forcing us to do their loathsome bidding, of which begging for coin is perhaps the least offensive. A person can only live like that for so long before you have to do something back. I know these people. They've slapped me about the head many times. If I lead you to them, would you . . . ?"

Darsho let the question dangle.

Gurga nodded. "I would."

"You would?"

Gurga nodded again.

Darsho did the same, slowly, as if realizing the potential worth of such a bargain. ". . . Excellent."

"I mean to kill them all," the enforcer said. "And if you try to stab me from behind—or from anywhere—I'll kill you too."

Darsho promised to never do such a thing with a vigorous shake of his head.

"Do you know someone called Linfur?" Gurga asked.

"I do. I know him."

"I've been told he . . . holds court . . . in a room behind a butcher's store."

"He does. I know the place."

That got the enforcer's attention.

"But . . ." Darsho said, "before we go there, might we go looking for his henchmen? These are Linfur's snakes. The very ones that strangle us."

"No. Take me to this butcher's place first."

"All right, I will. Most certainly I will." Darsho held up a finger. "Ah, might we get something to eat first?"

Gurga studied the grubby little wretch. He then considered the fountain and thought about throwing the louse in there, but that might summon the street watch.

The food stalls were another matter.

He sized up Darsho once again. "Wait here," he rumbled.

Some time later, perhaps early evening, well after they had both eaten something, Gurga followed Darsho through the intricate puzzle that was Sunja's backstreets and alleys. Lengthy narrows of stone and brick and spaces barely wide enough to slip through, which forced Gurga to turn his shoulders and suck in his gut. Even though Gurga believed Darsho was older than himself, the beggar kept a surprising pace. At times, Darsho stopped or slowed to scratch at his fruits and other cracks best attended to when he was alone . . . or at least when he wasn't walking ahead of Gurga.

At one juncture, underneath a drooping clothesline that crossed the space overhead, Darsho glanced back at the enforcer and slid a dirty hand along a wall overgrown with wild greenery.

This one, he mouthed, bobbing his head as he stressed the words.

Gurga reached out and grabbed the man's shoulder. "Wait here . . ." he whispered and handed over his spiked club.

The club was almost half Darsho's size, and he struggled with its weight.

"Lords above," he hissed, planting the weapon headfirst onto the ground.

Gurga ignored all that. "When I'm done, I'll return."

"If you can . . ."

The enforcer scowled at that and pulled his gloves tight. He left Darsho and turned himself sideways to better ease through the space, mindful of the clutter underfoot. A sound rose above the rush of everyday chatter generated by a busy populace, one that gave Gurga pause just to hear it.

A chopping. Heavy and relentless. Rhythmic and at times broken by a brooding silence before it repeated.

The alley ended just ahead, meeting a much wider street. There Gurga stopped, just out of sight, listening to that dreary *whuk* of metal into wood, at times followed by the distinct slap of meat being flipped over. He edged to the corner, ignoring looks from those passing by.

A butcher's store, different from the one he'd seen earlier in the day; this one was the size of a barn, and it had walls. The front was open, however, with a fence and gate facing the street. Inside, above a floor covered in hay, haunches of meat hung from overhead beams. Many haunches, as if the butcher worked to feed a large number of people. Slop pails filled with a bloody gurry dotted the straw, drawing the interest of flies. Dull, gleaming saws and large hooks hung from the walls and support posts. A series of barrels lined one wall all the way to the rear, where a broad wedge of evening light spilled from the ceiling.

There, with his bare back turned to the street, was a thickset man standing over a table. He reared back his arm, one that was holding a large cleaver.

Whuk!

The butcher shivered from the impact. He worked the blade free and shoved away something that landed with a splatter. As Gurga watched, he grew aware of another sound, one that surprised him, given the scene. The butcher *sang* to himself—or rather hummed—in a deep and melodious tune. One that he stopped when he brought the cleaver down.

Then continued when he pulled the blade free.

Gurga examined the gate.

Whuk! Another heavy blow. The butcher grunted as he freed his blade, his shape partially concealed by the many chunks of meat dangling from the ceiling.

Gurga opened the gate, the yawning squeal hidden by another chop. He entered and closed the gate behind him while the butcher continued working. Minding his step, he proceeded across spattered straw, stirring up angry flies as he went. At times, great slabs of meat blocked his way, as the butcher had hung them everywhere without any real order. Some of those chunks hung suspended over slop buckets stinking of dried blood. Red-white ribs and spines gleamed in the shadows as Gurga navigated that grisly maze, easing those great portions out of the way. A water barrel blocked him once, the rim wet and the contents as dark as wine.

The butcher continued to work.

Gurga threaded his way through the gloomy interior, toward his target.

"You want the chicken or the roasts?" the butcher asked, his voice coarse and rattling and in need of a cleaning just as badly as the floor.

The question halted Gurga at the halfway point. The butcher stayed at the chopping table, glimpsed between the hanging meat. He chopped again and studied the last cut with interest. With a nasty sniff he wrenched the cleaver free. Steel scraped wood as he flicked something over the table's edge. Gurga glimpsed a featherless chicken being worked upon. The sinewy crack of cartilage then, split down the middle. Another scrape of the blade and a plop of meat as it dropped into a great basket below.

Gurga shuffled forward again.

"You hear me?" the butcher asked. "The chicken is lovely. Just lovely. Have one or two if that's what you fancy. Roasts are hanging all around you. Cut and quartered. Some's been hanging a week or more. Some a couple of days. Some just today. You don't want that. My word to you? You want the older ones. Bled dry and ready for the spit. Or the soup. The warm air works on the meat, you see. Makes it more tender to the bite. Better flavor, even, I think."

Some five strides away and Gurga saw the butcher wasn't overly tall. The man wore black trousers and was amply wide across the hips, which made his bare, rounded shoulders appear narrow. Hair matted those shoulders, while fat rolls hung over and hid the waistband of the clothing.

Watching the butcher's every movement, Gurga picked the surest path through that hanging forest of meat. The closer he crept, however, the larger the butcher became, and those shoulders shivered after every downward blow.

"See anything then?" the butcher asked, still not turning around. "And be quick about it, would you? I'll be closing soon."

Gurga pushed aside a haunch tied off by the ankle. The rope groaned.

That cocked the butcher's head. He turned, curiously, revealing a huge gut hidden behind an apron spattered in red.

The man's eyes went wide.

Gurga charged.

The butcher whirled, bringing up his cleaver, just as Gurga lurched forward. He swung for the butcher's offended face.

Who ducked, darting under that sweeping catapult shot of a fist with surprising speed. As a reply, he swung the cleaver in a flat arc, looking to open Gurga's guts. That oversized shard of metal crunched into the enforcer's lower bits, delivering a troubling pinch as Gurga plowed into the smaller man. Grimacing, flailing, both men crashed over the chopping table and onto the floor. They rolled free of each other and scurried to their feet.

The butcher slashed at an ear. Gurga blocked the cut and punched the man's face, stumbling him backward. The butcher collided with two huge sets of exposed ribs before slamming into a wall.

Gurga went after him.

With a piggish snort, the butcher lashed out. Gurga blocked the cleaver on his bracer, the blow numbing his forearm to his shoulder. He crashed into the butcher again, flattening him against the wall. The butcher squealed and seized Gurga's throat. Digging in his heels, the smaller man forced him back. Gurga tore the offending hand away and shoved the butcher against the wall again. There the enforcer went to work, looking to do a little tenderizing of his own. He delivered three hard punches to that impressive gut, each one resulting in a puff of decaying breath. The butcher folded, dropped his cleaver, and stopped the last punch on his elbow. He countered with a surprising uppercut, smashing hard knuckles into Gurga's jaw and straightening the enforcer's neck.

But then Gurga righted himself and regarded the butcher, who clearly thought the fight was over.

Gurga grabbed the back of the man's head and pulled it forward to meet the hard tip of his elbow. Bone crackled and gore spurted, speckling the enforcer's beard and face. The butcher crumpled to the straw-covered floor. Gurga bent over and grabbed the man's hair. He lined up the bleeding face and struck again. Iron-shod knuckles shattered teeth and split skin in great gouts of color. Gurga drew back, deliberating another blow. The butcher's eyes were closed, and the pulped mess of his flattened nose pointed to the right. Blood flowed from a gash along the bridge, where red bone peeked through. A heavy sprinkling of teeth surrounded the unconscious man's knees, while his chin slumped as if unhinged.

Puffing, sweating, Gurga slapped that face, and the force of that alone snapped the butcher's head upon his neck. Gurga released him and the unconscious man fell flat.

The enforcer glanced over his shoulder, and saw he was still alone. Beyond the man at his feet was a single door, near the back. Checking on the butcher again, Gurga kicked the cleaver away and it clattered off a far wall.

On impulse, he stomped on the hand that had grabbed him. The butcher shivered but did not wake up.

Frowning, checking on his own hands before smelling them, Gurga pulled up his gloves and moved to the door.

Which he kicked in.

With a booming crackle and a dusty mist of splinters, the door bounced off the inner wall. Gurga glanced over his shoulder and through the clutter saw no one at the entrance or peering in from the street. So he shoved the door aside and entered the room belonging to a merchant. Boots clopped across bare floorboards as he kicked aside a chair. He stopped at a heavy desk, where a single unlit lamp rested. He lifted and sniffed at a bowl of herbs. *Pleasant smelling*, he thought, and tossed them aside. A chair and a well-made cabinet waited beyond the table. He heaved aside the furniture to get to the cabinet. A lock prevented him from opening it, so Gurga put his fist through the cabinet door, crumpling it. He cleared the fragments away and pawed about the inner depths.

A few small purses, all filled with coin.

Gurga hefted one and placed it in his pocket. While he did so, he noticed a black thread on his shirt, as well as a few dark spots just below his ribs. Frowning, he pulled at the cloth, widening the cut from the butcher's cleaver. Alarmed, he lifted his shirt to expose the leather band protecting his gut, and saw the barest split in the armor where the blade had cut the deepest, parting the cloth folds and just tasting the flesh beneath. No sooner did he see it than the annoying sting of a shallow lick tingled, announcing itself.

The cut he didn't mind. The split in the armor didn't bother him either. The shirt, however, had been a gift from Telda. Bought with coin given by Sindra.

His anger returned. Gurga stomped out of the office, to the unconscious butcher. Sparing a glance at the street, he stooped and grabbed an ankle. From there, he dragged the senseless man back into the office. The butcher was heavy, but Gurga heaved him into a corner, sat him up, and slapped his head, leaving it hanging and dripping over his chest.

Gurga felt the cut in his shirt again. He should have worn another. Fists clenching and unclenching, he watched the sleeping features of the butcher, very much aware of the anger building inside him.

Gurga took a deep, steadying breath, bleeding off some of the pressure gathering in his chest and head.

He reared back a fist.

"Sweet Lords above," Darsho spoke from the doorway, startling the enforcer. The beggar slumped against the frame and stared while covering his mouth.

Gurga glared at him.

"Do you know who that is?" Darsho asked.

The enforcer shook his head.

"That's one of Linfur's lads. He watches over the store here. Unfit bastard. Unchained *animal* is what he is."

That crinkled Gurga's forehead. "Not Linfur?"

"Oh no. Not him. Like I just said. One of Linfur's boys. One of his killers, truth be known."

Gurga regarded the unconscious man before he lifted a leg and smashed his huge boot into the swollen face. There was a nerve-jangling crunch of wood and bone and the butcher fell over, his bulk quivering. A bloody print marked the wall. Not yet finished, Gurga ripped a long wooden shard from the ruined cabinet door. He gripped the top of the butcher's head and leveled that raw spike to a swollen eye.

Not needing to see what happened next, Darsho looked away to check on the street. He still heard the dreadful sound.

"Is it done?" he asked after a moment.

"Aye that."

Darsho glanced back and wished he had not. He rolled his head, repulsed by the sight, and glanced away again. After a moment, he scratched at his belly. "Don't suppose you looked around any?"

"Only there."

The smashed cabinet, the doors crumpled with bits and pieces of wood scattered around it. Avoiding the mess, Darsho went around the discarded furniture to the cabinet, and swished his hand inside the space. A puzzled frown then as he pulled out the two remaining purses of coin. "Seddon above," he said and opened one. Then the other. "Sweet Seddon above."

Gurga watched him.

"Let's leave this place," Darsho said, moving for the door.

"No."

"*No?*" The beggar stopped, a purse in each grubby hand. "What do you mean *no?* You know what you've done here?"

"Killed one more."

"Well, yes, that you have. Killed him quite . . . yes. But this is a *store*. A butcher's store. There will be *people* about at any *moment*. People see *that* and they'll summon the street watch. You know about them, don't you?"

Gurga did.

"They won't take kindly to you killing that man, because when *he* killed people, he did so when no one was around."

Gurga glowered.

"Look," Darsho said. "You killed him. Excellent. You want to kill others like him?"

"I want to kill Linfur."

"You want to kill others like Linfur?"

That straightened Gurga's back. "Aye that."

"Then you follow me. Now."

With that, Darsho left.

With one last withering look around him, Gurga checked on his shirt and followed the beggar out of the room.

Darsho closed the door behind him, grimacing at the destruction to the latch and frame. "Well, they won't see anything unless they go in," he said, and examined the overturned chopping table. "Not too bad out here. Barely see it from the street. But they will find him eventually. This way."

The pair moved through the barn but halted when they saw a couple approaching.

A wife and her husband dressed in plain clothes stopped just outside of the pavilion. The lady brightened upon seeing Darsho for only a moment before frowning.

"Looking for a bit to roast, are you?" Darsho asked the couple. "Take whatever you want."

That surprised them both. "What do you mean?" the husband asked.

Darsho ignored them, however, and led Gurga down the very alley they had come through earlier. Once at the end of the barn, they turned and disappeared from sight. Again, they hurried through the secret maze of the city. After a time, Darsho stopped his companion in another alley, far from the well-traveled streets.

"Watch for people," he ordered and opened one purse again. Silver and gold coins pooled in his palm with a faint tinkle. "Oh dear, dear Lords. Look at this. *Look.*"

Gurga looked, but he was not interested.

"This is coin, lad. Coin. You know this, right?"

Gurga still wasn't interested.

"All right, but most people would be glad to see this. And wait . . ." He cupped the money and fed it back into the purse. When he had it stashed away, he opened the other one. "Sweet Seddon," he whispered. "There's more gold in this one than silver. A small fortune indeed. Well . . . plenty for both of us."

Darsho put it all back into the purse and held it out, to which Gurga scowled.

"Take it," Darsho said.

"Don't want to."

"It's yours."

"It's not."

"You don't want it?"

Gurga shook his head.

"None of it? There were two. This one has the most . . ."

"Keep it. All of it."

Darsho stared. "You don't want any of this coin?"

"Already took a purse," Gurga said.

"There were three?"

"Aye that."

"And you only took one?"

"Only wanted one."

Darsho winced as he scratched his head. "Boy, you see three, you *take* all three. You don't *leave* anything. Especially not to them. Linfur will kill you either way . . ." That stopped him, his bearded features going slack as he realized what he just said.

"We should go back there tonight," Gurga said. "When no one's about."

Darsho thought about it. "We could, but it'll be dangerous. Linfur will know you've been there."

"Good."

"Good, is it? The lad says it's good. You savage. Well, look. I've got coin now, but there's still unfinished business afoot. We can return to the store later tonight but it will be dangerous. Or . . . if you're agreeable, I have another bit of business we can do. Or, rather, you can do. If you wish."

Gurga studied his companion's face. A few heartbeats later, he slowly nodded.

Some time later, with the sky purpling to black, and the earliest stars shining overhead, a man stood in a secluded niche of the city. A rare dead end, really, where a crooked path between stone walls and buildings ended in a pair of huge wooden doors fit for a barn. There, in a corner dark as pitch, one man held a beggar by the throat.

"Stop squirming," the strangler whispered angrily, getting a second hand around his victim's neck. "*Stop it*, I said, or I'll wring your head off your shoulders. Unfit asslicker. What's gotten into your basket? Why did you run? You think you could outrun me? I *rule* this part of the city. It's mine. And all you who live *in* it are mine. All that you *have* is mine. And I've come to *take* what's mine. You understand that? Hm? You understand? Aye that, I know. Hard to get a word out when you're choking for breath. When your very eyes are set to pop from your face. Hard to say *anything*, really. You best have some coin on you. You best have some coin. If you don't, I'll . . . well . . . you know what I'll do. Perhaps that's why you bolted like you—"

A clatter of wood jerked the attention of the strangler away from his victim.

There, walking into the dead end was a great shadowy outline, the size not lost on the strangler.

"Who are you?" he demanded, shoving the beggar away.

"We're here for you, lad," a voice said.

"Darsho?" the strangler asked in a confused tone. "That you?"

"Aye it's me, Amplak."

Amplak took a step back. "You've grown a bit since last time I saw you."

The shadow split apart, the smaller one getting out of the way of the bigger.

"Ah, that's it then," Amplak jeered. "Got yourself a friend. Come to take a piece out of old Amplak, I see." The cornered street snake pulled a pair of curved knives from his belt, the steel twinkling. "Come on then, punce. See what's waiting here . . ."

Gurga advanced on the man. Anyone else might have hesitated at the sight of flickering steel, but not Gurga. He'd dealt with plenty of he-bitches sneaking knives into the alehouse. This one would be an exception, however, as he only smashed the others around a bit.

He intended to pound this one into the cobblestones underfoot.

"Come on," Amplak urged, flexing his shoulders.

Gurga lifted his spiked club.

Amplak froze at the sight, and Gurga crunched that morbid thing into an arm and the ribs beneath it. The weapon broke most of the bones it connected with, stealing a soft but shocked grunt from the man—before he bounced off the nearby wall.

Gurga closed in and grabbed his neck.

"*Yuh*," Amplak released, spitting and dribbling blood, before fingers as hard and overwhelming as dragon claws pinched off his air. Eyes bulged as he weakly clutched at a wrist and failed to remove it.

Gurga added another hand around that thick neck. He squared his shoulders and squeezed, squeezed so very hard. At one point he exhaled, the sound a hot and murderous hiss, and filled his chest again. He squeezed even harder.

Amplak's heavy frame hung lifeless in that awesome grip, and Gurga held on to him for a very long time.

"He's dead, my son," a nearby Darsho said in a low voice. "He's dead."

What might have been a tongue jutted from the corpse's mouth. Gurga checked on the dark sky overhead, needing more light yet failing to get it. So he lifted the body and brought him in close. *Dead.* Gurga jangled the maggot and nodded in satisfaction.

He lobbed the carcass into a pile of rubbish.

"Seddon above, lad," Darsho whispered. "You are a *beast.*"

"Who is he, Darsho?" whispered the strangler's victim in a pained voice. A woman's voice, and she struggled to rise while holding her throat.

Both men faced the shadowy figure.

"I've asked, but he ignored me." Darsho let a moment pass. "What is your name, boy?"

Silence, and just when there seemed like there would be no answer at all, "Gurga."

"Gurga?" Darsho asked.

"Gurga, Dar. He said Gurga. I'm Selve," the woman said.

"Her full name is Selvianna," Darsho said. "But we call her Selve."

"You saved me, Gurga," she resumed. "That one would have killed me this night. Without a doubt. This would have been my last few moments alive if not for you. For that, thank you."

"He led me here," Gurga rumbled.

"You led him here?" she asked Darsho.

"I did."

"Well, Dar. Aren't you the one to rescue me. Or at least half rescue me. If only you didn't smell like a public pisspot."

That silenced Darsho for a moment. "We're looking for Linfur's crowd," he eventually said.

"Linfur's crowd?" Selve asked. "For what?"

"He wants to kill them. Kill them all, in fact. That right, lad?"

"Aye that," Gurga answered.

Selve thought on that. "I might know where one or two of them are," she said.

"He's killed several, already," Darsho said.

"He has?"

"Gallwin's gone."

That lifted her head. "You killed Gallwin? He was *wicked*. Right and proper wicked. Linfur's just as wicked. None of them are like Strach, but they try to be. They certainly deserve a good killing. Or even better, a not-so-good one."

They stood in the dark, the city murmuring in their ears.

"Ah, may I ask why you want to kill them all?" Selve asked.

"They killed his employer," Darsho answered for him.

"Oh . . ." she said. "Apologies . . ."

"He's getting revenge for . . ." Darsho drew out, expecting Gurga to finish the sentence.

His features hidden by night, Gurga looked from one to the other. Speaking or explaining himself had never been something he was good at. So he held on to that swelling, uncomfortable silence until his patience came to an end.

". . . Where are they?" he growled, in a voice that sent shivers through both.

24

That same morning, Prajus opened his eyes and stared at the bare timbers of the ceiling. For as long as he could remember, he'd always woken up feeling replenished, his senses alert and thrumming. Perhaps it was due to how soundly he slept each night, or how calm and calculated his mind worked. Either way, each morning he awoke ready and willing to begin the day.

Prajus rubbed his forehead and held it before he swung his legs out over his bed. Men moved beyond the closed curtain of his quarters, their sleepy grunts and groans telling him all he needed to know. He wondered if this would be the day to make his presence known. Since his victory yesterday, there had been an unmistakable vibe of wariness emanating from his fellow pit fighters. Even a few uneasy looks, which Prajus met directly and turned away. Even the he-bitch Rigger kept clear of him, staying with his little pack of ankle-biting dogs consisting of Mison and Greygar.

Nexus had reinforced that wariness, right after Prajus's victory over Wocello. The owner praised his name, clawing at the very air while demanding the other gladiators to follow Prajus's lead.

"Every match is a war," Nexus had raved at them. *"And in war, there is only the victor and the defeated . . . and the defeated*

should be dead. Dead. Gutted, I say. You all saw what this man did. Do the very same! Kill whoever stands across from you!"

Or some such gurry. There was more but Prajus couldn't remember it.

He *did* remember the relaxing walk back to the compound belonging to Nexus. During that stroll, the one called Colcus stepped up beside him. Prajus remembered the gladiator from the very first day of joining the ranks of Nexus. Colcus matched his speed for a bit, just long enough to offer a quiet "Well done" and no more. Message delivered, he then dropped back among the rest of them.

And at the evening meal, the looks had continued, but nothing like the hateful scowling and teeth-grinding as before. It seemed as if the gladiators were having second thoughts about what he'd done. All except Rigger and his minions, but even they were mindful of their own business.

Someone slammed the post beyond his curtain, jarring him from his thoughts.

"*Out of your hole, maggot,*" Rigger bellowed. "Else we lop off your melon and prance about the grounds with it for a few smiles."

That arched Prajus's brow.

Else we lop off your melon and prance about the grounds with it.
Well, he thought.

After emptying the bull and washing as he normally did, Prajus pulled back the curtain and entered the empty hallway. On his way out, he turned around to consider the alcoves behind him. Glancing around, he walked back, passing several emptied nooks with their curtains pulled aside. He stopped beside the one place with the curtain still drawn across.

There he listened before hooking the material with a finger. He pulled it back and smelled several different salves and ointments.

Ansut.

The gladiator lay on his back, mouth agape, his beard glazed with thick drool from the night before. The bruised color of his face had deepened, perhaps from whatever healing shite was smeared over it. His ruined hand, kept together by sticks and cloth, drooped over the edge of his bed. Ansut's lower leg and foot—the same bits that caused the devastated pit fighter so much agony—ended in a bundle of cloth as well. Sweat gleamed upon whatever parts were not wrapped in bandages.

As Prajus stood there examining the man, sandaled feet clopped over the floorboards. The healer approached, a satchel thrown over one shoulder while he needled his teeth with a wooden pick. He was an older sort, like most in the profession. Freshly shaved, with thinning brown hair grown long in the back and knotted off.

"He awake?" the healer asked as he stopped and gazed in on the sleeping Ansut. "Good." He continued rooting around his mouth before regarding Prajus. "Rusmil roots I left him yesterday evening. You know of them?"

Prajus shook his head.

"Helps you sleep. Sleep *deep*. Like a corpse a week in the grave. Not that he'll sleep a week, mind you. He'll wake soon enough when I start rubbing the slop on him. Poor lad. Not the worst I've seen, but he'll have a few marks on him after all this is done. You his friend?"

". . . No."

The healer sized him up and down. "Well then. I've work to do."

"Good healer," Prajus allowed, widening the curtain for him to enter and then releasing it. The gladiator walked away, knowing full well Ansut would be wishing he was still sleeping soon enough.

I hope it hurts, he thought.

In the dining hall, Prajus ate his morning meal by himself as usual, taking his time with a handful of nuts, sliced fruit, and a cold leg of chicken. There had also been a pot of warm gruel, one smelling of burnt spices, but he avoided that, as did most others. He sat at a table, his back to the wall and elbows to the wood. There he gnashed at the chicken leg. His table was next to the door to the training grounds, so if he wished, he could lean forward and look outside. The rest of the gladiators sat in clumps in the hall, heads lowered as they ate and talked among themselves. The pair of cooks who had served them all were inspecting the contents of an iron pot hanging over a firepit. They peered inside that pot from time to time, as if wondering what else they might chance tossing into the gruel before it sickened the lot of them.

Sitting at a table two over were Rigger and his lads, Mison and Greygar. Rigger was picking at a chicken leg before firing the morsels into his mouth. Every now and again, Prajus glanced over to see Rigger watching him.

And every time, Rigger smiled.

Amused, Prajus looked away and finished his food. He wondered again if this would be the day to make his presence known.

Rezzo appeared in the doorway not long after the men finished their morning meal. The trainer placed his hands on his hips and eyed the lot of them. "Out of there," he ordered, his serious tone carrying farther than any of Bernd's shrieks. "All of you. Outside, now. Before you upset me."

The gladiators lurched for the door.

Prajus steepled his fingers and watched them leave.

"Waiting for your own invitation, maggot?" Rigger smirked as he left.

Prajus ignored that. He sniffed and looked elsewhere until they were all gone from the hall. Then he rose and went outside. A morning walk then, around the grounds with the rest of the pack, to get the limbs warm and loose. Once again, the gladiators marched in clusters of twos and threes. Prajus remained in the rear, this time mindful of them all. Not entirely unexpected, Rigger, Mison, and Greygar doubled their pace and got well ahead of everyone until they came up behind Prajus.

"There he is," Rigger whispered at his back. "The killer. Watch him lads, watch him. He's a killer. A real ruthless topper if there ever was one to walk these sands. In these *games*. Don't walk too close behind him. He might notice you. Might decide to take your head. Swing it about like a basket full of fruit. Make no mistake now, he hears me. He's been aware of me ever since coming out for a walk. Isn't that right, kog? Aye that, you're a *kog*. A twisted snake of one. I'd trust you only after you've been dead in the dirt for a week and the worms had just found you. Right evil, this one. Right evil. Watch yourselves lads, else he turn on you. On *me*, even."

Oh you right and proper eel, *you*, Prajus thought as he lowered his head and maintained an even pace. He had to admit, he appreciated Rigger's constant needling. Prajus had done it many times before, to lesser individuals. It made it easy for him to ignore the hellpup's poisonous yapping. Or so he told himself.

"Keep walking, topper. Maggot. *Kog.* Turn around if you dare," Rigger whispered, close enough that Prajus almost felt the man's breath on his neck.

"*You there, what are you doing?*" Bernd asked loudly, turning heads. "Back off a few steps. You look like you're about to sniff at his blossom. Back *off* I said. You really think we all looked away when you and your asslicking companions were hurrying around the sands to reach him?"

The resulting silence pleased Prajus, and he sensed Rigger dropping back, obeying the command. Rezzo cleared his throat and informed them all that the next bit of exercise would be sparring. Bernd then ordered them, in his usual throat-blasting volume, to choose their weapons and form two lines.

The pit fighters selected their tools from racks set against the wall. No one cut before Prajus as he reached for his wooden sword and shield, something which almost disappointed him.

"Prajus," Rezzo called out and motioned for him.

Prajus left the rack and the other gladiators, ignoring their curious looks. Not that there were many, as Bernd immediately ordered them to start swinging at each other, commencing the day's drills. Dust clouds rose as Prajus continued on, while Rezzo pointed to the raised platform, with a black canopy pitched over a single table and two chairs. Old Tino and Nexus himself sat there, facing the morning exercises. Tino watched with a slumped posture, as if he'd long conceded defeat in some matter. Nexus grimaced and fiddled with his tail of hair tied off at the back of his head. That facial rictus reminded Prajus of just how damn *skeletal* the man's aging face looked.

"That's him, Tino," Nexus said with a nod. "That's the one. The one who does what he's told. He'll reach the final eight. And he'll terrorize anyone facing him along the way. *Anyone*, because that he-bitch is absolutely *fearless*. How are you feeling this day, Prajus?"

"Good, Master Nexus, thank you."

That summoned an even fouler snarl on the wine merchant's face. "Hear that, Tino? Hear it?"

"I heard," old Tino replied, his thoughts hidden behind a tired expression.

"This killer, this *butcher*, *knows* when to speak. Especially when addressing his betters."

Prajus's brow knotted just a little at that, and he quickly unknotted it.

"Get on with it," Nexus said to someone behind the gladiator. The merchant ceased twiddling with his hair and reached for a nearby pitcher.

"You practice here," Rezzo said, indicating the exact place— directly before Nexus and the taskmaster, at the very head of two lines of gladiators.

Prajus cocked an eyebrow. Across the way waited a Sunjan called Porillan. A tall individual with a shorn head but a flourishing brown beard. Porillan had been one of the few who hadn't scoffed at Prajus, at least not outwardly, but he didn't speak with him either. Prajus did not know how the fighter fared this season, but a series of stitches glistened along the curve of his right shoulder, while his left eye barely opened due to several bruises along his profile. The rest of the Sunjan appeared fit and ready, however, and he nodded cautiously at Prajus.

Who graciously nodded back.

"Right, you two get warm," Rezzo addressed them. "You fight this day, Porillan. You take the offensive first. A hundred strikes at quarter-strength."

By his rather unmoved expression, Prajus believed Porillan had his bells removed long ago.

"Quarter-strength, Rezzo?" Nexus asked, goblet paused at his mouth.

"Quarter-strength, Master Nexus."

"Isn't that light?"

"Porillan does fight this day, Master Nexus. Anything more than quarter and he won't recover in time."

"Half-strength then," Nexus said and drank. "And let them use their combinations. Let them be dangerous. None of this sword-hit-shield gurry over and over again." He drank once more.

An expressionless Rezzo nodded without even a glance at the taskmaster.

"You heard the owner," the trainer said. "Mix it up a bit."

"Mix it up all they wish," Nexus corrected with a gulp.

"As you wish," Rezzo finished, uneasy with the command but unwilling to argue. "On my word, have at it, lads. Just don't kill each other."

Prajus regarded his training partner.

A determined Porillan had his shield and sword up and ready. The lad wasn't a punce after all.

"Begin!" the trainer yelled.

Porillan stepped into a sword thrust before swinging the shield's edge at Prajus's head.

Prajus avoided it all with a step back and then countered. He cracked his sword off an upraised shield before he quickly clipped Porillan's exposed knee.

The well-placed blow dropped the tall Sunjan, who fell into a crouch.

Prajus smashed aside the lowered guard with his sword and slammed the flat of his shield into Porillan's face. The force buckled the man backward, where he landed with arms splayed flat. A snarl and a headshake indicated the tall Sunjan was far from done. Prajus was, however, and he rushed in and placed the unwavering tip of his sword at his opponent's throat.

"Seddon above," Nexus exclaimed, spitting wine. "You see that, Tino? You see that? Did I speak falsely when I said we had a hellion in our ranks? No, I did *not*. You best do better than *that*, young Porillan. You know who you fight this day? An unfit bastard who's enjoying a little too much success in the Pit recently. You leap in there like you just did? Against *him?* You'll wake up in Saimon's hell without time to wonder how you got there."

All during the scolding, Porillan's swollen face flushed an even deeper red.

"Let him up," Rezzo ordered from nearby.

"No, don't let him up," Nexus countered. "Let him stay there for a bit. Get a good sense of what it's like to lie there, at the mercy of a killer." He nodded at Prajus.

Prajus considered the man at the end of his sword.

"All right, let him up," Nexus ordered, already bored as he finished off another drink.

The two pit fighters got clear of each other, while just beyond them, the other gladiators continued exchanging stabs and kicking up sand.

"Face each other," Rezzo said.

"What for?" Nexus grated. "Prajus will only put him down again. Am I wrong, Master Tino?"

A chasm of untapped wisdom, Tino answered with only a measured shake of the head.

"You see?" Nexus said. "I pay attention to your expertise in these matters. In this business, anyway. And a most brutal business it is. All right. Send him off to those wooden men over there and have him smash away at that. Get him as ready as you can. Porillan? Beat your opponent this day and I'll personally double whatever coin you wager on yourself. Hear me? Excellent. Off with you both, then. *Not you.*"

Holding sword and shield, Prajus halted in mid-turn.

Nexus flicked glares at the departing fighter and trainer while pouring himself another drink. "That's a dead man, right there," he said in a much lower tone. "A dead man. Doesn't even know it yet. Despite his previous matches, his experience, and your training. These are bloody times, Tino. Perhaps the bloodiest yet. Between you and me? I should place a wager on Gunjar instead of my own hellpup."

Nexus placed the pitcher down and watched Rezzo and Porillan walk toward the row of practice targets.

"Isn't it a bit early for the drink?" Prajus asked, getting the wine merchant's attention. "Master Nexus," he quickly added.

"Shaddup, you punce," the owner snarled. "You don't address me. I speak to *you*. For that bit of insolence? I'll have Bernd work you until your arms fall from your shoulders. I'm not some aged and broken maggot wearing a golden mask you can talk to as you please. You've done well, make no mistake. Burco hasn't come back with a blood challenge yet, which tells me he wants no part of you. And only after a pair of them were slaughtered. The House of Ustda. *Pah*. House cats fat on old mice. Weak-stomached bastard. He's in the wrong business. Keep killing, Prajus, and perhaps I'll share with you a drop of my time. Until then, mind your mouth, else I order this entire field to test you, and I mean *everyone*, all at once. Not to see how good you are, but to hear you howl when someone puts one of those wooden swords through your face."

Prajus lowered his eyes and clamped down on the smile threatening to spread across his face. He believed the wine merchant would do that very thing. He would do that very thing if he were the one sharing a table with the taskmaster.

"Now then," Nexus said, smacking lips after a swallow of wine. "Get your gurry hide back in line there. Your day is far from done."

The owner spoke the truth.

Bernd matched Prajus against another pit fighter, and the pair traded hard blows until the sweat began to fly. Then it was a short break for the midday feeding. For that, the men lined up to a table, where a pair of cooks handed each a bowl filled with a gruel of oats and mashed berries. The gladiators sat on bare ground or nearby benches, eating what was given them and sipping water cupped from a bucket. While they ate, Nexus and Tino spoke with the trainers before the wine merchant and taskmaster left for the games. Porillan went with them, as well as a handful of others, including Rigger and Mison.

Sitting in the shade with his back against the wall of the barracks, Prajus chewed and watched the men leave. Part of him hoped Porillan survived . . . so he could kill him later.

They finished their food. Bernd allowed them a short break to let the meal settle and then ordered them back to training. He directed them to the wooden practice men, their outstretched arms daring a person to lop them off. Prajus disliked this particular drill, as it was against an unfeeling target. Regardless, when he heard the call to begin, he lowered his head and did what he always did. He pushed himself, clacking sword and shield off the head and base and all points in between. Hard blows that shook the wooden man. A hundred strikes. Two hundred. From low to high, then high to low, all at alternating angles. Sword or shield, smashing the imaginary jaw of the practice man's head, with power enough to rip it from a real person's face. Prajus struck and struck again, until his arms burned from exertion. Sweat seeped into his eyes, at times blinding him. Annoying him. He welcomed the annoyance, however, as it made him angry, and anger was a secret reservoir of strength in all gladiators. He pressed on. Two hundred and fifty, then three, the combinations not nearly as fast or as powerful. His arms and shoulders were no longer burning, but blazing, close to dropping from his shoulders, and that made him angrier. He kept swinging, kept slashing, and fought on, seeking to either break his sword or the target.

Around the four hundred mark, however, Bernd shouted to stop, putting an end to it all.

A gasping Prajus swayed on his feet and stepped back. He sucked down deep breaths, taking a moment to inspect his wooden adversary and then the sword in his hand. Neither one had broken, which disappointed him. Glistening and dripping sweat, he still had enough strength left to sink his sword into the sand, though not as deep as he wanted.

Push, he told himself. He possessed a king's ransom in that commodity.

Prajus pawed the perspiration from his face while pacing a circle, awaiting the next exercise. He watched his feet, taking in great, calming breaths, while the hot air scorched him dry. In time, he grew aware of an eerie silence that prompted him to look about. Of the dozen or so men who had started training that day, all either sat on the ground or benches, clearly spent and done.

Prajus knew what had happened. He'd done it before, many times while training under that gold-faced prick Gastillo. He'd outlasted, out*performed* the entire unfit field. Over a dozen of them had started, hacking at their own targets. Around the two hundred and fifty mark, perhaps, they started to falter. The weaker ones first, then the stronger ones, emptying whatever stores of energy they had, until they physically and mentally buckled and staggered off the sands. From the edges they watched those who remained, until even those dogs slowed and dropped away.

Until only Prajus remained.

And because it was Prajus, the trainer had not called for a finish, content to see just how long the gladiator could keep swinging. So they all watched Prajus as he kept on smashing. As he blocked out the world around him and concentrated only on one thing.

Breaking the target.

The trainer Bernd, with hands to his hips, squinted in unchecked puzzlement at him. A reflective Rezzo lingered nearby, also watching and gauging. Even a handful of guards patrolling the walls of Nexus's estate had stopped to watch him. The other gladiators stared with a mixture of exhausted wonder, a little envy, and even hostility.

Sniffing hard, Prajus spat and lowered his head again and continued pacing. He passed buckets and barrels filled with water and ignored them all. Instead he checked his arms, flexing them even, favoring the prominent worms barely contained beneath the skin of his biceps, stretching up and into his shoulders.

I'm the dog warrior here, Prajus told himself, smiling grimly at his filthy feet. *I'm the terror of this pit. The one butcher no one dares visit, residing at the center of the blackest marketplace. I'm the enforcer they all must face, yet no one wants to cross. The executioner all fear. I'm the best. The* very *best . . . I'm . . . the* dragon.

Of endless forests. Of clutching nightmares. A dragon like no other. And all others are maggots beneath me.

He returned to his sword still in the ground. When he was close enough, he pulled that frayed length of wood and faced the target again. Without warning, Prajus swung that sword, up and over the shoulder, and broke it over the outstretched arm of the wooden man.

25

After Prajus broke his sword, Rezzo informed him his day was done and ordered him to the bathhouse. The trainer told him, in that subdued tone of his, to take his time, and that none of the other gladiators would bother him while he washed. Then the trainer told the rest of the roster that one man had outlasted them all, and for that bit of scalding embarrassment, Prajus would have the bath to himself. Rezzo also informed them that while Prajus enjoyed that rare luxury, the rest of the fighters would do another round of training.

Rezzo continued to lecture them as Prajus walked away.

The wealth of Nexus wasn't a secret. Clearly he had coin and plenty of it, and one glaring example of the wine merchant's riches was the bathhouse he had constructed for those fighting under his banner. One time, Prajus overheard a house servant boast about the extreme decadence of Nexus's own private bathhouse. Prajus didn't care. What Nexus did with his coin was of no matter to him. If the house master had a better bath, so be it. One day, he intended to have his own private bath, one to rival the pool he lounged in at the moment.

Steam billowed and wafted. Hot water engulfed Prajus to his chin as his whole frame stretched out on a submerged incline of marble tiles. Perhaps Vathian, perhaps not. Hazy cleaning oils glazed the surface of those blue-green depths, bespeaking the scrubbing just endured at the hands of an attendant. Glittering stones speckled the bottom of the pool. The walls, barely visible through the haze, twinkled with more fancy stones, arranged in artful depictions of men battling men. Many depictions, as if Nexus did not want his hellpups to forget why they were training.

If they did, they had no reason to be there in the first place.

The water threatened to cook him, so wonderfully hot it was. He laid back, just a flutter away from floating, and studied the ceiling. Dome-shaped, with more of those fancy stones showing a starry night and a full moon at the very top. A sleepy Prajus stared at that lovely heaven, supposing such a scene took some skill to craft. He wasn't one for such creations. His art was one of pain, his tools were the weapons of the arena, and the sands themselves displayed his destructive efforts before being swept away by his lessers.

Seddon above, he thought, appreciating just how pleasant it was to have the pool to himself. Especially when the pool was usually shared by a group of naked he-bitches recovering from a day of hard training. No sounds reached him from outside, which suggested the other fighters had exhausted themselves again.

Unfit, Prajus thought. These dogs were *all* unfit.

Images of them collapsed upon the ground, exhausted and aching, stewing in their own juices and suffering from the heat scrolled through his mind. Perhaps they even watched the entrance of the bathhouse for some sign that he had finished.

What was it that Rezzo had said to the others? As he was leaving?

"That one there outlasted the whole pack of you on the sands. You, who think yourselves gladiators. You, who think yourselves hard. Well, in my mind, he can outlast you in the pool as well. Get clean, Prajus my son. Take your time in there. Take all the time you need. It'll be a lesson for these lazy toppers thinking themselves pit fighters . . ."

Or something like that.

Take all the time you need, Prajus repeated to himself, his gaze flickering from one gleaming constellation of inlaid stones to the next, scrying faces among them.

He had to admit . . . he liked Rezzo's thinking.

Some time later, he pulled himself from those hot waters, refreshed, relaxed and dripping. He dried himself with clean towels left for him by the attendants, dressed in a tunic that reached his knees, and slipped into a soft pair of sandals. He left the bathhouse and strolled along the edges of the training ground, toward the dining hall. The air remained humid, but not so humid as that trapped within the bathhouse. He knew, without sparing a glance, that nearly a score of exhausted gladiators watched his every step. There was no way for them *not* to notice him.

Then Rezzo, the Lords bless him thrice over, raised his voice.

"All right maggots, off your arses and into the baths. Crawl if you must. And while you're stewing in there, remember *he* didn't make you wait. *You* made yourselves wait. Get on with you, you unfit lot. Get on . . ."

Oh, I made them wait, Prajus thought, entering the dining hall. He would have made them wait even longer except his fruits were beginning to take on water.

Alone, he dined on roast chicken, dressed up with a smattering of a cooked barley, rice seasoned with herbs, and a handful of roasted tree nuts. The clean cup of drinking water was perhaps the best part. He took his time eating, sitting in his usual place with a view of the training grounds, and enjoyed the solitude. As fleeting as it was.

When he finished, he was still the only gladiator in the hall, so he left, thinking of his bed. Within the living quarters, he heard Ansut's snores coming from behind the half-closed curtain. There was something oddly comforting in that sound, but Prajus didn't dwell on it. A hard day of training ending with a long, hot bath and a filling meal weighed upon him. He was tired. So when he reached his bed, he pulled the curtain all the way across, and fitted it just so from end to end. Then he glanced out the window, left open to allow a breeze, and eyed the paling sky. The bed was soft, the straw clean, as was the blanket covering it. Prajus lay back and propped his head up with one arm.

Lords above, he thought, examining the little bit of privacy he had, while his eyelids grew heavier.

In no time, he was asleep.

And in no time, it seemed, voices woke him. Loud voices. The place had grown dark, with the faintest light from beyond, outlining the edges of the curtain.

"Shaddup," someone grumped from nearby. "It's been a tiring day. Save your talk for tomorrow."

"The lad's dead," declared another. "That should mean something to you."

"Means there's a little bit more room in the bathhouse, now quiet down."

And to Prajus's surprise, they did quiet down. To a low rumble, anyway, one that was perhaps a door down the hall.

"Who do you think will be handed the task?" a voice asked.

"Colcus," another answered.

"Colcus would be my choice."

"Greygar was his friend, however."

"Greygar might have it. Anyone could, truth be known. Been a long day. We'll hear of it in the morning. Until then . . . no use talking anymore of it."

"Aye that, agreed."

And that was that. Prajus listened to the rustling of men in their beds, which carried oddly in the living quarters. Someone's ass whistled in the dark, a long, wet flutter of a note that seemingly lasted forever. That sound perfectly described the individuals fighting under Nexus's banner. Loud and blustery notes that gradually died away.

That etched a smile across Prajus's face, and he drifted off to sleep once more.

Until a mighty clap of wood against flesh roused him from his bed. His eyes flew open and he tensed, ready to kick anyone rushing into the darkness of the alcove. No one did, however, but an evil chuckle diminished in volume just past his curtain.

"Keep quiet out there, punce," someone moaned.

"Aye that, shut up," another added.

"Apologies, lads," spoke a voice belonging to Mison. "Rigger dared me to do it. Apologies."

Mison. Rigger. No doubt Greygar was nearby as well. Prajus waited, irritated by the disturbance, and waited for more. Nothing else happened, and the snores that ripped the silence before resumed once again.

Prajus, however, did not go back to sleep. He waited to see if he would have any late-night visitors, knowing full well who might dare. If anyone did visit, if anyone dared to enter his space, he would kill them with his bare hands.

He decided he might kill one anyway.

With a lengthy sigh, Prajus decided he had walked among these maggots long enough. It was nearing the time to announce his presence.

Morning once again.

As usual, Prajus waited until the others left the barracks. Rigger or one of his unfit minions slapped the post again, shivering the curtain. Another scratchy giggle, followed by Rigger shouting something about wasting the day away in bed.

Prajus rose after the three men had gone.

They all ate and later gathered upon the training grounds underneath thick, gray clouds. There they marched long ovals upon freshly swept sands. As before, Rigger, Mison, and Greygar marched behind Prajus, aiming evil whispers at his back.

"What are you about this day, 'eh savage one?" Rigger said. "Looking to embarrass us? Like you did the others yesterday? Bad manners, you dewy maggot. Very bad manners. You do that with us, with *me*, and I'll do something. Something very bad, indeed."

Prajus shook his head at the thought. He doubted Rigger would do anything. Dog blossoms like him liked to whistle before the eventual squat. He waited for more, however, just a little more . . .

"Don't think I will, he-bitch?" Rigger pressed. "Don't think I will? You'll see. You'll see soon enough. And when you do, you'll look back at this time and know I was speaking the truth."

That was enough for Prajus.

He slowed his pace, scuffing the grit softly beneath his sandals.

Bernd and Rezzo stood on the far end of the training grounds, puzzled at what he was doing. To their right, old Tino sat in the shade of that raised platform, also looking in Prajus's direction.

"Oh-ho, he doesn't like that," Mison remarked as he and a smirking Greygar walked by, watching Prajus. A sneering Rigger heaved a shoulder into Prajus as he passed, locking gazes.

Prajus stopped and smiled.

That halted Rigger. "Something amuses you, maggot?"

"Something does, little man. *You*. You amuse me."

Rigger scowled, exposing a rack of yellow teeth. "I amuse you?"

"You do . . . how someone like you goes about starting a fight—in a place where fighting is all we're supposed to do. The only thing we're supposed to do. You surprise me, Rigger. Usually the stupid ones die in the first few days of the tournament. Clearly Master Nexus has been feathering the Madea's nest with gold to keep you alive, for whatever reason. If not, then it must be because you're amusing to the rest of us. Or perhaps it's a little of both."

Prajus spoke calmly, not breaking the stare they were both locked into. A listening Mison and Greygar appeared every bit as insulted as the main target of his jabs. Rigger, however, became doubly offended but did not raise a hand at all.

The rest of the gladiators marched on, but one or two heads turned in their direction.

"Say that again," Rigger said, his shoulders tensing. "I dare you."

Prajus smirked and squinted, even though clouds hid the sun. "I've said it all just then. You've heard me. Punce. When you're *ready* . . . I'm right *here*. You can even swing first. Or . . . if you need lessons, real lessons, *I'll* swing first." He cocked his head. "But you won't like it if I do."

Rigger stepped in close, close enough to stare down his nose into Prajus's smiling face. A stern Mison blocked escape on Prajus's right, while an equally threatening Greygar did the same on his left. Surrounded as he was, Prajus did not back down.

"*What's going on there?*" Bernd shrieked, the sound startling.

Rigger didn't flinch. Nor did he attempt to fight.

Prajus turned from the man's furious expression. "This maggot wants to fight me," he answered the trainer.

"He insulted me, Master Bernd," Rigger added loudly. "Just now. Ask the lads, they heard him."

"What do you mean, *ask the lads?*" Rezzo cut in then, exchanging looks with the other trainer.

"He insulted Rigger, Master Rezzo," Greygar said.

"Aye that, he did. I heard it as well," Mison threw in.

"Been going on with the gurry all morning," Greygar added.

"Aye that, all morning," repeated Mison. "Ever since he arrived here, truth be known."

Silence then, swelling and looking to burst.

"That true, Prajus?" Rezzo asked in a calm voice.

"Oh, aye that," Prajus admitted. "Been telling all three they're no better than the crust upon sunbaked shite. But I ask you, Master Rezzo . . . is it an insult if it's the truth?"

All three louts stirred at that, their faces growing increasingly livid. Around the scene, the other gladiators stopped to watch. The show even hooked the attention of the guards posted around the grounds and upon the walls.

"Suppose not," Rezzo replied, scratching at his chin. "What do you think we should do here, then?"

"Well," Prajus said, spreading his hands. "We should fight. This one and me first, of course. He looks to be the angriest. Then either one of his friends next. I don't care which."

"I'll put you into the dirt first," Rigger swore.

Prajus met his eyes. "I'll slap your dead face like the post you enjoy slapping outside my curtain every morning."

That stuck deep, and a livid Rigger cocked back a fist.

"What's happening here?" Nexus demanded, standing a few paces away from the platform and the waiting Tino. All faced the owner, including Rigger, whose fist dropped back to his side.

Nexus waited for an answer. Two servants waited on his tail. One carried three bottles in her arms while the other carried fine goblets.

"He's an insult to your banner, Master Nexus," Rigger yelled. "An insult. He's the filth of the games for reasons we all know. He murdered his master and owner, and all of the arena wants him dead. And now? He's belittling me before my companions, my trainers, and even you, Master Nexus! My employer! Please, allow me to correct this insult and shut his mouth. And take his life."

The speech left all who heard it waiting for the response.

Nexus did not disappoint. He looked at his trainer. "Rigger, is it? Is that his name?"

A concerned Rezzo nodded that it was.

"Rigger," Nexus said sternly. "Let me explain something to you. The arena wants us *all* dead, you stupid punce. So finish your squat and realize that fact."

"Because of him," Rigger fired back.

Nexus silenced the gladiator with a single look of loathing. The wine merchant stared him down and kept on staring him down for moments, allowing it to simmer, to froth, while a handful of his prized Marrnite mercenaries, in full armor, reached for their blades.

If he was aware of it, however, Nexus didn't show it. The merchant regarded both gladiators and addressed them in a much calmer voice. "Rigger. Prajus. I have little use for fistfights on my training grounds, and I'll tell you why." He continued to the platform. "Yesterday . . . one of mine, perished in the Pit. Lad called . . ." he jigged a finger, fishing his memory. He finally looked to Tino and the old taskmaster provided it in a whisper.

"*Porillan.* Aye that, that's him. Porillan. Poor, poor Porillan. Got torn apart before my very eyes, he did. By a vicious, raving, froth-spewing mongrel from the Stable of Grisholt. I don't like losing to the Stable of Grisholt, but I did that day. I issued a formal challenge to correct such an insult, and Grisholt, the unfit strand of hanging gurry that he is, accepted. So, I need someone to avenge the stupid, stupid bastard *today*. A careless topper I truly have no desire to avenge, but I have to, because to do nothing shows weakness. Shows fear. That is unacceptable when all the houses are warring against us. And because we're at war, I cannot have my gladiators fighting among themselves here, when there are nine *other* houses, *filled* with gladiators, all looking to butcher you in the Pit. Do you see the problem I have?"

No one answered him.

"You hear me, you insufferable berry of shite?" Nexus yelled.

That shook Rigger. "I do, Master Nexus."

"*Prajus*," the merchant barked. "You insulted this man?"

"That I did, Master Nexus," Prajus reported pleasantly. "I'm willing to fight him as well, if you're willing to watch the punishment I'll put him through."

That widened Rigger's eyes. "You unfit bas—"

"*Shut your unwiped hole, lad*," Bernd shrieked from afar. "The master will speak."

Nexus nodded thanks at his trainer. He took his time sitting, pinching at his robes and getting them just right. All the while, his servants placed goblets and bottles of wine—unquestionably wine—upon the table. Nexus reached back and adjusted that stringy horsetail of hair hanging from the base of his head. Once finished, he noticed his goblet, already filled and waiting. His servants had filled Tino's goblet as well, but the old taskmaster was more concerned with the drama playing out upon the grounds.

"A fight you say?" Nexus finally asked.

"A fight, Master Nexus," Prajus answered.

"A fight will solve all this?"

"I guarantee it will, Master Nexus."

"You want to fight this man, Rigger? That's your name?"

"It is and aye that," he said, straightening his back. "I'll fight him. And I'll—"

"*Speak only when spoken to!*" Bernd screamed, his ruddy face close to bursting.

That blunted Rigger's enthusiasm just a touch, but he silenced himself with a withering glare at his opponent.

"Little early for a bit of bloodletting, isn't it?" Nexus asked Tino.

The taskmaster shrugged.

Nexus frowned. "Should I let them fight?" he asked his trainers.

Both men nodded.

"Very well," the merchant said. "Wooden swords only. The rest of you louts stand back. You two?" He addressed the combatants. "Only bloody the noses. The victor gets to avenge one of our fallen this very day. However stupid he might have been. Understood, Prajus?"

"Clearly, Master Nexus."

"Understood . . . you?"

Rigger frowned. "Understood, Master Nexus."

Nexus slumped, ruminating on matters. He remembered his wine and so he sipped, savored, and nodded. "Rezzo. Bernd. Have these two toppers square off. And have someone throw them their swords . . ."

Rezzo stepped to the center of the sands, pointing at where he wanted Prajus and Rigger to be. Prajus took his spot, casually catching the wooden sword tossed his way. The other gladiators cleared themselves of what would be the battleground. The household guard, along with the handful of Marrnite mercenaries, watched from their posts.

Nexus sat with one fist around his goblet, eyes shifting from the offended man to the offender.

Not ten paces from his foe, Rigger held his sword two-handed, then one. A huge grin split his face, as he clearly had wanted this moment for a very long time.

Prajus watched him while tapping his ankle with his wooden sword.

"Now then," Bernd said. "These are the rules. Fight's a fight, but we're in the season, so remember, any wounds you earn here, you'll carry with you into the Pit. First one hits the ground loses, however it happens. Or whoever makes the other yield. And try not to kill each other. Ready, then?"

An anxious Rigger nodded that he was indeed ready.

Prajus touched his forehead, as if remembering something.

"Then *fight!*" Rezzo bellowed.

At once, Rigger charged and stabbed, seeking to stick it through his opponent's guts with one powerful thrust.

Except Prajus blurred forward when his adversary stabbed—parrying the sword to the outside and punching an instant later.

A ridge of hard knuckles crunched into Rigger's throat.

A crackle of things best not broken split the air, and Rigger's legs flew out from under him. He dropped onto his back with all the grace of a falling barrel and clutched at his neck. Bloodshot eyes opened wide, on the verge of popping free of his face. His spine arched and his legs kicked and stomped, beating out a weakening tune. His tongue protruded and a ghastly hiss left him, weakening over time.

Prajus watched the dying man as the hissing changed into a soft but dreadful gurgling. Then his hands fell from his throat and his eyes glazed over.

In the chilling silence that followed, Prajus sniffed and tossed his practice weapon away. With resigned ease, he faced his employer, shrugged, and waited judgment.

A dour Nexus studied him in return, his eyes narrowed to thoughtful slits. Tino sat across from him, a rare look of disbelief on the old taskmaster's face. The fight rendered Rezzo and Bernd speechless, and they waited for their employer's reaction, as did most of the onlookers. Including an incredulous Mison and Greygar, whose shocked expressions flicked from their dead leader to his killer.

"You unfit bastard," Nexus drew out, pursing his lips. "You . . . you know what you've done?"

Prajus nodded. "Killed a piece of gurry."

"Killed a . . ." Nexus sputtered and drowned his response with a lengthy drink of wine.

"You don't need that," Prajus said, meaning the corpse. "You know his worth as well as I do. You also know the worth of his asslickers there. They aren't investments. They're losses. I'll fight each of them in turn or both at once and barely feel the sweat upon my fruits doing it. With your permission, of course, Master Nexus."

Nexus finished his drink and carefully placed the goblet upon the table. He wiped his mouth one corner at a time and did a very odd thing. A most odd thing indeed. Just when Prajus thought he might have made a mistake, the wine merchant smiled. Just a little at first, but it grew and stretched across his features.

Mison and Greygar, however, were not smiling. They dared not move.

"You would, wouldn't you?" Nexus asked, warming to the idea.

"And still have enough push for the likes of Grisholt."

"*Ha!* Seddon's glowing knob, I wager you would. Lords above. Lords above. Bernd. Rezzo. What say you? Should we clear the sands and let those two each have a turn? Hm? Or let them all fight at once? You know their worth."

The trainers traded looks. Rezzo spoke first. "We do indeed know their worth, Master Nexus. But perhaps that's a better question put to the lads."

"Well said, you crooked snake, you. You there . . . your name?"

"Mison, sar. Master Nexus, sar."

"Right. You want a go at that one?"

Mison shook his head.

Nexus leaned forward. "You sure?"

Mison checked on his feet, still shaking his head.

"He was a friend of yours, wasn't he?"

"He was that, Master Nexus."

"Well, then, your friend is dead right *there*. Your friend's killer is right *there*. I'll say it again. Do you wish to have a crack at him?"

With a deep reckoning breath, Mison shook his head again. "I do not, Master Nexus."

The wine merchant mulled that over, glancing at a stoic Tino, who perhaps had not blinked since the morning's events began to unfold.

"You unfit fool," Nexus said, pursing his lips. He gestured at one of his Marrnite guards. "Kill that one."

The Marrnite stood roughly twenty strides away from the suddenly speechless Mison. Twenty strides at least. The guard glanced at a companion, who tossed him a throwing spear. The Marrnite caught it easily, righted his grip, and took aim.

Naked except for his loincloth, Mison tensed, disbelief upon his features, and his mouth hung open.

The Marrnite took a step and flung the spear, the shaft flashing, where it struck and burst free of Mison's bare back in a spurt of gore. With the full dripping spearhead protruding from him, Mison staggered backward before he hit the ground. That heavy impact shoved the spear *back* perhaps a hand or more, but the rest of the grisly shaft remained a tilted flag post within Mison's chest. There was one last shiver, and the man moved no more.

Prajus combed his lower lip with his teeth and flexed his brow, casting a glance in Nexus's direction.

Tino reached for his wine.

"Now, then," Nexus asked as he settled back in his chair and focused on Greygar. "You. Don't worry about your name. I don't care anyway. Two of your friends are dead. One by him. The other by me. Aye that, I gave the order, so in effect, I killed him. Don't give me that look, you have other pressing matters to decide upon. Fortunate for you, since I've half the mind to make the same offer I made that one there."

He gestured at the dead man with the spear in his chest.

"I've lost *three* pit fighters in two days," Nexus explained as Tino gulped his wine. "And this day isn't even *finished* with." He let that sink in before continuing. "That's *coin* to me, you wretched bastard you. *Coin.* So, think hard on what I'm about to ask . . . Do you *think* . . . you can get *along* . . . with *that* one there?" With a flick of his head he indicated Prajus. "*Or* do you feel like *avenging* the deaths of your friends? Now then . . . what will it be?"

Greygar swallowed. "I can get along with that one there."

"What's his name?"

"Prajus," the gladiator said, a touch fearfully.

Nexus huffed relief and regarded Prajus. "That good enough for you? You unfit killer?"

"Good enough, Master Nexus," he answered with a gracious nod.

"So all this foolishness is done?"

"All done, Master Nexus," Prajus said.

"You there? This business is done?"

"Done, Master Nexus, done," Greygar sputtered.

"That's all good enough for me, then," Nexus said and pointed at Prajus. "What say you then? You ready to butcher another pig? And by pig I mean the one belonging to Grisholt?"

"A bit of butchery never bothered me," Prajus spread his hands. "Show me the pig, Master Nexus. And we'll feast later this day."

Another smile seeped across the wine merchant's face.

One that ended with a chuckle.

26

The arched window framed the arena sands and drew Grisholt closer until the lower brickwork stopped him. There he stood, hands on his hips, peering at the audience above as his group filled the chamber behind him. Outside, not an empty seat could be seen. People teemed the stands, right to the bustling top. The sight caused him to smile in satisfaction. His hand strayed to that little beard of his, to stroke the meager whiskers, as if encouraging greater lengths.

"Master Grisholt," greeted a familiar voice behind him.

"Ahhh," the owner said, turning to face his agent. "Caro, how goes the day?"

The question crinkled the agent's forehead, unused to such civilities from the owner. "Well enough, I suppose."

"Excellent. You've placed the wagers?"

"Wagers have been placed, Master Grisholt."

"Any crumbs of information to reveal?"

"The lad from the House of Ten—"

"The Perician?"

Caro shook his head. "Not him. The other one. Called Goll."

"Ah, I see. What about him?"

"Our spies say he's wounded. Fell on a sword in his fight the other day. Drove a length of pointed steel through his hand."

"A length of pointed steel through the hand," Grisholt winced, relishing the implications. "That must have hurt. Which hand?"

"His shield hand," Caro answered. "He won't be handling one anytime soon. And if he does, doubtful his grip will be as strong."

"So he's done?"

"No word of that," the agent reported. "Though I suspect he is. He's been tapped more than just a few times now. Hard shots to the face and head. Armor might protect you to a point, but the force still leaves a mark. Breaks skin. Bones."

"Unfortunate," Grisholt smiled, enjoying the news. "So the Ten is now just one?"

"Perhaps. I'll inform you if I hear of anything else."

"It's the other one that worries me," Grisholt said, suddenly serious. "The Perician. That one . . ." he trailed off with a flare of the eyes.

Caro peered outside. "Filled to the brim, I see."

"To the brim. And it's for us. I like to think it's for us. Did you know what happened this day?"

Caro shook his head.

"As we made our way into the arena, several commoners walked alongside us. Alongside me, in fact. Brakuss ensured they minded themselves, of course. You know I despise the common folk, but they were talking to *me*. *Praising* me on the dramatic turn of fortunes for the house. Well, the *stable*. I corrected the ignorant nogs on that point, but regardless, they were happy. Excited to see us arrive. Asked questions about the lad back there. They know it's a blood match this day."

"No doubt wagering on the contest," Caro said.

"No doubt. And no doubt they did the same before and won. And won quite the pot, I would expect. Still, it made me feel . . . good. Raised my spirits. *Inspired* me, in fact. I'm not the only one benefiting here. Those pink toppers are benefiting as well. Winning our fights is . . . enriching their miserable existence. In wealth. In spirit. We all know what it's like to have victory on the sands."

Caro, a former gladiator himself years ago, cocked an eyebrow at that.

"You know what I mean," Grisholt continued. "For me it's as an owner. I meant no disrespect. I know you were a destroyer back in your time. And I do well when you do well. Or the lads, that is. And when we do well . . . there are people out there who *also* do well. Who believe in the stable. Who wager coin on that belief. I tell you, Caro, that little bit of interaction with those unwashed pissers? Filled my black heart with a warmth I don't recall ever having."

Caro listened, taking it all in.

"Enough of that. To business then, 'eh?" Grisholt smiled. "Staying to watch the fight?"

"If you'll permit me, Master Grisholt. And if you have no other task for me to do."

"Not right now. Stay for a bit, Caro. I've brought firewater along this day. And a few bottles of Sunjan Gold. We'll crack them open and have a drink before the carnage. What say you?"

". . . I suppose, I—"

"Excellent, excellent. I'll have Brakuss crack open the Gold right now. Brakuss!"

Further back in the chamber, the one-eyed bodyguard turned.

"Pour us drinks. The Gold, if you will."

Orders received, Brakuss moved to do that very thing. The bottles of wine stood on the same table as an iron flask. Its brass crown of a stopper gleamed, while the crumpled folds of a red sack lay puddled around its base.

While Brakuss poured, Grisholt wandered back to where his gladiator waited. He was a Sunjan called Gunjar, armored in a shirt of dull ringmail. The lad wasn't overly tall or thick across the chest. Nor was he pleasing to the eye or unfit to look upon. Skillwise, his trainers had deemed him average at best, and even taskmaster Turst admitted the lad wouldn't go far in the games. Gunjar's ability with an axe and shield, his chosen tools for the trade, was passable. Capable, even, on truly good days. His only redeeming quality, however, was his total willingness to follow an order. Gunjar would split a man down the middle if commanded to, and later heave everything into the deepest sewers of the city. Whatever Grisholt wanted, Gunjar was up for the task. So, when Grisholt decided to follow Turst's advice and give all his gladiators a taste of "Victory," starting with the very next fight . . . Gunjar was the first lad to have that taste.

Like most everything else about him, his record to that point had been unremarkable, consisting of four victories and four defeats. All that had ended yesterday, however, when Gunjar sipped from the iron flask before his match, because Grisholt allowed him to do so.

Whereupon the pit fighter became . . . remarkably *frightening*.

Powered by the potion, Gunjar devastated his opponent—a topper called Porillan. Energized with the same maddening vigor experienced by his sword brothers before him, Gunjar split Porillan down the middle, from collarbone to sternum. Spewing froth and madness, he freed his axe and proceeded to hack off the dead man's limbs.

Grisholt smiled at the memory, believing he heard Nexus's cursing across the arena.

That death had been punishment to the wine merchant, for taking in the murderous pig bastard who had killed his owner. That pig bastard was Prajus, and this day, Nexus would send Prajus to avenge the death of Porillan. Just as Grisholt had planned. Oh, he knew Curge and the others agreed to bleed Nexus of his fighters slowly, to rob the merchant of his gladiators. But Grisholt had his own thoughts on that. What better way to punish the merchant than to kill off his prized pit fighter? Oh, he knew of Prajus. Knew the murderous knob was a handful. Didn't bother him in the least, because with the potion Gunjar was a *monster*.

Nexus had taken the baited hook, and now . . .

"Gunjar," the owner greeted, stopping before the pit fighter.

"Master Grisholt."

"Your time nears again."

"So it does, Master Grisholt. Ah, anything you wish me to do?"

"Merely the same. Just like yesterday. Sip from the flask there—just a sip, mind you—and become the brute within you.

A thing to be feared. And kill Prajus. You know he killed his owner in single combat?"

"I've heard others talk of it."

"Well, he did. And we can't have gladiators turning on their owners, violating that long-honored agreement we all swear to uphold. An agreement as old as the games itself, built upon the games, even. And upon trust. Owners provide gladiators the lodgings, food, armor, weapons, training, and support they need, in their quest to become champion of the games. And gladiators . . . provide the *victories*, to pay back their debt, and to ensure the continued success of the stable. Prajus has not only broken that agreement but he's right and proper *pissed* on it. And for that, he dies. Today. Nexus will be punished as well, for accepting that killer into his house, and breaking trust among owners. You kill this one . . . and every one after that. Every unfit maggot Nexus sends after you. Until he has no more to send."

Brakuss interrupted him then by handing him his wine. The owner took it without thanks, inspected the drink, and tasted it. With a smacking of lips he sighed before regarding Gunjar again.

"I'm very much looking forward to this match. If you remember, Wocello from the House of Ustda killed our Olibo. I was a touch careless, as I should have issued the blood match right then. For the very *next* day, Prajus fought and killed Brontus, from the very same *house*. And Burco Ustda, prompt bastard that he is, sent his demand for a blood match that same day, before I could send mine for the death of Olibo. The gladiator he sent after Prajus was *Wocello* . . . the same lad who killed our Olibo. Prajus killed Wocello easily. You, however, will *butcher* Prajus . . . because he killed his owner. And because he belongs to the same house responsible for Olibo's death."

Grisholt saw confusion on his gladiator's face. "Don't be troubled by my prattling. Clear your mind. When your time comes, you go out there and finish Prajus. Make him a horrible warning, a story of *remember when*, meant to frighten anyone thinking to do as he has done. Today, you're the hammer of the Stable of Grisholt. I want you to crush any maggot belonging to Nexus. One by one. I will prepare you for those contests, the same way I prepared you for yesterday's contest. As I will prepare you *this* day."

Grisholt gestured at the iron flask and its shining brass stopper waiting upon the table.

"All right, you unfit hellion," Nexus said, facing his gladiator. "This contest will be a war. A *war*, you hear me?"

Prajus nodded that he did.

"This is Bojen," Nexus introduced his companion, wearing a heavy cloak. "Bojen is my agent. You know how all that works. Bojen has been watching the pit fighters of Grisholt and he has some information for you."

With that, he indicated Bojen should speak. Not overly tall or broad across the shoulders, the agent had a full head of clean white hair and a matching beard. He elbowed his cloak back and held his hips. The cloak was a bit much in Prajus's opinion, especially during the sweltering summer months, but underneath the garment it was clear Bojen enjoyed spending coin on the good stuff. A princely shirt of silk covered his torso while well-made trousers draped his lower bits, all ending in a set of quality sandals.

"Good Prajus," the agent greeted. "You have quite the task ahead of you today. Quite the challenge. However, you do have a chance, if you'll listen for but a moment."

Prajus nodded a wry *Of course.*

Bojen cleared his throat. "It's interesting to me that a man of Grisholt has managed to . . . improve his fortunes so dramatically in one season. Especially when he has retained the same training staff and has not added any significant sword arms to his roster. The men under his banner are the same lads who started the season. In most cases, they were struggling and usually losing, with one or two exceptions. But recently, they've become . . . well, *terrors.* Adopting a . . . rage, if you will. A furious, dare I say, frightening rage, that allows them to overwhelm most of their opponents. Now, there have been fighters who are clearly not in a rage, and their opponents make quick work of them . . ." Bojen held up a finger. "This Gunjar was just another pit fighter struggling through the season. Until his last match, when he clearly adopted the same style as those winning around him. This is interesting, as no one has defeated any of these brutes . . . except one. Only one man has faced these rampaging screamers and not only survived, but soundly defeated him. *Without* freeing his own *weapon*. You might have already heard of that fight?"

"No," Prajus admitted drily. "Carry on, please."

"Yes, well, this fellow—Junger of Pericia—simply avoided *all* attacks being thrown at him. He dodged and darted about like a hen escaping a kitchen, while Grisholt's lad swung and swung again. Missing at every opportunity. Eventually, Grisholt's lad wore himself out. Wore himself out and sank to the *ground*, where the Perician forced him to yield. And that was that."

Still holding his hips, Bojen smiled at his retelling.

"So . . ." Prajus cast out, unimpressed. "I should . . . 'dart about'? 'Avoid' all attacks? And wait until this topper becomes so tired that he should fall over?"

"Aye that. You should. If this Gunjar comes out as he did yesterday, which I expect he will—"

Nexus held up a hand. "At least consider it, lad. I've seen the fits they get themselves into. It's frightening, as Bojen has said. He will come at you, swinging for your head—"

"For anything, truth be known," the agent corrected.

"For anything," Nexus allowed. "The Perician defeated him soundly. You can defeat him soundly. And by defeat, I mean take his head off. I *demand* it."

"We all demand something one day," Prajus said.

That little remark rubbed the merchant the wrong way, and he leaned into his gladiator's face. "You listen to me, you sun-soaked stain of *piss*. You're *indebted* to me. A considerable fortune in coin. The financial risk I've absorbed by simply taking you on? The deaths of my fighters? My *other* investments? That's all because of *you*. I *own* you. As long as this season goes on, you're mine. And I have roughly two *dozen* reasons why you'll clean that brazen look off your face this instant . . ."

Prajus sighed and tucked away his saucy expression. He supposed the wine merchant had a point. As for the two dozen reasons, well, a dozen pit fighters accompanied them this day, making the room tight indeed. An equal number of Marrnite mercenaries stood guard outside the door. There was no doubt Nexus would order both groups to discipline him if needed. Probably most severely. Unlike dead and gone Gastillo, the merchant followed through on his threats.

"Apologies, Master Nexus," Prajus said in a softer tone. "Pardon my insolence. I'm insolent by nature, I suppose. I very much . . . appreciate all that you've done for me. Truly. You wish to have his head?"

"I do," Nexus said.

"Then you shall have it . . ."

Sunlight blazed through the rising portcullis, marking the steps to the arena floor. Prajus took his time climbing them. He hummed faintly while going over the conversation he'd had with Nexus and his agent. *He dodged and darted about*, Bojen had said. *While Grisholt's lad swung and swung again. Missing at every opportunity. Eventually, Grisholt's lad wore himself out.*

Chains rattled as the portcullis lurched to its highest point. A puff of dust blew over the top steps. The Orator's voice reached him, just beginning his introductions. Prajus paid little mind to that.

Heat cooked the places where he wore no armor. Sweat already coated his forearms, slicking them under ill-fitting bracers with leathers pulled a touch too tight. His legs felt no better with his greaves. Another sigh left him, the flash of daylight narrowing his eyes. He tightened his grip on his sword and felt an unfit itch take him under his helmet, around his right ear, where he couldn't get at it.

A hateful welcome greeted Prajus as he walked into the Pit. Curses and insults scorched the air, while a few half-eaten apples bounced off the ground. He supposed he had earned it. He also hoped he would one day meet each and every punce throwing their gurry at him.

That rain of garbage gradually ceased as he strolled out of range and into the open. He ignored the crowd, not bothering to acknowledge them at all. Instead, he concentrated on the rising portcullis across the way, where his opponent would emerge.

He dodged and darted about. Bojen's voice repeated in his head.

Prajus rolled one shoulder, loosening the uncomfortable cuirass he wore. An even thicker cloth padding lay underneath the leather—every bit as foul as the scrub rag he'd worn in his last fight. He hefted his sword and shield, a small, rounded thing of wood and reinforced with iron.

A great, throat-splitting roar erupted from the opening across the way. A feral scream not unlike one of pain—angry pain, as if belonging to a prisoner finally freeing himself from a torturer's table. A prisoner who sought revenge upon his tormentors. That single, skin-shivering rattling of vocal cords reached the onlookers and seized their attention. They knew what was coming. The foul curses and insults changed into a rumble of anticipation, where they hoped for the very worst for Prajus.

When the arena gate was halfway open, the gladiator behind it bawled again. He ducked under the rising gate and threw his arms wide. Another blistering howl. The crowds answered it with one of their own, which distracted the pit fighter and whirled him about. For only a heartbeat before he noticed Prajus and shrieked again.

And charged.

Gunjar pounded across the hot sands, his ringmail and pieces of assorted armor gleaming in the sun. A wicked, long-shafted axe swung in one hand while a rounded shield covered the other. His helmet was a dark-gray bauble, the features growing more distinct as the space between the pair shrank with alarming speed.

Thirty paces, and Gunjar did not slow down.

Prajus believed the angry pisser might have even *gained* a stride.

The roaring of the audience rolled over him as he steadied himself, aware of the hammering of his own heart. Not in fear, however, as fear would be as crippling and defeatist as stabbing one of his own legs. Concentrating on the man coming at him, Prajus held his shield before him and drew back his sword.

Twenty paces, and Gunjar's head bobbed with every galloping step.

He dodged and darted about, Bojen repeated in Prajus's head. He set his feet and bent his knees, thinking the Perician might have had the right idea . . .

Ten paces, and that frothy ocean of screaming from everyone reached a deafening peak. Prajus saw Gunjar's eyes, framed in the generous cuts of his helmet, and they blazed with fevered madness.

Dodged and darted about.

After running all that distance across sand, Gunjar flung aside his shield, the disc spinning off several strides to his left. He gripped his war axe with both hands and had the unfit power to scream again.

Dodged and darted . . .

Well, Prajus thought, *I'm not doing any of* that *shite.*

Within a teeth-baring five strides from his victim, Gunjar whipped his war axe over his head, intending to split his foe down the middle in one fell chop . . .

When Prajus reared back and *flung* his sword at the hellion bearing down upon him.

There was no time to duck. No time to dodge. Not that Gunjar would have done anything of the sort. Sunlight flashed off the sword as it snapped forward, as if launched from a tightly wound ballista, at a target practically in front of it. The blade punched through Gunjar's neck in a life-snatching burst, just as his axe started its downward cut. Gunjar's roar ended in a *Yurk!* and his momentum carried him two more stumbling paces . . . which Prajus sidestepped.

Arms and axe dropped as Gunjar collapsed face down into the sand.

The dead gladiator landed hard, the impact shoving the killing blade deeper into the corpse's gushing neck. In one startling display of life, one that put Prajus on guard, Gunjar sank his fingers deep into the sand. The fighter clawed grooves, as if refusing to perish. A wheeze came from the man then, a horrible death rattle of a sound, where blood flooded his cheesepipe.

The gladiator did not rise, however, and his gurgling eventually died away. Those hooked fingers stopped clawing at the sands and relaxed.

Only then did Prajus realize how damn *quiet* things had become.

Aware of the hushed audience, he tossed his shield away and nudged the carcass with a boot. Satisfied the man was indeed dead, he gripped his sword, took a firm hold, and yanked it free. The head lifted and dropped with a thud. A couple of flicks cleaned the blade somewhat, and Prajus took a moment to appreciate the killing blow. Armored and rushing in as Gunjar was, Prajus had been given only a precious instant to spot and act upon the crack of flesh around the screamer's unprotected neck.

And what a fine toss it had been.

Prajus circled the corpse, admiring his work.

Then he remembered his orders.

He sized up matters a little more and, once certain of the best way to proceed . . . he removed the head. Two hard chops and a bit of sawing and he had it. It was grisly work. Horrifying, really, but Nexus wanted his trophy, and Lords above, Prajus didn't mind getting it.

In fact, he might have enjoyed it.

When it was done, and the sands drank deeply of what flowed, Prajus straightened. He was filthy, as if he'd just fought a war singlehanded. Gunjar's head swung from his left hand as he located the box seats belonging to Nexus. There, framed in brick, stood the wine merchant along with old Tino. Prajus couldn't see the taskmaster's expression, but Nexus held up both hands and clapped. Several times, in fact, the noise stirring the audience back to life. Some moaned disappointment while others cursed, but they were finding their voices.

With a brazen smile, Prajus raised his arms in victory, holding both dripping sword and head. He turned, basking in the rising anger, soaking in the hatred. When he had had enough, he ambled for his side of the arena, where the portcullis had opened.

Halfway to the gate he dropped the head.

The heat lessened with every step as Prajus descended the stairs. At the bottom stood the gatekeeper, with a lantern burning brightly behind his head. The old man's shoulders tensed upon seeing the returning gladiator, and his eyes flashed like those found on a dungeon rat. Behind him stood the first of many Skarrs, ready to be called into action if needed.

"You missed it, old man," Prajus said to the gatekeeper, who jerked his head up as if he'd been pricked by a needle. The flab of flesh under his nonexistent chin shivered as he did so.

Prajus resisted the urge to slap the old topper and kept on walking, past the city guards lining the walls. He turned at a juncture and continued along a white corridor. Torches fluttered as he followed his shadow. Thoughts of the fight replayed in his mind, and he congratulated himself on a match well fought, such as it was. Beheading his opponent didn't move him in the least. In his mind, a few more of those and his name would be right and proper feared.

A pair of men walked toward him, breaking his thoughts.

Both lads had swords strapped about their waists, and their hands dangled close to the hilts. A warm tingling flashed up Prajus's neck, placing him on guard . . . until they drew close enough to see their faces.

He stopped and smiled. "Saimon's black hanging fruit, are they allowing just anyone to wander the underguts of this place now?"

"You see, he remembers us," Tulka said to the other one, who grinned.

"Kall," Prajus said, inspecting the man. "Best you stay away from the bakers. All that dough on you will only tempt them to push you into an oven."

The remark put a frown on Kall's bearded face, but only for a moment. Tulka and Kall were nearly equal height, with thick heads of hair and matching beards. Tulka was the leaner one and definitely the meaner. Kall carried a heavier frame, most of it through the middle, and had the mentality and work nature of a sleepy bear. Despite those qualities, he nodded fondly at his old companion and gripped his shoulder.

"He wouldn't fit into an oven," Tulka remarked in a dubious voice.

"There are big enough ovens about," Kall said.

The comment reminded Prajus how dense the lad could be. He removed Kall's hand from his shoulder. "Where's Savul?" he asked.

"Gone," Tulka said, his eyes widening for a moment. "Long gone. Shortly after Nexus drove us away."

Kall nodded in agreement.

"He had a few coins," Tulka reported. "Mostly ours, unfortunately. Since Nexus didn't take us on, I decided to fight in the Pit as a Free Trained."

Prajus cringed.

"Aye that, fighting among the slop. Who would have guessed that? Anyway, we pooled our coin and placed it on my head for my first contest. Kall and Savul went to place the wager while I stayed below, waiting my time. Killed the pisser fighting me in three chops. Returned to where I left the lads and only Kall was waiting."

"He took the coin and ran," Prajus stated, remembering Savul to be the devious one.

"Took it and ran," Tulka repeated. "He told Kall he'd go get it from the Domis and instructed to wait for him. Never came back. Left us both. Treacherous kog."

"You didn't look for him?"

"'Course we did, but it's a big city. Not a hair of him to be found. He's probably living like a king in Vathia by now."

"Or Mademia," Kall muttered. "He always said he liked Mademia."

Tulka frowned. "Wherever he went, my only hope is some Dezer overtook him along the way and strung him up by his fruits. Take everything and leave him swinging from a tree."

Prajus chuckled, thinking Savul had made a smart decision.

"He always was a schemer," Tulka continued. "I suppose he decided we weren't worth the company. So I said to this one," he prodded Kall's arm, "we'll have to seek out Prajus. See what he's doing. And you're doing just as well as you ever did."

"Even better," Prajus answered. "Nexus has a thirst for spraying blood. Like I do."

That slackened both men's faces.

"He doesn't mind you killing everyone?" Tulka asked.

"He's *telling* me to. Take that one's head. That one too. See that one there?" Prajus drew his thumb across his gullet. "It's all damn refreshing, truth be known."

"Damn frightening is what it is. You'll be fighting blood matches until the end of the season. If you make it that far."

A concerned Kall nodded agreement.

Prajus frowned. "Lad. I explained this before. Every one of them I put into the dirt? One less I have to face at the end."

"Well then, perhaps if I sleep outside of Nexus's gate, maybe he'll take me on one day," Tulka said.

"He just might," Prajus said, but thought definitely not. "So you lads are wandering the city then? And the arena?"

"I've fought two more matches against the Free Trained," Tulka said as if not hearing the questions. "I wear the Free Trained shite. It's shite, but it's better than walking into the Pit bare-assed and expecting not to be scratched. Gurry they might be but even the Free Trained will hit the ground if they drop a blade on it. This one has no interest in fighting, so he wagers, leaving me to risk life, limb, or worse. We've been successful enough doing that. Living at an alehouse with the winnings. It's good enough." Ever the talker, Kall nodded.

"So we decided to find you," Tulka smiled. "And here we are."

"Here you are," Prajus repeated with feigned affection, though the sight of them was enough to twist his guts. He considered driving them both off, but a thought stopped him. "What happened to Gastillo's property?"

"Ah, that?" Tulka waved. "The city claimed that. And right quick, too. Gastillo had no heirs. No wives. No one to claim what was his. All the training staff and whatever lads there were? Gone. Some probably returned home, *but* I've seen a few familiar faces below. With the Free Trained. I suppose they figure if they cut up enough meat, someone might notice them. Or earn enough to keep them until next season. Or a trip to Vathia."

"Suppose so," Prajus said, inwardly scoffing at the very notion. "Well . . . you ever go back there? To Gastillo's property?"

They shook their heads.

"Lads," he smiled. "I have something for you to do . . ."

27

The clouds had pushed off from the city, ending the threat of rain and leaving only the deepest blue, with the shadows retreating along brightening cobblestone.

Feeling the strengthening heat, Zelia moved through a street filled with wandering crowds. A summer shawl covered her head while yellow robes draped her from shoulders to ankles. She dressed plainly to avoid attention, even deciding not to wear a belt, as it would draw eyes to her figure. When she had walked with Sorban, one look at him would discourage anyone from approaching her. Even when he'd been away, training with the likes of Slavol and his dogs, Zelia had known he was nearby, and she traveled the same streets with a sense of security. Since her husband's death, however, the city felt more dangerous, resulting in her concealing herself as much as possible, despite the heat.

Over the last few days, she'd met with most of the owners of the gladiatorial houses participating in this year's games. Dark Curge had been the first and perhaps the most difficult, as she chose to talk with him during a contest at the arena. The near-constant screaming, blood-mad people distracted and even repelled her. Only once before had she watched a contest, when Sorban fought, and that was perhaps the second-worst time in her existence. Her man had won, and won cleanly, as he didn't kill his defeated foe. But since then, she'd promised herself never to return to such organized spectacles of violence. Sorban had smiled when she had told him her feelings about the games, and he'd said, half in jest, she should find another man. She did not, however, loving the one she had, understanding his participation was for a short time only, and for their future.

Those memories stirred up a mood of sadness, tightening her throat and reddening her eyes. *Their future.*

No longer. She had nothing. *Nothing.* Except that ever-present craving for revenge.

A knot of women walked toward her, arms linked together to form a wide barrier. A family, from the looks of them—daughters, mothers, and wives—perhaps on their way to a marketplace. Children bounced before them. Two little girls held on to their mother's hands, their round faces lit up with broad smiles.

Zelia skirted around the edge of them. Another woman approached, carrying a swaddled baby. Zelia hurried past her as well, only to face another mother and her children. Everywhere, families were enjoying the morning, as families should. Children played before the tired faces of watching grandparents, racing in and around arched entrances to private homes.

Setting her jaw, Zelia walked by them all.

A day ago, she had visited the House of Tilo where the owner, like Curge, met her and listened to her proposal. Tilo was the oldest of the lot and listened intently while occasionally scratching at his beard. When she finished, he informed her that one of his men had fought Goll just *yesterday* and failed to defeat him. He promised that if any of his lads battled Goll again, they would have explicit orders to take his life, for her and for the memory of Sorban. Tilo then spoke fondly of her husband, heaping praise upon Sorban's name as if he had been a distant son.

When their time was done, she left with that familiar sensation of a constricted throat, red weeping eyes, and a terrible loneliness that clung to her all the way home, where no family waited for her. Where she called out upon closing the door behind her in the hopes that her husband might answer.

That had been enough misery for one day.

Zelia concentrated on the two owners she had yet to visit. To this point, all had been gracious enough to meet and listen to her, and they all stressed that if a fighter was matched against Goll, that the fight would be to the death. That pleased her very much, but all the owners had seemed preoccupied with some other concern. One only Dark Curge had actually revealed.

War has come to the Pit this year.

War. She scoffed, wondering if their war was any worse than the organized displays of mayhem within the arena. They could have their little wars, all of them, as long as they knew her bounty was out there, and whoever killed Goll first could collect. Only Curge had said that his gladiators would take Goll's head for the memory of Sorban, and not for coin. Strangely enough, Zelia believed him.

Those thoughts weighed upon her as she navigated through the cobblestone sprawl that was Sunja. At times she asked for directions, as the walled compounds belonging to the owners were built far and away from each other. Grisholt's training grounds lay beyond the city walls, perhaps half a day's travel away. She could never remember which was a school or stable or house. Didn't know if there was a difference and, truth be known, didn't care. Regardless, she would attempt to meet that one when he was in the city rather than travel beyond.

At the moment, she was on her way to see Razi, of the House of Razi.

Just before noon, under a hot sun nowhere near its full power, she arrived at her destination. A stone wall four times her height loomed before her with its gates closed. The defensive structure appeared old and blackened by fire along the base. Crumbles of mortar sprinkled the ground while pointed tangles of animal horns lined the top. An imposing front door of black-stained wood and studded iron bands faced her. Slivers curled from the wood in places, while dents and gouges scarred others, as if someone had once knocked upon the surface with a mace. A closed slot marked the center of the barrier while a metal ring hung just below. Standing before the entrance, in the growing summer heat, she glanced around. After pushing through crowds for most of the morning, this particular side lane was eerily empty. No one walked along its considerable length. An opposing stone wall stood at her back, rivaling the one before her. In the distance, people continued on their way, but not one turned onto this lane.

Steeling herself, she reached for the iron ring. Rust speckled the metal and it took both hands to move the thing. She knocked twice and, upon the second strike, the door slot snapped open. A set of annoyed eyes filled it. The glare softened upon seeing who it was and quickly studied her from head to feet.

"What do you want?" a man asked.

Zelia squared her shoulders. "I wish to speak with Master Razi, the owner of this house."

"You what?"

"I wish to—"

"Why do you want to speak to him?" the man demanded, his gaze meeting hers for a flickering instant before studying her robes once more.

"That business is between Master Razi and me."

"Does he know you're coming here today?" the man asked, peering at her chest.

"He does not. Not until you inform him I'm here. And that I wish to speak with him."

That lifted the guard's gaze. "I don't know. I'll ask him. He doesn't usually talk to ordinary folk. Especially one so . . . well-dressed."

Well-dressed, Zelia's mind repeated, knowing full well what the pisser meant. "It's my intent to speak with him either today or another. Here or someplace else. It's only a matter of when, and when I do, I'll tell him of you preventing me from seeing him earlier."

"Oh, you will, will you?" the eyes narrowed.

Zelia did not look away.

"All right. Hold on."

The slot slammed shut.

So she waited, enduring the heat. People chatted in the distance. An unseen dog barked nearby. Zelia lifted her chin, listening, but eventually returned her gaze to the door. The wooden base looked worn and frayed with peeling splinters. The thought of leaving occurred to her, as she didn't like the guard eyeing her in such a manner. Only yesterday she'd seen Boh the weaponsmith again. Boh . . . who had plagued her with his lecherous stalking—despite his wife and children. That one had a head as thick as the anvil he routinely pounded with his hammer. The burly weaponsmith had been walking through the nearby marketplace, perhaps looking for materials for his work. Zelia stopped when she saw him, as did he, and they shared a look.

Hers had been one of loathing.

His was lewd and something else.

And just before she could walk away, he brazenly pulled off his shirt, right there in the marketplace, baring his thick torso for all to see. Not that Zelia waited, for no sooner was his shirt being hauled over his head than she had turned and hurried off.

That display warned her that Boh had not abandoned his lecherous pursuit of her. She knew she would have to be doubly careful in the days to come, until she had finished dealing with Goll. After that—

Latches clicked and scraped against the inner door, jarring her from her thoughts. The thick barrier swung inward with a noticeable creak. The guard opened it halfway, huffing as he did, nodding at a job well done.

Zelia decided it was better when she could only see his eyes.

He was tall, lanky, and unshaven, with a scar down one cheek. His hair had been shorn to a prickly fuzz and, as she watched, he jammed a finger into one ear and rooted it around.

"Come in, my missus," he said much too sweetly. "The master of the house will see you. If you'll take my hand."

"Many thanks," Zelia said, ignoring the offered hand. "Please lead the way."

He smiled thinly, not minding the rebuff, and waited until she was inside.

When he closed the door, Zelia's alertness truly took to the sky. Her hand grazed the hilt of her hidden dagger, the very weapon her departed husband had gifted her. The blade would be her only protection within these high walls.

Steadying herself, she followed the guard, her attention split between him and the property grounds. From outside, the place had seemed huge. Inside, however, it felt cluttered. Confined. They walked past a smithy, a barn, and some squat structures that looked like living quarters for the residents before entering an open area covered in white sand. Two lines of gladiators filled that space, stripped down to undergarments and holding wooden swords. They waited for a crack at a pair of tall wooden frames resembling headless men. A pair of older men addressed the lot, explaining the drill they were about to start.

"You're visiting at a good time," the guard said. "The lads have a good shine on them."

Zelia said nothing to that. When visiting the cave of an ogre, it was wise to know when to speak and when not to say a word.

The guard led her to a low house with a heavy roof upon it, the stone slats piled high. Through a wide entrance they went, into an even more expansive chamber with floor stones freshly swept. Tall vases filled the corners, each holding green and white flowers that scented the room. The guard stopped at one of two inner doorways and nodded at someone out of sight.

"Here she is," he announced. "A yellow flower of the city."

"Yellow flower of the city," a voice scoffed. "You think that gurry charms the ladies? I should be looking for another guard if you do. Get out of the way and let her in. Wait out by the door."

Color rushed to the guard's cheeks as he frowned and backed away.

Zelia entered a study with two walls filled with shelves and books, and an open window fixed with bars. Razi stood at the window, a curious look splitting into pleasant surprise. He was only a few fingers taller but outweighed her considerably. Perhaps in his late fifties, with brown, graying hair. A loose brown shirt lay open all the way down to his upper belly, where a single straining button sought to keep everything from bursting free. The man's gut was enormous, and whoever had stitched his shirt knew the trade well. The dark pants below the gut were ordinary, but she didn't linger on those.

A desk filled the rear of the room, every bit as scratched and dented as the outer door to the property. Two white candles rose like spires on the corners, their bases fixed by melted wax. Parchments and scrolls filled the middle of the surface, placed neatly beside each other. Razi moved to the side of the desk, smiling broadly, showing widely spaced teeth. He flicked a few fingers over his face, perhaps checking on how well-shaven his jaw was, and studied her with piggish eyes.

The owner beckoned for her to sit in the chair before the desk. She nodded thanks and did so.

Razi remained standing. "You're quite the berry, now, aren't you," he said, ending the sentence with a soft nibble of his lower lip.

"Master Razi," Zelia greeted cordially. "I wish to speak with you about the season's games."

"The games?" he asked in confusion. "You follow the games?"

Outside came a rapid clacking of wood against wood. That harsh pattering continued for a short time before stopping, only to be replaced by another smashing.

The noise distracted her. "Not really, no. However—"

"Thought as much," Razi interrupted. "You don't have the look. I can tell. Those robes you wear? Soft and pillowy. Covers you well. Many of the women who frequent the games are dressed to hook the eyes and attentions of the dogs who fight. Not you, clearly. But you're here all the same. Maybe you're more interested in the men who handle the dogs?"

That last comment stunned her for a fluttering moment before she pressed on. "My husband was a gladiator."

That ripped the smile off his jowls. "He was? Who?"

"Sorban."

"Sorban?" Another confused look. "Yes, yes, I know of him, but he's with Slavol's lot. Or *was* with Slavol's lot. He's been dead for days now, hasn't he? Even weeks?"

The bluntness of his question stunned Zelia.

Razi interpreted it as permission to continue. "Sorban, yes. Cut down by one of those Ten mongrels. What was his name?

What was it? The he-bitch is still fighting, I know that much. Still killing, too. Gark? No, that's . . . *Goll.* That's the one." He patted his belly as if it had helped in some way. "A Kree called Goll. Aye that. I knew I knew. So then, you're Sorban's widow?"

Unable to answer and struggling to control her emotions, Zelia nodded.

"Apologies," Razi offered, seeing her reaction. "I speak much too fast at times. Or perhaps always. Well . . ." he patted his gut again. "That is that."

That is that, she repeated in her head. No words of sympathy for her husband. Nothing about how great or how skilled he was, which she'd heard many times over from the other owners. Simply, *that is that.*

Worse still, the man leaned against his desk, drumming a tune on his stomach. He smiled, with a hint of regret, and edged toward her. "Well, then, what is it you wanted to speak of?"

Zelia clenched her jaw. "I . . . am offering coin. To the person who brings me the head of Goll."

That arched the owner's eyebrows. "You are? Interesting. Where are you getting this coin?"

"Let your men know," she pushed on, ignoring the question. "If one of them faces Goll in the Pit, then kill him. If they can. For my husband. If they can do that, tell them to find me and I will pay them coin for their effort."

That cocked Razi's brow and he leaned forward. "You're not Sunjan, are you?" he asked in a curious voice, his tongue visibly touching the roof of his mouth.

"That is all I have to say," Zelia said curtly and stood, which Razi mirrored. "Many thanks for your time, Master Razi. I must leave now, as I have other matters to attend to."

Like escaping here, she thought, backing away from the larger man.

A reflective Razi did not pursue, however. Instead he leaned back and folded his arms. "You're a fierce one. I can tell. You play these games long enough, you develop a feel for these things. Sorban did well to have you as a wife. Very well indeed. He was a fortunate man. One question then, before you go. Does Goll know about this price on his head?"

That stopped her. "He does not. Not yet. And though it is a bounty, I want him killed in the arena and not in some dark alleyway."

"Killed in the arena," Razi said in a low tone. "Won't be easy. Mongrel dog he might be, but the man's a skilled fighter. Very skilled in fact. He's also battered. Cut. These games . . . they're more than just a string of bloody contests, you understand. Much more than skill with a blade or whatever. It's a contest of wills. To push on, even when you're bleeding your guts onto the sands. To *keep* pushing, even when taking a step brings you pain enough to double you over. When your brutalized frame pleads for you to stop . . . and, yet, you can*not*, because you have to fight tomorrow. Or the next day. Or the day after that. If you wish to win it all, that is."

Razi squinted and smiled. "Before you leave, let me tell you this . . . it may help with your thoughts of revenge. Everyone gets cut during these games. Everyone. No one gets through without a mark. This Goll? He has collected his share of wounds thus far, and there is still much further to go. Worse, the competition will become even more difficult. More . . . intense. Until the final eight, when the blood will truly start to fly. Why? Because the last eight are not only the most skilled of the games, they are usually the only ones still standing."

The owner nodded. "So, good lady . . . I apologize if I have offended you. I probably have. It's my nature. But just remember . . . these games are long. Even longer this season, as ordered by the king. What I say may be little comfort, but . . . I daresay you *will* have your revenge. Eventually. So ready your coin. Or any other payment you might be considering."

That left Zelia staring, and when she realized she was staring, she turned to go.

"*The lady is leaving now,*" Razi bawled, startling her. "Apologies again, my lady. That's my usual tone of voice in this place." He looked past her. "See her to the entrance. See to it no one bothers her, else they'll answer to me."

The guard—the same lout who had led her in—nodded and spared a glance at the departing lady. They retraced their steps back to the main gate. Upon the training grounds, the gladiators continued hammering their targets in short savage outbursts. One would step up and unleash a combination of strikes before going to the rear of the line, allowing the next fighter to practice a similar set.

They held her attention for only a heartbeat.

The main gate drew closer. A sapling tree she didn't notice before grew to the side, already bearing green fruit. The tree threw shade across the door, where two stout timbers lay to one side. Already she longed to be free of the place.

"You impressed him, you did," the guard said. "I can tell. He's usually shouting his way through a conversation. Usually. Foul-tempered at any time but you impressed him. He didn't shout when you were with him. Makes me wonder . . ."

The guard gripped the door's inner handle and regarded her. "What was it you were talking about?"

A smirk slid across his face as he pulled the door open.

Ignoring him, Zelia hurried through and marched toward the closest street filled with wayfarers. Her heart pounded as she focused on rejoining civilization while listening for sounds of pursuit. Any moment she expected sandals scuffling along the stones, or even the guard calling out with his unwanted attentions. Nothing of the sort happened, however, and the crowd drew closer, faces took on features.

One last owner to see in the city. Only one, and from what she had learned, he might be the worst of them all . . .

Zelia returned home later that evening, her shadow stretched out before her. The meeting had gone as well as anticipated, and Nexus proved to be every bit the unfit topper she'd expected him to be. Through the brief encounter, the merchant fumed and fidgeted, clearly believing his time was being wasted. All that changed when she mentioned coin, however, noticing a distinct flutter of his eyelids. At the end, Nexus had frostily thanked her for visiting, and he assured her that if his lads were scheduled to fight the man, they would have orders to execute him.

Which was all she wanted to hear.

Those thoughts and hopes stayed with her on the long journey home. A growing ache in her feet and calves told her she had walked a good distance this day, with Nexus's walled home being perhaps the farthest away from her own. She had ample time to reach her door before dark, which was a relief. Some loved the night, but not Zelia. Even when Sorban was alive, she had no desire to be caught outside after nightfall. With him gone, she fortified her door in the evening, shuttered and barred her windows, and kept her dagger at her bedside.

With relief she turned onto the street of her home, but that comfort only lasted a moment as she knew she was returning to an empty house. Tall trees grew on either side, planted evenly along the cobblestones and providing some shade during the day. A few city folk passed by, their backs to her while their long shadows stretched out before them.

She had filled her water barrel before she left for Razi's residence, and a washing appealed to her very much. She also wondered what she might have left in her cupboards. She remembered some fruit from the marketplace, as well as some vegetables and a small basket of eggs, all of which would need to be eaten soon.

Her front door beckoned, and her weariness grew with every step. She would have to bar her door and windows once inside, and that slowed her just a little more. Perhaps she would not eat anything at all and just wash herself instead before sleep.

On impulse, she glanced over her shoulder.

Boh casually followed her a dozen paces behind, smiling that evil smile.

And one stride of his equaled two of hers.

Startled by the sight of him, Zelia screamed and lifted her robes to run. The other doors along the street blurred by as she hurried to her home. Other families lived there, but they no longer talked to her after Sorban had died. Nor did they seem to be around when Boh made his presence known. And the street watch, normally patrolling regularly at this time, was nowhere in sight.

She reached her door and fumbled about her robes for the key. *There*, she felt the piece, grabbed it, and yanked it free.

The weaponsmith strolled toward her, less than five strides away.

In her haste, Zelia missed the slot, jamming the key against the door hard enough to pry it from her fingers. She bent over and snatched it off the ground before straightening and shoving the key through. With a turn, the door opened and she plunged inside, skidding upon her floor. She slammed the door shut and quickly fitted the first of two planks across its width.

The windows! she realized and rushed into the sitting area.

A wave of relief washed through her when she saw the shutters already closed and secured, done when she had left in the morning. She hurried to the kitchen and saw the window there also closed. Not fully safe yet, however, she raced back to her front door and stood there. She dug into her pocket again, forced her hand through the cut in the material, and gripped the dagger strapped to her thigh.

With a rip of cloth, she pulled the weapon free. Ready to defend herself, she glared at the door.

Footsteps, then, scuffling along, perhaps a bit louder than need be. A shrill whistle followed without a tune.

Her knuckles whitened with pressure as she tightened her grip on the dagger. If he tried to enter, if he forced the door, she would stab the man dead, street watch be damned. So she waited, her heart hammering, holding the blade as Sorban had taught her, ready to thrust.

Boh was just outside, perhaps with his ear pressed to the wood. The brazen pisser would regret coming to her home. She would *make* him regret it. Lords above she would cut him for his pursuit of her. Cut whatever he tried bringing into her home. And she intended on screaming when she did cut him. Screaming long and loud, so that anyone nearby would be forced to come running. Someone would if she made enough noise. *Anyone.*

She faced the door, waited for the scratching that would be the signal of war.

Perhaps even a heavy knock. Or a kick.

Except . . . nothing of the sort happened.

The footfalls drew faint as Boh walked by her door and his nonsensical whistling faded away. Puzzled and confused, Zelia put an ear to the surface and listened, listened until she could hear nothing at all.

The unsavory bastard had marched on, leaving her be. Or so he wanted her to think.

Fuming, dagger swinging, she went into her kitchen. There she lit a candle and then lit two more, lighting up the room. She went from room to room, searching for any potential threats. There was no place to hide in such a small dwelling. Her shutters and doors remained closed and undisturbed, and she took a moment to inspect them. Made of strong cuts of wood, there would be considerable noise if anyone attempted to break through, and she would be ready.

In the sitting room she looked about, dagger still in one hand and glowing candle in the other. She listened, wondering if she was indeed alone or if a siege was about to take place. She waited, hoping Boh had walked on but refusing to relax. Sorban would not be pleased if she did lower her guard with danger so close. Her anger flared and she quietly cursed the weaponsmith.

And with every curse to leave her mouth, her anger grew.

28

Daylight bled through red curtains, coloring the room a deep shade of carmine. Lying atop a snarl of sweaty blankets from the day before, Linfur rubbed at his face, attempting to massage away his weariness. He couldn't sleep. Dared not to, really. Moving the bales of hay containing hidden snow orchids from one secret place to another had been a harrowing affair. One that had them all working until dawn. All during that time, he and his lads were nervously mindful of the shadows.

Troubling thoughts filled Linfur's head as to who was killing off their lads. And why? Whoever they were did not know the snow orchids were hidden at the storehouse. The same killers had executed Morg and his enforcers but blatantly ignored a sizable collection of coin behind the bar. Certainly not riches like the orchids but coin all the same. He wondered if, by chance, the killers *had* simply missed finding it, but that seemed doubtful. The coin was right *there* for anyone who looked.

Assuming they were interested in coin at all.

Blessed Lords and Seddon above. Linfur ceased rubbing his cheeks. Someone was striking at the Sons for reasons unknown to him, in the territory assigned to him, to replace the long-gone "king" called Strach.

Could it be someone at odds with Strach? Wouldn't surprise Linfur. Wouldn't know, however, until they discovered more about what was happening. Ideally, he preferred catching the killers and cutting them apart a little at a time, right in front of each other.

With a huff, he realized he wouldn't be doing any of that while lying in bed. So he got up, threw on his shirt from the day before, and slapped his cheeks with scented water. The strain of the previous night weighed on his frame. He was exhausted, and yet he had to present himself to the kings—the Sons—in their court and reassure them everything within the realm was well. That stopped him, long enough to consider some firewater to steady himself. *No*, he decided. Half-pickled and swaying before the Sons would not do. Any gurry might come out of him then, and he had his secrets. Besides . . . he had finished the bottle in the room the night before.

Linfur dipped his hands into the washbasin and ran them over his hair. He took a moment to arm himself, being careful while doing so. At the door, he paused and listened, hard, before undoing the latch. When he went out, he marched, hurrying past a few doors, eyeing each one in case it might fly open. The stairs came into view at the end of the hall, as well as the impressive sight that was the interior of the alehouse.

Boot soles blurred and fluttered as he went down the stairs, fast enough that the barkeep paused in wiping out a mug and watched him.

Linfur glared back, raising a hand as he did so, warning the other not to say a word.

So the barkeep kept on cleaning.

Snores rattled the sleeping lumps of Chur and Grohk. Both murderous louts had slept on the main floor, behind a pair of tables. Grohk snored the loudest, as if inhaling—and choking upon—bowls of cold stew. Chur lay face down in his arms, rising and falling as he rumbled through a dream.

"*Up*, asslickers, up!" Linfur bellowed as he thumped onto floorboards and hurried for the door. Squawks of wood shoved over wood and heavy footfalls soon followed him.

Dense and steamy humidity slapped Linfur's face, stopping him as he stepped outside. The unchecked moisture almost stole his breath, and it took him a moment to get down a full chestful. He grimaced, studying the flow of people struggling against one another in the street. The sight annoyed him. The thought of having to cut through all those pissers *poisoned* him.

Damnation, he fumed, already sweating. He just might stab someone this morning.

"Anyone perish last night?" he asked his killers at his back.

"No word of anyone," Chur answered.

"Did you sleep?"

"No," they answered in near unison.

Linfur had thought so. "We'll sleep better this night," he vowed and strode into the masses. He stopped among all those unwashed bodies and smelly blossoms and scowled at the cloudy sky. It was much later than expected.

"Is it noon?" he blurted.

"It is," Chur said.

Damnation, Linfur mentally shrieked again and glanced from one lout to the other. "Why didn't either of you tits *wake* me?"

He left them before they could answer, knowing what they would say, and knowing he would probably kill them both. Right there in the street. Two quick stabs to their faces and leave them screaming.

A food booth caught his eye, the same one where he'd gotten the fancy pastries for the Sons yesterday morning. The smell of fresh baked goods wasn't in the air, but he spotted the same little old woman. Her button eyes widened at his approach. No doubt because he looked the fright, but then he saw the real reason . . .

There were fewer than a third of the pastries for sale.

"What happened?" he demanded.

The little old woman's mouth dropped open, her lower lip trembling. "I sold them."

"You *sold* them?"

She nodded, her gray bangs bouncing over her eyes.

"You sold them to *who*?"

The question frightened her badly. "To everyone . . ." she replied, gesturing at the crowds around them.

Linfur snatched up a cloth satchel and stuffed the remainder into the bag. Again he ignored paying her and stalked off, stuffing half a pastry into his mouth.

Unfit things didn't even *taste* good, but he still didn't offer his dogs a single scrap. A familiar alley came into sight and Linfur marched into it. He halted after a few paces and looked around. Piles of rubbish lay heaped against the walls, and a puddle of stinking pisswater stained the cobblestones, but there was no sight of the beggar he usually found here.

"Where is that rosy blossom?" he muttered.

Neither Chur nor Grohk answered, deeming it wise not to remind their leader that collection day was just once a week, and that day had been yesterday.

"I'll kill him," Linfur seethed. "If I see him again, I'll kill him. Come on, then."

With that, the three continued on their way. Linfur did not seek out any of his other collectors, instead deciding to head straight to the storehouse belonging to the Sons. In short order he stood before the three remaining brothers.

The stoic Jaro took the satchel from him and delivered it to Calagu.

"You're late," the enforcer said with a dangerous look.

That set Linfur to blinking. "So it is. Too much into the firewater last night. Won't happen again."

"Any news then?" a bored Brejo asked while his brother pawed through the contents of the satchel.

"This is only half full," Calagu interrupted, pulling out a pastry. "Did you eat the rest?"

"Of course not, good Calagu," Linfur said, straining to be pleasant. "Merely rose late in the morning. When I found the merchant woman who sells them, she'd already sold off much of her stock."

"Doesn't even *taste* good," a grimacing Calagu said through a mouthful.

"Perhaps he's trying to poison you," Brejo suggested.

It was the wrong thing to say. Calagu's eyes flared wide. He ceased chewing and retched a gummy mouthful onto the floor. Wheezing and grunting, the pale man spat brown strings until he stuck fingers into his mouth, to hook whatever remained. Worse still, no sooner did Brejo mention the very word than Jaro questioned Linfur with a menacing look.

"*Treacherous bas—*" Calagu croaked out before a spasm of coughing gripped him. He bent over as veins swelled along his temple.

Uninterested, Brejo plucked the bag from his brother. He peered inside and selected a pastry.

"*Don't do it,*" a flushed and red-eyed Calagu squeaked while clutching at his throat.

Ignoring the warning, Brejo ate half of the morsel in two bites. As he chewed, Calagu slowly recovered. "You were joking, weren't you?"

The brother held up the half-eaten baked good. "This is a joke," he said when he was ready. "Daresay you purchased last night's fare. The bites she couldn't sell the day before."

With that, he popped the remainder into his mouth.

Linfur relaxed. "Aye that," he agreed, trying hard to sound normal as Jaro looked elsewhere. "No question that's what it is. I ate one while on my way here and thought the very thing."

"Why didn't you get anything fresher?" Brejo asked while covering his mouth.

"I looked," Linfur lied, "but as I said—I rose too late. Apologies. I'll do better tomorrow."

"Clean that up," Calagu said, wiping his hands in his shirt and leaving stains.

A dreadful, considering silence followed those words.

Anyone else even suggesting such a revulsive undertaking and Linfur would have stabbed the topper through the throat. Repeatedly. Anyone else would be lying on the floor, clutching at multiple wounds. The order came from Calagu, however, the youngest of the remaining Sons, but still one of the kings of the ruling street clan. Worse still, the clan's head enforcer stood nearby, and though Linfur believed he had some favor with Jaro, he dared not refuse the man's brother. Not in front of him. Or Brejo, for that matter, which was perhaps even twice as condemning.

Jaro would only kill you.

Brejo would order you tortured for a year before finally killing you.

So Linfur did the only thing he could do. He looked for a cloth.

"Use your hand," the flustered Son ordered, glaring, shoulders heaving.

Nodding, Linfur did just that, scooping the wad of warm slop off the floor and picking up whatever moist fragments remained. He was no fool, not in this court. After disposing of the handful in a nearby pisspot, Linfur replaced the lid and inspected his hands.

"You didn't answer my question," Brejo said.

Linfur wiped his palms clean on his fine pants. "Your question, Master Brejo?"

"Any news this morning?"

"Apologies, Master Brejo," he said and lowered his eyes. "Your joke unnerved me there. And then Jaro looked my way. In all honesty, I thought I was about to perish."

"Only if you had poisoned them," Brejo grumbled as if it were no matter. "Now, then, that news?"

News.

Linfur could have told the truth and responded with something like, *Someone's slaughtering all our lads for some reason, including the ones guarding the storehouse where we had hidden a large supply of Osgarman snow orchids. Not only are they killing off the lads, but they're ignoring any nearby coin.*

What actually came out of his mouth, however, was "None."

"Boring morning," Calagu said.

"Unfit boring," Brejo complained and eyed Linfur. "What were you saying yesterday? About those paying us for staying at our storehouse? About the patrols being more numerous about the border?"

Linfur nodded, thankful his lie had worked.

"We've asked some of our people recently come from that way," Brejo scowled. "They say there's no issue with patrols. None. Because there are hardly *any* patrols."

That crinkled Linfur's brow. "What?"

"All the regular patrols have vanished," Brejo said.

"All of them?"

"All," Brejo answered. "Not a horseman or Lancer in sight."

"Well, the Lancers *are* a notch above—" Linfur started.

"None," the Son's leader cut him off.

"Perhaps it's best to say they've gone *somewhere*, instead," Calagu said.

"Word is they're gone," Brejo repeated.

"They can't be *gone*," Calagu argued. "They merely haven't been seen in a while. Which tells me that the patrols have *diminished* because the forces there are *less* and have yet to be reinforced. The border is a huge swath of open territory. And there *is* a war on, you know. There is someone guarding our hides. Has to be. Else Marrn might invade us."

Brejo scowled. "Foolishness."

"Well, they could."

Brejo dismissed that with a wave. "I'd be more concerned with Vathia, and Vathia isn't going to invade us either."

"You don't know what the Marrnites are planning."

"The Marrnites won't do a damn thing, I said. Not until we're finished with the Nords. I don't like the Marrnite asslickers any more than you do, but to suggest a war from them? They love their coin as much as we do. In their minds it's best to let Nordun smash us about the heads until we've had enough, and *then* lower a lance and charge in. Anyway, enough of that. Linfur . . ."

An attentive Linfur cocked his head.

"Go back to those dogs sleeping in our storehouse. Talk with them. Tell them what I just said to you."

"Then maybe Vathia is planning something," Calagu said, turning heads.

Brejo acknowledged that with a withering frown and chose to ignore it. "I don't know what those storehouse toppers are talking about, but in this business they're either lying to us for reasons we'll have to find out . . . or someone's lying to *them* for reasons *they'll* have to find out. Either way, go talk to them. Ask your questions. Return if you learn anything. If not, come back tomorrow."

"And make certain these are fresher," Calagu warned, holding up a second pastry.

Linfur absorbed all that, grateful that his slack face had successfully hidden his growing concern. He nodded and considered revealing what was going on with him and his minions, but he knew the answer. *Deal with it, then*, they would tell him, and give him that one chance only, considering it a test. And if he couldn't deal with it, he would be quickly killed and replaced with someone else who could.

Brejo watched him, expecting him to say something.

"Apologies, Master Brejo," Linfur explained. "Merely wondering if there was anything else needing to be done."

"Just don't get killed," the leader of the Sons said and reached for the bag of food.

Don't get killed, Linfur grumbled to himself, washing his hands at a small public pool. Several small children played nearby with their leggings rolled up to their knees. He ignored their splashing and scrubbed himself clean of the filth that had fallen from Calagu's mouth. Chur and Grohk, very much aware of their leader's anger, guarded his flanks, glaring at anyone venturing too close. Children included.

"*Fah*," Linfur released, inspecting his hands before dipping them again. His skin crawled despite his best attempts. Images of cleaning Calagu's gurry off the floor plagued his mind. Anyone else and he would have gutted them, but because it was Calagu, he obeyed, and he hated himself a little bit more. It wasn't the first humiliating session with the Sons. There had been plenty of others. Enough where he had imagined killing all three of them . . . all three kings.

In the end he reminded himself that he had done the wise thing. He obeyed, and he was still alive because of it. *That was a test*, he thought. *Of your loyalty to the Sons. Just remember. That was a test and you passed it. You're still alive.*

One day, however, it would be Calagu picking up *his* gurry from the floor.

Linfur studied his hands and wondered if he needed to see a healer. For some medicinal slop guaranteed to purify his hands of Calagu's foul mouthful. Once finished washing, he decided to see what was going on with the secretive lads in the Sons' storehouse. So he hurried through the familiar maze of Sunja's backstreets, with Chur and Grohk on his heels. Until Linfur lifted a hand and stopped his henchmen in a familiar alley.

"You both wait here," he ordered. "I'll talk with whoever's at the door. See what I can see. If you hear fighting, then come running. If you don't hear anything and I don't return in a timely fashion, then go back to the Sons. Tell them they have me, round up as many cutthroats as you can, and return for me."

"Why do you say that?" Chur asked.

Linfur winced. "I don't know . . . just wait here until I return. And if I don't, you know what to do."

Hunched and ready, Chur and Grohk nodded, their eyes narrowed and thoughtful, resembling wolfhounds wondering what would be thrown their way.

Linfur left them, one hand skittering along a wall as he proceeded alone. The alley narrowed, turning him sideways as he continued between a pair of empty barns. When he reached the end, he checked on matters before easing around a corner. The storehouse belonging to the Sons loomed before him, where the secretive Sunjan-speaking Mademians lurked.

Or so Linfur thought. Lords only knew what was going on in there. The lot of them might be strewn about the interior, enjoying the very thing they came to Sunja to sell. Which raised another question in his mind . . . The lads in the storehouse wanted to sell the orchids themselves but had given a substantial gift to the Sons, who were not only enjoying the orchids but also selling it. Thus, they unwittingly created competition for themselves with a very dangerous adversary. An adversary that would, without question, seek to control all their business affairs one day.

Not very smart. Truth be known, it was unfit stupid.

Unless that was the plan from the very start . . .

To what ends, however, Linfur didn't know. Certainly was a puzzle when one thought about it. Almost . . . like a distraction from whatever they were truly doing in the city. That hooked in his mind. The whole agreement had been arranged by Strach. Linfur had only been tasked with collecting coin and safeguarding the orchids. And the other Sons, perhaps enjoying the orchids a touch too much, hadn't really thought matters through. Or were unable to . . .

He snuck along, mindful of the gurry underfoot, keeping one hand on his sword and the other against the storehouse's wooden hide. At times he glanced overhead, in case the maggots within had decided to place guards on the roof. One didn't live long in his business without developing a healthy sense of caution.

On impulse, he stopped and carefully placed an ear to the wall.

At first, he couldn't hear anything, so he adjusted his head a little, flattening his ear to the boards. An empty hush filled it, lasting long enough that he wondered if there was anyone inside at all. The place was big enough for a couple dozen men or more, especially if they didn't have anything in there with them. Be *boring*, he thought, and then wondered again what they could possibly be doing in there. Perhaps they might only come out during the night or—

Someone coughed.

Close enough that Linfur dared not move, for fear of being heard himself. His shoulders tensed as he waited, eyes wide and searching.

"That roast was good," a voice remarked from inside.

Linfur's mouth opened in a voiceless *Ahhh* and he strained to hear more.

"It was good," said another. "The Sunjan cooked it up just right. Not too salty. Not too many spices. Too much of that and I'm squatting all night."

"I'll go back there this evening, I think. See if there's any left."

"*Pah*, you're not going back there for the roast."

Silence to that. "What am I going back there for?"

"*Poltu*. The cook's *wife*. I saw you eyeing her."

A soft chuckle then. ". . . Perhaps I was. *Basten* . . ."

Then a third voice broke in, but low, making it difficult to understand what was being said. Words were exchanged, growing fainter, as the two speakers moved away from the wall. Licking his lips, Linfur slid along the wood, listening for more. The conversation had ended, however, replaced by that empty rush of nothing in his ear.

Linfur straightened, thinking over what he had heard. He didn't speak Mademian, so the meaning was lost upon him. Considering the earlier conversation, he figured it was merely jabs traded between two men known to each other.

Poltu. Basten.

Linfur decided the words might have meant something about rutting or nogging or the like. That they called the cook "the Sunjan" was of no matter to him, as they were Mademian. No doubt they called anyone they encountered in the city a Sunjan.

He listened once more, but the voices ceased to be, so he made his way out front. Rusty nailheads dotted the old wood, and thick planks barricaded the nearby windows. The faint smell of piss offended his nose. Frowning at the stink, he felt for his sword. All set, he faced the smaller gate inset within one of the two larger doors and frowned again. *Damnation*, he thought blackly, knowing he'd have to knock for himself. Rolling his eyes, Linfur scowled and rapped three times. The very contact deepened his disapproval, and he checked the edge of his hand afterward, wanting to wipe it somewhere.

Something moved inside, a subtle scratching upon wood that hooked his attention. A clatter followed, jarring Linfur enough to retreat a step. Gripping his sword, he hoped he hadn't made a mistake leaving Chur and Grohk behind.

The door opened in a puff of foul air and a different face peered out at him.

"Yes?" the face asked, blinking at the day.

"Greetings, young sir," Linfur said, inwardly cringing at his buttery pleasantry. "Ah, I'm not familiar with you. Might I have a word with the fellow from before?"

"You are the collectors?" the face asked somewhat sleepily.

You are the collectors, Linfur repeated in his head, detecting the slightest accent on the words. "I am. But have no worries. I'm not collecting today. I would like to speak with the other lad. The one I usually speak with. About matters he mentioned the other day."

The fellow stared, clearly thinking hard, when the same lad from before—brown hair, eyes, and neatly trimmed beard—appeared behind the puzzled one. He slapped the doorman on the shoulder, turning him around. With a jerk of the head, the bearded man sent the other one away and took his place. He smiled at Linfur. "You again? Is all well?"

"Oh, aye that, all is well. My, ah, employers sent me to talk with you, about what you mentioned the other day. The border patrols hindering your shipments."

The barest hint of concern flickered upon the bearded face. "Yes?"

"They have talked to others on that very matter, and they say there should be no troubles for bringing your goods across Sunja's borders and into the city. The horseman and Lancer patrols are not as . . . regular as before."

"Aye that. We have learned the same."

"You have?" Linfur asked, his senses flaring, detecting an untruth.

"Some lads arrived with news from Mademia. Our problem isn't with the Sunjan patrols, but with the Kree and Vathian ones. The countries between Sunja and Mademia."

"I know where they are," Linfur said drily, studying the speaker.

"We have had several problems with them. Our orchids are highly prized. Very much in demand. And there are clans such as yours in those places who have considerable influence upon those patrols. Enough influence that they send out those same soldiers to hunt for our deliveries with the intentions of robbing them."

"Robbing them, you say?"

"Aye that. But have no fear. We are already, ah, looking into revenge against these helldogs."

"Hellpups."

The bearded face frowned.

"You said helldogs," Linfur explained. "No one says that. It's hellpups."

"We say helldogs in Mademia."

Linfur smiled coldly. "You're in Sunja now."

They faced each other, the conversation gone frosty.

"Well," the bearded man said and patted the door. "While we are here. In *here*. *This* place . . . is *Mademian*."

Linfur shook his head. "Of course it is. Call it whatever you like in there. Call it Nordun if you like."

He meant it as a joke, but the bearded man stiffened as if he had been stabbed under the chin.

"Dear me," Linfur said with suspicious amusement. "Seems I've upset you. Apologies. Well . . . I'll let my people know what you've just said. About those meddling clans. My lads are very anxious to purchase more of your orchids."

"Many people are," the bearded man said, becoming pleasant again.

But it was also forced. Linfur detected that right away. "I'll return another day," he said, turning away. "To collect our fee."

Nodding, the bearded man closed the door. Someone secured it by slapping a pair of planks into place.

Pretending all was well, Linfur strolled away, but his mind was racing.

Nordun.

The lad's mood had clearly soured at that, as if he'd sipped from a full pisspot. Linfur wondered why. All those countries lay stacked upon each other, if one looked at a map of the day. The mountain range known as the Gray Teeth lay on Sunja's left shoulder. Those mountains stretched south, all the way down to Mademia and far-eastern Borja. A natural barrier that prevented the passage of any army through them. If the Nordish bastards wanted Mademia, they would have to cut a path through Sunja, then Vathia, and finally Kree before reaching that country. Sunja was the doorway to the greater southlands, with Marrn playing a somewhat smaller role to the northeast.

An undertaking that not only seemed quite unlikely, but even foolish.

Still, Linfur felt odd about the interaction, mulling it over all the way back to Chur and Grohk.

"Follow me, boys," a distracted Linfur said. "Time to visit my favorite butcher . . ."

29

Linfur stood over the corpse of his favorite butcher, whose name was Pomak. Pomak the Butcher, they called him, but it wasn't always livestock stretched across his chopping table. Not at all. Sometimes, Linfur even helped hold down the dog blossoms stretched across the butcher's table. Good times, those were. No longer. Pomak had departed this life in the same eye-widening manner as the others under Linfur's command.

Lying in a pool of his own thickening juices and smelling worse, Pomak had clearly sustained a savage beating. One eye was horribly swollen, both lips were fattened, and his nose was crushed so badly that the gruesome nub of red and pebbly pink looked mashed into his right cheek. Just looking at that thing threatened to turn Linfur's guts. None of that had killed him better, however, than the spike of wood protruding from his other eye. Linfur didn't know how deep that thing went into Pomak's head, but he guessed it scraped the inside of the skull.

"Quite the . . . eyeful, isn't he?" said the Koor officer—called Kelmo—of the local street watch.

Linfur tongued the inside of his cheek. "Quite the eyeful, indeed."

"You lads having it out with another clan?"

Linfur shook his head.

"Are you certain?"

That turned Linfur away from the dead man to face Kelmo. The Skarr wore full armor, as if he expected to be attacked at any moment. Tall and broad-shouldered, the armor widened him even further. Three slots in his helmet revealed hard green eyes and a bit of mouth. Linfur sized up all that armor, thinking it wasn't a bad idea these days. It might have helped old Pomak.

"No," Linfur sighed.

"No what?"

Lords above, he thought, but what he said to this insufferable guardian of the city was, "No, we're not having it out with another clan."

"So what's this then?" Kelmo asked, indicating the corpse.

"An accident."

"An accident, *fah*," the officer scoffed. "You lads best find out the reason behind that accident before I'm ordered to do something."

"What do you do again?" Linfur asked and regretted the question the moment it left him.

The Koor didn't like that jab, or the implications. He glared, and his hard green eyes appeared very serious indeed.

"Look here . . ." the officer ordered.

A resigned Linfur nodded, waiting for the threat he knew was coming.

"All that's required of me is to look that way," Kelmo nodded left. "And look that way," he nodded right. "And then . . . walk away. That's all. If you wish me to do more, you know what to do. Understood?"

Linfur knew. Another one of Strach's duties was to channel a small percentage of profits to the local street watch commanded by Kelmo. In return, the city guard allowed the Sons and their criminal activities to flourish, provided they did not disturb the peace and kept matters in relative secrecy. It was a small amount paid, trivial really, but Brejo warned Linfur to act as if it were a painful sum, an agonizing sum, to convince the Koor he held the Sons by their swollen bells. And, thus, all would remain well and good.

Linfur glanced at the smashed cabinet. He had already checked earlier, when Kelmo stepped outside to order his soldiers around the butcher's store. As expected, whatever coin was stashed in the cabinet was gone. He cocked his brow at the watchful officer.

"What?" Kelmo asked.

"There was coin in that thing."

"There was?"

"Aye that, there was."

"Well, I didn't take it. Nor did any of my lads. You certain there was coin in there?"

Sighing, Linfur nodded.

"Well then, perhaps he was murdered for it. A robbery, then." Kelmo dipped his head with the air of a job well done. "My thanks in helping solve this mystery. I'll leave you now, to do whatever it is you need to do. Ah . . ."

"What?"

Kelmo gestured outside. "There's a fine lot of meat hanging about."

"So?"

"A few are missing, but that was to be expected. Not all people are honest. Still a lot left, however. S'all right if me and the lads take a few cuts? What's fit, that is."

"You're asking me?"

Kelmo waited.

"Yes, yes, go on then," Linfur groaned, knowing the man would do so anyway. "Take what you like."

Kelmo left to bark at the men outside, leaving Linfur to study the cabinet again. He checked on Chur and Grohk at the wrecked doorway, mindful of the Skarrs examining the best cuts hanging from the ceiling. He caught Chur's eye and sent a silent message, and the cutthroat smoothly faced the activity beyond—blocking the office's interior from sight. Picking up on the move, Grohk did the same a heartbeat later.

Ordinarily, Linfur would return later when there was less activity outside, but he had to know. Dread filled him as he stepped to the cabinet and steeled himself for the next part. He sized up the mess, probably made with a heavy mace. With a glance over his shoulder, he gripped a familiar spot and pulled the furniture away from the wall, just enough to peek behind it.

The wall looked intact.

Linfur reached back there and pressed until he heard a soft click. With a gentle touch he slid open a panel, revealing a hidden shelf and a dozen or so purses upon it. He let his breath out in a grateful hiss. The Sons wouldn't kill him after all. Not right away at least. Whoever had killed Pomak took the not-so-well-hidden coin in the cabinet but failed to search behind it.

"Come here, my loves," Linfur whispered and collected one, which he slipped into a pocket. He quickly extracted a few more and stashed them away. Once he had taken what he could, he walked across that gore-splashed floor, avoiding the thicker pools, and got Chur's attention. His henchman went back to the hiding place and retrieved the rest.

Linfur watched him tuck the purses away, periodically checking on Kelmo and his Skarrs, fussing over a great haunch they cut free from a rope. A soft cheer went up from the soldiers.

Chur pushed the cabinet back to the way it had been.

"Ready, then?" Linfur asked Chur, who nodded. "Excellent. Follow me then, lads. We're off from this place."

"What about the food here?" Grohk asked.

Linfur shrugged.

"I can take some of that chicken there," Grohk suggested. "Bring it back. Have it cooked up."

"You have no idea how long it's been there."

"Does it matter?"

"Punce. Do what you want but just be quick," Linfur muttered and left him to do just that. "Kelmo," he called, walking across the straw-covered floor. "I have a question. You're a learned man. I heard a few words today I didn't know. Perhaps you do?"

"Let's hear it then," Kelmo grumped with mild impatience.

"We say *hellpups*, that's understood, but do the Mademians say *helldogs*?"

The Koor officer nodded. "Some do. In southern Mademia. Not so much the north."

"Excellent, excellent. Two more then. I overheard *Poltu* . . . and *Basten*."

Kelmo frowned. "Where'd you hear that?"

"In an alehouse," Linfur lied with experienced ease. "From a Sunjan pickled on cheap mead speaking Mademian."

Kelmo checked on his men hauling up the claimed food. "That's Nordish you heard. *Poltu* means punce in our tongue. *Basten* is the rank of an officer. Same as Koor, from what I know."

A chill gripped Linfur's spine. "Where did you learn all that?"

"Drunken Sujins. On the mend from the front. But well enough to crawl about the alehouses. They mutter on about anything while they're being heaved into the streets."

A chill spread to his limbs. He nodded at the huge haunch the Skarrs were about to hack into smaller bits. "You enjoy that," he said. "Pomak's the best butcher in the city. Or was the best . . ."

With that, he left the city guards. Once in the street, he looked about and found Grohk and Chur behind him. Grohk had a chunk of something wrapped in a cloth. Chur held on to a bundle of what might have been a pair of chickens. Linfur didn't comment on either.

That's Nordish, Kelmo had said. Poltu *means punce in our tongue.* Basten *is the rank of an officer.*

The pig bastard Koor had learned that from drunken soldiers, which Linfur supposed was true enough. The words he heard had been spoken by a Sunjan-speaking Mademian. Or rather a Mademian speaking Sunjan. *Damnation*, Linfur wasn't certain anymore, and he made a living from being certain. But he was certain of the guarded reaction from the bearded pig bastard at the door upon mentioning the word *Nordun*.

His senses buzzed with suspicion, a familiar low and unfriendly tickle at the base of his skull, reaching for his ears. He'd have to further investigate that pack of vermin nesting in the Sons' property.

Maybe they were Sunjan-speaking Mademians?

Or could they be something *else*?

Something other than bumbling merchants who sold all their goods and had only excuses as to why they hadn't brought in more. But if they had sold all their goods, then why were they still in the Sons' storehouse? Sure, they'd given him a reason, but the Sons had already revealed the truth of one lie, which made Linfur suspicious about their recent story. And there seemed to be a great number of them in there. Almost as if they were hiding. Or preparing. But hiding from who? And preparing for what? And who would *want* to hide in Sunja, keeping their identities a secret, who used Nordish words in their conversation? Deserters, perhaps? But they said they were from Mademia.

They *said* . . .

The chill overtook him again, and Linfur had learned long ago to pay attention to it.

He'd have to return to the storehouse. Perhaps with a group of men armed from head to prick. Or, even better, with Kelmo and a group of Skarrs. Make that cracked pisspot of a Koor earn the few coins they tossed his way every month.

Seddon above. Lords above. Saimon below. Linfur's unease swelled by the heartbeat, knowing something was dreadfully wrong about the group sheltering in the storehouse. Dreadfully wrong. Without question, he would have to return that day and investigate further.

But first, and more importantly, he had to find a safe place to hide the coin they carried.

Without knowing it, he'd already increased his stride.

A short time later, he hurried toward the alehouse he usually resided in. The place was far from grand, but his room was the best of the lot. He was, in fact, the sole owner of the establishment, and he went to great measures to hide that information from the Sons, even sleeping at other alehouses or inns about the city, to keep his enemies from guessing his whereabouts. This place, however, he considered home, and he stayed here the most.

The two-story alehouse squatted upon a stone foundation and dangled limp banners of gold, green, and white from its heights. Weathered planks covered the building, nailed to a frame of thick timbers. Several food carts and stalls peddled their wares along the same street, while merchants in neighboring stores sold all manner of goods, from perfumed water to sandals, boots, and fancy caps. All that business pulled in customers, and a healthy stream was strolling through that afternoon.

Linfur glared at anyone in his path as he closed in on his alehouse. He quickened his pace again, shoving aside anyone too slow to move.

The crowds parted and the entrance came into view.

A beggar with a slovenly bush of hair on his head sat on the first step, staring one way before swinging his gaze to the other. A second beggar sat beside him. The first one was an old man, decrepit and dying day by miserable day. The other was a woman, younger by a few years, but every bit as deplorable as the wrinkled knob beside her. She glanced around more often than her companion, and she locked onto Linfur first.

Her face filled with fright. She fled, bolting into the crowd without warning her crusty companion. The abrupt departure startled the old topper, and he looked about in puzzlement.

Then he spotted Linfur and his dogs, not five strides away, and his mouth dropped open.

"*Ah-ha*," Linfur snarled and lunged for him. He grabbed the old pisser by his beard and cringed at the oily feel. That nasty sensation angered Linfur all the more, and he viciously rattled the beggar's head.

Chur and Grohk guarded their leader's flanks, staring down anyone thinking about interfering.

"What do you think you're doing?" Linfur challenged harshly, getting a whiff of an even nastier smell. "Lords above, man. You bathe in pisswater this morning?"

"Might've been," the other rasped.

"You best get on then," Linfur warned, releasing the beggar and immediately checking on his hand. "Find an empty shite trough to perish in. Go on. You're keeping paying customers from me."

"From—"

"Aye that, *me,* you unsalted strip of pig shite. You perched your ancient ass upon *my* front step. Now *leave* before you anger me further."

With that, he shoved him off.

The beggar stumbled away. Linfur watched him go, believing the louse looked familiar. No doubt he collected coin from the unfit bastard. His hand tingled from grabbing that filthy beard and that brought him back to the current business.

With Chur and Grohk at his back, he bounded over the steps and entered the alehouse, opening the door with a hard push. Boots trampled over floorboards as an unusual sight stopped him cold. Daylight outlined the shuttered windows, barring both the sun and much needed fresh air. Besides the light from the open door, few rays illuminated the deeper section, leaving most of the cavernous interior in shadow. Several thick log columns divided the main hall, holding up the second floor, four of which stood in a group some five strides apart at the center of the room. The bar waited beyond, dark and moody, and eerily empty. Tables and chairs cluttered the left side of the alehouse, but on the right was a shadowy figure slumped against the wall.

Linfur checked on his two killers behind him, with their backs to the half-opened main entrance.

"That's the enforcer," Chur said calmly, nodding at the figure.

"I *know* that's the enforcer," Linfur said sweetly. He hardened his voice as he pulled steel. "See to him."

Chur proceeded to check on the man, while Linfur brandished his sword and treaded softly to the bar. He leaned one way and then the other, peering around the mighty logs holding up the ceiling. Turning about, he reached the bar and glanced over at Chur, who crouched near the unmoving man. Behind them all, the light from the main entrance slowly diminished as the door swung shut. The distant murmur of the street crowds lessened. Linfur cocked his head and leaned across the counter.

Sandals and boots. Six of them. Piled upon each other, with the legs attached to a collection of bodies. Fresh corpses all. One lay face down atop another, his head sunk deep into an armpit, while the other's face was stretched back on the shoulders, as if looking at the stairs to the second level.

"Chur?" Linfur called out, glancing back to see Grohk's dark expression, standing not a stride away.

"The lad's dead," Chur replied.

A door slammed.

The front door.

And standing there, upon the same floorboards Linfur crossed only moments ago, stood a man. A monster of a man, his head nearly reaching the ceiling. A beard of steely gray hung off a dark face, and eyes simmered with a malevolence that gave Linfur pause, caused Chur to stand, and turned Grohk around. The monster beheld all three, his sinister gaze flicking from one to the other as if sizing up the task before him. Outside, the parade of city folk passed right by, blissfully unaware of the showdown happening behind a single closed door.

Linfur barely moved, tapping his sword against his lower leg while studying the man blocking all escape.

Grohk pulled out a pair of curved daggers.

Chur had his own short sword in hand, poised and ready.

Watching them all, the monster flexed a shoulder, connected to the arm and hand that held on to what looked like a club.

One studded with spikes.

Silence then, swollen with a tension as thick as the humidity in the streets.

"You the one killing my boys?" Linfur finally asked, his voice unnaturally loud in that empty place.

". . . Aye that," was the low but earnest reply.

"And you killed these lads here as well?"

To that, the monster only nodded.

"Well, my thanks," Linfur said, freeing his dagger and flipping it into his hand. "You saved me at least a day's hunt. Now then . . . lads . . . ?"

Like a pair of obedient guard dogs freed of chains and waiting for the command, Chur and Grohk stood stock still, their gaze locked onto the monster.

"Kill that one."

His killers rushed in, converging on their foe.

The monster swung his spiked club, batting Chur's head away and lifting the rest of him off the floor. Chur flew aside while the monster whirled upon Grohk. Grohk stabbed for the monster's guts and face. The first knife struck, but the monster swatted aside the slash for his eyes. Grohk still crashed into him, releasing a rapid stitching of thrusts where he could.

Until a massive fist crashed down upon his shoulder.

Grohk tipped, the connection driving him to a knee.

The monster seized the henchman's throat with a meaty clap. Yanked him off the floor and slammed the top of Grohk's head into the ceiling, into one of the solid crossbeams there. There was a clop of bone and Grohk's head squished into his shoulders. His arms and legs shivered to an ominous patter of droplets upon the floor. A deep and rhythmic breathing rose over that as the monster exerted enormous pressure. The breathing peaked with a satisfied grunt, low and mean, signaling the final, killing squeeze of pressure.

The monster dropped his victim to the floor.

Chur stayed where he landed, among a thorny briar of overturned chairs. The spiked club remained stuck to his head.

In the whispering stillness that followed, Linfur shook his head with rising fury. "Oh, you big bastard," he swore softly, fingers flexing upon his weapons. Blades weaving, churning, he edged to the center of the four posts. "Come on then," he goaded. "Come on. Come see why I'm the master here . . ."

The monster studied him for a moment. Then he reached for a chair.

"That won't save you . . ." Linfur sneered behind his bobbing weapons. "Truth be known, I haven't killed anyone in *days* . . ."

The monster lifted the chair and charged.

And as he did, he swung the furniture.

Hearing, *feeling*, a roar that didn't come from him, Linfur nimbly dodged that improvised club and ducked behind an enormous log. The chair exploded against the base of the thing, sending pieces flying past his eyes. More fragments rattled across floorboards.

Linfur rushed his towering adversary and stabbed for a thigh.

Except one huge fist slapped aside the crippling thrust. The force ripped the weapon clear of Linfur's grip and twisted him off-balance. He recovered faster than the monster, in time to face the ogre square on. Linfur stabbed for the guts, seeking to open this creature up from waist to chin.

Except the first thrust struck a tough band of leather hidden beneath the shirt.

That unexpected impact buckled Linfur's arm, sending a shot of agony from his wrist to his elbow, bright enough to slow him.

Slow him long enough for one of those huge, bludgeoning fists to fall.

There was an explosion of force, a concentrated clap not unlike wood on wood, taken fully upon the forehead. Linfur's chin bounced off his chest and his jaw snapped shut, his teeth snipping off the tip of his tongue. The room spun and tumbled, and the floor slammed against his back. Linfur bounced and buckled, suddenly choking on a gout of his own blood. He barked a cough, misting the air before him.

The monster grabbed him by the scruff of the neck. The seams of Linfur's shirt let go in an alarming rip, and he dropped flat on his face again. Dazed, confused, spitting blood, and leaking fury, he propped himself up on one elbow.

A hand clamped down on his throat. The overwhelming strength in that grip yanked his senses back with breath-stealing force. Linfur's eyes narrowed to slits. He clawed at the thing holding him, his tingling fingers weakening.

"*Guh*," he spat, flowering the air again. He was turned over, flailing as he went, until his fingers scrabbled against an unforgiving grain, and the insteps of his boots skidded across the floor. A second hand held him by the rear waist of his trousers, the fingers hard and invasive against his rump. The room dipped and whirled as he was swung about, while a disturbing darkness bled into the corners of his vision.

Blind, was Linfur's last bewildering thought. *I'm going blind.*

Still, he had sight enough to glimpse the log before his face crunched into it.

Gurga mashed that head into the post thrice more, each blow harder than the previous. The body in his clutches slumped, but the enforcer held on to it like a bleeding, battering ram. A red rose marked the point of impact while a handful of teeth scattered about the base. After the third strike, Gurga adjusted his grip and shoved the face into the wood, grating it up and down. After a time, the fury left him and he straightened, the corpse hanging from his hand. He eyed the thing and, after a considering moment, let it drop, where it landed in a heap.

All became quiet.

Until Gurga stomped on the dead man's neck.

With no one left to kill, the enforcer turned this way and that, fuming through his nose. In time, the distant perhaps even calming buzz of an unaware populace reached him. Shoulders heaving, Gurga looked about, tired from the short but intense struggle. No one else came at him. No one else tried to gut him. With a sinus-clearing sniff, he saw the other two bodies where they had fallen. Not that a second smashing bothered him.

A slight pinch distracted him, somewhere down below. A pain not unfamiliar. Gurga patted himself down and checked his fingers. Darkness stained them. Scowling, he lifted his shirt and found the cut. Not much. A finger's length and no longer, just above the leather bound across his lower self, nicking his ribs. The line wept, wept even more when he pressed it, but failed to penetrate deep. It stung, however. Stung terribly. And bled rivulets anyone else might find worrying, but Gurga knew a wad of cloth would stop it.

A knock on the alehouse door lifted his head.

Grunting, favoring his wound, he plodded to the entrance. A sprawled-out leg attached to one dead bastard sought to trip him, so he kicked it out of his way, twisting the whole torso. Gurga reached the door and pulled it open a crack.

There, looking about furtively, was an anxious Darsho. Selve stood behind him.

"Is it done?" Darsho asked, the hope unmistakable in his voice.

Gurga stared before shaking his head. "Not yet," he growled and opened the door to allow them inside.

30

A familiar metallic rattling roused Pig Knot.

He'd been sleeping restlessly, drifting in and out of consciousness, suffering through the midday heat in his little prison. Dreams of Sunja's bathhouses had tantalized him when the yawning creak of hinges jerked him awake. He snorted and wiped away a string of drool clinging to his chin. A slick sheen of perspiration coated his entire frame, gluing the smallest particle of dust or debris to his hide.

The paltry water bucket drew his eye, and he remembered his dream of steamy bathhouses.

Odusk stopped before Pig Knot's cell, leading four guards. One of them was Slok, but the others were unknown to him. Odusk inserted a key into the lock, opened the door, and motioned the others to enter.

Alarm fired through Pig Knot. When the Skarrs appeared in numbers, it meant he was about to be held down and pounded about the face and shoulders.

Not this time, however, as the men shoved a prisoner bound in chains into the cell. Once inside, they forced the newest man to sit. Two Skarrs unshackled him from his rattling bonds while the others watched, their hands on short swords. Metal shook and plinked, and one guard fondly patted the cheek of their prisoner, who snarled as if ready to bite. That stirred the pot. The other guards tensed and pulled steel, poised to thrust. Even Odusk and Slok snapped to attention, ready to join in if matters got bloody.

Nothing of the sort happened, however. With a poisonous glare at all opposing him, the newest addition released a huff of frustration, drew up his knees, and hung his head between them.

"Smart one, isn't he?" Odusk noted.

"Oh, he's right smart. Right and proper vicious as well," one Skarr remarked. "You're a right and proper eater of men, aren't you, Poza?"

"Aye that," Poza answered, wise enough to know what might happen if he didn't reply.

The Skarrs withdrew, the last man backing out while watching the prisoner.

Odusk locked the door, the keys jangling.

"What were his crimes again?" Slok asked pleasantly with a glance in Pig Knot's direction.

"You said he killed a man?" Odusk added.

The Skarr scoffed. "*Three* that we know of. But his sort leaves corpses all across the land. Just a matter of finding them before the crows. Isn't that right, Poza?"

Poza kept his head lowered, his long hair, straight and greasy, hid his face.

"So he's dangerous, eh?" Odusk asked.

The Skarr regarded him. "What gurry are you getting at?"

"None," Odusk said, somewhat taken aback. "Just wondering, is all."

"Just wondering? You're certain that's all? I mean we did just throw the bastard in there, did we not? That should be clue enough. And didn't you ask for him to be brought here?"

That narrowed Pig Knot's eyes, but Odusk was already leading the Skarrs out of the cellblock. "Yes, yes," the jailor explained, "but as I've said . . ."

The door slammed shut, muting the voices.

Pig Knot studied Poza, sitting some two strides away. He still had his head down and legs pulled up. Not overly meaty, but lean, filthy with dirt, grime, and smelling of smoke. The burned meat kind, not campfire. Poza possessed narrow shoulders, but what really got Pig Knot's attention were the man's forearms corded with thick muscle. His hands ended in fingers that resembled segmented spikes, well suited for strangling necks.

A right and proper eater of men, Pig Knot recalled, watching his cellmate.

Feeling the other's gaze, Poza abruptly looked up and stared right back. Just for a heartbeat before he leaned to one side and checked on where the jailors might be. He had a hawkish face in need of a shave, with dark eyes and hair shorn to the stubbly skin just above his ears in a most unflattering way.

Satisfied the jailors were gone, Poza smirked and sat back. He studied Pig Knot in turn. He lingered on the missing legs, sizing them up this way and that, before continuing with the rest of him. Poza took his time, not meeting the other's gaze until he finished his inspection. Whereupon he leered, displaying half a rack of rotten, overlapping teeth. The sight reminded Pig Knot of Halm of Ziberia, but he didn't want his memory of the Zhiberian marred by the menacing individual sharing his cell.

"Lost your legs, 'eh?" Poza whispered.

Pig Knot frowned.

"I said . . . Lost. Your legs. *'Eh?*" Evil flickered in the lad's eyes, raw and bright.

"Aye that," Pig Knot replied evenly, wondering how bad it had just gotten for him.

Poza continued to leer, even poked his tongue out of one corner of his mouth before pulling it back, as if sensing an easy meal. "Unfortunate. For you."

"Unfortunate," Pig Knot echoed softly. "For me."

"You look like someone I killed once."

That put Pig Knot on guard.

"Even sound like him," Poza continued. "Big brute. Like you. Except he *had* legs. Not like you. Had that look, though. Thought himself tough as steel. Walked and talked like he pissed iron. I didn't like the look of him. Told him so, and when he saw I meant it, well . . ." he smiled, and his tongue appeared in the other corner of his mouth. "He knew he had to do something. Before I did something. So you know what we did?"

Though he might guess, Pig Knot slowly shook his head.

"We fought. In an alley. He knew he had trouble then. You could see it on his face as he walked into the place. You could see he was thinking, *I'll have to kill him, because he'll kill me.* And he was right. So we fought. Aye that we did. You see this?"

Poza held up his right thumb, which ended in the foulest hook of a fingernail Pig Knot had ever seen.

"Know what I did with this?"

Pig Knot shook his head.

"I stuck this into his *eye*," Poza grimaced, baring the bottom nubs of his teeth. "Sank it deep. Into that soft cheese behind the eyes. And I gripped it. The whole head. Until I felt the inner curve of his ear. Tough lad screamed the whole time. You've never heard a man scream like that . . . until I bit out his throat."

Poza smirked in lazy fashion. "He stopped screaming then. Became more of a gurgle. While it lasted. He tried to stop it, but that's hard to do, right? When it's all . . . flying out of you like that. Killed him in Pericia, I did. You know how far Pericia is from Sunja?"

Pig Knot sighed. He knew but shook his head anyway.

"Ten days," Poza said. "Depending on matters, you understand. If you walk or ride. If you have prisoners or by yourself. If the weather's fit. All that, right? Took me nearly *three* weeks to get to Sunja. Three. I took my time."

Poza stretched out his legs so that his feet almost touched Pig Knot's stumps. "And every day I traveled, I killed a person. Sometimes two or three. Sometimes families. The small ones. You kill the parents and the children hang about, like lost lambs. Making that noise."

Lords above, Pig Knot thought.

"Wanted to tell you all that," Poza leered. "So . . . when they bring us food? You'll give yours to me. Every last crumb. When they bring us water . . . You'll give yours to me. Every last drop."

"So I'm to have nothing?"

"Only what I give you."

"Not very fair."

Poza bared those horrible teeth. "Suppose not," he chuckled, unbothered. "But fair to me. And that's all that really matters. Really."

"Suppose if . . ."

"Shhhh . . . don't. Don't talk. You talk . . . when I *say* you can talk."

That took a moment to absorb. When he did, Pig Knot raised his hand.

Evil eyes glittering, Poza again stuck his tongue into a corner of his mouth and thought things over. In time he nodded.

"Suppose if I . . . decide *not* to?" Pig Knot asked, feeling a familiar heat rising within him, one he hadn't felt in a very long time.

"Decide not to?"

"Aye that."

Scowling, Poza shook his head. "You don't decide on *anything* anymore, topper. Any decisions you *might* have made before? All that ended the moment they brought me in here. I decide for both of us now. Me. And if you disagree . . . *I'll* decide if I use just this . . ." he held up a thumb. "Or both."

The other thumb came up, and Poza made the point of wiggling them before he made fists . . . which he flaunted before lowering.

Pig Knot blinked at the display, and he put on his best face of being worried. For only a moment, before the mask broke into a lazy scratch of a smile.

Poza smiled as well.

Pig Knot rubbed at an eye and chuckled. Poza chuckled with him.

Pig Knot *laughed*, starting in little amused hitches until something inside broke. He laughed hard, until water sprouted from his eyes, and great, belly-wracking guffaws bounced off the stone walls.

Poza did not laugh like that. His chuckling ceased and his smile faltered. In fact, all his amusement bled away to annoyed confusion.

Pig Knot's own laughter eventually died away to nothing. There he sat, one hand across his guts, and shook his head.

"Lad," he smiled in a tired tone. "There's only one thing you'll get from me. One thing only . . . Can you guess what that is?"

"What?"

"Can you guess it?"

"What *is* it?"

"I asked if you can *guess* it."

"I guess . . . I'll kill you slow," Poza whispered, watching him from beneath a lowered brow. "I don't think I like you at all. Not at all. I think . . . I'd rather have this cell for just myself."

With that, Poza took his time getting to his feet, his hide whispering against the wall as he did so. He stood tall, imposing himself over the other, and let his muscular arms dangle. He examined the helpless, legless man for a short, considering moment, during which his expression flowed from being horrid to that of a killer making a final decision . . . about the best place to start inflicting pain.

"Only one thing you'll get from me," Pig Knot whispered, raising a finger. "One—"

Poza kicked for his victim's face, the flat of a filthy sole blurring forward with the full weight behind it. Pig Knot slapped it away with his upraised hand, as fast and as hard as he could muster while twisting away. The calloused foot still grazed his profile, just barely, flattening hair and clipping his ear before it slammed into the wall.

Pig Knot grabbed that offered leg with every bit of strength left to him.

And pulled the offending limb to his chest.

An off-balance Poza toppled, arms flailing, glimpsing the top of a head and then the flashing ceiling. He fell onto the grimy cell floor, and the one thing that went through his mind as he went down, the one thing that caused him to worry . . . the first worry of the *last* few moments of his life . . .

Was how surprisingly *strong* the legless topper was.

Shortly after the Skarrs left the street watch jail, Odusk, Slok, and Sharo sat, relaxed, and talked. Truth be known, Odusk and

Slok talked only to each other, while Sharo mostly ignored them. He kept himself busy by stitching up a pair of old leather gloves.

"I don't miss patrolling, I tell you," Slok said. "We're much better off here. Let them nogs stroll about the city. Suffering in the heat. Mucking up the drunken shite."

"Drunken shite indeed," Odusk agreed. "Had my fill of that."

"As I. That's what I'm saying here. Here, we can—"

Odusk held up a hand, silencing his companion, who stared back with a questioning frown. Then he heard it.

Sharo stopped mid-stitch, also cocking an ear.

A muted thumping, only because it was behind the thick door that led to the cellblock. A fleshy drumroll of limbs and torsos that ended in brief bouts of silence, until the next solid rolling about. A grunting squeal of pain followed, then even more rolling, along with heated mutterings not understood at all.

A knowing smirk flashed across Odusk's face. Slok matched it with one of his own, and for a beat of time both men smiled and listened. Which was right about when the shrieking started. A sharp, terrified screaming fueled by several short breaths but quickly evolving into one maddening squeal of suffering.

That unlocked the jailors. All three rushed to the cellblock door. Slok grabbed the one timber barring it and heaved the thing away. Odusk nearly ripped a fingernail off pulling the door open. Sharo was the first to enter, however, and the first to see.

The sight before him robbed him of both speech and thought.

Odusk and Slok pushed their way inside and gathered on either side of him. The eagerness upon their features froze, then melted into stunned surprise.

On his chest, his face stuffed into the latrine hole up to his ears . . . lay Poza. A trail of bloody teeth and other fleshly matter led to the cavity, as if someone had mashed and smeared those unpleasant features all the way across the stone floor . . . before finally shoving the head down the drain. Dark rivulets flowed from Poza's ears, which remained attached by the barest of fleshy threads.

Poza didn't move.

Pig Knot rested against one wall, one stump nearly touching the dead man's leg. Blood covered his hands and spattered his chest. Breathing hard, he winced before regarding all three jailors with a defiant, if not predatory look.

Then he adjusted himself against the wall, hoarked, and spat on the corpse before him.

31

After killing Gunjar, Prajus returned to the underground chamber of Nexus and experienced two things.

The first was Nexus heaping a surprising amount of praise upon him. Even the trainers congratulated him, though with less enthusiasm than the owner.

The second was receiving wary looks from the other gladiators.

The day's events at the arena had come to an end, and Nexus ordered them all to return to his private grounds. The gladiators rode in covered wagons with the trainers and taskmaster, while Nexus went off in his private koch. The ride in the wagon was a solemn affair, as if they'd just lost another sword brother to a rival house. No one spoke. Not even the trainers. And when Prajus glanced around, the other fighters avoided his gaze. Prajus recognized it for what it was. *Fear.* Fear of having underestimated him, of having insulted someone smarter, stronger, than any of them.

And wondering if—and how—vengeful he could be.

Their silence said it all, and Prajus let them wallow in it.

Upon returning to the walled compound, Bernd ordered the returning pit fighters to assemble on the training sands, which brought about a few scowls of confusion. They did so, however, joining the group of warriors who had not taken in the games that day, who were standing about waiting for word of the day's results.

Prajus headed that way himself before Rezzo gestured for him to stay where he was. When the pack left him behind, the thick-bodied trainer motioned for Prajus to follow him. They walked by taskmaster Tino, who acknowledged the fighter with a guarded nod.

"You pleased Master Nexus this day," Rezzo explained as they approached the bathhouse. He stopped before the door and eyed Prajus. "He's instructed me to allow you to have the baths in solitude once again. As reward for your performance in the arena."

Prajus smirked. "I'd rather have a stroll to one of the local alehouses, truth be known."

"You might have gotten that with Gastillo—"

"I did," Prajus interrupted, and received a glare for doing so.

"But that was then," Rezzo said in that level tone of his. "And here, a night of drinking is something Nexus doesn't easily permit."

"Perhaps you should mention it to him?"

Rezzo possessed dull blue eyes, set below gray hair cut short but not overly so, as well as a neatly trimmed beard. He had the look of an officer and the stoicism to match, and he trained that emotionless gaze upon Prajus.

Not that it bothered Prajus.

"You can go on and enjoy your bath in solitude, or you can decide not to. Makes no difference to me."

"If I do so, won't that anger the others?" Prajus said, nodding at the gladiators still on the ground. At that moment, Bernd began yelling at them.

"You don't care about them," Rezzo said. "We all know that. Have this bit of luxury and be glad you have it. Refuse it if you dare, but if you do, know that I'll inform Master Nexus that you declined his reward."

"I can think of better rewards."

"And you'll step out of Master Nexus's favor after only just earning it." The trainer sighed, his gaze now more steely. "Not very wise, lad. You should know by now, Master Nexus is not one to be taken lightly."

Prajus agreed on that point.

"Well," he announced brightly and nodded at the trainer, "I believe I'll take that bath . . ."

Which he did, and enjoyed it to the fullest, stewing in the warm waters until his low-hanging fruits urged him out. Even then he took his time, standing on the edge of the pool, studying the water. Clear, marred by whatever oils the attendants had smeared upon him.

Sniffing, Prajus gathered up his manhood and pissed into those waters. He finished in good time, his stream dribbling off, whereupon he forced a few more drops just to see them dapple the surface. The bathhouse attendants stood nearby with horrified expressions, but neither one dared say a word to the gladiator.

Which Prajus expected.

When he finished, he dabbed a towel over himself, dressed, and left the pool. When he left the bathhouse, he paused at the doorway and waited until he caught Rezzo's eye.

Whereupon he signaled he was done.

Still basking in his victory, a relaxed and refreshed Prajus strolled the house grounds, wondering what might be served for their evening meal. A guard standing at the main gate spotted the gladiator and waved. Prajus checked behind himself and realized the man was waving at him.

"What?" he asked, pinching his damp tunic and pulling it from his chest.

"Some lads here," the guard asked. "Asking for you."

Mildly curious, Prajus noticed Bernd inspecting a rack of wooden swords. "Master Bernd," he called out, turning the trainer around.

"*What?*" Bernd yelled back.

"Apparently, I have some visitors at the gate. Permission to see what they want?"

"*At the gate?*"

"Aye that, at the gate."

"*Well go see what they want. And be quick about it.*"

The reply surprised Prajus, as he expected his request to be loudly declined. Nothing of the sort, however. Not even a well-intended *punce* or *flick of shite* or the like. Wonders over wonders. Private baths. Permission to see visitors. It amazed him what a little bloodletting in a public arena did to elevate one's worth. Now if only he could get out every now and then to visit an alehouse.

Prajus strode over to the entrance where three guards waited. The one that had spoken earlier nodded to the others, and they unlocked the gate.

"Don't be long," the guard informed him. "Find out what they want and get back in here."

Prajus smiled a reply, intending to take as long as he wanted.

He stepped outside and saw his visitors. "Tulka," he greeted neutrally. "Kall."

"Prajus," Tulka grinned, his last meal clinging to his teeth. "How have you been?"

"Since the last time I saw you? Well enough. What is it you want? I've been told to be quick."

"Haven't broken them yet?"

Prajus did not answer, suspecting those very shaggers were listening. He noticed Kall carried a sack and pointed at it. "What's that you have?"

Tulka grinned. "That's the reason for the visit. You wanted your armor returned to you."

"That's not my armor."

"Clearly not. However, if you will allow me to finish . . . you wanted your armor returned and so . . . we went looking. As you asked."

Prajus sighed while only half listening. He eyed the sack, discerning a familiar shape. "Is that my shield?"

That stopped Tulka, who traded looks with Kall.

"Aye that," Tulka said. "It's the shield."

"Give it here."

Kall held it out.

"Take it out of that hide first. Where did you find that? I smell rotting potatoes off that thing."

"All the better to hide it from the unwanted sorts. Keeps them away."

"Really? So if I keep it, it'll keep you away?"

That scrunched Tulka's brow. "Bit harsh."

Prajus offered no apology as Kall pulled the thing out of the sack.

"Give it here," Prajus said impatiently. He took the shield and turned it around, inspecting the piece. "Ah, yes . . ."

Stout iron and wood, with a metal grip and a leather strap for the forearm. Hard and strong and near perfect weight. The artwork upon the shield itself was the prize, however. Etched upon the surface and positively fine-looking was the head of a dragon, rearing back as if to strike. Prajus had paid good coin for the artwork. In his mind, if one were to be a dragon, he should at least *look* it. Or wear it. Or both.

"Yes, indeed," Prajus whispered in approval. "Where's the rest of it?"

"Well, ah," Tulka said, nodding at the shield. "That was the easy bit. The armory was plundered, but that piece was left on the floor. Simply left on the floor. I didn't think it was yours until I stood over the thing. Whoever looted the place must have forgotten it or . . . well. There you go. The rest of it? Gone. Didn't find a piece."

"Did you search the property?"

"Aye that, we looked. Place was looted. There were some things left behind, but whoever went in there gutted whatever had value. Except that shield. We might go about the city, see who sells scavenged armor. I mean the good pieces scavenged from a battlefield. Not the repaired gurry. Some of yours might be there. Can't believe whoever took your armor was able to fit into it. That was all made for you. Maybe the greaves and bracers, but the scale?"

"See to it, then," Prajus said, admiring the shield at arm's length. "Buy it if you can. Steal it if you must. But get it. All right?"

Tulka looked offended. "Of course, Prajus. We said we'd find it for you, and we will. Just might take some time, is all. If it's in the city, we'll get it. Since we're talking here, have you had a chance to speak with Nexus?"

"About what?"

"Taking us on?"

"Oh that. He won't say," Prajus lied. "He keeps changing the subject, and I risk being slapped in chains or worse for pestering him. Give me time. Every victory I claim here gives me a little more influence. But if you can retrieve the rest of my armor, I can wear it, and he'll notice. I can tell him you brought it back to me. That might grease his chains even more. Might. I can't rightly say anything more about his thinking other than he's not Gastillo. Nexus would cut me down if I give him reason to. He wouldn't hesitate giving the order."

"But you're winning in the Pit *now*," Tulka pointed out.

"I am, but . . ." Prajus checked on the guards before whispering, "he's *ruthless*. Positively cold-blooded. You couldn't squeeze a drop of kindness from that one. Or pity. I actually admire him for those qualities."

"Perhaps it's the reason he's rich."

"Daresay. Well. Thank you for this, lads. But your work's not yet done. The armor next. Don't return until you have it. Or some of it."

"When do you fight next?" Tulka asked.

"No idea. Check with the Madea. Every day if you have to. Seems I'm something of a favorite there. Place your coin on me and enjoy it afterward."

That lifted their spirts.

Having no interest in continuing the conversation, Prajus nodded. "Lads," he said and went back inside, leaving them in the street.

The evening meal consisted of chicken pieces in a tasty broth seasoned with herbs and spices, and served with soft vegetables. Prajus ate alone, from his usual spot in the dining hall, and watched the other gladiators file into the bathhouse. An evil smile creased his features as he watched them go in.

When he finished his meal, he retired for the evening and returned to the living quarters. Ansut was back there, as evident by the closed curtain, but no sound could be heard. Prajus left him and entered his little alcove. There, he pulled the curtain all the way across, leaving no cracks to see outside. Patting his belly, he sized up the serviceable quarters, shook his head, and settled down for the night.

The rest of the gladiators returned, and Prajus listened as they entered.

No one spoke a word as they passed his little enclosure.

No one slapped the posts.

In the morning, Prajus rose with the rest of the pack. He ate, squatted, and later exercised with the others. His training partner was a tall lout named Lirvo, who had amassed an uninspiring record of four wins and three losses thus far into the season. Quarter-strength was ordered, and Lirvo appeared uneasy as he squared off against Prajus.

Prajus could have been easy with his strikes.

Could have. He was not, and he exposed glaring holes in Lirvo's defense and attacks, dappling the man with several red marks. Red marks only, but if the heavy-footed punce tried Prajus's patience or, even better, got saucy, then he would draw blood.

Greygar practiced with another fighter beside Prajus. Whenever Prajus connected with a strike, the slap of wood on muscle rang out, and he stepped back for a moment to allow Lirvo a chance to reflect on his mistakes. It wasn't a gesture of mercy on Prajus's part, but an opportunity to look directly at Greygar's sweating profile.

The big Sunjan did not look back.

Prajus continued sparring with Lirvo, huffing with boredom at times, until Rezzo motioned for him to step out of line. He did so, and when a hurting Lirvo offered his sword for a well-done tap, Prajus ignored it and walked away.

Rezzo showed him where to go.

Prajus stopped before the raised platform of Nexus and taskmaster Tino, who studied him with the barest smile upon his wizened face.

"You fought well yesterday," Nexus acknowledged. "Very well, in fact. You keep fighting like that and you'll be a wealthy man when all this is done."

"I expect to be, Master Nexus," Prajus said.

The words caused Nexus to frown in amusement. "You hear that, Tino? He expects to be. He *expects* it. You surprise me, Prajus, you truly do. Tino has spoken frequently of the minds of gladiators. How they must be in the right state to push through to the end of the games. To do what they do, over and over again. How they must truly believe that they are the *best*, in every possible way. Physically. Mentally. With a weapon. I've heard the little speeches Bernd and Rezzo give these dogs. Even heard old Tino whisper a few words to a gladiator. Words of encouragement. Savage praise, really, meant to . . . motivate a pit fighter, to impose their will upon an opponent before cutting them apart piece by piece. He tells me those words have to be spoken to all the fighters, to lift their spirits. To ensure the best possible performance in the arena. I understand the purpose of it all. I see some worth in such gurry."

Nexus paused for a drink. When he finished, he lowered his goblet and studied Prajus again. The wine merchant pointed at him. "I've heard these little speeches. And I've seen the eyes of the gladiator being addressed. They all *believe* they can be the best . . . they all think it . . . but *you*? I see your eyes. You right and proper *know* it."

Prajus nodded ever so graciously, acknowledging the compliment while a rush of pride flooded his person. All his days with Gastillo and the gold-faced shagger never offered a good word at all to him, and yet, this *wine* merchant just did. An individual some would say should not even be in the games. And yet, it was a *merchant* who recognized Prajus for what he was. Certainly what he was worth.

"You fight again this day," Nexus said, "and as before . . . you keep doing what you're doing. Keep cutting up the sheep before the rest of the herd. Before them all. Incur as many blood matches as you like, because I like it. I demand it. They wish to ruin me? By attempting to cripple my fighters? *You* . . . Prajus . . . will be the ruination of *them*."

"As you wish," Prajus said, struggling to conceal the elation surging through him. "Who am I to kill, then?"

Nexus raised his goblet . . . and provided the name.

Some time later, beneath the arena, Prajus sat in the chamber assigned to the School of Nexus. The wine merchant stood with Tino at the window. Bernd and a handful of gladiators had also been permitted to come along, in addition to the dozen Marrnite mercenaries guarding the entrance in the corridor. Unlike other times, however, there was a decidedly different atmosphere hanging about them all. No one glared at Prajus. No one invaded the space about him and, if someone did walk by, he made certain to avoid Prajus as much as possible. No one spoke to him either, but he didn't mind that. Granted this rare moment of solitude, he used the time to prepare himself for the approaching contest, lowering his head and reminding himself who he was.

I'm an unfit hellion, he mentally intoned. *I am a killer among pigs. A butcher let loose among sleeping cattle. I am the mountain that stomps upon the plain. The angry sea that swallows ships whole.*

Prajus scoffed at that last one. Cottony gurry. He could do better.

I am the ruination of them all, he began again, knowing it to be the truth. *I do not fear, I am feared. I do not spare, I kill, and have been unleashed to do so at my whim, because my owner knows what I know. I cannot be beaten. I cannot be defeated. I defeat. I put down all who face me and they fear me for it. I am deadly. I am* lethal. *I am unleashed upon these games and all that face me tremble in terror. I am* . . . Death, *come to claim what is mine, and I will take them* all *and demand* more . . .

"Prajus."

He lifted his head to see the stern face of Nexus studying him. "It's time, lad . . ."

Only then did Prajus look around. They all watched him. They all waited for him to move. So Prajus nodded and got to his feet.

"You know what I want," Nexus reminded him.

"Another head for your wall," Prajus said with cold humor. "I'll return shortly with that very bauble."

With that, he left them all.

Outside in the corridor, he walked past the Marrnite mercenaries guarding the chamber. In time, the Skarrs appeared, lining the white tunnel. Weapons at the ready, their visors impassive. Oozing unshakable confidence, Prajus sauntered by them all and spared them not a glance.

They all fear me. They all know what I can do. What I am capable of. Who I am. For I am Death walking. I am the one they all wish to defeat, but they cannot, for these are my games. These are my *games, and this is* my *time. My time. In this place, I am not to be ruled, I rule.*

"Lad?"

Standing at the base of the steps that led to the arena, Prajus glanced at the hunched shoulders of the gatekeeper.

"Go on," the old man nodded, indicating the opening portcullis far above.

"My thanks, gatekeeper," Prajus said, and jogged up the stairs toward a rising heat and a blazing blue sky. The very air shimmered above the white sands and sweat moistened the cloth padding underneath his armor. The audience erupted in a rolling cascade of displeasure when he stepped into daylight—not nearly as loud as before, but the hatred was there and spitting. Crackling. Curses and insults scorched the air, and he raised his arms to welcome it all. Half-eaten fruit fell about him, missing their target, but Prajus ignored that. He strode onto the sands and halted a dozen strides out, eyeing the lowered portcullis on the other side of the arena.

You unfortunate maggot, he thought and smiled.

The audience's shouting lessened, as if smothered by the thickest blanket, before ending entirely.

"Ladies and gentlemen of the Pit," the Orator's voice boomed. "Welcome to the last contest of the day, and what a contest it promises to be. Between two very different, very skilled, and very dangerous opponents. Two men that walk very different paths in these games, and who now face each other, to see who will prevail, and who will continue. I know . . . I often . . . paint grand scenes with such descriptions, preparing this celebrated stage for the mayhem, the carnage, and the sheer *spectacle* that is this most brutal business. This day, however . . . I fear whatever I might say . . . will not be enough. Will not *nearly* be enough. But, as always . . . I will try."

Groans and mutterings of disbelief answered that, but the Orator held up a hand and continued. "Allow me, ever your servant, to introduce to you the first of our gladiators upon the sands."

"In all my days as your servant, in all my years holding the title and duties of your Orator, never have I witnessed the terror standing upon the sands right now. I know . . . I've often used such colorful and dramatic words as *a destroyer of men. A mauler of spirit. A collector of heads.* But I know you will agree . . . this man is *all* these things. He is indeed a destroyer. An absolute *butcher* upon our grand sands. And, aye that, most certainly a collector of heads. He has been killing daresay *everyone* facing him, taking on all challengers, and not caring in the least whose head it is he lops off at the shoulders. With no fear of the consequences. We have seen him not only dispatch his opponents in his last few fights, but absolutely *decimate* them without mercy. With an eagerness that is absolutely chilling. And this day, I expect nothing less from him once again. Whenever he steps into the arena, we can all be certain the match will be to the death. He is a son of Sunja, sent to us from the . . . School of Nexus. He is . . . *Prajus* . . ."

Hearing his name, Prajus lifted his sword and dragon shield in a *V* over his head. Though his helmet hid his smile, he smiled anyway, embracing the hateful welcome of the crowd.

I am a collector of heads, he thought, very much approving of the title. *I'm to be feared. To be terrified of.*

The Orator held up both hands, pleading for quiet and restraint. When the roar simmered to a dull rumble, he spoke.

"The man Prajus will fight this day—"

And the arena exploded with cheering. Not just cheering, but an ear-bursting rush that shook the halls of brick and marble deep into its ancient foundation. A wave of noise that threatened to bring that ageless structure down in a cloud of dust. That awesome frenzy of excited delight spilled over the heights of the arena and rolled into the city beyond, to once again turn the heads of citizens going about their day.

Across the way, the portcullis pulled upward, the cranky gears and chains smothered by that tumultuous discharge of thousands of voices. Excited faces blurred into an undulating mass. Smiles flashed in the sun. Fists pumped the air and arms and hands waved.

Prajus faced the opening gate. *They all fear me. They all—DYING SEDDON!*

The audience, deafening before, doubled their efforts when a figure holding a sword still sheathed in its scabbard entered the arena.

The overwhelming welcome hammered at Prajus's ears, distracting him. As much as he tried, he could not, for the very life of him, hear his own thoughts.

Bare-chested, wearing nothing but grayish pants tucked into low boots. Sunlight shone across the man's slim but powerful torso. He took his time, perhaps basking in that tremendous reception, and when he was a dozen strides away from the gate, he lifted a hand into the air and did a quick turn. To acknowledge the people watching him.

And that endeared him even more to the masses.

I know what . . . What I can—WHAT I CAN DO. Prajus roared in his head and barely heard it.

Junger, the Perician Wonder, lowered his arm and regarded his opponent, taking stock of the challenge before him. There was the slightest pause there, not of hesitation, but of the deepest reckoning, of seeing the one who had dispatched so many in recent days.

Then Junger, his head lowered just a notch, walked straight for him. Sheathed sword swinging at his side.

With rising anticipation, the cheering grew a few notches more.

Intending to shock them all, Prajus smiled viciously and went to meet his next victim.

"My time!" he shouted against the praise of thousands and barely heard his own voice. "This is *my time*. My *place! I rule here! I rule!*"

If Junger heard him, his pace did not lessen in the least.

"I've killed many during these games!" Prajus shouted, dragon shield at the ready and sword at half guard.

At a dozen paces apart and quickly closing, neither man slowed.

"And I'll kill you as well," Prajus screamed at Junger.

With all his speed and might, Prajus swung at the amused head of his Perician opponent bearing down on him.

And *missed*.

32

Prajus swung with everything he had and split only air.

Moving with a speed that made his foe appear forty years older, Junger slipped under that slow-moving, head-hunting cut and struck back. *Repeatedly.*

Tong! His leatherbound blade slammed into the Sunjan's stomach, buckling him.

TONG TONG! Junger struck Prajus twice more on his way to meet the ground.

The first blow took the Sunjan's helmet off in a violent, sparkling puff of sweat and hair. The *second* blow, an uppercut delivered with a sorcerous speed too fast to see, *upended* the man mid-fall, and pitched him *back.*

Prajus landed on his spine in a puff of sand, arms splayed and sword and shield out of reach. Not that he would have reached for either, as he did not move upon the ground.

Junger waited several heartbeats before approaching his fallen adversary. Then, satisfied the gladiator wasn't rising, the wary Perician walked over and knelt upon Prajus's sword arm, pinning it. He placed the sheathed sword at the unconscious man's exposed neck, right under the weakly bobbing throat nut. Junger pulled a hand's worth of edged steel from his scabbard, the metal flashing, and held it at the knob of Prajus's kinkhorn.

Having a blade that close to his throat roused him. It reached down into the Sunjan's pitch-black cauldron of his unconsciousness and reattached the strings of his senses.

Prajus stirred and slowly opened his eyes. Realization, as he met the steady gaze of the man who had just defeated him. He sighed, more dazed than anything, but aware that he was expected to raise his hand to yield.

Except he wasn't about to.

"Do it," he croaked, hearing his words that time.

Junger put the edge to his throat.

Prajus kept still. "I . . . said . . . *do it.*"

Another notch of pressure, enough to summon blood, to widen the Sunjan's eyes, to bare his teeth.

"*Now*," Prajus insisted.

Junger's gaze narrowed, becoming as cold as the killer's beneath him. The sword he held did not waver, did not relent, and for the briefest moment, the Perician's shoulders tensed. His expression hardened, as if weighing the consequences of taking the man's life. It would be welcomed by many, perhaps even all, if only to save the lives of future gladiators.

Prajus braced himself. Any moment he expected to feel and see a spray of scarlet across the cloudless sky of cobalt blue.

Except nothing of the sort happened.

Junger blinked, awakening from conflicting thoughts, and pulled back from the gladiator. He stood, his sheathed sword at low guard, watching Prajus all the while.

The audience voiced their disappointment.

"You *punce*," Prajus seethed weakly, dabbing at his throat. "You think you won this day? You did *nothing*. You *are* nothing. *Nothing* I say." He rose to one knee, eyeing the Perician. "We'll meet again, you and I. We'll meet again. And I'll cut you from chin to prick in a flash of red. I'll open you up for the world to see, to show them you're nothing. And become a legend in doing so. You hear me, you motherless kog? You hear me? I'll *end* you . . ." Prajus checked where his sword lay nearby. "You Perician—"

An instant *before* he lunged for the blade, Junger lashed out and cracked the Sunjan across the face, toppling the man. Prajus crumpled, eyes crossed and closed upon hitting the ground.

And the very last thing he heard as he once again plummeted into that black pit of unknowing . . . was the approving roar of the crowd.

From where he watched in his private chambers, Nexus clutched at a silver goblet. Taskmaster Tino stood nearby, his near-toothless mouth hanging open. There were others around them, but Nexus stood at the center of the brick sill and had the best look of all.

Defeated. Downed in three blistering strikes he had barely had time to count.

But *alive* and able, and no doubt willing to cut through however many it took to once again fight the Perician.

On another day.

That's what Nexus told himself.

He released a throat-stinging bark of frustration and whipped the goblet of unfinished wine out the window.

In the private chambers belonging to the House of Curge, several gladiators rested their elbows on the sill and watched the Perician's performance with unblinking eyes, for fear of missing anything.

The one called Gair, in particular—Dark Curge's prized knife fighter. As of that day, Gair possessed an undefeated record himself. Once again, he absorbed every one of the Perician's moves. Gair knew full well, if death did not claim him first, he would eventually face the man they called *the Wonder*.

Above it all, in his private roost overlooking the arena, Dark Curge leaned back in his seat. He watched Junger disappear into the tunnel, the awesome applause and cheers barely lessening. A great sigh escaped the one-armed owner. He rubbed his chin uneasily, feeling as defeated as Junger's most recent victim, left unmoving upon the arena floor.

With every contest the Perician fought, it became painfully obvious that no one could match him. Curge shook that troubling thought free of his skull, knowing it both untrue and unfit. They all had their weaknesses. All of them. It was only a matter of finding it. And then exploiting it.

He regarded his thick-necked taskmaster, Baris, sitting beside him. Baris had watched the same spectacle. He glowered at the departing gladiator and, in time, observed the attendants hurrying to Prajus's side. The taskmaster looked as if he'd downed a mouthful of sour wine and sought to spit it out.

"Well?" Curge asked, growing impatient.

For many heartbeats, Baris didn't say anything. Just as Curge was about to ask him a second time, the taskmaster turned his stern stare around to face his once student. Prickly gray speckled his chin, but it was his eyes, usually deep with knowledge and at times frightening with intent, that silenced the owner. Those eyes held a troubling uncertainty that Curge had not seen since . . . well . . . ever.

Baris held that stare for moments before looking back at the arena.

He did not say a word.

33

That same morning, squeals of children playing woke Zelia. She lay on her side and lingered in bed, listening to their sporadic laughter. If there was anything finer than waking to the sound of happy children, she did not know it.

She closed her eyes again. *Children*, she thought and sighed. Before long, she was sitting with her husband in their kitchen. Crouching, he leaned forward and fussed over something hidden from her.

"What are you doing?" she asked sleepily.

He shook his head and continued working.

"Are you fighting today?" she asked, her chest aching with sadness.

Sorban shook his head again. "No, the season isn't right."

"The season is never right," she added, staring at his bare, muscular back. "When will you go?"

Sorban didn't answer.

Which puzzled her, enough for her to find herself standing behind him, not remembering rising or crossing the floor. "I have to leave soon," she told him.

He nodded.

"Will you come with me?" she asked, placing a hand on his shoulder.

Sorban didn't answer. He pulled on whatever it was before him, as if completing a knot, and sighed. "Remember, he is stronger than he looks," he finally said.

"I know," Zelia agreed sadly.

"I knew him well. He'll help you."

"Why would anyone help me?"

At that her husband faced her, plainly amused at the question. The scent of honeywood filled the room then, strong enough for her to believe they were walking in a forest full of it. He reached out and placed a warm hand upon hers.

"When it's time," Sorban whispered and smiled, "see past the colors."

Feeling the end slip away, Zelia covered his hand with her own, and that contact opened her eyes. She lay on her side in a dark room, barely holding back the strength of the beginning day. The memory of honeywood lingered beneath her nose . . .

And her hands folded upon her chest.

She rose shortly after, wiping her eyes while remembering her husband. He'd spoken to her in her dream, and in that moment he was alive. That pulled a little croak of misery from her. She remembered his words but didn't understand the message, if it *was* a message. *Oh my husband*, she thought, staring at the shuttered window. After a moment she told herself to stop it, that she had things to do that day, and that perhaps, later that night, Sorban would again visit her. And stay until morning.

With a quick check on her shutters and door, ensuring all were still secured, she went about her business. She quickly washed herself and dressed in fresh, earth-brown robes and a grayish-white vest. Once done, she reached back, gathered her long hair, and pulled it over her shoulder. On impulse, she held on and smoothed out its light-brown length.

Sorban had loved her hair as much as she did. Perhaps more.

Perhaps Boh the weaponsmith liked it as well. Along with the rest of her.

She remembered her dagger and realized she had dressed before strapping the scabbard to her thigh. So she sat, pulled the hem up, and secured the scabbard. Then she opened the pocket of her robe and cut a new slit inside the material. Making that alteration might have poisoned some women, but not her. For her, it was very much needed. Once the dagger was in place, she felt around down there to ensure she could pull the steel without much issue. When all was ready, she straightened everything out so nothing looked amiss.

With Boh stalking her, she would have to adjust all her clothing in the same manner. Until she dealt with him. Which was her task that day—reporting him to the street watch.

She opened one window just a crack to peer outside her door. The citizens of Sunja went about their business as always, and there was no sight of the despised weaponsmith. Shutting the window again, Zelia barred it and went to the door. She let herself out, glancing around while she did so. No one paid any attention to her, which suited her fine. Locking her door, she left her home and made a mental check of where to go. The street watch wasn't that far from where she and Sorban lived, but that morning, it felt as if those guardians of Sunja's law were in far-off Vathia. As she made her way down the street, she glanced back several times. The weaponsmith would be working this morning but she kept looking anyway, unable to let down her guard.

After a good walk, the white stone wall surrounding the street watch compound came into sight. When Sorban was alive, she had barely noticed it. The quarried stone was smoothly fitted, without a crack to be seen, high enough to hide everything beyond it except for a long, black ridge of a roof. Most people passing by paid no mind to the little fortress.

Zelia hurried toward a handful of Skarrs standing at the main gates.

"Greetings, good Skarrs," she said. "I wish to report an offense."

"What's the offense?" asked one behind a full-face visor that slightly muffled his voice. Blue eyes scrutinized her, warning her not to waste his time.

"I'm a recent widow. Lost my husband to the games. A man has been pursuing me since then, with unwanted affections. I've made it clear I want no part of him, but he persists. Last night he followed me home, where I had to shut all my doors and windows as if under siege."

The blue eyes studied her. "Did he take advantage of you?"

"No," Zelia replied, not expecting the question. "But I fear for my safety."

The Skarr nodded. "Wait here."

With that, he walked through the gates, armor clanking as he went. The soldier ambled over flagstones and approached the main building some ten strides away. The other soldiers remained at their posts and didn't speak with her. Instead, they watched the street traffic as it flowed by like a river.

A short time later, the Skarr returned and gestured for her to follow him. Without a word, Zelia entered the compound. The central building was an imposing structure, with thick walls and an eerie silence hanging about it. A second Skarr waited at the entrance, a rough-looking individual with dark hair shorn to his perspiring scalp and a noticeable piece of flesh missing from an ear.

"Greetings, good Skarr," she said.

"Lady," the man replied in a tired voice. "This way."

They moved out of the heat and into a large interior filled with stagnant, foul air despite the open slit windows. Two racks of weapons caught her eye. The shorter rack against the west wall held a collection of ready swords and spears, while a much longer rack against the south wall displayed an impressive assortment of bows and quivers of arrows. She found herself surrounded by so many weapons, in fact, that she wondered why such an amount was needed at all.

A pair of formidable doors stood at either end of the shorter rack, and a heavy table stood before it all. A few open scrolls lay discarded upon the surface, as if someone had stopped reading them to do something else. Two other doors were squarely set in the north and east walls.

"You say you were attacked?" the Skarr asked as he went around the table.

"I was not attacked," she replied evenly. "I simply fear for my safety."

"Your safety?"

"Aye that, my safety. He followed me to my home last night and it was not the first time. He's made it known that his intentions are less than honorable."

"Less than honorable," the Skarr repeated. "Your husband is dead, you say?"

That caught her off guard. "He is," she said, keeping her voice level.

"Killed in the games?"

Zelia nodded impatiently. "He was a gladiator, yes."

"Harsh," the Skarr grunted but offered no condolences. "Wait here then."

With that he went to the door behind him and rapped upon it. A voice answered and the soldier entered. Zelia waited, a touch offended by the Skarr's stark assessment of Sorban. *Harsh*, he said. *Harsh* was pinching your finger between some rocks. Losing the man she loved was so much more.

The Skarr returned and pointed at her. "Here she is."

A second man appeared, a few fingers taller than the first, also without a helmet but wearing a polished vest of chainmail. Broad in the shoulder and strong, with a sharply trimmed beard and green eyes that locked onto hers.

"Lady . . . ?" he asked.

"Zelia."

The man halted at the table, towering over her while the other soldier stood off to the side. "You lost your husband, I've been told."

"Yes, and—"

"And another is pursuing you?"

Zelia nodded.

"Following you?"

"At night, to my home. He's made his intentions known to me. He wants me as his own."

"And you want no part of him."

"None," Zelia said. "I don't want to see him ever again."

"You know this man?"

"I do. His name is Boh. He's a weaponsmith in this part of the city."

"I know the man," the Skarr said. "I'll talk with him later this day. Make it clear you want no part of him. Shame. He's a good weaponsmith."

"He's unfit. The man is married. Has children, even. And he *pursues* me, a widow still mourning the loss of her husband."

"You did nothing to entice him?"

That horrified her. "I did nothing to entice *anyone*. In my mind, I am still married."

The Skarr grunted neutrally and huffed. "I'll look into this, Lady Zelia. I'll . . . make it clear he's to leave you alone. He won't bother you again."

"Many thanks . . ." she trailed, waiting for a name.

"Kelmo. I'm the Koor officer in command of the street watch here, in this part of the city."

"Many thanks, Koor Officer Kelmo."

Another grunt, and those hard green eyes flashed at the other soldier. "Take this lady to the gate and walk her home."

"There's no need for that," Zelia said. "I have some other business to attend to, but thank you for listening to me, Koor officer. And addressing this nuisance who threatens me."

Kelmo held up a hand, not bothering to meet her eyes. "Lady Zelia," he muttered.

The soldier went to the door and Zelia followed him outside.

Kelmo traced the grooves in the table, idly watching her leave and taking note of the robes she wore. When she was gone, he went back into his private office. Without a word he closed the door and rounded his desk to a padded chair. There he sat down heavily, scratched at his neck, and flexed his brow.

"What do you think of her?" Boh the weaponsmith asked, sitting across from the officer.

Kelmo shrugged. "She's dressed like an old woman in those robes."

"Ah, yes, she's not wearing her belt. Hides everything. I've seen her curves. Oh, she's a dish, cousin. A fine dish. Believe me when I say that."

"She says she's a widow."

"She is."

"And that she has no interest in you."

"They all say that."

Kelmo lowered his brow and stared at him. "Look. Why not go after another? She's not interested in you. Clearly not. She's only just lost her husband."

"In the games," Boh scoffed and waved a hand. "What gurry is that? I knew her husband. The man was a Balgothan asslicker. If he had any sense at all he would have stayed in Balgotha with that pink flower out there. No, instead he brought her here so that he could perish in the Pit and leave her all alone. I'm not complaining, mind you. Gives me a chance at her. She's worth it. I tell you, cousin, under those robes . . ."

Boh smiled and sighed, as if finishing a very fine meal.

"I don't know, cousin," Kelmo said. "What about your missus?"

The other man scowled and dismissed that with a wave. "You can have her. I'm not going to marry the Balgothan."

Kelmo didn't comment on that. "I don't like you following her at night," he finally said. "Noise carries then. If you *must* pursue her, be a touch more careful about it. Give her time to mourn her husband. Court her like any other."

Boh leaned forward, placing his elbows on the desk. "Look, cousin. As I've said before . . . let me go about this in my own way. All right? I'll be quiet about matters. Don't concern yourself with that. All I need to know from *you* is . . . that you'll be someplace *else* when I see my time. Agreed?"

The Koor shook his head. "You'll never change, cousin."

"Not when there are honeypots like that walking about."

"I don't find her so attractive."

"Excellent," Boh said brightly. "Then she's all mine."

Kelmo exhaled slowly. He thought matters over before a resigned smile spread across his face. "You'll never change . . ."

34

At dawn, Sunja's southern gates creaked open.

The sleepy lines of people waiting to enter the city rose, rubbed at their faces, and checked on their belongings. The sun was nowhere to be seen, hidden behind a dense blanket of clouds that stretched far and away over the fields below the bluff. Dark clouds promised rain, and the sight of them made the weary travelers before Sunja's gates all the more restless. It had been only a little over a week since the last summer rainstorm drenched the city. No one wanted to be caught in another downpour.

Beneath those dreary clouds were the jutting battlements of Sunja's formidable walls, where squared watchtowers rose up at precise intervals.

The gates swung open, pulled from within, and those who had camped before them hurried inside, into a squared tunnel leading through the massive stone wall. Overhead, murder holes pattered the cobblestones in gray daylight. A score of armed Skarrs waited beyond the tunnel, just past a huge portcullis smelling of wood, iron, and grease. Two inner walls of stone rose on either side of the entry point, where more city guards waited with crossbows and spears at the ready. Others stood around huge cauldrons set up along points of the walls, ready to tip their contents into the channel below if needed.

Skarrs stopped traveling individuals and questioned them before granting permission to enter the city. People with carts, wagons, or traveling in koches were directed to one side, where another dozen Skarrs waited to inspect them.

One by one, group by group, people from all over flowed into the city.

One Skarr waved a family through and looked to the next group.

"Come on then, step forward," the guard said, before checking on his companions behind him. A knot of metal and piercing glares, with hands on the hilts of swords or holding spears.

"Right, stop there," the guard grumbled, pushing up the visor on his face. His name was Neris, and he knew he was in for an unfit day of minding the gates. His guts were in a state of early-morning turmoil, and every inner muttering deepened the frown on his bearded face. He had no one to blame but himself, as he and the lads had gotten into the local beer the night before. Plunged face-first into the wicked drink, truth be known, and all had partaken mightily of it. That was the problem with beer—it tasted so damn good, once it got flowing, well . . . morning surprised you.

Oh, Neris had been well aware that he had guard duty when the drinking started. He just didn't care. He cared *now*, however, or rather his innards cared, warning him to be ready to sprint for the nearest pisspot. Still, he was a guard of the city—a Skarr— and had a job to do.

"Stop right there," he repeated at the newcomers clustered together. Three of them. Young men in their twenties, well-built if not a touch buckled at the shoulders, as if mercilessly whipped the day they dropped into the world. Quiet faces, unshaven, carrying next to nothing, not even a blade, and dressed like asslickers looking for work.

"You lot together?" Neris asked with an uninterested sniff and a rub of his nose.

The three of them exchanged looks, each expecting one of the others to speak.

The one on the right decided it would be him. He hitched up one side of his face to reveal yellow, overlapping teeth. "Aye that. We're together."

The lad's breath stank as bad as a moist cow kiss dropped in the street.

"What's your reason for entering the city?" Neris asked while sticking a finger in his ear.

"Our reason?"

"Yes, your reason. Your purpose for being here? Whatever it might be, let's hear it."

"We are looking for work. We have heard there is work here, so . . . we came."

Neris ceased all rooting about his ear. "You speak oddly. You're not Sunjan."

The lad nodded as if this was an old conversation for him. "My father was Sunjan but my mother was Mademian. We're all from Mademia, but . . . we speak Sunjan well enough."

Yet you smell like you just escaped a cow's wet blossom, Neris thought. His guts rumbled agreement. His guts also sent notice to forget about the pisspot and start thinking about the nearest, deepest shite trough.

To add to it all, a pair of horses pulled a wagon past Neris and the three men. One of those horses decided to let slip a stream of hot gurry, right on the clean cobblestones of the city.

Lords above, Neris thought and winced at the newest stink of the morning.

"We're all from Mademia," the lad continued, every breath a puff of poison. "You'll catch us on a few words, but otherwise . . ."

Neris held up a hand. "What do you do?"

"Anything, really. We just need the work."

Neris waved that off. "That the same for all of you?"

No sooner did the words leave him than his stomach knotted and unknotted painfully.

Nods from the three lads.

Neris fought down another painful twisting, of things seeking exit. "Any weapons?"

They shook their heads.

"Can you handle any weapons?"

"Axes, mostly," the lad with the shite breath admitted. "We chopped wood before coming here."

"Chopped wood," Neris said and clenched his blossom, knowing the moment was fast approaching. "All right you lot. In you go. Stay well out of trouble. If you're up for training, the city Skarrs might consider you."

"Oh no," said the lad, "We couldn't—"

But Neris was already waving them through while turning away. He stopped by one of his nearby companions. "Take over for me, will you? My blossom's about to spray fire . . ."

Sparing only a glance at the Skarr moving away from the gates, the three Sunjan-speaking Mademians entered the city. At times, they slowed and stared, clearly impressed at the many armed men patrolling the inner walls, until one of their number pulled the other two along. Eventually the walls turned left and right, and the three men stopped to behold the sights. And what sights there were. Roads led deeper into the city. Barns and houses lay before them in well-planned clusters, some with fences, some without. Merchants stood beside booths and wagons filled with all manner of goods, from leather to livestock, bottles to little cloth bags. Above it all, clothing hung on lines, drying from recent scrubbings. Fences kept in uninterested horses and a few cows. The newest arrivals to the city rumbled straight into the activity, quickly disappearing in those moving about. People stood everywhere, moved everything, absorbed in conversations, bargaining with merchants, and ignoring the newcomers.

The lad who had spoken with the Skarr stopped and rubbed his forehead, as if overcome by everything to see. His companions stopped as well, looking about and appearing fascinated by the local sights. Anyone paying attention might have noticed that the young man rubbing his face did so for several heartbeats before switching to his left hand—then returning to his right hand.

A single man wearing plain clothing emerged from the crowds and scratched vigorously at his head. He was brown of hair and eyes, with a neatly trimmed beard. The Sunjan-speaking Mademian locked eyes with the head scratcher, and both shared a look before they ceased what they were doing.

The head scratcher walked away.

The Sunjan-speaking Mademian walked after him, and his two companions followed.

Through the streets of Sunja they went. The head scratcher no more than five strides ahead of the three newcomers.

They walked down streets less traveled and met fewer people along the way. The ones they did meet did not spare them a glance.

In time, they passed no one at all.

The head scratcher led the three others past several old properties in need of repairs, until he stopped before a small door inserted into one of two larger gates. Thick planks barricaded the nearby windows. There, the head scratcher gestured for the three to come closer.

"Do you have something for me?" he asked.

"Only us three," replied the lad with the foul breath.

"You speak well."

A faint smile at that.

The head scratcher rapped twice on the door before checking on his followers. Wood squealed overhead somewhere. A short time later, the door opened. A tall individual wearing a shirt of chainmail motioned for them to quickly enter. They did so, and the door shut behind them.

Smiles then, from all around. "Excellent," the head scratcher said. "You didn't have any trouble?"

"None," reported the lad with the bad breath. "I think the Skarr needed to squat."

"Excellent. We'll send word to have all the lads come into the city during the morning then. I am Harbin. This way."

Harbin led them deeper into the barn, through a shadowy interior smelling of old hay, toward the rear. They passed perhaps a dozen men standing or sitting in various stalls, nodding at the arrivals as they went by. One stall held racks filled with short swords, bows, and even arrows. Three men sat around a bucket in one stall working on arrows, while another fixed iron heads to finished shafts. One stall held a collection of toughened leather vests, chainmail vests, greaves, bracers, and even helmets of various designs. Yet another stall held a patchwork display of assorted swords, maces, and axes. Another still resembled a small but respectable kitchen, with two individuals working therein. Other stalls were empty.

"The place used to be a barn but was changed into a storehouse," Harbin explained as he walked along.

Daylight filtered down from above, revealing a wide stairway to the second level. Harbin led them upstairs, past three spearmen sitting on stools and one axeman positioned next to a rope that held up a heavy door, which could fall upon the opening and block passage to the upstairs.

"We can speak now, if the Sunjan tongue hurts your ears," Harbin said in a low voice and gestured at an individual leaning against a table. Not so tall but lean and alert, perhaps in his forties, with his beard streaked gray.

All four men nodded at the leader.

"This is Basten Crazavo," Harbin introduced quietly, in the Nordish tongue.

The three men greeted the officer and waited on his word.

"Lads," Crazavo said in near-perfect Sunjan. "The *poltues* gave you no trouble?"

"No trouble at all," answered the one with the bad breath.

"Excellent. Now then, dog, what's the word?"

"The Ikull gathers its strength," the man reported in a low voice, speaking Nordish. "We're to remain hidden and gather our own. Until the command to strike."

Crazavo frowned. "Still gathering their strength? Seems they've been gathering their strength for years now."

The three men before him said nothing.

Not that the Nordish commander expected them to say anything. "Did you bring coin?" he asked.

Straightaway, the three reached into their pants and pulled away small bags of leather hidden upon themselves. Harbin took everything and passed it along.

Crazavo's frown deepened as he weighed each one in his hand. "This is all?"

"That's all, Basten," one replied. "But we've been told to tell you that more is on its way."

The officer shook his head. He untied one small bag and opened it, shaking free the contents. Fancy stones sparkled in the dim light. Just a few handfuls, however, and that was all. The trouble was he needed more, a lot more, if they were to buy weapons and armor from the local smithies. Even more if they wished to continue using this place as a nest. Crazavo wondered if his commanders perhaps thought he was frequenting the legendary alehouses of the city.

"Well met, lads," Crazavo informed them with a sigh. "Well met. You're in the chop, now. What will be the chop, one day. Speak Nordish while you're up here, if you wish, but only up here, and keep your voices low when you do. I don't trust these walls, and if the right rat overhears you, well . . . I'll kill you myself. Understood?"

Nods from the new arrivals.

"Hardin is my second. He'll give you your duties if I don't. When you're below, you speak Sunjan. Always. You must live in complete secrecy now. When you're outside wandering the city, you most certainly *always* speak Sunjan. Your very lives depend upon it. Do nothing to allow anyone to remember you. No drinking. No carousing. And stay clear of the arena. I'll tell you now that, yes, a handful of captured Jackals are fighting in the games. And yes, they are cutting their names into whoever they face upon the sands. Otherwise, stay clear of it. Mind yourselves with the tasks given you. And mind yourselves around the Sunjans. Always mind yourselves around them. Never let your disguise slip, because if you do . . . if the Sunjans don't gut you, I will. Understood?"

More nods.

Harbin glanced at each new arrival in the weight and warning of those words.

"Welcome to Sunja," Crazavo said finally and smiled grimly. "It shouldn't be too long before we rip out her heart."

About the Author

Keith C. Blackmore is the author of the Mountain Man, 131 Days, and Breeds series, among other horror, heroic fantasy, and crime novels. He lives on the island of Newfoundland in Canada. Visit his website at www.keithcblackmore.com.

JOIN THE FELLOWSHIP

follow us on our socials

podiumentertainment.com

@podiumentertainment

/podiumentertainment

@podium_ent

@podiumentertainment